Praise for *Con*

M000119153

"Three lives collide with tragic results in this propulsive and transporting novel. At the center of *Conch Pearl* is Dede, a twelve-year-old British girl, dragged to Grand Bahama Island by her mother who finds work and love in a casino. Dede, unsupervised, lonely, yearning for home, seeks companionship from two neighbors, Ethel, an aloof Bahamian woman, and the too-friendly handyman Johnnie McGuinn. Justicz's profound insights into her characters and her unfolding of the risks they must face are stunning. *Conch Pearl* is a grip-you-by-the-throat page turner about love and survival, that is profound and deeply satisfying. This is a novel you won't forget."

—Lynn Sloan is the author of two novels, *Midstream* and *Principles of Navigation*, and the story collection *This Far Isn't Far Enough*

Praise for *Degrees of Difficulty*

"*Degrees of Difficulty* is heartbreaking and enraging, even chilling, as it exposes, in straightforward and never-maudlin terms, the stresses and strains of providing constant care to someone who will never be independent. Different coping styles are also beautifully explicated, without judgment. A stunning, heartfelt, and poignant debut."
—*Kirkus Review*

"Julie Justicz asks 'Could a child ask too much of his parents? And... what should a parent ask in return?' *Degrees of Difficulty* is the totally absorbing story of the many kinds of devastation that can wrack a family, no matter its passion to survive intact. Justicz writes with deep feeling and saving wit about her characters who leap, alive and hopeful, off the page."
—Rosellen Brown, author of *The Lake on Fire* and *Before and After*.

"Justicz emerges as a master storyteller in what is left unsaid, not just by her characters but in the narrative as well. What the author makes immensely clear is how fragile Ben's life is. Each seizure feels like a heart-stopping moment. Caretakers range from inept to violent. Although not necessarily a novel about how ill-equipped our society is to aid the most vulnerable among us, Justicz, who works on civil rights issues in Chicago, can't help but illuminate that very fact. Self-hating, ambitious Ivy emerges as the most interesting character. She has the most to grow emotionally; she's been disappointed by her family count-less times. This heartbreaking, loving novel about a family struggling to survive offers a redemptive opportunity for them to finally connect."
—*New City Lit Review*

Conch Pearl

Julie E. Justicz

Fomite
Burlington, Vermont

ISBN-13: 978-1-959984-11-5
Library of Congress Control Number: 2023942624
Fomite
58 Peru Street
Burlington, VT 05401
08-30-2023

for Mary

What are the words you do not yet have?

      "Sister Outsider," Audre Lorde

Blue,

Here is a shell for you

Inside you'll hear a sigh

A foggy lullaby

There is your song from me

      "Blue," Joni Mitchell

PRELUDE

The Hobie skips waves and shreds seaweed, racing ahead of the storm. Dede, flattened on the mesh trampoline, grips its laces. If she lets go now, rolls off the side and into the crazed sea, could she make it to shore? She swam 400 meters at the Freeport Y once—but this? When she dares to lift her head and angle her eyes left, the island—a charcoal smudge above the wild green water—melts into a darkening sky. Too far, too rough to try.

A massive wave lifts the left hull, slams it down. Her body jerks like a hooked flounder. The laces cut into her finger grooves, knuckles threaten to burst through the back of her hand, but she holds on. Another monster catches the Hobie and her stomach heaves and plunges, heaves and plunges. Land, there and not, there and not. The boat swerves and jerks her sideways, her belly hits a metal bar. Hard. Sick rises in her throat. She tries to swallow, tries to catch her breath, sucks in air, and then vomits onto her chest.

Think, Dede, think. What to do? Let the storm carry her until it passes? If she keeps holding on, how far will it take her?

Grand Bahama Island is an outstretched arm, one long finger beckoning to Florida. Freeport fills out the lumpy wrist with its resorts, rentals, and the casino, then sixty more miles of bone straight-lines towards a fractured elbow. All the scattered East End cays. She knows the names, McLeans's Town, Sweeting, Michael's—even now can picture them, south and east of the main island, small and smaller and then disappearing into the sea.

Fear pins her to the boat. Wind thwacks the sail; the main line sings its tension: Hmmmmmwww. Hmmmmmwww. Hmmmmmwww. Dede spread out like the Cuban tree frog they dissected during science class in April. A metal skewer pinned each frog limb to a wooden board and its upturned belly shone pale as a sickly moon. The frog sliced open, its heart thumped rapid red, rapid red, rapid red 183 times before it died. Maybe now is her punishment. For things she's done and for things she's let be done. Her heart beats hard and harder, fast and faster, rapid red, rapid red. How many beats? No one is counting.

Will anyone look for her?

She tries to telepath an SOS. Please, Mum, Please, but the main line thrums like a bass string, Hmmmmmwww, Hmmmmmwww, drowning out her message.

How fast does sound travel? Wind to line to air to ear? Her body is an idiot, but Dede knows some things. The speed of sound—768 miles per hour. And if she doesn't act soon, she'll be miles offshore. She could drown. She will drown. She throws up again—bile this time.

Maybe her friend Ethel is parked at High Rock now, shut inside her El Camino, waiting out the storm. If she could see Dede, if only she could sense Dede, tossed along on the horizon line, she would race her car eastward keeping an eye on the catamaran the whole way.

Ethel, look across the sea and save me.

Black-green clouds getting darker, too dark for anyone to see.

Waves crash against the fiberglass hull. Waves spray her face, salt bites her eyes, her skin, her lips. Waves spit and foam and slam the boat, growing the space between Dede and Ethel, here and there, lost and land. Should she try? Let go and try? No. Stay on the boat, stay with the boat. Stupid, bloody stupid, to climb on board, to not jump off in the first fifty yards when she could have swum to shore. Now she has no chance, no choice. Now she must hold on until the end of this storm.

Hands on fire. Waves season her cuts. Fear rattles her brain. Just hold on.

Please. I don't think I can.

Even if she holds on all night, outlasts the storm, she could still die out here. Her body would wash up somewhere—an East End cay, or somewhere farther still—the Tongue of the Ocean, where the deepest, darkest waters fill an underground canyon.

The storm sucks her in, lashes her with rain and wind and chop. Waves crash over her body, again and again, trying to push and pull her into the sea. She grips the laces tighter, even tighter. The ropes shredding her palms. The mainline shrieking louder: Hmmmmmwww, Hmmmmmwww. I can't. I can't. I can't hold on anymore. Please. Someone. Anyone.

She sees his face, his smile, his hand reaching for her.

No.

Eyes squeezed tight, she feels her stomach drop before the next wave lifts and slams the catamaran sideways. Her body crashes against the lower hull, shoulder, rib, hip, whole body screaming, but somehow, somehow, her hand finds a fiberglass ridge to grab onto for as long as she can.

PART I

FREEPORT, GRAND BAHAMA ISLAND

1975 - 1976

CHAPTER 1

The fresh catch that landed on Grand Bahama Island in mid-November came not from England, like her predecessors, but from a Welsh hamlet. In every other way, she fit the species of teacher Dede was used to: twenty-something, glue-white, and way overdressed for Freeport's shoddy grade school. She showed up Wednesday morning wearing a turquoise top and a black skirt, clicked across the floor in her heels, and unlatched her leather briefcase to pull out paper and a grip of pencils. When she turned to the blackboard, sweat islands dotted the silky ocean of her blouse.

Miss Evans. Her script was tidy, but the chalk skipped and shrieked when she tried to spell out her village: *Llanrhyr—r—n....*

Turning to face the class, she brushed yellow dust from her hands and skirt.

"Well, I'm delighted to be here," she sing-songed in that Welsh way, as her wide-set eyes scanned each row with a mixture of curiosity and fear.

Dede smiled as encouragingly as she could, while the other students smirked or stared, trying to intimidate another teacher into quitting. Island idiots. Dede had been stuck with this group for almost three years now. Packed into a tin can classroom, three rows, eighteen desks, but only about ten kids bothered to show up most days. Twelve today, including Dede. Faces spectrumed from white to pink to brown; hair long or short, straight or curly, some spit-slickened, some plaited, some matted into thick coral branches.

"I'm sorry we couldn't begin the year together. But we'll make up for lost time. I've got lots of interesting lessons planned."

"Oh, I bet you do," number one idiot Jethro said from his seat behind Dede, loud enough to get the class going. Hoots, chuckles, loud fake coughing from every row.

Miss Evans looked for something to lean against, found the edge of her desk. "Let's be respectful of one another."

Half past nine but already muggy in the tin can, even for the well-acclimated, like Dede. Miss Evans probably wouldn't make it through the day, never mind to the end of the term, if she didn't get a glass of water soon. And she needed to learn how to dress for the heat.

Dede raised her hand, threw a lifeline.

"Ye-e-es?" Miss Evans' vowels rolled like Welsh hills.

"How do you pronounce the name of your village, Miss?" Dede lilted too. Sometimes her voice mimicked people, all by itself. She liked Wales, the seaside town where her family had holidayed when she was seven or eight and Mum and Dad were still happy together. They'd borrowed Gran's caravan for a fortnight, driven west from Birmingham, and parked at a campsite near the estuary. Slate beach, glaucous sea, sky softened with drizzle—beautiful in a monochrome way; nothing like the color dazzle of the Bahamas.

"It's Lan-Rick-Win," Miss Evans said, her voice like two wine glasses clinking. "And you are?"

"Domini Dawes, Miss. People call me Dede." She sat up straight in her chair. Another new teacher meant another chance to present herself as well-liked and plucky, a class leader with a sporty nickname like Pippa or Kit or Tippy, the heroines from those boarding-school books... girls who climbed out of their dorm windows and hosted midnight picnics for their clever but mischievous chums.

Nothing like the truth.

Dede knew she wasn't well liked at Sunland. When she'd first arrived, her thick brown hair got so tangled from the sea, sun and chlorine that the boys nicknamed her Cave Lady. This year, they'd taken her down another peg, dubbing her "Doodoo." They threw it at her every chance they got.

"Well, Dede, it's very nice to meet you." Miss Evans' bright green eyes hovered on her for a few seconds; Dede wanted her to keep looking. She wanted to hold her teacher's attention and then ask her all sorts of questions, like *Why did you choose to teach here? What's your middle name? Couldn't you get a job somewhere decent, like London?*

Dede's mother didn't like it when she asked too many questions. *No one likes a precocious child*, she'd say, as if precocious meant rude, instead of intellectually mature and naturally inquisitive. Mum was so English... sprinkling praise on her criticisms and criticisms on her praise.

"Now, class," Miss Evans moved forward a step. "I'd like to get to know all of you a bit better. So how about an interesting fact from each of you... shall we go down the rows? Or alphabetically? Actually, is there an attendance list?"

Dede hadn't seen a list of students since the first week of school when their original teacher, Miss Morley, had put it in the top drawer of the desk. Jethro or one of the other idiots had left a dead fish in there one morning and Miss Morley quit soon after. Several students left, too—Polly Kottler to go to boarding school back in England because her parents were fed up with all the Sunland teachers coming and going. Robbie had returned to the States because his parents divorced. Natalie said she was heading to England next summer for certain. No one knew what happened to silent Bertram from Eight Mile Rock.

Dede raised her hand. "There might be an old attendance list in the desk drawer, Miss."

"Shut up, Doodoo," Jethro said. His father was some bigwig Bahamian politician, so he thought he could get away with anything. He was probably right. He was the tallest and oldest kid in the middle school trailer, a straw-haired Conchy Joe who hated school. She pulled down the class average in height and weight, but at twelve she was smack in the middle age wise. And cream of the crop in the brains department.

How could she demonstrate her perspicacity to Miss Evans? Would Miss Evans know what that word meant?

Coming up empty-handed after a quick search of the desk drawers, Miss Evans persevered. "While everyone thinks of something to share, let me tell you a bit about myself. As I wrote on the board, my name is Miss Evans, and I was born in Wales. That's part of the United Kingdom, of course. My parents breed border collies. I have four younger brothers who are lots of fun. The youngest, David... we say Di in Welsh... he's about your age."

"Wanker." Jethro coughed into his hand. Trevor and Nigel, loyal followers, copied, of course, "Wanker. Wanker," in between loud laughs.

"Quiet," Miss Evans tried. "Settle down or I'll have to..."

"You'll have to what?" Jethro challenged.

Miss Evans backed up, bumped against the blackboard.

Hold your ground, Dede thought. *Don't let him push you around.*

Miss Evans gripped the chalk ledge. "Who'd like to go next? Something interesting about you or your family? Anyone? Dede?"

What to say? What personal detail would intrigue Miss Evans? That she and Mum had left England three years ago after Mum spotted an advert in the Birmingham *Telegraph* and decided to apply for a job in the Bahamas. That back then saying Grand Bahama Island felt like an adventure. That when Mum learned she'd been hired as a Hospitality Clerk at a newly constructed casino, the real fun began. She'd taken Dede out of school to go shopping for a bathing suit at the center Birmingham Marks & Spencer, and they skipped down the aisles holding hands. That a fortnight later, they said good-bye to Dad and another damp sooty March in the Midlands. That Dad didn't fuss when they left. That like always, he sat in front of the telly watching his football team fall apart mid-season. That Dede didn't fuss either, because she thought they'd be gone for a few short weeks. That in the past three years Dede had learned how to swim well and could complete two whole lengths underwater at the apartment pool.

Dede raised her hand, but Timmy started talking without waiting his turn. About pirates, of course, his favorite topic, along with shipwrecks off the Abaco islands. Pieces of eight and all sorts of buried treasure.

Miss Evans nodded her head and asked questions, but she'd tire of these facts soon. She'd get bored and lonely here, like all the other teachers before her. None of them stayed more than six months, a year tops, before they returned to their real lives in the UK. Dede was so tired of being stuck in a stinky trailer with a bunch of sub-tropical idiots. She had to get away, too. If Mum wasn't ready to go back home, couldn't she at least agree to send Dede back—find a boarding school? Somewhere, anywhere, if not in England, then even the States would do.

But Mum didn't give a damn about Dede's education. All wrapped up in her not-so-secret boyfriend Silvio, who'd recently given her a promotion so she could work nights at the casino. *The first female croupier*, Mum bragged when she left for work in the evenings. Silvio had also helped Mum get a work permit that meant she could stay on now when other Brits had to leave. Did that mean Dede would end up going to high school here too? The thought of Freeport High with the likes of Jethro made her feel sick.

She had to get away. She needed to talk to Dad. He wrote to her every couple of months, but he never phoned, and he hadn't visited once in three years. His last letter mentioned that his beloved Blues had been relegated to Division 2. As if Dede cared one iota about football. Did he still have to watch every second of every bloody game? Sometimes Dede's thoughts echoed Mum's words, just as Mum's words sometimes interrupted her thoughts. *No one likes a precocious child.*

Timmy was still going on about Calico Jack Rackham and Anne Bonny, now. How they stole the sloop *William* from Nassau. How they later got caught, and were tried in Jamaica, but Anne Bonny avoided hanging at the gallows because the governor found out she was pregnant.

"Probably faking it," Jethro said, "too scared to die like a man."

Miss Evans wiped her brow. Her smile had melted. Her skin mottled pink and white. Dede raised her hand again. When Miss Evans called on her this time, Dede offered to fetch her a glass of water. She said she'd run fast, be back in a jiffy.

"That would be lovely, Dede. Thank you."

"Yes, fuck you very much, Doodoo" Jethro said as she stood up to leave. "And don't hurry back."

She walked across the scabby playground, past the dodgeball square, past the tetherball poles. In the rock garden outside the office building, lizards scurried, disappeared into holes. Rock garden? Ha! Rubbish heap, more like. She jumped over a coral chunk, skidded on the landing, fell and cut her leg. A raw red spot, the size of a Bahamian quarter bloomed on her kneecap. She could cry. Just sit there and cry. *But it's no good feeling sorry for yourself, young lady.* Plus, she had to get back to the trailer before all hell broke loose. She stood up, brushed the grit off her legs, and hurried inside the office.

Cool air hit her face. She closed the door softly behind her because the school's secretary, Mrs. Hibbert, hated slamming. She was on the phone, but put her hand over the mouthpiece, "What do you need, Dede?"

"A glass of water." Dede whispered. "For the new teacher."

Mrs. Hibbert pointed to the teachers' lounge and went back to her conversation.

The lounge was empty. The Mr. Coffee on the counter had burned a thick smelly paste in its carafe. Dede turned the machine off, then pulled a paper towel from the roll, and dabbed at the cut on her knee. A hibiscus blossomed on the white square. Blood art. She tossed the paper towel in the rubbish, then found a clean glass in the cabinet over the sink and filled it with cold water. She didn't bother looking for ice because Miss Evans was new on the island. British expats didn't know to ask for ice until they'd been on the island for at least a few weeks.

On her way out, Dede quietly asked if Mrs. Hibbert had a list of students in the middle school trailer. Still on the phone, she shook her head, covered the mouthpiece. "If any of the usual troublemakers start acting up in class, tell Miss Evans to come and see me during lunch. We'll sort them out."

Dede nodded, opened the door, stepped outside into the heat, and let the door slam behind her before she remembered not to. She could almost hear Mrs. Hibbert's excruciating sigh. Never mind. She'd say sorry on her next visit to the office. Now, she had to get back to the trailer, give Miss Evans the water, keep her hydrated and calm through lunch time, then give her a few encouraging words for the afternoon. Later today, she'd offer to write out a class list; she could do that from memory. She knew all the names of the students who usually showed up as well as the names of those who rarely did. She could even asterisk the troublemakers... she'd double-star Jethro's name.

Maybe Miss Evans would want to give Dede something in exchange? Tit for tat. Yes. She would make a deal with the new teacher. Dede would offer useful information about all the island idiots and, in return, she'd ask Miss Evans to help her get a scholarship to a boarding school in England. Maybe Cheltenham Ladies College, or Roedean, where Natalie planned to go next year. Or somewhere else; it didn't matter too much if it were halfway decent. Even Wales would do if Miss Evans had connections. Dede had heard of Gordonstoun, up in Scotland, where Prince Charles went when he was a boy. England's Prince of Wales sent to boarding school in Scotland. That was absurd. But not as ridiculous as Dede being marooned on this cragged and crooked island.

CHAPTER 2

John McGuinn had been careful, left the States before things blew up again, was working shit jobs, hands busy and head down, staying out of trouble. No temptations for going on a year now. But mid-island, mid-week, mid-December, and just shy of midday, he felt it again. Dear God, the want, the goddamn want. He'd tried to ignore it, tried to snuff if out. Might as well spit on a bushfire.

He parked the Olds across from Sunland Academy, engine running, AC blasting, and his mind spinning through the same old promises—a quick look, just this one time, it need not go any further, it can't go any further, one look is all. His mind told the usual stories, but his body knew the truth. He'd been a goner from the moment he first saw her, three or four weeks back, standing by the pool, in her sagging, faded swimsuit.

She'd bounced over to talk. "Excuse me, sir." Her voice so English, so very polite. Her legs skinny and brown, her hair a bleached and shaggy mess, her nose and cheeks lightly freckled. "Are you the new building manager?"

His heart already skipping, he'd bowed and said, "Johnnie McGuinn, at your service."

"How do you do, Mr. McGuinn?" She extended her hand to shake his, and her well-chewed fingernails grated against his wrist.

"Call me Johnnie, please."

He'd watched her tongue twist around a few more pleasantries. She lived with her mother in apartment 1C. She was twelve years old. Her favorite color... definitely blue. "Cyan blue," she'd said. The sweetest lisp, enough undo him.

She was there in the pool the next afternoon, and then every one thereafter, swimming underwater or lying on a deck chair with her nose stuck in a library book, clad always in the same faded one-piece, loose as an elephant's skin. Same color too. When he did the chemicals, she'd skim the water for him. She was sort of shy at first, but soon enough she let herself chatter.

He'd taken the apartment manager job when Silvio offered it, because a one-bedroom unit and the use of a car came with the position. Two things McGuinn needed, even if he didn't care much for his role—glorified janitor and occasional gopher for the boss. There were only twelve apartments in the building, all well-kept, occupied by decent tenants—mostly casino workers—who paid their rent on time. He planned to save a little money, stay a year or two tops, until things settled down and he could head back to the States. And Silvio—a hustler if there ever was one—had promised that there'd be opportunities for extra pay—for resourceful employees.

But now... here McGuinn was, lovesick all over, waiting outside the girl's school, willing to what? Risk it all? Christ. Sixty-three years old last year and here he was waiting in front of another school. *Sunland Academy.* A bullshit name for a bunch of doublewides, dropped like Matchbox toys on a plot of scrub land.

With all the money dumped into Freeport, it seemed that one of the billionaire investors, Wallace Groves or Howard Hughes, might have spent a fraction of it on education. Donated a decent lot by the water, underwritten the costs of a couple of air-conditioned buildings. But those misers didn't give a rat's ass about kids. No, they'd bull-dozed the bush and built their harbor, their tax-free paradise for British investors, their gamblers' playground for American tourists.

Kids not even an afterthought.

McGuinn wiped his brow. The girl was stuck in one of those trailers. Baking in the late morning heat. He'd like to get her out of there, buy her a cold Coke, or an ice cream, take her for a drive, and get to know her better, without all the eyes of the school or the apartment building looking on. No father in the picture, as far as he could tell, so she'd be wanting an uncle, a male friend. His heart pulsed in his ear.

No. Stop. He shook his head, tried to rattle her from his skull. He had work to do, stuff to get from the store. Commonwealth Building Supplies. The tenants in 2D locked themselves out last night, and instead of doing the reasonable thing, waking him up, asking for the master key, they'd tried to force the lock. Broken a penknife in the shank and destroyed the faceplate, too, before remembering an open bathroom window. "So verrry sorry," the faggoty French one said this morning. "We couldn't bear to trouble you in the middle of the night." Like it was no trouble now for McGuinn to have to drive into town, buy and install a whole new mechanism to repair the damage. But he'd smiled and said no problem. He didn't need them complaining to Silvio.

He checked his watch. A little before noon. He should drive to the store, buy the lock, pay the fucking island markups, go back to the apartments and do his job. Stay out of trouble. Wasn't that the whole reason he'd picked this island in the first place? He looked across the street at the empty schoolyard. Maybe the kids would come outside soon for recess. They couldn't keep them boxed up all day. Must give them a half hour after lunch, a little air? He'd wait a few minutes more... five, seven at most. What harm was there in sitting, waiting, watching? He wasn't hurting anyone. He'd been a good boy since he'd arrived on the island. What was it that Sister Mary Pat used to say to help the piano students remember the notes? "Every Good Boy Does Fine."

The sun overhead. If she didn't come outside by 12:05 he'd go. He wouldn't return. He'd take it as a sign that this wasn't meant to be. 12:05—that would be the cut off. He crossed his heart and hoped to die. Promised Sister Mary Pat. Swore on his own mother's grave. He thrummed his thumbs on the steering wheel and waited. Three minutes, three and a half, four. He'd have to leave.

Then, like a blessing from above, some battle-axe walked out of the school office and started shaking a hand bell. She looked across the street, so McGuinn sank a little lower in his seat. What if she came over to ask what he was doing? He could say that he'd come to pick up his... niece... for an outing. Would granddaughter be more believable? She clanged the bell again and again until children started tumbling out of their classrooms and scattering across the yard.

He opened the car window and turned off the engine.

Voices sing-songing, the rhythms of play. Tall black boys racing towards tetherball poles. Clusters of white girls unraveled jump ropes. Double-Dutch. His head spinning, a whirring in his belly, as he strained his eyes to see the girl, his girl, among them, as he strained his ears to hear her voice, so pretty and polite. If he could tease out a thread of her sound. If he could will her to come his way. His face dripped with effort, dripped with the day's muggy heat. Yes, he was too old for this, but still just a kid inside.

He closed his eyes. He could almost hear the words, the rhyme, the ditty that the first girl whispered in his ear so many years ago. *My mother said, I never should, play with the gypsies in the wood. If I did, she would say, naughty little girl to disobey.*

When he opened his eyes, he'd conjured up the new one. She stood behind the fence on the asphalt—alone, a few yards away from the jump-ropers. What was she doing? She spread her arms wide and spun in a circle. Spun and spun, making herself dizzy. Skinny arms, blue-plaid skirt. Pencil legs. Both white socks slouched around her ankles. She didn't know it yet, but she was already performing for him. A girl mixed with guile, like so many before, shyness cloaking seduction.

She stopped spinning, stood perfectly still, then looked across the road, angled one hand as if to salute him, or maybe to shield her eyes from the sun. Did she recognize the car from the apartment lot? Too soon, too soon to wave at her. He turned the engine back on, raised his window, ready to move on with his day. But he'd come back. He'd show up after school next week, ask if she'd like a ride home. She'd say no at first, but he'd come back a few days later, try again, just out running errands, he'd say, it's really no trouble, and soon enough she'd get accustomed to his presence, so used to the pale-yellow car on the shoulder of the road, so ready for a ride home that she'd rush toward him, still shy but wanting to accept. *Are you sure it's no trouble?* She'd ask. *Thanks very much.* The snag of her tongue. The smell of playground sweat. He could almost taste the salt on her skin. He'd drive her home that day and again and again and again, transforming himself into her devoted servant.

Chapter 3

Ethel had seen Dede playing in and around the pool every day for the past week, and early this Saturday morning she was at it again—bouncing up and down in the shallow end, turning somersaults in the deeper water, and then lying on a chaise longue reading one of the library books she had piled beside her, before giving up and jumping in the water again. How many hours could she entertain herself doing handstands in three feet of water? The girl was bored, of course. And who could blame her? No school to go to during Christmas break, no playmates in the building. And the mother— what was her name—Angela? Anna? —a night shift worker, probably catching up on her sleep during the holiday rush, but surely, she shouldn't leave the girl alone this much.

In a moment of inexplicable weakness, after she finished packing her car with painting supplies, Ethel returned to the pool deck and invited the girl on her expedition. Now thirty minutes into the drive, Ethel was beginning to regret extending the offer. The girl was a chatterbox and Ethel needed quiet today. She was heading to Deadman's Reef, a place she hadn't visited in years. She had a notion she wanted to explore. A series of paintings beyond her usual seascapes, her tame watercolors. She wanted to capture something real about the island. The people, her people, fishermen coming in with the daily catch—not tourists with their sailfish trophies. Women drying sponges in the high, hot sand. Children chasing crabs in the shallows. Even potcake puppies lounging in the scrub. Like the Newlyn School, but peopled by Bahamians—before Wallace Groves and his fellow tycoons built their tax haven on Grand Bahama. This morning's goal was simple: get the lay of the land, the rocky shoreline that she remembered from her childhood in Eight Mile Rock, and maybe sketch out a few scenes.

Dede sat cross-legged on the front seat, chewing on her fingernails, and peppering Ethel with questions. Why had she opened this day, this private time, to an outsider, not to mention the drive through the settlements where she grew up? This was exactly the kind of self-sabotage that Nora used to blame her for—*I am not stopping you from painting, Ethel—You're the one who won't stick to it.* Nora's words made Ethel wonder if she lacked the discipline or a certain something—muscle, endurance, insanity—to be a real artist. A real artist protected her workspace. A real artist never would have invited Dede—a white child—along. True, the girl was usually polite, always appreciative of any attention coming her way, but she hadn't stopped jabbering since she got in the car—and not just reciting facts or telling the kind of school stories that Ethel could tune out while she steered the long, thin highway west of Freeport. No, the girl was full of questions, questions that required a response.

What kind of bird makes that machine gun sound?

What's the best color for painting a shallow sea?

Worse, some responses required introspection before answering.

Why did you leave England and move back to Freeport anyway?

Ethel half-grunted half-answers, hoping to stall the interrogation,

23

but it continued past the holiday-packed resorts of Freeport, through the unfinished network of roads and waterways beyond town limits.

Is painting your passion?

Did you ever have a boyfriend... other than Art?

Ethel grew edgy and irritable whenever she drove into the settlements—but of course the girl couldn't know that it was best to pipe down because her driver had pangs of guilt about not staying, a healthy dose of shame, too, at how her own people still lived in such shabby conditions, couldn't know what it meant for Ethel to drive through here. Couldn't know her constant chatter chafed on Ethel's already flayed feelings. How could Ethel be so stupid as to bring her?

Dede switched to "Would You Rathers:"

Live every minute of the rest of your life in a shack in the settlements or locked up in a penthouse like Howard Hughes?

Eat nothing but raw conch or only sea grapes for a year?

"Good gracious girl, doesn't your mouth get tired," Ethel snapped.

Dede withdrew like a hermit crab. But no time to apologize as they approached Hepburn Town, a half mile of pastel shacks lining both sides of the highway. Ethel wanted to race through, but she slowed her El Camino to twenty; last thing she needed was to sideswipe some mangy potcake or, God forbid, a child.

"Is this Eight Mile Rock?"

"The start of it. This is the first settlement of maybe ten or eleven in Eight Mile Rock. You'll see."

"A girl in my class lives here. Prudence Simms. Do you know her?"

"I haven't lived here in years."

There was a group of kids on the roadside just ahead. Four or five boys, all bare-chested and scratching around in the dirt in front of a squat building. A store? A church? A ramshackle school? One of the boys leapt up as Ethel approached. He had what looked like a broom handle in his hand and swung it at the corner of the building. A sag-bellied potcake and three pups scurried out from an alley and darted across the road right in front of Ethel's car. She slowed to a creep, honked her horn, two, three times, then stopped, but the kid ignored her and chased after the dogs, his legs grazing her front bumper, as he brandished his stick, whooping and yelling.

"What's he doing?" Dede asked.

As the dogs disappeared into the bush, the boy turned to cross back over the street. He smiled at Ethel, then raised his arm like a conquering hero. He was skinny as a runt himself with a belly protruding over his shorts—probably the same age as Dede—and he patted the hood of the car with his free hand before returning to the other boys.

Ethel started driving again. Slowly picking up speed to a steady, safe 25 mph.

"Why did he chase those poor puppies?"

"Because potcakes are a nuisance. Get into the rubbish, steal food. So the boys scare them off."

"That's terrible."

"That's settlement life. Would you rather the boys chase them, or the shop keepers poison them? This is not Freeport."

"Where do people work?"

"These towns started when folks came from the Turks and Caicos Islands to work the lumber mill at Pine Ridge. They joined freed slaves already living on Grand Bahama and built their homes along this road. Lumber's long gone, but the families eked out a living from sponging, bootlegging during prohibition, fishing, of course, and a little farming. And now... well, they do whatever they can."

"Why did you leave, Ethel?"

"Because I could."

"But what about your family? Your Mum and Dad? Don't you miss them?"

How could the girl understand any of this? "This is not like your world. My mama died when I was a baby. My daddy went off on The Contract—farming in the States when I was two or three years old and I lived with my Auntie Gert; my father sent a little money, but he never came back. Stopped writing altogether before I was in the all-age school. I was an extra mouth for my Auntie to feed so I left as soon as I could. Scholarshipped off to Government High in Nassau, and then, when I got the chance, all the way to university in England."

Another pack of scabby looking dogs darted out from the bush ahead of the car. Ethel swerved to miss them.

"Dear God."

"Can't we stop and help them?"

Ethel shook her head. She should never have brought the child here.

"But what's going to happen to them?"

"Some will survive, others won't. It's tough for people here, too, Dede, not just dogs."

They drove slowly for another couple of miles. Ethel's skin prickled near Old Mt. Olivet Church. What became of Mr. Reverend Pike? He'd always welcomed her, even when she was barefoot and dirty, smelling of fish and sweat, and the only one in Auntie's family who found her way regularly to Sunday services. She'd gone just to get out of the noise of that shack—all the children with snotty noses scrapping for food. Her skin itched with the memory of it now and she wanted to drive fast and faster away from this place.

"Are we near to where you grew up?"

Ethel nodded. "Getting close. Hanna Hill." She couldn't help laughing when she added, "My hometown." She felt exposed and judged and wanted to add something —that the place had been better, cleaner, a notch up from what Dede saw now: buildings lined up like chipped and broken teeth—some still roofless from the last big storm. Laundry flocked and snapped on lines. A few women sat on chairs placed beside the road, watching cars that passed, maybe only one or two an hour at this time of day. A couple of kids hopscotched on the sandy verge. Ethel saw them without turning her head. She didn't want the girl to think she was judging the people. She wasn't. But how could she explain that not once since she'd been back on Grand Bahama—over five months now—not once had she returned to visit her relatives in Hanna Hill.

"Can we drive by your old house? I'd love to see where you lived?"

Ethel shook her head, found a lie. "That place is long gone. Hurricane Betsy took it in 1965. I was in England at the time."

"Did anyone die? I mean in the storm?"

"Not here in Hanna Hill; lots of homes collapsed though." That was true. Just not the case with Auntie Gert's place; it had survived the hurricane and was still standing, as far as Ethel knew, only about a half a mile along the next road to the right. Gert had died in 1968. Ethel got a telegram in Bristol from her cousin Angus. *Gert at peace.* Ethel bought a condolence card with red roses on the front, the best choice she could find at the local Boots; mailed it to her cousins. That was the last contact she'd had with any of them. Some of them probably still lived in the old place, patching it with cardboard and corrugated tin between storms. One relative gone, another filling the spot. When Ethel left Hanna Hill, no one would have felt the void.

None of them knew she'd returned last summer, was living in

Freeport, working in a local branch of a British bank. She'd told herself for years that they'd never accept who she'd become—all educated and uppity—not to mention what they'd think of her proclivities, the life she'd lived with Nora. But it was not that, or not only that, keeping her away. Somehow, she didn't feel she'd come far enough to return. She didn't want to visit with her relatives and realize that even though she'd changed everything about herself and her circumstances, she was still not happy, still not satisfied. As a kid, she'd been miserable most of the time, but always thought that her misery was about lack: no parents, not a cent to her name, hand-me-down clothes, scarcely enough food. What she hadn't expected or understood was that a strain of unhappiness would always run in her blood, no matter how far she went in school, in her professional and even in her romantic life. No matter how far she wandered away from her Hanna Hill clan, a familiar loneliness would cling to her, like salt on her body after a swim in the ocean.

She accelerated through the last part of town. Just a couple of miles farther west to Deadman's Reef. She wanted to try something new, to stretch herself. She didn't know how... so why didn't she pack up and return to Bristol, paint scenes from the river-walk, the coal gray skies, the gloomy waters? What was she trying to prove? Her foot extended against the accelerator, and she squeezed the wheel. Would Nora take her back after all this fumbling and bumbling about where she belonged? Christ. She was thirty-four years old—too old for mind games with herself. The car's speedometer hovered near seventy-five. Too fast for these sun-cracked roads.

Dede silent beside her.

"It's important to have family, Dede. Or at least a special person who knows where you come from and how you tick."

"Do you have someone like that?"

"I lived with Auntie Gert... but she didn't really understand me. There was another lady who used to live out this way, Jestina Lawler. I went to school with her son, Clarence, and she looked out for me, too. She knew I wanted to learn. She had more time and more energy for me than my Aunt Gert. When I was sad, she'd listen to me; when I was lonely, she'd treat me like one of her own."

"But she's not here anymore?"

"I'm not sure." Ethel bit her lip. "We've lost touch. I feel badly about it." She meant that didn't know how to go to Jestina, how to apologize for the time and the distance between them. She meant that she didn't know how Jestina would understand her choices and behaviors. She meant that she was afraid of not being accepted for who she was. She meant that she'd grown used to keeping secrets.

"Well, at least you've still got your boyfriend." Dede said.

"What are you talking about?"

"Art. You spend every single night with your art, don't you? In your flat?" Dede made a kissy face.

"Christ." Ethel spat out, "Not every woman needs a man in her life." All the women she'd known—women like Dede's mother—who used their femininity as bait. So many of them at Bristol University; they'd been clever enough to do well on A Levels, yet they still chose sex as their currency. It infuriated her.

"Sorry," Dede clutched the handle above her door.

Ethel's anger had startled the kid but was it so bloody difficult for her to understand? Why was she always probing around the same old topic? The stupid joke about a boyfriend named Art.

Ethel released her death grip on the steering wheel. "I'm driving too fast?"

Dede nodded.

"I apologize for snapping at you. This place brings back some memories."

"No one likes a precocious child."

"No. It's my fault. It's just that seeing these places shakes me up. Maybe that's why they say you can't go home again."

"I can," Dede said. "I'm going back to England soon."

"Really?"

"Yes. I'm going to get a scholarship, just like you did, and go to a proper boarding school."

"Well, good. Good for you. Ask your teacher about the Port Authority grants; they send a student for school overseas. All expenses paid."

Ethel turned off the highway and drove a half-mile on the crushed coral road toward the water. To the right, about a mile down the beach, was the West End dock. To the left was the stretch of rock where she remembered folk sat and fished. Ethel parked the El Camino next to a sea grape bush as big as a house—the fruit on the tree was still firm, and green-purple—a few weeks shy of edible. They unloaded supplies from the back, then carried everything— cooler, canvases, paints, canopy—to the low-tide beach. No one else was around. A great painting day—the sky clear except for pink, gauzy clouds stretched above the horizon line. Wind pushed lightly off the land and the sea quilted green and turquoise and blue —the surface barely rippling. Ethel felt her good spirits returning.

Dede kicked off her sandals, pulled off her t-shirt and shorts, and raced across the fine white sand and into the ocean. Angled sunlight turned her silver, sprite-like, in the shallows; she was a hundred yards out, and the water still not up to her knees. She stopped and bent down.

"Conch," she yelled, holding up a shell.

Ethel couldn't make out the shell's color or definition, except to see it was huge.

This: a silhouette of a girl, not white or black, but silvery—a dream child conjured up by the waters. You could fight so hard to get the right idea, nothing, nothing, and in a moment, it would find you and you'd know that it was right. A wave of relief, then belief. She had been right to bring the girl. Right to be kind to her even when she poked and probed the sore spots. Right to capture this moment.

She laid out a straw mat on the sand, set up the easel, unrolled the umbrella and planted it in the metal holder; she unfolded her stool. Though she painted on her feet indoors, out here, on the sand, she needed the stool, the shade from the umbrella—even for a quick value study. She'd brought four small canvases and a suitcase of paints, but for the first runs—twenty-minute drafts that she wanted to do today, she'd rely heavily on ultramarine, burnt umber, sap green, and quinacridone gold—colors deep enough to get the contrasts. In her studio, when she had the time, she'd review the values and pull up all the details—the feelings and thoughts about the day—find shapes and colors to paint the memory. What was memory but a series of images—each one beautiful or mundane or ugly in its own right, each one asking the bigger question: Who caught this and held onto it? And why?

Dede yelled from the water, closer to the beach now. "Come in, come in. It's incredible." She had a shell in each hand and was hopping in place, "They're all over!"

Ethel pulled off her painting shirt and tossed it on the sand. Beneath she wore a black tank top and men's khaki shorts. No swimsuit. But her clothes would dry quickly in this weather. Her legs felt out of shape; years since she'd really worked them, but she'd been a good 800-meter runner once, and she raced across the firm sand and leaped through the water toward the girl. When she pulled up beside Dede, they looked at one another, both hit with a sudden shyness.

Dede let go of the two conch shells in her hands. They shuffled off on the white sandy bottom. The pair joined dozens more conch, a little farther out.

"What do you think they're all doing here?" Dede asked.

Ethel had seen them on sandbars, reefs, and in turtle-grass before. In deeper water, too, but never in such a large group. On the ocean floor, they seemed to be headed westward, each rolling movement took them a half body length.

"I'm not sure. Let's leave them alone for now," Ethel said. "Maybe later, when we're ready to go home, we'll grab a few. Did you ever make fritters?"

Dede shook her head. "I've had them at restaurants, though."

"There's nothing like homemade. I'll show you. The friend I was telling you about, Jestina, she had the best recipe. With onion and peppers from her patch."

They walked out farther. Shoals of silvery fish scattered as they neared. Dede stepped on a sand biscuit, pulled it up to show, then dropped it back in the water. Another, then another, dozens of them, white and slightly prickly, lying under a thin coating of sand. Ahead of them, the sea surface flickered from shimmery turquoise to a greenish-blue. They were approaching the reef, and beyond that the drop-off into the Providence Channel.

"Can you imagine trying to paint the underwater world?" Ethel said. "The coral, the sea fans? All the half-hidden lives? And the movement of the sea? How would you recreate it on canvas?"

32

"Maybe if you had special underwater cameras you could catch a snapshot then paint later."

"Yes... but how to show the movement? The fleeting light? You'd have to somehow catch it... the full moment. The best art does that— not capture an image but recreate a full sensory experience."

The water reached Dede's waist now. "I wish we'd brought snorkels."

"When I was a kid, we'd come dive here to get our relish—that's what we called fish back then. No masks. We'd dive with our eyes open. Come on, let's keep going a little way. We can swim out over the reef. Just as long as we don't go out where the water turns dark."

Dede leaned forward, swimming British school-girl breaststroke. Ethel waded a little longer, until the water came up to her chest, then she too began frog-kicking. So easy to stay afloat in these waters, just relax, breathe, let the ocean lift you. They stroked side-by-side wordlessly, another fifty yards or so, until they were right over the reef, then stopped and tread water. Below, sea fans swayed, coral brains bulged with their own memories, angelfish darted in the water. They took deep breaths, then dived down, eyes open, lungs blazing to get a closer look at the underwater settlement: the large platters and swaying cups, the spiders and flowers, the tubes and the bowls, each coral colony an accretion of the living and the dead.

Before lunch, Ethel suggested they walk along the beach; she wanted to see the rocky landscape she remembered farther east. Maybe they'd find a few fishermen. They started out, collecting shells, and the odd bit of sea glass, dropping them in a bucket Ethel had brought along for this purpose. They talked easily now—the tension of the car ride washed away—talked about coral growth, conch fishing, painting techniques. They agreed that next week, before school started back, they'd each try to paint reef life, they'd put their own memories on the canvas and compare the images and the feelings evoked. What would they remember in common? What would be lost or forgotten to them both?

After a half-mile or more of walking, no one else, no footsteps on the sand, their clothes had dried, salt-crispy against their skin. Ethel hadn't thought to ask the girl about sun cream. Ethel didn't use it herself. Her own skin these days was a lighter brown than it used to be in her childhood, when she lived on the beach; but she didn't burn, never had. After a day in the sun, her skin would pull tight across her face and turn a shade darker. Dede's skin glowed red-brown across her back and shoulders, the color of a good wood—natural cherry, but her face was pink and freckled, and her nose was peeling. No hat, either.

"You're getting burnt. Maybe we should get back so you can cover up."

"It doesn't matter. I fry every weekend. Then I peel and start over again. Like Johnnie Angel."

"Johnnie Angel?"

"Mr. McGuinn. It's my nickname for him. He's always sunburning his forehead."

"I've seen you two cleaning the pool together. Does he pay you to help?"

"He gives me Cokes and he lets me watch his telly sometimes because ours is broken and I get bored at night when Mum is working."

"She might not like that, I mean, if you're supposed to be asleep."

"Oh, she doesn't care, as long as I'm not bothering people. I don't knock on your door after eight because I know you're usually painting or sleeping. But Johnnie Angel said anytime is fine." Dede bent over to pick up a shell. "Anyway, I've told Mum about a hundred times that our telly is spazzy."

Ethel didn't like McGuinn—he seemed like the worst caricature of America that anyone could conjure, tall and brash, sunburned and potbellied—but she certainly wasn't going to offer to entertain the girl in the evenings. "Well, I suppose no one likes being left alone at night."

"You do." Dede dropped a shell in the bucket. "You're alone every night."

Ethel shook her head. Ethel didn't love solitude; it was more that she feared the alternative. "I like my time to paint, of course, but I still get lonely." She missed Nora. But how to explain. What could a twelve-year-old understand? "I had a special friend I left behind in England. Someone I miss quite a lot. I wanted to come home to the island—I thought it's where I belong—but now I am not sure. And I actually miss this person more than I thought possible."

Last summer in England, the day after her school term at Red Maids had finished, Nora had packed a picnic basket and they'd gone on an outing to Bristol Bay. Spent the day talking, lounging on a tartan blanket, drinking wine, eating bread and cheese—Nora sketching out her plans for the summer holidays. Maybe they could add a studio onto the back of Nora's house so Ethel would finally have time and space for her art. The new rose bushes Nora wanted for the back garden— some climbers for the fence, too. Nora took Ethel's hand and held it in hers, fingers intertwined right there in the open, big and small, black and white, woman and woman, on display. At least until a couple of girls from the school came running along the path, swearing and yelling, cigarettes in hand. Ethel pulled her hand back. The wind off the water was cool, the sky brushed with clouds, but when they got home that night, Nora's pale English skin had flushed hot pink. She'd had to take aspirin and go to bed. Beside her that night and on into the early hours of the next day, Ethel had never felt more like a stranger in a strange land. Who was she kidding? Settling into a steady job, living with a small, efficient white woman in a distant gray land. A week later, Ethel left. Time to think, she wrote, in her coward's letter.

"Maybe you should go back to England and see your friend," Dede said. "I'd leave today if I could."

"Well, it's not that simple." She'd flown back into Grand Bahama, mid-July, intending to go home to Hanna Hill and find her cousins, to visit Jestina and to make amends with Clarence. She believed in time she'd figure out what she wanted. She'd told Nora that she'd be gone a month at most; instead, she found an apartment in Freeport for a decent rate and requested a transfer from the bank. Barclays agreed to post her immediately in the Freeport branch; a shoo-in, her boss in Bristol said, because she was a well-educated Bahamian woman. No work permit problems. She could really go far.

Ethel wrote a second longer letter to Nora in September, trying to explain—said she needed more time to make peace with her past, more time to work on her painting. She never got a reply.

"But if you miss this person so much... maybe they could at least visit you."

They rounded a curve in the beach. A rocky plateau ahead. Three people squatted on a wide, flat gray stone, next to a sloop in the water. Fishermen coming in from the sea. She wished she had a Polaroid to snap this. Even a pad and pencil for a two-minute sketch.

"Come on," she said to Dede. "Let's go see what they've caught."

"Plenty of conch, I bet," Dede said.

But as they got closer, Ethel's stomach dipped. The men were dressed wrong for fishing—in shirts with collars; one even wore long slacks and black leather shoes. She wanted to turn back, afraid of what they'd stumbled onto. She reached for Dede's hand. As she did so, one of the men saw them and yelled; all three stood and starting walking towards them. Fast.

"What do they want?" Dede said.

Ethel squeezed her fingers. "Hush now. Let me handle this."

"Morning, sister," The man in the middle said as they closed in. "What are you lovelies doing out here on my beach?" Clearly, he was the oldest of the three, his hair and trim beard grizzled with gray. He wore trousers, and his long-sleeved shirt was unbuttoned at the top to reveal a gold coin dangling from a thick chain around his neck. The two younger men flanking him stared at Ethel with no trace of welcome.

"Just out walking," Ethel said, "collecting shells." She rattled the bucket. "Thinking to head back now. Too much sun for this one."

"Who this bright beauty with you, then?"

"She's my young friend."

"Does she have a name, your young friend?" He took a couple more steps toward them; the other two men did the same and Ethel saw that the one on the right had a machete in his hand. He poked at the sand with the tip of the blade. Stay calm. Lots of folk carried machetes. Machete for cracking conch. Machete for chopping off fish heads. Ethel glanced at the boat. A fishing skiff all right, but no nets, no rods, no coolers. A drop spot then? Had she and Dede stumbled onto a drug deal? Machete for intruders?

"What's your name, beauty?" The old man said directly to Dede this time.

37

If the girl was worried or scared, she didn't show it. She held her ground. "Domini, but most people call me Dede."

The old man laughed. "Domini is better."

Dede nodded.

"Then why you let them call you that? Why don't you stick up for yourself?" He spat out on to the sand.

Dede smiled nervously.

"Why you bring your little friend out on this here private land, Sister?"

The land wasn't private; never had been, but Ethel didn't disagree. The West End had always had its smugglers—so close to Miami. Rum-running during prohibition. Now, it was cocaine. She'd read about it in the *Freeport News*. She didn't need to know what these three were up to but fleeing now was not the answer. Not with the girl. Not with the machete. She wanted things to go smoothly. She knew they could go otherwise. Time to lose her hard accent, her white woman's voice.

"We come out this way for a picnic and we got to walking," Ethel said. "S'pose we done lost track of time and walked too far. No plans to trespass."

"You from Freeport?" One of the sidekicks.

"That's right."

"Come out all this way for a picnic?" The old man again. "Where's your food? Your scrumptious picnic?"

"Back that way."

"What kind of car you drive, Sister?"

Was he going to take her keys? Money? She'd left her wallet on the beach under a towel. Where were her keys? She felt her pockets.

"Don't play with me, now." He stepped closer and cupped Dede's chin in his hand, tilted it up. "Domini. You a smart girl, I'm betting you can tell me what kind of car this nice lady drive."

"It's an El Camino," Ethel said quickly, trying to stay calm, keep herself from panicking. "Please don't hurt her."

"Hurt Domini? Why would I do something like that?" The old man ran his fingers through Dede's tangled hair. "Someone needs to tame her hair though." He reached toward his sidekick for the machete. "Or chop it all off."

"Wait. Take the vehicle if you want it. Don't belong to me, no how." She kept her tone even, and willed Dede not to talk, not to add fuel to any fire burning inside these men. "This one's Daddy—He a big man in Freeport. Casino boss, Mr. Silvio, you know. He told me I could use the car to bring the child out here. See the Rock. Meet my own family—all them Hanna Hill Tootes."

The old guy stroked his own chin, then scratched above his lip. "Gertie Tootes? Old Albert's wife?"

"That's right," she said. "She my auntie." Ethel was glad for her salt-crusted shorts, the sloppy tank top. Her hair was a mess. And Dede was too much of a child—God she hoped it was true—still too stick-boned, sun-speckled for them to fool with her in that way. "My family living in these parts since sponging days."

"Sponging ain't shit." The young man who'd given up the machete said. "Only the outfit got rich off sponging. None of the settlement folks got paid nothing for that kind of work."

"You right about that. My own father gone off on the Contract in the forties. Carolinas. I grew up with my Auntie and all her childrens. She made extra straw-plaiting, but it's a hard living, so I be nannying in Freeport town these last years."

"Slaving for white children." The old man spat on the ground

39

again, just missing Ethel's bare foot. "Tell your Casino boss, tell that Mistah Biggety, he best not be bringing his powder business through here. This here's my landing place, been in the Rolle family since rum running days."

He turned and walked back to the boat, raising the machete with his right hand to dismiss them. The younger man followed, dragging one foot behind him in the sand.

The third man spoke. "The Rock's not like what it used to be, Miss Tootes. You best get going, before that there real boss changes his mind."

On the drive home, Dede should have been full of questions. Lord knows what she must have thought about the confrontation, about Ethel's evasions and omissions and downright lies. Was she aware of drug dealers on the island... or the possibility that Silvio was involved? Unlike the drive down, when she wouldn't shut up, the girl was silent for a couple of miles then fell asleep on the road through the settlements. Exhausted from the stress of what she'd witnessed? Or maybe she was worn out from the too-many nights she stayed awake while her mother worked. Ethel didn't want to worry about the girl; she didn't want to care. She shook her head and shivered with the thought of what might have happened on the beach. She raced toward Freeport faster than safe, past the shacks, the churches, the schools, the women, the hens, the children, all running together, her past blurring, blurring beside her, then left behind.

When they got back to the flats, Ethel pulled into the car park and shook Dede's arm. "We're back. Earlier than expected."

Dede had a line from the seat imprinted on her cheek, and her face was flaming from the sun.

"Thanks very much," she said as she yawned and gathered her towel. "I enjoyed the day immensely."

She was so damn earnest that Ethel had to laugh, "Oh, what a mess." She pulled her into an awkward hug. "I'm sorry for dragging you into all that." She looked into her bloodshot eyes. "Are you all right?"

Dede nodded and got out of the car.

"Would you like me to come over and talk to your mother? Explain what happened?"

"No, no, no. She'll be asleep." Dede's hair, knotted, dried, and coarse as sisal rope, swinging side to side. "It will be our little secret."

CHAPTER 4

Showered and fresh-shaved. Wearing white tennis shorts and a collared shirt. A splash of Old Spice on his cheeks. In the mirror, iron hair glistened, most of the white covered by an application of Grecian Formula. He slicked a wayward strand into place on his temple. As a kid, he'd had a thick blond forelock, forever dropping across his left eye—a mark of his incorrigibility that drove the nuns crazy. Especially Sister Mary Pat. *A boy's boy*, she must have muttered to herself, with an exasperated headshake. *Young Johnnie McGuinn.*

He'd bought a gallon of mint chocolate chip ice cream. The girl's favorite—but he'd got Gibson's Deluxe—only available at a specialty shop on the other side of Freeport. He didn't mind driving a few extra miles, forking out another couple of bucks. He wanted her to know the best: Gibson's was white and creamy—not the bright green fake stuff—and the chips were irregularly sized, plentiful, as if someone had pick-axed a chocolate mountain. A princess should be picky, he'd told her more than once.

Her favorite show was on tonight. *Happy Days.* He knew she'd come. She was lonely when her mother worked; she'd prowl the pool deck most evenings looking for company. Oftentimes, he'd take her a

Coke or one of those piss-colored Goombay Punch drinks, sit on the deck chair and talk to her, make her laugh. Tonight, though, would be different. He'd been patient. As he pulled on his socks, the phone rang. He ignored it. The clock radio by the bed said 8:30 pm; too late for tenants to be pestering him. He slipped into his tennis shoes, then fumbled with the laces, like a schoolboy in a hurry. Nervous, yes, he didn't mind admitting it. He'd planned everything down to the smallest detail, but he would do one more walk through, then take the ice cream out of the freezer ten minutes before show-time, let it sit, top off, on the kitchen counter, so it would be easy to scoop, but not too melted. Right before nine, she would knock on his door, come inside. He'd ask her to sit down. He would serve her in a glass bowl. The mother would be long gone by then because she worked casino hours.

He'd cleaned up the apartment before his shower. Vacuumed the floors. Made his bed—pulling sheets over the mattress on his floor. Washed the dishes and wiped the counter. All his dirty clothes hidden in a hamper inside his closet; his three pairs of shoes lined up on a mat by the front door. But as he walked through the living room, he straightened cushions on the couch, moved the only armchair into a distant corner and turned on the TV, to make sure it was good and warmed up, that the reception was as clear as it got. Her television, she'd told him more than once, had blacked out during a pivotal scene of *Happy Days*. She'd missed Richie Cunningham's first kiss.

The phone rang again. If it was a tenant with a problem, they would have to wait until tomorrow. But what if it was Silvio needing a last-minute job done under the cover of dark? Perhaps an unscheduled delivery of goods at the West End? The crew would dock on the island when and where no one expected, and then McGuinn would need to unload the product, transport it to an makeshift airstrip for the next leg of the journey. He had to be ready for a pick-up whenever Silvio or one of his men called. That was the deal. So... "Hello?"

A garbled voice.

He tried again. "Who's this?" Nothing. "Well, it's your dime, buddy."

He'd done his part; he'd answered. It was almost 8:40 pm. He grabbed himself a beer from the fridge and took a long pull. God, he was nervous. He got out a tray, then bowls, glasses, spoons, napkins, arranged and rearranged them. A knock on the front door reverberated in his heartbeat. He'd assumed the girl would walk across the pool deck and rap on his sliding door, like usual, not come around to the front of the building.

He opened the door and took a step back. Not Dede, but that oversized woman from 1A.

"Can I help you?" What the hell was her name? Had to be nearly his height, even without the afro. She could easily pass as a man, especially with the way she dressed. She didn't even work in the Casino, so God knows what she was doing in this building.

"Mr. McGuinn. I'm Ethel Edgecombe—we've met a few times before, I believe?"

McGuinn looked her over; she had paint on her shirt and a few drops of yellow splattered on her cheek.

"I tried ringing you up just now, but perhaps I had the wrong number?"

He looked at his watch. "I got a call. All static."

"Be that as it may... my lavatory is blocked up, and I don't have a plunger. I'm happy to do it myself if I could borrow one."

44

Damn right she could do it herself. McGuinn sighed. "There's one in the supply shed by the pool. I'll get my keys. Meet me out back."

He closed the door on her. Christ. Sweating again, despite his shower. Goddamn tenants, all the demands. It was bad enough with the Europeans, Brits and French who worked the Casino, but a black woman? Why was he catering to her too? He pulled open the drawer, found the right key. The kitchen clock said 8:45 pm. Almost time to take the ice cream out. He had to hurry, didn't want to miss the girl.

He met the woman by the shed, at the end of the building. He opened the padlock. Pulled on the light string and fumbled around inside.

"What do you know?" He said, "You've got a choice." There were three cheap wooden plungers in the back, and a plumbing snake hung on a hook. He'd already showered, for Christ's sakes, and she'd said she could manage. A big gal like her probably had to do all sorts of work for herself. "Yellow or red?"

"Either one will do.

He passed her a plunger. "You know how to use it, right?"

"Of course."

"Call me in the morning if you're still having problems."

"Oh, I know how to find you," she said. More threat than fact? Did she suspect something? She turned and walked across the pool deck and into her apartment through the sliding glass doors.

He hurried back to his unit, slipped inside. 8:51 p.m. He drained his beer, applied more cologne and changed his shirt again. From royal blue to navy this time; with an alligator patch. His new girl liked all kinds of blue. He needed to settle his heart, still going nuts because of that busy-body Bahamian bitch coming around like the Queen of Spades.

At last, the knock on the glass he'd been waiting for. Five to nine. Heart skipping now, he pulled back the curtain. "Hello, Princess," he said. He showed her into his living room.

"Hello, Johnnie Angel," she replied with that shy smile. She'd started calling him that after a song she'd heard on his car radio a couple of months ago. The Carpenters. Karen and her brother, Robert, or was it Richard? He slid the door closed, pulled the drapes again, to keep the air nice and cool inside.

"Is your mother at work?"

"Like always."

"She'll be out all night then, I guess?"

"Like always."

The girl had been in the pool earlier—he'd seen her there five-ish—but now her hair was parted with a line straight down the middle and combed out, neater than usual, and she smelled not of chlorine but of something soft and powdery. Love's Baby Soft? He'd seen the ad; he loved the ad: *Because innocence is sexier than you think*. She wore brown overalls and a too-big, tie-dyed t-shirt, stepped into the living room, chatting about her day. She said the teacher had given them another spelling test and she'd made top marks. The only word she didn't get right was the challenge word, for extra credit: paleontologist.

"Do you know how to spell it?" She asked.

"I.T.," he replied, and she giggled into her hand.

She checked his shelves and kitchen counter, picking up things: the set of keys to the supply shed he'd left out. A bottle of Heat that he used for his rheumatism last night. His Dictaphone.

"What's this for?"

"Business, mostly."

"How come you don't have any photographs?"

"I do," he said. "I have a whole collection."

"Why don't you have anything hanging on your walls? Don't you have a family?"

"Sure, I do. I've got four kids living in the States." She questioned him like she was Kojak on a case.

"Don't you like your family?"

"Of course, I do. They're all grown up. I just haven't gotten around to framing any pictures yet. But I'll show them to you sometime. I promise. Got a whole case full of photos."

"What do you use this tape recorder for?"

"Oh, all kinds of things. Making lists of things to buy, to fix, to remember. And just for fun sometimes, I record things, songs and voices I like. You can make your own song for me if you want." He picked it up. "Go ahead, say something." He clicked record.

"No thanks. Where are all your books?"

He rewound and played it back for her, her light voice, the slight lisp: "No thanks. Where are all your books?"

"Stop it," she said. "I hate hearing myself talk."

He turned it off and put it down. "You sound beautiful to me. Best thing I've heard all day."

"Where do you keep your books?" She repeated.

"Never been much of a reader. But you—you're always reading. Every time I see you sitting outside you have a book in hand. That's good."

"I finished the St. Clare's and Malory Towers boarding school series last year. Now I'm reading books and magazines from the Bahamas section at the library—history and geography—only they don't have much here. I asked Miss St. John, the librarian, to order me more stuff from Nassau, but it takes forever. Did you know that

47

the Taino people lived here before Columbus arrived? Did you know that most of them died from infections that the Spanish brought? Did you know that the islands are made from skeletons? Not the Taino bones, but layer on layer of marine life, and we are walking around on desiccated bodies."

McGuinn laughed. "Desiccated," he said and put a finger to her lips. "The moment I laid eyes on you I could tell you were whip-sharp. Maybe you should be a journalist or something, have one of those notepads and pens, like Brenda Starr. Then you'd probably want a tape-recorder of your own, too. But, hey, look, it's show-time."

He led her to the couch, told her to make herself comfortable, while he went to use the little boys' room. He walked through his bedroom and into the john, his heart still going a mile a minute. He needed to take a leak, needed it bad, but he couldn't get it out. Buddy boy was all jacked up with excitement over the girl—hard and willful and inpatient as always. Jesus, calm down. He ran the faucet, tried to breathe; he knew what to do. He closed his eyes, listened to the water running. Easy. He thought of certain things that always brought Buddy down. His mother when she had that terrible cough towards the end. His ex-wife, Joan. What a fucking ballbuster she turned out to be.

At the first commercial break, he served Dede her ice cream in a glass bowl, delivered it to her on a tray. Two large scoops. Perfect and soft. Like that perfume ad said: *You can love them hard, and you can love them soft. Soft will get them every time.*

"Is this mint?" she asked. "I like *mint* chocolate chip. Not plain chocolate chip."

"Just taste it. Looks can be deceiving." He patted her leg, felt a shiver to his core. Dear God.

She took a tiny taste. She smiled her appreciation and took another bite. "Mmm. It's actually quite good."

"Only the best for you, Princess."

He sat down beside her, let his arm stretch across the back of the couch and tried to focus on the show. Marion, the TV mom on *Happy Days*, with hair pulled up into a tight red bun, was learning to dance. Secretly. Her husband didn't know what she was up to, or why she kept disappearing. Her kids—the snot-nosed Richie and the chubby little sister—had no clue. Only Fonzie was in on the secret; he was Marion's secret dance partner. McGuinn caught fragments of the show, the laugh track grating his nerves. Mostly, he breathed, smelled, sensed, touched the girl. When he could, he stole quick glances. Her green-blue eyes fixed on the TV screen, her mouth moving. She had such full lips, her tongue licking the ice cream off the too big spoon, stockpiling the chocolate chips. Her feet up under her thighs and her body relaxed against the side rest. She was getting used to having him near her. Yes, he'd been patient, taking his time. What had it been? Two, three months now? She seemed ready—ready to accept more —to embrace him like a giant teddy bear—all hers—or to school him like a pound puppy that she was teaching tricks. Good boy. That's a very good boy. Key was to let her believe she'd chosen this. That she was in charge. He did not want to rush; the crossover had to be invisible, seamless, so that in looking back she would never remember when, how, why it had happened.

"I need a glass of water," she said, during the second commercial break.

"Please," he prompted.

"I need water now," she repeated, and pointed to the kitchen. She gave a brat smile, one that Joanie had just used on the Fonz. And

McGuinn caved, of course. He filled a glass at the sink, drank it down, then refilled it and added ice cubes and carried it out to her; set it on the side table. She'd be drinking from his glass; her baby soft lips where his had been seconds before.

"Thanks for the water," McGuinn prompted, half-joking, as he sat back down.

"You're welcome," she replied, without taking her eyes off the TV.

Yep, the spoiled-princess routine. Part of him liked being told what to do. He loved how she manipulated his thoughts, made him crazy. All he was, all he'd ever been, a little boy in love. He moved a little closer, so his thigh pushed up next to her crossed legs. She still had the ice cream bowl in her lap. The chocolate chips stacked next to a pool of white. He reached over to sneak one.

"Hey," she rapped on his knuckles with her spoon.

"Please," he said. "I just want one little bitty chocolate chip."

"No."

"Pretty please," he tried.

He got down on the carpet in front of her. On his knees, put his hands together and looked into her eyes. "Pretty please, Princess, with a perfect cherry on the top." He held his palms open, cast his eyes down at the floor. "For your favorite Johnnie Angel?"

She picked up a chip—the smallest she could find—with her thumb and index finger and dropped it onto his hand. When he put it to his lips, he could taste the chocolate's bitter edge.

"Now move out of the way," she said. "I am *trying* to watch my show."

So beautifully imperious. He pushed himself back up off the floor, turned and sat, let his hand drape across the back of the couch again. Her t-shirt was too big for her slight frame and it slid off her shoulder. He reached over, pretended to pull it up, but then let his first two fingers start moving, right there in the notch above her collar bone. Back and forth and up and down, in a perfect two-inch square. Did she feel all that he was holding back? She didn't recoil from his touch; the ice cream bowl in her lap, the chips sitting in a white pool, her eyes transfixed on the TV, while his fingers, deferential and constrained, moved up and down, back and forth, informing her of his patience and desire.

CHAPTER 5

Dede lay stomach down on her twin bed, writing about her day in the Betsy Clarke diary she received for Christmas. Mum knocked on the door before eight p.m., dressed in her work outfit—black pants and slinky shirt with the Lucayan Princess logo on the pocket: a brown-skinned girl wrapped with pink bougainvillea vines. She gave the same old song and dance about bedtime—*9 o'clock, lights out and no telly*—as if Dede were still a little kid who needed a babysitter.

"It's spazzy on all three channels now. Can we *please* get a new one? There's nothing to do when you're gone."

"You'll survive. Read another book. Or tell your diary how mean I am. I'm sure that will fill a few pages."

Mum's shift at the casino ran from 9 pm to 5 am, five nights a week. Usually, she pulled her hair up off her face so that drunk Americans wouldn't tug on it for good luck before they rolled the dice. Tonight, her hair rippled long and blonde over her shoulders, the way Stupido Silvio liked it. And she was wearing his Christmas present again—a string of 22 conch pearls in shades of pink and rose. Dede didn't know why Mum liked him. Yes, he was rich and bought her nice things, but he was nowhere near as handsome as

Dad. Silvio's hair was gray and wavy—a poncey do. His nose was flat and wide and ugly. Mum said it was because he used to box as an amateur and it made him "rakish." He seemed much too old for Mum, but when Dede said so once, Mum told her to mind her own beeswax. *At least he knows how to treat a woman.*

"And no more Coke at night," Mum said. "I found several cans in the rubbish last week. No wonder you don't sleep well." She tapped the end of Dede's nose with a fire-coral red fingernail, kissed her goodnight.

It was a ten-minute drive to the restaurant and the Casino, where Mum could run all the tables now: Blackjack, Caribbean poker, baccarat, roulette. Craps was best, she said, because it kept her thinking and time passed quickly. Quickly for her maybe.

Dede reached for the phone beside her bed and dialed the time. The man with the sandpaper voice said: "For the finest drinks under the sun mix them with friendly Appleton rum. Time 8:03." She synchronized her Timex. Another eleven hours and twenty-seven minutes until Mum returned. Would she think about Dede while she was working? Or did all the tourists with their big bellies and stuffed wallets occupy her thoughts?

Loneliness filled Dede's mouth like a fat fist. A year ago, when Mum first started the night shift, the flat felt so restless and creaky that Dede would have to walk up and down the hall until it settled. Now the walls seemed to moan in frustration when Dede tried to sleep. She wanted to sleep through the night, but she could never drift off when Mum was gone. Midnight to three a.m. was worst; if she closed her eyes, the walls shuddered and the bed jostled, trying to get rid of her. And if your home gets sick of you and tries to push you out, where are you supposed to go?

Johnnie Angel wasn't sick of Dede. Never once had he told Dede that he was too bloody tired to talk, like Mum always was in the mornings when she got home. Never once had he given her that empty television stare that Dad used to do when he was watching football. And unlike Ethel, he didn't act like he was her friend one day and then avoid her the next. Whenever he saw her around the building, Johnnie Angel stopped what he was doing to ask her how she was and to tell her she looked beautiful. For the past few weeks, he'd picked her up after school to save her from walking home in the afternoon heat. No problem, he said, because he often had business in town. Maybe tonight he'd let her come over to his place again. *The Bionic Woman* came on at nine—she could fill him in on the background of the story—Jaime's love for Steve Austin, her tragic skydiving accident, her amnesia.

She sat on the edge of the bed, tugged on her brown dungarees and clasped the straps over her t-shirt. She walked down the hall, into the living room, pulled back the drapes and slid the glass door, and stepped into the throbbing night. Cicadas whirred the air. Gray-tailed lizards skimmed over rocks. The muffled grunt of a tree frog. Surrounded by vines and bushes, the swimming pool flashed six underwater eyes at Dede, trying to entice her. But she was tired of being the only swimmer it could count on. Most of the other tenants were night-time casino workers like Mum, and the pretty boys, Sebastian and Leo, who shared number 2D upstairs; they slept all day.

Sometimes in the early evening when Dede was swimming, Ethel came home from her banking job, changed into a tank top and shorts, and worked in the garden before her supper. She wore men's gardening gloves because her hands were so large. Ethel didn't talk much about herself, but she'd speak about the island flowers and plants that she loved, their colors and scents, and about painting. She'd told Dede once that *Art saves lives* and then laughed softly when she said it, as if she didn't quite believe it. Dede wanted to ask, "Did it save yours?" But Ethel was tricky: she'd give out little pieces of information and then clam up.

A few of Ethel's frangipani blossoms floated on the water's surface tonight. The pool was shaped liked a lima bean, so it didn't really have a length or width and calculating surface area would be next to impossible. Even Pi was useless when the shape was all weird curves. Most of the petals gathered on Ethel's side of the pool. Johnnie Angel didn't like Ethel's gardening; he said that all the leaves and petals gunked up his filters.

Dede walked across the deck and lifted the pool net from the hooks near Ethel's door. She skimmed the pool's surface and dumped the soggy petals in a pile beneath a giant bougainvillea vine. As she worked, she felt the pool watching her. *Please, it said. Pretty please, come swim.* Dede's yellow bikini was still wet from earlier in the day; but she did have that old stretchy Marks & Spencer one-piece from way back; Birmingham blue—she'd chosen the swimsuit because it was Dad's favorite color. If he ever made it over here to visit the suit would be almost threadbare.

Who was she kidding? He would never come.

She carried the skimmer back to the wall and accidentally on purpose rapped the pole end on Ethel's door.

"Sorry," she yelled. Then she hit it again, a little harder. "Sorry."

When Ethel didn't come to the door, she replaced the net on the hooks. Either Ethel hadn't heard her, or, more likely, she couldn't be bothered answering. She was probably annoyed by Dede's ceaseless prattle. That's what Mum called it. Ethel's living room curtains were

55

drawn; the lights off. Maybe she was already asleep. Or painting in her studio? Dede tried to peek in between her curtains but the living room was dark, too dark to make out any shapes or movement.

She walked across the courtyard to Johnnie Angel's flat. She hadn't seen him after school today, so she'd had to walk home alone. Come to think of it, he hadn't been cleaning up around the building when she got home, either. Sometimes he went off for a couple of days on a business trip, didn't answer his phone or open his door when tenants needed something done. Ethel said you should be able to count on the caretaker to handle basic repairs. She'd had to get out a stepstool and change light bulbs in the laundry room when she couldn't find him. She'd even called Silvio to complain when the washing machine broke, which made Johnnie Angel furious. She's a pain in my ass, he'd told Dede. She pressed her ear against the wall of his flat. Nothing.

Three purple and green striped loungers lined up on the deck; like the pool, they never got much use from the other tenants. Dede sat in the middle one. You could adjust the seats between 90 and 180 degrees. Dede liked an obtuse angle—around 110 degrees. In the early days on the island, she used to imagine her family reclining side-by-side-by-side, with cold drinks in hand—a Pina Colada for Mum, a Coca-Cola for herself and a Guinness, of course, for Dad. Only rarely would Mum come out now and even when she did, she was no fun. She'd stretch out, after slathering coconut oil on her body, and fall asleep. Mum's breasts were big for a thin lady, but they flattened out when she lay down. Dede's breasts were growing, and they had tender spots in the middle when she squeezed them at night. But she wouldn't like it if they got as big as Mum's.

The night wind rustled the bougainvillea on Ethel's trellis, and her sea glass mobile that Dede had helped her build tinkled. If only Ethel would come out tonight and keep her company for an hour—but she had to be an early to bed, early to rise kind of person. Oh yes, she had to be an I-like-my-privacy kind of person. Mum working; Dad too far way. Ethel sleeping or more likely, ignoring her. Johnnie Angel who knows where. Dede tried to telepath a message to him: *I'm bloody bored. Please come and find me. Now. Now. Now.* She tried to make out his response, brain waves transmitting through the thick night air, but only heard cicadas arguing. *No, no, no, yes; no, no, no, yes.* Petals dropped and settled on the turquoise water. Maybe she should cool off in the blue. Blue was best for calm and clarity, Ethel said. Cerulean perfect for painting the sky. Phthalo or cyan for the sea, because of its bias towards green.

The pool called. *Come in. Come in.* Its underwater lights cut geometric patterns. She felt tired but knew she wouldn't sleep if she went back to her desolate flat. Maybe she could nod off out here. She reclined her chair to about 150 degrees, closed her eyes tight. She sang softly, trying to capture the achy sadness of Karen Carpenter's voice. *Johnny Angel, Johnny Angel, Johnny Angel. You're an angel to me.* She let the song cycle through her brain again and again but did not open her eyes.

"Hello, Princess."

Had she fallen asleep? His voice from across the pool.

She didn't open her eyes because he was better in sound than in view. She waited until she could feel his slow walk closing in. "Shouldn't you be in bed?"

"Shouldn't you mind your own business?" She pushed herself up onto her elbows.

"Well, I am glad you're still awake because I brought you payment for all your work on the pool. I can tell you skimmed it while I was away."

He had a bottle of beer in one hand, and a Coca-Cola in the other. Wearing tennis shorts as usual, but at least he had on a decent shirt with a collar. He bent down to hand her the Coke.

"Thanks very much," she said. She sat up and took a sip. "But not cold enough."

Johnnie Angel stood beside her. "Are you mad at me about something, Princess?"

"Of course not."

"Maybe you're angry because I didn't pick you up from school. I was away on business, but I missed you like hell, you know?"

Now that he was here, he wasn't so great. Be careful what you wish for, Mum often said. Dede would rather Johnnie Angel were Ethel. But she didn't have the willpower to pull Ethel outside. She looked back to Ethel's flat—still blacked out.

"I brought you something back from my trip." He dug a hand deep into the pocket of his shorts, pulled out a coral pendant, the kind Bahamian women sold to tourists at the Straw Market, and dangled it in front of her face. "Want me to put it on you?"

When he leaned over Dede, he smelled like beer and hair grease.

"No," she said, pulling away.

He dropped the necklace between her thighs. She picked it up and closed her fingers around the coral's ruts and ridges. Rubbish.

"Don't you like it?"

"Of course, I do." She laughed in that way Mum did for Silvio, half cough, half throaty sigh. "It's *awfully* nice. So *terribly* kind of you."

"I'm gonna be real sad if you don't like it."

At Christmas, Mum cried real tears when she unwrapped Silvio's present. "They are conch pearls," Silvio explained as he lifted her hair and clasped the necklace around her throat. Dede hadn't known until then that conchs could make pearls, but she didn't let on in front of Silvio. She asked Ethel later, and she said, "Very rare. Maybe one in ten thousand conchs make them. Very expensive, too." Dede felt sad for her dad, even though he hadn't called her once in the New Year.

"You sure you don't want to wear it?" Johnnie Angel leaned in close again and his breath hit Dede with a gassy heat. He had a dab of toilet paper on his neck where he must have cut himself shaving. A fat white lip of belly showed between his shirt and shorts.

"No," she said, her voice louder than she meant it to be. "Stop breathing on me." She stuck the necklace in the front pocket of her dungarees, vowing never to wear it. Coral was dead animals gunked together. Grand Bahama meant *big shallow sea*, and coral was everywhere: Under the ocean and under the island, under every building and pool and resort and casino and school. This beige lump in her hand had a circumference of about 5 cm and hung on a cheap wire— not even silver. It sold at the bazaar for under $5. Mum's necklace must have cost Silvio thousands. He gave Mum lots of things and she got a super good deal on rent, Johnnie Angel said, because she was a sexy mama. Way more sexy, he said, than Silvio's fat Cuban wife who spent most of her time alone in their Miami home. Alone with a dozen servants, he added.

"Listen, Princess, I'm really sorry that I've been away. I will make it up to you, I promise. Next week, I'll pick you up every goddamn day if that makes you happy. No more pouting." He held out his hand. "Now, do you want to come inside? Watch some TV and stuff?"

Dede sat up. A light had come on in Ethel's apartment. The living room. So, she was home after all. Home and not sleeping. Or maybe she'd just returned from an outing?

"I'm sick and tired of the telly," Dede said. "Besides, Ethel asked me to pop by for some dessert tonight. She made guava duff." She stood up quickly, ignoring Johnnie Angel's outstretched hand and walked right past him, hopped over a flowerbed that separated Ethel's patio from the pool-deck, and rapped hard and harder on the glass door until she saw a tall silhouette approaching.

CHAPTER 6

Sunday morning, Ethel was stirring dirt and ground coral and water in two five-gallon paint pails in the bathtub—the walls and floor splattered with brown clumps and dribbles, the containers full of sludge, a good metaphor for her current understanding of where this project was going. A knock at the front door. She pushed up from the bathmat where she'd been kneeling, washed her hands in the sink, and grabbed her wristwatch from the window ledge. 9:22 a.m.—an especially obnoxious time for an uninvited visit.

No one ever knocked on her front door. But there it was again, tap-tap-tatap, not loud but with a definite "I'm not leaving" cadence. Tap-tap-tap-tap. Dede? No. When the girl wanted something, she'd bang on the sliding glass doors. Besides, Ethel had expressly limited those interruptions to weekday evenings—*Before 9 pm*, she'd said, firm in tone, if not always in follow through. Sometimes, the girl tried her luck anyway—but never on a Sunday morning. Never the front door. Ethel held her breath, as if her stillness could stop the sound. A brief pause and then a fusillade. If it were the girl, Ethel would let her have it.

Sweet Lord Jesus. I'm coming. I'm coming. She caught a side-glimpse of herself in the hall mirror: untamed hair, mud splotches on her white tank-top, something tacky—last night's paint or this morning's guava jam—on her cheek. Well, if you show up uninvited, what do you expect?

Through the peephole, she caught the fish-eyed distortion of someone's head—a woman, short, with shoulder-length brown hair. Ethel's stomach lurched. Nora—Nora looking small and nervous and white, God, so white. Nora, peering anxiously at the door, then raising her hand to knock again. Ethel turned the deadbolt and opened the door and Nora took a step backwards, stumbling over her suitcase.

She composed herself, waved awkwardly. "Surprise."

"Lord, woman! You almost gave me a heart attack."

"I know this is absolute madness. I know that I should have called you first. If you want to send me away, you can, but it's half-term and I have a week off and I miss you, Ethel, I really miss you and I knew if I called, you'd say no, don't come, and I didn't want to hear that, so I bought my ticket and packed and... please don't hate me."

"Hate you? Oh, Lord. Never" Heat rose up Ethel's chest and neck. How she had wanted and dreaded exactly this. "It's only that I'm a bit surprised." A bit? Where was this British understatement coming from? "Come in, come on in."

Nora carried her red tartan suitcase into the entry hall, set it down, peeked into the kitchen off to the left—which was a mess, of course, breakfast plate, dirty mugs, and last night's dinner dishes piled on the counter—then walked toward the living area. She was wearing bell bottom jeans, an embroidered white cotton smock top that she was swimming in. Had Nora shrunk? Was she always this slight? Her pageboy had grown out, no more fringe. Maybe the long hair made her look smaller, paler. She certainly looked, well, less prim and schoolmarmish, more... hip? Was that the right word? She stopped at the edge of the carpet.

"I've tried to picture your home here, so many times, imagine you living here."

"And? Were you close?"

Nora turned slowly, taking in all in, and Ethel saw the place through her eyes: dropped ceiling, beige walls, nondescript art—a framed map of Grand Bahama Island above the couch, and across the room, a long macramé hanging, and a bad watercolor seascape—all these belonging to a prior tenant who'd left in a hurry, all pieces that Ethel had intended to replace at some point in time which obviously had not arrived. The orange shag rug, the brown sofa, and a gold swivel chair that she'd purchased cheaply from another man, a young British banker who'd lost his work permit and was heading back. The room was, Ethel realized now, dull, perfunctory, a waystation to a real life. Certainly, none of the flair, the whimsical orderliness of Nora's cottage in Bristol.

"It's... it's... certainly sufficient."

Damned by faint praise. What was Ethel doing living here? And why had Nora come? Nora dropped her handbag on the ersatz coffee table. Well, at least that was a unique creation—Ethel had repurposed four wine crates she'd found in a rubbish pile outside Butler & Sands imports after New Year's. She'd meant to buy a colorful Androsian batik to cover the crates but hadn't gotten around to it.

"It serves my purpose. For now, at least."

Nora didn't ask what this "purpose" was, how long "now" would be. She didn't re-raise the still unanswered question of what the hell Ethel was doing here. Did she know Ethel had no idea? Did she know that Ethel's worries and doubts visited her each night when she tried to sleep? Could she guess that Ethel had no more understanding of why she'd up and left England nine months ago, without warning, with barely any explanation?

Nora walked towards the long white curtains, pulled them aside.

"Now this... Wow!" She opened the sliding door and stepped onto the small patio, looked out on the courtyard in its splendor: pink bougainvillea, red hibiscus, and the fuchsia ixora. "It's brilliant. If I were you, I'd spend every moment out here."

Beside her, Ethel had to agree. Sometimes she forgot how incredible the colors, the scents could be. "It is brilliant, yes. The thing is, though, when you live here any length of time, you take it for granted. Even the beach, the water, you can get used it it—lose that sense of awe."

She followed Nora onto the pool deck.

"The smell is incredible too—what is it? Honeysuckle?"

"Frangipani, probably. It's much stronger at night. You may be getting some wild unction... see those yellow trumpets over there? They've got a sweet, fruity smell, too."

They walked around the courtyard, Ethel pointing out flowers she'd planted or tended, naming the squawking birds and flash of insects showing off, even as she kept an eye on the other ground-floor apartments, feeling self-conscious about how unkempt she looked, worried someone might come outside and see her in this state, might see Nora and wonder what was going on.

But the courtyard was quiet, pool and deck still empty as they finished their perimeter walk. Not even a sign of the pool's favorite customer. Ethel glanced at Dede's flat—the curtains drawn across the sliding doors and the bedroom window. Maybe she was sleeping in—she was, after all, not that far from being a teenager—was it possible she'd succumbed to this age-appropriate behavior? When they walked back inside Ethel's flat, Nora left the door open, but Ethel drew the curtains. They caught a light breeze and waved half-heartedly as Ethel and Nora, a little shy, a little unsure, stood close, not speaking. That line, that sonnet that Nora had always loved, used to read out loud to Ethel: *When our two souls stand up erect and strong /face to face, silent...*

Nora took a step back. "I bet the beach is incredible. When my plane was landing this morning, the sea was a patchwork of blues and greens—I'd love to go there, maybe now... after I change?"

"Oh, baby, you'd fry at this time of day. Look at how pale you are. Mad dogs and Englishmen..." She reached out to touch Nora's cheek, *drawing nigh and nigher,* but stopped herself. "I like your hair longer like this. Your fringe all grown out. So pretty."

Had she said too much? What rules were they playing by?

Nora held the distance. "Your tips are ginger; I love it. The sun? And are those new freckles? Or is that paint? Oh, I'll be so glad if you've been painting."

Ethel felt the heat from her chest redden her neck and face, too, no doubt highlighting the specks of mud or whatever else she hadn't had time to wash off. She turned away—hating how her body betrayed her, the uncontrolled blushing when the topic was her art. Another subversive passion unveiled.

"I have been working on something new. I'm not sure what it is right now, other than a big mess in my bathroom. I've worked steadily though, since I've been here. I've been... disciplined. Several new paintings."

"Can I see them... or anything you want to show? I mean, whenever you're ready and only if you want to."

"My second bedroom, well, there's no bed in there. I've made it a sort of studio." A sort of studio? Jesus. Pathetic. Cheeks burning. "I usually spend most weekday evenings in there. Weekends I try to go to one of the quiet beaches and paint outside." Her armpits prickling.

"Hey." Nora took Ethel's hands. "What's going on?"

Ethel stared at her feet—they were splattered too. She was what? Embarrassed or ashamed? Drowning in the same old feelings. Should she mention the clay?

"Hey," Nora repeated. "I have missed you so much."

The curtains listless now, filtered the sounds of birds, of frogs, and insects into the room. Ethel's heart pounded; she wanted to run, she wanted to stay. Who were they to each other at this moment? Not "companions"—the oh-so-effective euphemism they'd used when Ethel moved into Nora's cottage. Lovers or exes? Nothing had been resolved before Ethel fled. How could they be together in this world, in any world? Black and white, solid and petite, banker and schoolteacher, Bahamian and Brit. What could their life ever be? Hidden or dangerous.

"I've missed you too." She lifted her eyes, held the contact with Nora's for several seconds, wanting and not wanting to want, needing and not wanting to need. Did Ethel, after what she'd done, how she'd left, deserve another chance with Nora? *A place to stand and love in for a day?*

Yes.

She pulled Nora closer, wrapped her arms around her. Nora's head beneath her collar bone, the familiar scent of cheap Herbal Essence shampoo—because even though she came from a long line of bluebloods, Nora did all her shopping at Boots. Nora. Here. She squeezed her body tight.

"Gentle, Killer!" Nora laughed and pulled back. "You're going to crack my ribs."

"Sorry. It's just that you came. You came to find me."

After Nora had used the toilet, washed her face—Ethel told her to ignore the mess in the tub—they ate toast and jam, sipped hot tea at the kitchen table, and nattered on about everything, like a couple of old spinsters, Nora said. Red Maids news, the cranky new neighbor on Grange Court. The Maguire Seven convicted two weeks ago—wrongfully, Nora thought. Soon, though, she was rubbing her eyes, swallowing her yawns, and Ethel led her into the bedroom. Nora hadn't slept at all on the plane, she said. Too nervous. She lay on the bed, fully clothed. Ethel sat on the edge, feet on the ground.

"Still nervous?"

Nora nodded. Ethel lay down beside her and took her hand. They both stared at the ceiling, the cheap tropical fan circling slow as it could go.

"And now?" They turned to face one another simultaneously, and then laughing, crying, and kissing, tasting tears, relearning the rightness of their mouths together, shedding clothes, and muscle memory kicking in—the way their bodies, large and small, had always wanted one another, would always fit. This.

Later, Ethel woke alone. A palmetto bug clung to the bedroom wall. Nora must have slipped out. Had she left the door open and let the bug in? Had she even slept? Ethel walked out to the living room. Sliding door still open, but the screen pulled across at least, curtains immobile in the afternoon doldrums. She heard the voices, laughter, and walked to the patio. Ah! So predictable. Nora by the pool where the girl had found her—the two of them sitting in adjacent deck chairs, like a couple of schoolgirls, prattling excitedly—Nora giving the girl what Ethel often would not: unfiltered attention, lively conversation, time. Nora was generous like that; it's why her students loved her.

The kitchen clock confirmed the sun's angle, the tide-over wind. It was 3:45 pm. Ethel needed a shower. She lifted the two large pails out of her bathtub and carried them into her studio, placing each on an old beach towel. The silt was settling, the top water hazy. Later, she'd need to sieve the slurry. Her studio was a mess; paints everywhere, finished pieces lying against the far wall, her worktable covered in newspapers and small mounds of clay, some shapes—her first efforts brittle and crumbling. She'd need to clean all this up before she let Nora in. Not wanting to expose this nascent project, she closed the door behind her.

She showered quickly, scrubbing at the mud on her cheeks, arms, and chest, then pulled on fresh underwear, a clean pair of shorts and a yellow tank top. In the kitchen, she juiced six lemons and six limes, added a cup of sugar, mixed in water and ice—taste-tested the tart and pulpy drink. The girl's loud giggling and Nora's lower, rumbling laugh coming in through the opened doors. She tried to shrug off her annoyance. What could it hurt, really, for them to meet? She sliced and plated a ripe mango and two bananas, added a handful of genep she'd picked at the East End yesterday. Then she carried a tray outside—three glasses, three paper napkins—her effort to be more generous than she sometimes felt with Dede.

"I see you've met my favorite neighbor," Ethel said.

Side by side on the lounge chairs, both wearing bathing suits—faded and blue—British school-girl style. Granny-style. Ethel had to laugh. "You two are a sight... tiny white people sitting poolside. And me, bringing you ladies your afternoon tray, like a good Commonwealth Citizen."

"Ha! Come sit with us. We've been talking about all sorts of things." Nora said. "I've learned a lot about the islands."

"Oh, I'm sure. Dede's a fountain of knowledge. Always got her nose in a book—reading or writing or researching."

"Pull the other leg," Dede said.

"What are you up to today, then?" Ethel asked. "I see that thick book. Doesn't look like a fun read."

"Bahamian history—I got it from the library. I've been swotting all morning for the BJC exam. We take it in a few weeks."

"I remember that one well." To Nora, "BJC is somewhere between the 11-plus and O Levels. Kids take it for secondary school admissions—scholarship opportunities, too."

"Dede was asking me about Red Maids," Nora said.

"Are you still thinking of boarding school next year, then, Dede?"

"Absolutely. I'm hoping Roedean but Red Maids sounds brilliant. Do they have a lacrosse team?"

"Oh yes. And netball and tennis. It's not as well known as Roedean, but it is highly selective."

"Do you, I mean, does the school give scholarships?"

"I'm not sure about all the financial aspects of that... we do have a few foreign students now and then. Though you wouldn't really be foreign, I suppose. I don't know how that would work for an expatriate. I promise you, though, it's a top-notch education." Nora went on about the extravagant and quirky things that came with being the oldest girls' school in the United Kingdom: the Founder's Day march through Bristol. Intramural competitions among four houses named after four of the founder's ships. She tapped them off on her fingers. "*Speedwell, Maryflowre, Discoverer* and *Seabreake*."

Ethel felt her anger surging. "Slave ships," she said.

Nora looked at her. "Surely not."

"Surely," Ethel said. "Where do you think your benefactor got the money to build a school? In Bristol—the vertex of the triangular trade between England, Africa, and the Caribbean. I'd bet my black behind that your founder was a slaver."

Nora shook her head. "I've taught there for ten years and never heard such a thing. Anyway, Dede, the point is, whatever its history—even if there were some unsavory parts—Red Maids, the school *I know* is a wonderful and welcoming place to learn. I can send you a brochure when I get home."

"Thanks. I'd like that. I should go inside. I need to read a bit more. Pleasure meeting you, Miss. And thanks, Ethel, for the fruit."

Ethel nodded.

After the girl had gone, she picked at her thumb nail—flaking off dried clay that lined her cuticle. The clay was whiter than she'd hoped—to much coral in the mix?

Nora finished her drink. Set it down on the side table. "What was all that about?"

"What do you mean?"

"I felt as if you were interrogating me... or rather, accusing me of something in front of Dede... the slave talk?"

"Well, it's not as if it's a secret, is it? Bristol's role in the slave trade. And the girl said she's studying for her Bahamian history exam. Seems that both of you would want to know some of the hard facts."

"You've never mentioned the Red Maids connection to slavery to me before. In all the time you lived there, shared a house with me, it never came up."

"That doesn't mean I didn't think about it. How could I not, with statues of Edward Colston everywhere? Colston Street, Colston

70

Hospital. Bloody Colston buns in every bakery in town? That man alone is responsible for bringing over 80,000 slaves to the Caribbean. How could you not know? That's the real question."

"Why do you keep everything so bottled up? You were stewing on this the whole time and didn't even give me the chance to talk about it with you before you left me? Do you think that's fair?"

"Fair? We're not talking about a bloody cricket match, Nora." Ethel stood up.

"Don't run away from me. Tell me what has got you so angry with me."

"You were talking about those boarding schools with the girl. Roedean, Red Maids, all of them, Cheltenham Ladies, Badminton like they're heaven on earth. They're not. They tell you you're lucky to get plucked from a life of misery and dropped in jolly old England for secondary school or university. You're supposed to be eternally grateful for the opportunity. But believe me when I say that it's not all that it's cracked up to be. People like me, Blacks, browns, islanders... even kids like Dede, white but lower class—we're always going to be outsiders in those places. And now I'm back here, well, I come to find that thanks to my education and ten years abroad, I'm an outsider here too."

"Why have I never heard any of this before?"

"Maybe I should have told you. Or maybe you should have known."

"That's putting a hell of a lot on me. To read your mind..."

Ethel picked up the empty glasses, the plates. "Is it? To ask you to put yourself in my shoes? To ask you to think about what it's like to be Black in Britain?" She started to carry them indoors.

"Don't leave, this is important. Don't just walk away. I want to hear what you have to say. Please."

Ethel should have kept her mouth shut. "Perhaps I didn't let myself feel all of these things when I was living with you. Perhaps I didn't trust you to understand. But I don't want to have to sit here now and teach you about what it's like. You were there... you saw how the shopkeepers looked at me if I walked in first. How they relaxed when they saw you were right behind. Don't act like you didn't see any of it. You heard the comments they made under their breath."

"I... I don't know what to say right now."

"Look, it's bigger than we can get into today. Can we please change the subject?"

"Okay."

Ethel sat back down. She exhaled, tried to calm her racing heart. Her anger. She didn't want to hold onto it. "Okay, then." She drank her lemon-limeade, already regretting her outburst.

Nora waited a minute or two, staring across the pool, before changing course. "So, tell me more about Dede. Why is she living over here in the first place? What do her parents do? She adores you, by the way."

Ethel filled Nora in—lonely girl, bored, single mother from Birmingham, brummie accent and all—Casino worker— no dad in the picture. Dede was certainly clever, but the boarding school idea was likely fantasy on the girl's part—out of the family's reach. Nora shouldn't make any promises, or even talk too much about Red Maids. If the girl sensed an opening, she could be quite persistent, desperate for company. "She traps me when I'm gardening, talks my ear off. She's even wormed her way into some of my painting sessions. Sometimes I feel as if I am sneaking around in my own flat—curtains drawn, light out—so she doesn't come knocking."

That evening, while Nora showered off the plane trip, their sex, the sun and the pool, their cross words, Ethel packed them a picnic for the beach: cheese and tomato sandwiches, a bag of crisps, two apple guavas she'd bought from a roadside vendor near High Rock, a large thermos of the lemon-lime quench she'd made earlier. She found a bottle of white wine she'd received from her boss at the Christmas party in the cupboard above the oven. It was warm, but still, a nice Bordeaux for a toast, maybe. She found plastic tumblers, threw in her penknife with the corkscrew attachment. Then she sat on the couch, waiting for Nora to finish dressing.

She drove them toward the Lucayan waterfront, the miles-long, white sand beach on the island's south side. A picture-perfect first beach. Later in the week, maybe they'd drive toward the East End, stop at Ethel's favorite spot in High Rock—a more rugged, isolated spot. Nora would be staying for almost a week, she said, her return flight booked for next Saturday, so after today, they'd have five full days to talk, to walk on the beach, to try to figure things out. When Nora said maybe they could visit the town where Ethel grew up, meet some of her relatives and friends, Ethel tried to push down the wave of fear. Exposure. Remembered that awful gut-wrench of showing Dede the settlements in January. How could she share any of that with Nora? And what if they couldn't decide anything different from before... being apart, living on different sides of the Atlantic, but not being over one another? How could this go?

They cruised slowly along Royal Palm Way, Ex-pat Parkway more like, turned onto Sea Gate Lane, found a parking spot at the end of the road. Ethel lifted the cooler and thermos out of the truck bed, Nora carried a beach blanket, and they walked the short path to the water, left their shoes near the dunes. Sunday evening, this stretch of beach was quiet, empty in both directions. All the home-owners would be inside for their Pimm's cocktails, their G&T's, Sunday dinners, roast beef and Yorkshire pudding, or whatever it was the Brits ate in their émigré world. A mile down the beach was the Holiday Inn, where early spring break crowds from the States were no doubt drinking poolside. But rarely did the American tourists come up this far. Last stop on their beach pilgrimage would be the Sandpiper disco.

Nora and Ethel walked a quarter mile to the east, passing several ostentatious mansions before settling in front of a clump of casuarina that grew tall and shaggy in the dunes, creating a dense barrier between beach and beach houses. Nora unfolded the blanket on packed sand, a few feet below the dry sugar of the dunes. She crossed her legs, yoga style, and Ethel, not nearly as flexible, sat beside her with legs stretched out in front, watching clouds streak the evening sky.

"Is it low-tide?"

The water was barely moving.

"Half-way. It will recede another twenty yards, I'd say, before turning."

"I've never seen colors like that before. At least not in real life. It's as if I'm wearing glasses with the right prescription for the first time. Everything is so clear."

"Let's eat and then take a walk towards that waterway—see it jutting out there? Maybe then a glass of wine while the sun sets?"

Nora reached out and held Ethel's hand. "I am sorry that I've been so damned naïve. You're right. You shouldn't have to explain the evils of British slavery to me. I should have been more tuned in to what it must have been like for you, living with that history, living with the continued racism. I'll try to do better."

Ethel squeezed Nora's fingers. "Thank you." She felt the warmth of the sinking sun on her bare legs, the fine sand between her toes. She had missed Nora so much when they were apart, but how would this go? Nora loved everything about that oh-so-British school—the red and green tartan skirts, red jumpers, and red blazers with the white trim. The stupid houses. Nora would never leave Red Maids or England. And while Ethel didn't feel settled in Freeport, she also wasn't ready to go back to Bristol. Which left them where?

As if sensing Ethel's roving thoughts, Nora yanked on her hand. "Hey, I thought you said we should enjoy the evening. Let's not try to figure it all out on our first day."

By the time they'd finished the picnic and taken a walk along the beach—to the waterway and back—it was low tide. The sun had set; the sky mauve and gray, holding onto its last traces of color. The smallest waves tickled the shoreline. A self-satisfied moon watched its reflection. Side by side again on the blanket, Nora and Ethel each finished a second glass of wine and kissed between sips. When they'd emptied their glasses, Ethel lay down, tried to pull Nora on top of her, but she wriggled away, laughing.

"What's the matter?"

"Nothing. Nothing at all." She stood in front of Ethel; her white limbs whiter in the night.

"Come back here and kiss me."

Nora spread her arms wide, as if trying to capture the whole sea. "This is as good as it gets. Almost..." She started walking toward the water.

"Hey, woman," Ethel laughed. "Don't leave me."

"If you want me, you'll have to catch me."

Nora shook her hair and started to run. She stopped half-way down the beach and pulled off her skirt, tugged off her smock top. Ethel watched her, full of desire and terrified of who might be watching them. She looked both ways on the beach to make sure they were alone. The casuarina whispered, "go to her, go to her." Ethel stood up, looked around again, then gaining courage, moved faster, walking as she unzipped her shorts, running after she stepped out of them, lifting her tank up and unhooking her bra as she chased down Nora. Just ahead of her, at the edge of the water, Nora stopped and turned to give Ethel herself in full frontal nudity. Her breasts gleamed in the moonlight and she arched her back, then turned again and raced recklessly into the shallow sea.

Back in the flat, after Nora had passed out—it was, after all, four a.m. English time—Ethel, lying beside her, was still jazzed, wide awake from the day, her earlier nap, their fight, the beach, the picnic, the make-up sex. Sex! God that felt good. Her mind was racing around Nora and again, what would they do, how could this go? She tried to shut the worries down but when she couldn't, she decided to work, to finish what Nora had interrupted this morning.

In the studio, she tested the sludgy mix in the two large pails— ready for a first sieving. She carried each pail—so heavy she had to lift them one at a time—out to her patio and poured the contents into the sisal sacks she'd prepared, hung them from the railing, with a large baking pan beneath to catch the drippings. She sat in her deck chair, put her feet on the wine crate footstool, and listened to the slow plips and plops. It would take hours for the filtering to finish.

Then that watery sludge would need to go through another filtering process, until she had what might work. If she'd got the recipe right this time. So much effort for a few pounds of clay.

She'd been painting for ten years now, modeling her watercolors on artists like Elizabeth Forbes, plein air paintings that captured everyday scenes. First in Bristol, those were all a lie. Lately, her attempts at scenes from the West End settlements; those too felt wrong—prurient, invasive. Maybe that was why she'd felt the shame. But in her few botched attempts with clay, she knew she was onto something. And at night, lately, the ideas that came, insisting themselves into her brain like memories of things she'd never seen, were a strange combination of ceramics and biology—visions of worlds she would make, where things moved at a different pace, and people didn't matter, different species would be interacting and following their roles in the ecosystem. Yes, she would teach herself to make the perfect clay, she would learn about reef life so she could shape biologically accurate corals, sea sponges, mollusks, anemones, and urchins. She would capture and recreate the fragility of the undersea world. This was what she must do.

CHAPTER 7

Two weeks before Easter holiday, Miss Evans took attendance and announced that it was time to get serious. For the next three days, the class would spend several hours practicing for the Bahamas Junior Certificate, an exam that was administered to Lower Secondary students in late April. Highest scorers from the islands had the possibility of receiving scholarships to Government High School in Nassau, possibly even top schools in other Commonwealth countries. If they all worked hard, she said, there would be a surprise for them before school break.

She patted a pile of booklets on her desk. "Think of this as an assessment to see where you are... to identify areas for improvement," she said. "This is not a test."

But it sounded very much like one: three days, five different hour-long sections on English, Bahamian history, geography, maths, and science. Dede had been around long enough to know that when a grown-up insisted that something was not what you suspected—*not a permanent move, not a boyfriend*—then it most assuredly was. She could play the same game, though. She could stare right back into any lying adults' eyes and say, *Not a problem*. Besides, unlike most of the idiots in her trailer, Dede liked tests. Mum had pulled her out of school in England when she was ten, gypped her out of the Eleven-Plus exam, so this would be her first chance to shine in quite some time. She cracked her knuckles and asked Miss Evans if she could help hand out the first assessment. Subject area: English.

When Miss Evans replied, "Why yes, thank you," Dede grabbed a pile of booklets and distributed them along each row, trying not to flash glee as she placed them face down on students' desks. "Here you are Prudence, here you are Jeremy. Trevor. Nigel. Here you are, Natalie."

Dede knew she could out-assess them all, even Natalie Fryer who'd been accepted to Roedean for next autumn. Dede was tops in every subject except for maths. And when Miss Evans looked over all the answers on the English section tonight, no doubt she'd see Dede's intelligence and ring up Mum to talk about options for her secondary education. Mum would have to agree that Dede needed to get back to England and into a real school. Like the ones she'd read about in a book at the Freeport Library: *The top British boarding schools, like Badminton, Cheltenham Ladies, and Roedean, now offer scholarships to the very brightest pupils from England and Commonwealth countries.* She added Red Maids to that list too. Nora had said it was highly selective. Dede knew she'd fit in.

"Here you are, Enid. Jethro, best of luck, because you'll need it."

Having a dad who was a Member of Parliament, having a mansion off Royal Palm Way, did not make Jethro any less of a wanker.

After Dede returned to her seat, Miss Evans pulled a stopwatch from her briefcase, told the class to turn over their tests and start. Dede's heart thumped. She needed to do well. She had to show Miss Evans exactly what she was capable of… she pictured herself in a new school uniform, plaid skirt, white blouse, navy blazer, and a straw boater rimmed with the school colors. In a few years, she'd be Head Girl.

The first section was on vocabulary. *Pen is to writer, as sword is to*_____ *(shield, soldier, steel, stone)*. Dede snaked her left arm around the test, hung her head low to obstruct Timmy's line of sight. He was such a snot-digging cheat, always copying her work. *Colt is to stallion, as filly is to* _____ *(chariot, saddle, mare, stable)*. She'd been out of the UK for a while, but she still had horse sense, thanks to all the pony club books she'd checked out of the library. Unlike Jethro who liked to brag that he'd neither set foot in England nor finished a book. He also claimed he could trace his ancestors to a 1650 settlement on Eleuthera. He'd have no excuse for bollocksing up the afternoon section on Bahamian history. She peeked over his way. He was picking at a scab on his arm, and it started bleeding, dripping onto his assessment. Disgusting.

The air in the trailer thickened. Prudence, who was always a bit of a nutjob, began to rock and moan. Miss Evans walked over to her desk and patted her on the back. "Just do your be-est," she lilted."

Dede progressed through the twenty analogies and turned the page to reading comprehension.

"Miss Evans," Jethro said, "I'm bleeding. I need to go to the bathroom."

"No breaks during the test," Miss Evans said, contradicting her earlier assertion that this was not, in fact, a test. She brought Jethro a box of tissues and went back over to Prudence and whispered something in her ear. Prudence came from Eight Mile Rock; she lived with her Auntie since her parents died in a storm a few years ago. Supposedly Prudence had stopped talking for a whole year after they died and only spoke rarely now, even though she was quite clever.

Prudence kept rocking in her seat, starting to cry.

"You're going to be all right, Pru," the teacher whispered. "You know how to do these." She walked back to her desk at the front of the class.

"Miss Evans," Jethro insisted, "I really need to go."

"Jethro," she warned. "Quiet."

"Or what?" Jethro asked. "What will you do?"

All the idiots snickered. Why did everyone think Jethro was so special? Yes, he was tall and had muscles on his arms, but he was also disgusting and mean. Dede tried to focus.

> From 1940 to 1945, Edward VIII, Britain's Duke of Windsor, served as governour of the Bahamas. He had abdicated the throne to marry Mrs. Wallis Warfield Simpson, an American divorcee. At first, many Bahamians thought the Duke was callow, untested and unlikeable. During a terrible fire in Nassau in 1942, he helped battle the blaze. His valour helped win the hearts and minds of the Bahamians.

Several vocabulary questions followed the paragraph. *Abdicated. Valour. Callow.* Easy, easier, easiest. Mum loved that song from *The Fantastiks... Try to remember the kind of September when you were a young and callow fellow.* Callow: immature. Is that what Mum thought of Dad? Is that why she dragged Dede to the Bahamas and abdicated her role as a wife and mother?

Two more paragraphs, a dozen more questions; almost half-way done with the English non-test. Dede shook out her wrist.

Jethro stood up and stomped to the trailer door. His arm had stopped dripping but the tissue he pressed against it was soaked with blood. "Sorry, Miss. But I've got to take a piss."

Miss Evans watched him turn the handle, push open the door, and disappear. Maybe she was stunned by him using the word "piss." Maybe she believed he was telling the truth and was about to wet his pants. Maybe she was too scared to stop him. Did she know his dad was a bigwig? Maybe she had no clue what to do.

Dede raised her hand to offer a suggestion.

"What is it now, Dede?" Miss Evans wiped her forehead with a handkerchief.

Dede caught the reprimand. "Nothing. Sorry." Fine. Let her handle Jethro her own way. Let Jethro handle her, more like.

Next section. Grammar. Subject/verb agreement. *None of us need/needs this.* Ha. Dede worked through several questions. *All of them is/are quite happy with the results.*

Something pinged against the back of the trailer. Miss Evans left her seat and hurried toward the sound. Stupid bloody Jethro. If he left dents in the aluminum, he'd get more than a tongue-lashing from the headmistress this time. A limestone clump meteored through the trailer's window, just missed Miss Evans' head and landed in front of the blackboard.

Outside, Jethro whooped.

Miss Evans walked quickly to the trailer door. "Keep working, class." She kept her voice calm as she stepped down onto the playground.

Nigel and Jeremy snickered in the back row. Trevor stood up and ran to the rear window. Several other kids started talking.

"Sit down," Natalie said. "Everyone should finish their work."

Finish *his/her* work, Dede thought. Maybe Natalie wasn't so clever after all.

Dede pressed on for another five minutes and finished her booklet, turned it over, and put her pencil down. Nothing to do now but wait for the slowpokes to finish. She bit her fingernail, tore at a piece of flesh around it. She felt she'd done well. But well enough to beat everyone else in her class? Well enough to get away? When school let out for Easter Holidays, she'd make sure she was better prepared than everyone else. She would keep swotting all week. It was the end of tourist season so Mum would still be working nights and Dede would set up a study space in the dining area.

The rest of the class was finishing up, one by one, turning over booklets, sighing, stretching, leaning back. A few were starting to talk quietly. Dede stood up and walked to the side window. Across the playground, Miss Evans had Jethro in a corner by the office building and seemed to be giving him a bloody good tongue-lashing. Jethro hung his head and stared at the ground. He shuffled his feet and followed her into the office. Dede couldn't help but smile. Maybe she'd call his dad. Maybe Mrs. Boatwright would paddle him. Maybe Jethro would be expelled this time? Sent away to boarding school? Did he dread what Dede hoped for?

"Sit down, Doodoo," Timmy said, "Or else."

"Or else what, you little snot," Natalie said. "Don't talk to your olders and betters that way."

Natalie joined her at the window. "Where'd they go?"

"She took him into the office."

"You know who his dad is, right? Barry Ingraham? I bet they'll ring him up. Jethro will end up in military school if he doesn't shape up. That's what Mr. Ingraham said to my dad. He won't have Jethro ruin the family name."

"Thanks for helping just now with Timmy."

"My pleasure," She whispered, "I can't stand that little twerp. I was going to ask… do you want to come over this weekend? Maybe spend the night?"

"Yes, absolutely."

When Miss Evans stepped into the trailer a few minutes later, she seemed unfazed by whatever had happened with Jethro. The tough Welsh farmer in her showed when Jethro slunk in behind her like a remorseful border collie and hurried to take his seat. What could she possibly have said to him? He had a plaster on his arm now and a red flush on his cheeks. If Miss Evans could get him to bow his head, heel, and obey, then she'd have the wherewithal to help Dede get a scholarship.

Miss Evans clapped her hands twice. "All right, class. Time is up. Will someone please help me collect the papers and pencils?"

Dede raised her hand.

"Jethro," Miss Evans said, even though he hadn't volunteered. "Would you be so kind?"

He completed the task slowly, proceeding along each row, not saying anything, not annoying anyone. When he finished, he walked back to Miss Evans' desk and set all the papers in a pile then patted the edges even. He arranged the pencils like a bouquet in a plastic container—their points all aiming at the trailer's tin top.

"Thank you, Jethro," Miss Evans said. "Class, you may have fifteen minutes outside. Use the toilets, get a drink. When you return, we will try our hand at the history section. Jethro, please stay inside with me."

Jethro put his hands in his pockets, kept standing by her desk with the lightest smirk on his face. Dede's gut churned a warning. She wanted to say something, alert Miss Evans to whatever he might be planning. Miss Evans pulled over an empty desk, set it next to her.

"Have a seat Jethro."

Maybe she did have control. Maybe Dede had it wrong this time.

An hour before the end of the school day, after Jethro had collected all the tests and returned to his seat of shame at the front of the class, Miss Evans announced that it was time for some fun. She was dividing the class into four groups for an *experiential learning opportunity.* She wrote out four fish names on the blackboard—*Grouper. Snapper. Amberjack. Wahoo*—and then laid out the plan. For the last two days of this week and all next week each learning group would come up with a lesson for the rest of the class; each group would be given a morning to teach. The lesson had to involve natural life in the Bahamas; other than that, they were free to come up with a topic and a method of instruction. She turned to the board again and listed the members of each group. Dede was a Wahoo, along with two other clever students, Natalie and Prudence, probably because Miss Evans thought it would take all three of them to balance out the impact of the fourth member: Jethro. Dede stifled a groan when Miss Evans chalked his name.

Jethro raised his hand. "Please, Miss Evans."

"What is it?" Miss Evans said.

"Can I switch groups?"

"No, you *may* not."

"But I'm the only boy in my group."

"Then you'll have to act like a proper gentleman. Remember what your father said when we called him. I don't think he was joking, do you? Now, class, find a place to meet with your team members and start your planning. Jethro, you may join your group."

Jethro sighed but complied. Had he come to fear Miss Evans? Or was Natalie right about his dad's threat of military school?

"Come on, Dede," Natalie called. "Over here."

All the Wahoos circled around Natalie's desk. Since she would be leaving in the summer, heading back to England, everyone assumed she'd be the group leader. Even though Dede was cleverer.

"We need a lesson topic," Natalie said, "Then, we can arrange some time this week or over the weekend to plan the lesson. We can use my house if we want."

"Why don't we try to grow conch pearls," Dede suggested.

"How do you propose we do that, Doodoo?" Jethro said. He winked at Natalie who smiled back at him. Whose side was she on? Did she fancy him?

Dede felt her face burning, but she continued anyway, "We'd get live conch from the reef, maybe ten? Then we could inject a tiny speck of sand or grit inside each one. That makes a nucleus—an irritation inside the shell, and the conch secretes a protective lining. It makes a pearl, just like an oyster does. A non-nacreous pearl. I read all about it at the library last week."

"What the hell are you talking about?" Jethro snorted and punched Natalie lightly on the arm. "Non-nacreous." He repeated the word several times, until he sounded as if he were throwing up.

"Is everyone in the right group?" Miss Evans called. "Natalie—is everything all right?"

"Fine, thank you, Miss."

Dede pressed on. "We would need a saltwater pool to keep the conch. Maybe an aquarium?"

"You can't grow pearls in a week, Doodoo. You'd probably just end up killing a bunch of perfectly healthy conch." Jethro winked at Natalie again. "Any other brilliant ideas? How about you Pru? I bet you've got lots of deep thoughts buried in that nappy noggin."

Prudence stared at the blackboard. She seemed lost in space, but then she made a suggestion: they could make paints using the island's flowers—hibiscus, poinciana, bougainvillea—extract color from them and then find a way to preserve them. "Salt, maybe. My Auntie preserves fish that way."

Dede added that Ethel Edgecombe, her neighbor, was an amazing artist, and would probably let them borrow some supplies—brushes and stuff. They could create a giant canvas; and on their day to teach they could show off all the paint colors they'd made and let the other kids paint.

"Sissy stuff," Jethro said. "Let's trap lizards, cut off their tails and document regeneration."

"Haven't you created enough havoc for one day?" Dede said.

"Or we could find an island frog," Jethro said, "We could pin it down, slice it open, so we can watch its heart beating. Ba-boom, ba-boom, ba-boom. We could count the heart beats until it died."

Prudence started to cry. She was even softer than Dede when it came to living things.

"No," Natalie said firmly. "I've seen your so-called animal research before, Jethro. It's rather—barbaric." She laughed a snobby girl sort of laugh and touched him on the arm. "Please behave yourself, or you know where you'll end up."

He swore under his breath, but he didn't seem especially angry, "I need another boy in this group. Me against three girls: It's not fair."

"Snot fair?" Dede said, "How do you propose we do that?"

He grabbed one of Dede's pigtails. "Watch yourself." He gave it a quick tug before Miss Evans saw. "If you're so brilliant, why aren't you going off to boarding school with Natalie? She's the real brain in our class."

"Quit quarreling, you two," Natalie said. "We're on the same team, remember?" She smiled at them, as if she were the teacher, and then she offered a compromise: the group would make the paints—as Pru had suggested—but not just with flowers. The kids could come to her house every day after school this week and collect flora and fauna from the land and the water. They'd use berries, flowers, leaves, mud, rocks, coral, to make an island palette.

"Can we use dead animals?" Jethro asked. "Ones we find in the bush or on the beach?"

Natalie weighed the question. "I don't see why not," she said. "As long as it's not—you know, fresh dead. Stinky."

After that, they took turns calling out suggestions for paint sources, and Natalie wrote them all down: sea cucumbers, sea sponges, sea fans, sea grapes, cocoplums, tamarind, wooly-nipple cactus, mangrove, guayacan, palmetto, oat grass, sargasso. They added what was shed or dead or ocean-fed: Flamingo feathers, fish skeletons, lizard skin, jellyfish, horseshoe crabs, conch shells, sand dollars.

"How about agouti?" Jethro said.

None of them had ever seen a live agouti, which supposedly looked like a squirrel-rat mongrel, but Jethro said he'd seen evidence in the woods behind his house.

"Their shit is like mini-bananas. Same color as your hair, Doodoo."

Over the next few days, together and apart, they collected ingredients and met at Natalie's house every evening to create pigments and test out recipes. As presentation date approached, Dede asked Ethel to help them, and now that her friend Nora had somewhat reluctantly gone back to England, Ethel agreed to give up her precious Saturday to assist. She drove over to the Fryers' beachside home in her El Camino and offered up brushes, paint containers, palettes, stirrers, linseed oil, rags. She stayed and watched, then joined in and helped, as the Wahoos tore and crushed, pestle-and-mortared, and added casein and borax to turn their island finds into an impressive collection of paints. They filled dozens of Ethel's jars with watery blues; bone-flecked whites; clay-browns from the brackish inland waters, and oozy green gels from the seaweeds and evergreens. Ethel said the best thing about homemade paints was how color kept evolving: What was phthalo blue on a morning application might lighten into a cerulean sky by afternoon.

As they all worked into Saturday evening on the Fryers' porch, Dede found Johnnie Angel's coral pendant in the pocket of her brown dungarees. She pulled it out, stomped on it, mixed the chunky granules up with a fresh batch of Jethro's agouti dung and a few drops of linseed oil. It made a color so ugly, a paste so thick that no one would want to use it.

The Thursday before Easter break was the Wahoos' lesson day. Ethel transported all the materials, as well as a large canvas she'd prepared, to the school in the back of her El Camino. Dede rode shotgun. When they arrived at Sunland, she and Ethel carried the canvas across the schoolyard and propped it up along the shady side of the middle school trailer. Jethro, Prudence, and Natalie helped unload the rest of the materials they'd made and set them up on a table Miss Evans had carried outside.

Fifteen students showed up for the painting session: Jethro and Natalie and Prudence and Dede, of course, because they had to talk about their work, but also, Jeremy and Timmy and Trevor and Nigel and Enid and Miles and Leroi and four or five others from Eight Mile

Rock who barely bothered with school. Miss Evans wore a sundress that she covered with an apron. She asked if Ethel would be willing to stay to hear the students' presentation and then talk briefly about the life of an artist. Ethel laughed and said *I'm no artist,* but she stayed on, nonetheless.

The paints and pigments and painting supplies filled up the table. For each color, Dede had hand-written a placard, giving the paint a name, and describing its contents. Prudence and Dede doled out colors on giant scallop shell palettes for everyone who wanted to paint, and Natalie described their basic paint recipe and the reasons for each ingredient. Then Dede and Prudence took turns speaking about the various plants and minerals they'd used, and Jethro demonstrated how he had made a variety of applicators from sea oats, grasses, shells, and dried natural sponges. Finally, Ethel spoke about art, what it meant to her. "Colors answer feelings; shapes answer thoughts," she said quietly. "Use paintbrushes, sponges, rocks, leaves—anything else you want to apply the paints. Turn off your brain and see what questions your body wants to answer with your art."

Everyone, even the headmistress, Mrs. Boatwright, and the secretary, Miss Hibbert, who'd come outside, decided to have a go. Some kids dipped their palms in oily paints, made handprints around the edges of the canvas. Others used the shells Jethro had collected to stamp patterns. Trevor used his fists, making cool patterns with his knuckles. A couple of the idiots wrote dirty words then took off toward the tetherball court. Towards the end of the morning, when most of the students were done, Dede found a patch of white space on the lower right corner of the canvas. Using her first two fingers as applicators, she rubbed the dull brown sludge that she'd made from the coral pendant, agouti dung and oil, up and down, back and forth, up and down, back and forth—the same motion Johnnie Angel used when he rubbed her shoulder—making a small gritty box from the color of her shame.

CHAPTER 8

Just ahead and to the right of the highway, black smoke mush-roomed above Mary Star of the Sea Church. McGuinn slowed as he approached; he couldn't see any flames, but ash floated around the white spire. Had lightning hit a dried-out palm frond somewhere deep in the bush? Maybe sun glinted off a broken beer bottle and ignited the brush. More likely, some stupid SOB tossed a cigar out of the car on the way home from the casino. Did it matter how? Sparked by nature or idiots, bushfires burned hot on the island, turning scrub to cinder, leaving nothing but charred pines pricking the rock-bed. No one stopped. No alarms sounded. No firefighters on call. *Live and let burn*—could be the island motto.

He scanned the church property as he passed by. Over a year on the island already and McGuinn still had not gotten used to the sight of buildings backdropped with smoke. A parking lot half-filled with cars separated the facilities—chapel, convent, and the Medical Center—from the bush. A nun in a white habit hurried across the asphalt towards one of the white-washed buildings. Small, stooped and focused only on her destination, she was as familiar as the back of McGuinn's hand. He'd been a Catholic school boy growing up in

Elizabeth, New Jersey; a thousand miles and a thousand years ago, but he still got that embarrassed feeling, that shoe-shuffling inadequacy, whenever he encountered men and women of the cloth. You could take the boy out of the church. He rolled the window down, spat out onto the asphalt, and continued along the highway. Driving through Paradise on fire.

He accelerated again until he hit the second traffic circle. American cars, British roads, what a nightmare, drivers on the outside trying to control the speed and the force as they looped around, trying to hold it all together. McGuinn knew he wouldn't last long in this beautiful, fucked-up island world, but he had to wait a little longer, at least until things cooled off in the States. He took the third exit onto Gambier Road.

Outside the school, he turned the engine and AC off while he waited for the bell. No breeze today and the three spindly casuarinas at the edge of the bush offered no shade from the afternoon's angled sun. He'd worked outside most of the morning. No rest for the wicked. His arms ached, his shoulders were sore, and despite wearing a bandana to keep sweat out of his eyes, his forehead had fried all over again. Christ, he was too old for this shit—three hours spent waiting for and then unloading packages from a fishing boat at some makeshift dock near the West End. Just he and a Colombian guy who said his name was Bob White (a fake name if ever there was one) doing the heavy work, while the boat's captain complained about them taking too much time, putting them all at risk.

School let out at three. He'd had just enough time to haul the product to the drop off spot and then drive home, take a quick shower and change his clothes. He didn't want to be late and miss her, like last week, when she ran off somewhere instead of waiting ten minutes. Today, he'd buy her a cold treat: an ice cream or a snow cone, her choice, then take her for a drive with the AC blowing full force so they'd both feel better. He scanned the playground and then checked his watch. One minute before the hour.

The bell sounded; his heart jitterbugged. He adjusted his shirt collar to hide the wrinkle lines around his throat. She liked blues best. He spat into his hand and smoothed back his hair. Across the street, girls and boys streamed out of their trailers. As they got closer, walking along the concrete path past the white administration building and out onto the front driveway, each one came into focus. Each child who was not Dede was a disappointment. White kids climbed into vehicles waiting in the semi-circle driveway. The blacks walked along the shoulder of the road towards Sunset Highway where a bus route ran in both directions. A few loitered on the playground. He strained his eyes, tried to make out if she was there among them.

Why would she make him wait? She knew he'd be here. She was starting to get full of herself, and only a few months in. Little tease. He loved and hated this part of the game—his girls asserting themselves, as he'd coached them to do. He closed his eyes, waited another couple of minutes. If he trained this one just right—with care and patience—she'd come into his room at night; he'd leave his glass doors unlocked so she could slip in, sidle up to him in bed, brush a hand over his shorts. A real bed instead of a car seat. *Christ.* A horn blasted through his reverie. Some idiot parent backing out of the school driveway. McGuinn opened his eyes, too antsy to see the fantasy through. Despite the shower just an hour ago, he was starting to sweat again. His skin itched. He wanted a cold drink. A beer. He'd left a six-pack in his refrigerator before he left the apartment; it should be good and icy by the time he got home tonight. He

94

checked his watch again—twelve minutes after the hour. Should he go? Should he try to find her? Much too old for this crap.

A skinny black kid walked beside his car, looked in with a shit-eating grin on his face.

"You need Kamalamee, man."

"What?"

"You all fried up like a tourist. Need some Kamalamee bark. I'll pick you some right now. Five dollars. American bills."

"Get out of here." McGuinn waved him off. Fucking hustler. Fucking mumbo-jumbo.

The kid ran off, hitching his shorts as he went; a few yards down the road, he picked up a rock and tossed it back toward the car; it hit the hood. McGuinn started to get out and give chase, but the kid took off. Long-legged, fast, laughing over his shoulder. Little shit.

Had Dede left out the back of the school lot somehow? He'd told her last night he'd be waiting here. He was going to be pissed off if he'd showered and rushed over here for nothing. He opened the door and stepped out onto the street. He could feel the heat of the pavement through his tennis shoes. The whole island was burning up, the sun and the bush fires and the air thick and smoky. Crazy hot. Where the hell was she? He'd worked a long day already. He wanted to start the car, turn on the air, and take her for a drive. Was that too much to ask? He couldn't exactly enter the school grounds and start inquiring after her.

Or could he?

People at the school—some of them—must know he picked her up now, several days a week. Kids, parents, schoolteachers had seen him here before waiting on the side shoulder, seen her scramble into the front seat. So why shouldn't he ask if anyone had seen her? Why should he act guilty? He could be… hell, he could be her grandfather. On a good day, her Uncle. Uncle Johnnie. If he were dressed a little better, he could be her chauffeur. She loved that game, anyway. *Chauffeur, get the door. Chauffeur, take me home. Chauffeur, give yourself a jolly good tip.*

He crossed the street and walked through the now-cleared driveway. As he passed the main office building, he ducked his head, looked at the ground. Old school guilt catching up with him. Christ, those nuns had done a number. In the back yard, four boys bounced a ball in the four-square court. Two taller kids punched a tetherball back and forth between each other, yelling "Boosh. Boosh," with each fist-hit. Did they have nowhere to go? Like hell out here on the asphalt. The middle of the island was always ten degrees hotter than the beachfronts where the fat cats built their porticoed mansions. Could Dede still be inside her classroom? Had to be roasting in there. Was she playing some kind of game with his heart? He loved when his girls asserted themselves, hated when they switched up the rules of the game. In the end, all of them turned out to be teases. In the end, all of them turned out to be fucking heartbreakers.

He turned to the boys playing tetherball.

"Either of you fellas know Dede? Domini Dawes. Little English girl?"

One guy stopped the orange ball, held it by the rope. "Miss Evans' class?"

"Yeah, I think that's right. You see her leave already?"

"Dunno." He shrugged. "Could be in there. Middle school trailer." He whispered something to his friend and they both laughed.

McGuinn stared at the yellow tinder box, just twenty, thirty yards back from where he stood. He should walk over and rap on the door. Talk some sense into that teacher. Fucking crime to keep kids in there in this heat anyway. He looked at his watch again. It was already twenty after. He should walk over, open the door, peer in, and say, polite as can be, *hi there, I'm looking for Dede.* If the girl caught his eye, he'd wink at her. If the teacher asked why, he'd add *I'm a friend of the family.* His throat felt dry. Or *I'm her chauffeur.* Too risky. There'd been that Orlando incident. He'd had to go to the station, police pressing him... how he knew the girl, what he'd been doing at the school, why he'd offered to drive her to tennis. Even here in the lawless islands—too risky to enter a classroom again. He shouldn't have stepped on the playground. He'd have to go home without her today. Or he could sit in his car and continue to wait. His fucking life.

It had been a long year and he'd been so patient with this girl, but Christ. Sometimes she played him. If this were Dede's idea of a game, he'd show her that he could play too. He'd go back to the car and sit and wait, and when she came out, he wouldn't bat an eye because he hadn't even noticed it was three fucking thirty. Or maybe he should leave. Let her walk home. He turned and moved slowly, steadily (in case she or any busy body teacher was watching) across the street, and back to his car; he opened the door and sat on the burning vinyl. Five more minutes.

␗␗␗

When the bell rang Dede watched the rest of her class grab lunch pails and satchels and push for the trailer door, ignoring Miss Evans' words, "Calmly, class, let's exit like civilized people."

Dede sat at her desk until the last of the idiots had gone, and then took a deep breath for courage. The trailer trapped the usual smells–sweaty armpits, Fritos, chalk dust. She swiped her forehead with her fingers, pushed her damp hair behind her ears, stood up, slung her satchel over her shoulder, and approached her teacher's desk.

Miss Evans looked up, "How are things, Domini?"

"All right, thank you Miss."

"Did you need another book to read? I've got the new James Herriot in my briefcase if you'd like to borrow it."

"No thanks. I'm just on my way to the library to pick up some things, but, actually, I have a bit of a favor to ask."

She pulled the form out of her satchel. She'd carried it around so long now that the edges were curved by humidity and the pages pocked and nicked by stray pencils. GRAND BAHAMA SCHOLARSHIP APPLICATION – typed in capital letters across the top of the first page. She'd already filled in all the blanks on the cover sheet with blue ink, in her best penmanship, already signed her mother's name with a plausible right-leaning cursive in the space on the bottom. She'd agonized over the three-paragraph personal essay, written a draft over the past two nights, and copied it out neatly into the space allotted on page three. She get BJC scores soon. Now she needed a teacher's letter of recommendation on the third page, along with a report card, and the headmistress's signature at the end.

She held the form out towards Miss Evans. "I was wondering if you might be so kind as to recommend me for this."

Miss Evans took it and looked it over. "I'm familiar with this scholarship." She frowned. "But I'm quite sure it's meant for a Bahamian pupil, not an expat. The thing is, Dede, I've already written a recommendation letter for one of your classmates." She handed the form back. "I'm sorry, Domini. I really hate to disappoint you, but the school can only put one name forward. Mrs. Boatwright wanted it to be someone without many other opportunities."

Dede bit her lip and tried not to cry. It had to be Prudence. She was the only one clever enough to deserve it; she was the one all the teachers tried to help all the time because her parents had drowned. Poor, poor, poor Pru. Dede could throttle her, the way she always rocked and moaned and wailed through her maths tests. Bloody great faker. She probably knew that all the crazy behavior would help get her something in the end. What did being polite and good ever get Dede?

"Besides," Miss Evans said, with a head tilt and an awkward smile, "You're such a clever girl there will be plenty of chances for you to excel. You'll see."

Dede stuffed the scholarship application back into her satchel, started toward the door. She turned the handle, then let go, and spun around. "At Freeport High?" She could hear the disdain in her own voice. "Bloody brilliant." Miss Evans flinched behind her desk. Dede wanted to hit her in the face, so she'd feel real pain. Then punch her in the belly, double her over. Take that, and that, you stupid Welsh cow.

She slammed the trailer door. Fuck you very much, as Jethro would have said. She stepped out onto the blazing playground and ran across the patchy field to the back fence. Johnnie Angel had said he'd collect her after school today, but she didn't want to see him, even if he would buy her a snow cone. She'd rather be alone and miserable. She'd rather spend the afternoon in the back corner of the library, reading and napping and hating her life.

At the edge of the lot, she pulled up the loose section of the chain link and slipped under, snagging her thigh on a metal prong. "Fuck," she said again, and it felt good to scream into the brush. "Fuck Miss

Evans and all the bloody island idiots. Fuck Mum and Silvio and everyone. Fuck you too, Dad, for never ever coming to get me."

She pushed through the tangled yellow vines and turned onto a wider path, a horse trail that led from behind the stables, where the stench of sweating animals and steaming manure blasted her, towards the south shore beach where the horses carried the tourists three times a day. She jogged a half mile on the choppy path until it spit her out in a gulley by East Sunrise Highway. This was where the trail riders crossed on the way to the beach. Dried pancakes of manure baked on the coral shoulder, too flat and dry to smell much anymore. But she did smell smoke. A bushfire? To the right down the highway, just beyond Mary Star of the Sea Church, a dark cloud. The library was a mile beyond all that smoke. Hard to tell how close the flames were. Fires like these could spew for hours, even after the blaze was gone. She hitched the satchel strap on her shoulder and hurried along the roadside where broken bottles and fag ends accused each other of arson. As she approached the church lot, she realized the blaze must be deeper in the bush. Though she could taste acrid pine smoke in her throat, there was no heat, or rather, the flames did not make the already stifling afternoon any worse.

Past the Antonio Medical Clinic, she turned right at the next main intersection onto the Mall, headed towards the library. Miss St. John, an old English woman from Dorset, worked the desk, and she liked Dede. She always had a few books set aside for her, and sweets—usually Quality Street chocolates that her sister sent over from England every month, along with a shipment of donated books from her village.

Dede opened the front door and the cool air hit her forehead; she pulled at her white blouse, to unstick it from her back and stomach.

The downside of the air-conditioning was that she'd be freezing in here in a few minutes, her wet shirt would cling to her and goose-pimple her flesh and she'd want to leave again.

"Hello, my dear," Miss St. John said. "Are you quite all right? You're terribly flushed."

Dede nodded. "I ran through the bush; there's a fire. I probably smell like a chimney."

"Not to worry. Get yourself sorted. The books you wanted from the Nassau library finally came in."

Dede stopped first at the loo, washed her hands, and swigged from the tap. In the mirror above the sink, her face looked ridiculous, red and tear-stained; she rubbed hard at the smudges under her eyes with a paper towel. Stupid fat cry-baby. What makes you think you deserve a scholarship? She dabbed at the scrape on her thigh and then carried her satchel to her usual seat in the back corner, at a small wooden table, between two sets of shelves. She pulled out a thick volume called *Island Memories: Bahamian Voices from 1900 to Independence*. She grabbed the big book of oral histories and started reading the chapter on beliefs, values, and customs, an interview with several bush medicine practitioners, and a section on Obeah—a form of religious belief using witchcraft and sorcery—medicinal herbs, manmade charms, incantations. She'd see if she could check out the book, maybe learn how to get revenge on some of the idiots. After finishing the chapter, she put her head down on the desk and closed her eyes.

✻ ✻ ✻

He found her asleep in the back corner of the library, rubbed her shoulder and she startled.

"Dreaming about me, Princess?"

She looked up at him, confused. "What are you doing here?"

"I told you I'd give you a ride home today. I waited at school until after three-thirty. Then I saw your teacher leaving. She told me you might have come here; said you were upset. Come on. We had a date."

Dede carried the large volume she'd been reading to the front desk.

The old biddy said, "Here are the other books you ordered, dear." She picked up a pile of materials on a back table and handed Dede several check-out cards to sign. "Two weeks for all these," she said, while stamping the date on each card and in each book. She looked at McGuinn. "Your granddaughter's quite the reader."

Dede nodded her thanks and stuffed all the books she could fit into her satchel. The rest she carried in her arms and walked ahead of McGuinn out the door.

Halfway across the lot, she turned around and said, "Carry my satchel."

She handed him the heavy book bag. *Satchel.* That's what she called it. And God, the way the "s" caught on her teeth was enough to do McGuinn in. Just remembering it made him forget his anger, the wait. He wanted to grab her in his arms and embrace her. Kiss her on her throat and chest. She reached the car and stood beside the passenger door. When he reached his door, he tossed the book bag on the floor and climbed into the driver seat. She tilted her head and tossed her hair the way she must have seen her mother do a thousand times. Damn if she didn't stand there waiting. He started the car, turned on the AC, leaned over and lowered the passenger-side window so he could talk to her.

"Aren't you getting in, Princess?"

"Door," she said.

"Ah. Yes. Of course, Princess." He let the engine run while he climbed out, walked around the front, gave her a gallant bow, and then held open the door. "Forgive my oversight. Please step inside."

She threw her books on the floor, attempting to be regal with disdain, but she still had chalk smudged yellow across the side of her skirt. He wanted to brush it off as he closed the door. He wanted to touch her baby soft cheek, smell her sweat from the day. He wanted to bury his face between her legs and sob into her belly, *why did you make me wait?*

"Snow cone," she said, as they came to the first traffic roundabout. "Pronto."

"As you wish."

A guy from Eight Mile Rock parked his truck in front of Freeport High every weekday afternoon, 3-5 pm. Cedrik's Sno-Cone painted on the side panel of his truck. His store was a chest of shaved ice on the ground, two cement blocks and a plank of wood for a counter. He organized his syrups in rainbow order. No cash register—only his right pocket for bills, his left for coins. He reeked of rum and sweat, but unlike a lot of the black guys on the island, he had a work ethic. The cops let him be, too; bigger fish to fry than a vendor from the settlements. Or maybe he gave them kick-backs.

Cedrik was a skinny little shit, scruffs of gray hair stuck to his head and his clothes just shy of rags, missing several teeth and the ones that remained were too big for his mouth. His product was— well—sugar water. But still Dede liked to visit him and often chose his snow cones over gourmet ice cream from Gibson's. McGuinn parked behind the truck on a rocky patch of land. She opened her own door this time and walked toward the makeshift counter.

Cedrik shuffled forward, scratched his chin. "Hello again, young lady. Extra-large, Ocean View?"

"Yes, please," she said.

McGuinn watched her weight shift from one leg to the other, one of her knee socks slumped mid-calf, the other wrapped around her ankle. Her white blouse had untucked from her plaid skirt. How could her voice, that lisp, that accent not have any effect on Cedrik? Why didn't his ancient dick jump? How could some men, so-called normal men, be immune to these girl powers? Not react to something so tender, fresh and perfect?

Cedrik scooped an extra pile of ice from the chest into a red plastic bowl. He used the back of a spoon and then some kind of metal file to shape it as though he were an artist. "Rough water, today," he said, forming waves in the ice.

Dede laughed, covered her mouth.

McGuinn knew there were others like himself. He caught them on occasion, watching one of his princesses. He could tell what was happening for them inside, the churning stomach, the dry mouth, the torment of desire. He should commune with these men—share this miserable blessing, this holy affliction. Instead, he would glare at them and turn away. *Sick fucking bastard*, they might read in his look, and, if so, too bad. He had to be cautious. And they had to be able to take his feigned hostility and a whole lot more if they were going to survive in a world that wanted to extinguish their sort.

Cedrik went for the syrups: green, and light blue, a splash of dark blue to deepen the sea in a couple of places.

"A stormy sea like this gonna sweep your boat right into the Tongue of the Ocean." Near the end, he added a few extra shavings of ice.

"White caps over the coral reefs." Dede said.

"One Ocean View," he said, handing Dede the bowl. "More like a Hurricane Warning."

He flashed McGuinn a toothy grin, working on his tip. "Yessir—hurricane season coming early this year, I reckon."

McGuinn paid him a quarter for the treat, tipped him another, and nodded good-bye.

As he drove her east on Sunset Highway, McGuinn watched Dede cradle the bowl between her thighs. In the heat of the afternoon, even with the windows up and the car's AC on, the treat wouldn't last long. Dede liked to let the snow cone melt a little before she tasted it; she liked the flavors to blend into what she thought would be a perfect rainbow sensation but, of course, was always a let-down. McGuinn saw it in her eyes every time. She never said so; he never mentioned it, but they both knew. How could it possibly live up to expectations?

"What did Cedrik mean about the Tongue of the Ocean?" she asked.

"No idea."

"Do you think it's a place—part of the sea—or maybe a language, a dialect that people speak?"

"Aren't you gonna taste your icy?"

"Miss St. John found me a book from Nassau about coral reefs, and one about medicinal plants in the West Indies."

"Why are you reading all that mumbo-jumbo?"

"I was going to do a report on island remedies for our next big project on Bahamian culture. But I'm not going to do it anymore. If you want to know the truth, I'm not even going to try at school anymore. Miss Evans is so biased you wouldn't believe it." She held her snow cone and stared out the window.

After they exited the second roundabout and headed east on Atlantic, she took the first suck, pulling blue from the top of the concoction. The top of the snow cone formed a round, white head. Buddy Boy stirred at the sight.

"Can you take me home, please," she said, "I'm feeling really tired today." She'd lost her imperiousness. He gripped the steering wheel. He didn't dare speak. He tried to get himself under control. He glanced at her a moment later. Was she going to fuss? She knew the routine. She stared ahead out the windshield; worked slowly, with building disappointment, on the snow cone. He didn't respond to her question. He just accelerated, pushing the car to eighty, eighty-five, empty road and straight highway. She didn't ask again.

By the time they approached their usual site ten miles out of town, her lips and her tongue and even the tip of her nose had sponged up the blue dye. A few weeks back, they would have laughed at this together. He would have told her to look in the rearview mirror and she would have giggled into her hand. *Oh Chauffeur!* A shy school-girl. But today, she was finished with her treat, pouty-mouthed, bored, and ready to be done? Was she losing interest in him like she was with her schoolwork? At the abandoned High Town project, he turned left, into a barren grid of unfinished roads. The 88 rattled on the crushed coral underlay as he drove down one, then another, half-imagined street. He asked if she wanted to drive the last bit and she said no. She used to love this part too, sitting on his lap, while he worked the gas and brake, she'd steer them to this place. He already missed those first few rides, the pressure of her body, the feel of her cotton plaid skirt on his thighs, McGuinn concentrating still on the road, even as Buddy Boy rose and sang.

"What's wrong, Princess?"

She shrugged.

"What happened at school?"

She shook her head.

"Are you in some kind of trouble with your teacher?"

She started to sniffle. "Of course not."

"Then what?"

"I'm not getting the scholarship for boarding school. They're giving it to Prudence even though I'm smarter. Just because she's Bahamian. Miss Evans said that it's meant for poor island children, so they can get away to a good education, even though Mum can't afford to send me. It's not fair."

So that was why she'd kept him waiting? That was why she'd run off through the woods. Left him sitting in the car for over half an hour. Jesus H. Christ. He tried to calm himself. He had to relax. He had to make her laugh and relax, too, or this trip would be worthless.

"Well, it would break my heart if you left me, Princess. I'd die without you."

"No, you wouldn't."

"I would. I would miss you so terribly, I would die of grief." He reached across the bench seat and took her hand. "So, I am glad you didn't get the stupid scholarship."

"Stop it," she said, pulling back her hand and pressing her body up against the passenger door. "Stop trying to cheer me up. Stop buying me treats and things that I don't even like, just so I do what you want."

She'd kept him waiting today and time was precious, and he would not get enough of her as it was. She was still small, but he'd seen the signs. The bra she now wore; her breasts had grown in the past three months, and she was shaving under her arms. If she hadn't already, she'd soon go through the change that ruined them all. If only he could find a way to freeze time—to keep her in that delicate stage—girl on the cusp, supple and sun-kissed, pouty and lisping. Dear God, don't take her away yet, not when the real fun had only just started.

He parked by an unfilled waterway in an aborted development and took the empty snow cone container from her stained hand. He rolled the window down and tossed the trash into the wide rocky basin.

"Give a hoot, don't pollute," she said.

"Come here," he said.

She gave him a snotty look and moved closer to the passenger door. "Never be a dirty bird."

She was watching too much TV, getting too American. Too much of an attitude and he was suddenly so sick of the patience and the pretending and the hiding and the games. He had been a good and careful and gentle suitor, every time he'd taken it slow. He slid over on the seat and put a hand on her thigh, circled an inch of skin with his two fingers. She sat rigid, still, staring straight ahead through the windshield. A quarter inch, a half, a half-hand length and he was under her skirt.

"You know you like this," he said, as she started to relax. He could feel her body respond, loosen, move with him, even though she was fighting it. He pushed her book bag onto the floor, watched her notebooks and the library books spill out. He pulled her lower body across the seat, her legs across his lap. She let her head fall back on the seat, her crown pressed against the door.

"All girls like this," he said as he kissed her belly, and between her legs, "All women. This is what Silvio does when he's getting ready to make love to your mother."

Buddy had been patient today and Buddy had needs.

"I would never hurt you," he said and repeated it again. He adjusted her body then let himself down on her, let himself go, because this was Buddy's time, Buddy's show. Be gentle, he warned Buddy. But sometimes big, old dumb Buddy had to push and push to have his way.

Afterwards, he let her sob for a while, curled up in a ball, against the car door.

"What's the matter?" he asked after a while. "You know I would never hurt you."

"I'll tell my father." She would not look at him.

Tears were expected the first few times. Even accusations and threats. But she should be used to this by now.

"My dad will be so angry. He will fly over here as soon as I call him."

He wiped her thighs and the seat beneath her. He ignored the words that came more sporadically now, between her softening sobs. "I'm going to call him tonight. I swear."

McGuinn bent down to pick up her books from the floor mat, and stuffed them back into her bag, one by one. He started the car, let the AC blow on his face, no need to panic; she just needed time and he had plenty of that to give. He wouldn't move until she stopped making threats.

She stared out her window. "I'll tell Silvio," she whispered.

"What did you say?"

"Silvio. I'm going to tell him what you do to me when you drive me out this way."

He grabbed her arm. "Tell him what exactly?" She'd gone too far. He made her turn to face him. "That you knock on my door at night? That you climb into my car after school every day? That you sometimes steer us right to this spot? It's not my fault you're a little cock tease."

She threw off his hand and sat up. She wiped her nose on the sleeve of her blouse. She pulled the biggest book out of her bag and clutched it on her lap. *Bush Medicine*, it was called, and McGuinn laughed out loud, seeing it there between her legs. She ignored him. He watched her open the cover and start reading, and he tried to figure out what to say next to fix things between them. He could be patient now. A little more time would be all it took.

She read a few pages and sure enough, she soon stopped crying. Ten minutes or so and she got over herself, remembered the rules and the limits of their game. In her most imperious voice, without taking her eyes off the page she was reading, she said, "Well what are you waiting for then, Chauffeur? Drive me home this instant."

CHAPTER 9

Seaweed hemmed the beach from Natalie's house all the way to the Coral Cove Hotel. Below the line, sand packed hard, flat, and beige. Above, it blew fine and white as castor sugar. Dede toed the Sargasso gingerly. A jellyfish welt across her instep insisted that dangers hid along with treasure. Stowed safely in the pockets of her shorts, though, were several good finds: Two Tiger Cowry shells (speckled like leopards, not striped), a Sunrise Tellin, and six chunks of sea-chafed glass, including best of all, a prize amber piece, smooth and round as a Bahamian quarter. Ethel had told Dede that amber glass comes from old medicine bottles, odds of finding it at around one in two thousand. Ethel had just a handful of ambers in her collection of mostly greens and teals and blues. And only two true reds—*treasure among treasures,* she called these—odds at one in ten thousand.

As Dede followed the seaweed fringe, her pockets jangled congratulations: *Not bad, Dede, not half bad.* Of course, she'd had no competition this morning; the beach empty in both directions, except for herself and Natalie, who raced ahead. Summer had washed in the jellyfish but swept out all the tourists. Midway through hurricane season, late-August now, and no more American white-whites, with their sunhats and zinc-noses, scouring the shoreline for sand dollars and conch shells. Natalie didn't give a damn about Dede's tide finds. She said beachcombing was for tourists and old farts. A quarter mile down the beach, she zigzagged in and out of the turning tide, her long hair flagging behind. She gripped and twisted an imaginary lacrosse stick, as she dodged phantom defenders. She'd be leaving for England next weekend and all she'd talked about was London, where she'd end the summer holidays with her *brilliant* cousins, and *lax*—which she'd be playing at Roedean come September.

Dede didn't give a damn about Natalie's pending departure. Or at least she wasn't going to admit she did. It was just like a stupid rich Brit to scarper off to boarding school. What bothered Dede most was Natalie's sudden obsession with sports. She had never seemed remotely interested in athletics before; now she charged up the sand toward a clump of straggly pines and took a diving shot at an invisible goal, fell flat on her stomach, jumped up, and raised her hands in triumph. She turned and ran back to Dede. Striding across the sand, she seemed taller and tanner and faster than yesterday. Already a breed apart.

Dede pulled the tellin shell from her pocket and scraped its razor edge against her knuckles. Natalie might have a new school and a ton of new friends in her future, but Dede still *knew* some things. *Private* things Natalie would not want her to tell. Dede twisted the shell deeper, wishing she could scrape her whole body clean, and when blood trickled over the back of her hand, she wiped it off on her droopy t-shirt. One secret—Natalie claimed to be a vegetarian but ate beef burgers at the Coral Cove Grill whenever she could. Another—Natalie had started her period when she was ten and knew how to use tampons. Dede had only had two sort-of periods since Christmas when hers first started. A third secret: Natalie's birthmark—a raised, pink, and vaguely heart-shaped patch behind her left ear. Like a strawberry. Last night when Natalie was sleeping and Dede's brain wouldn't turn off, she'd reached over and pushed Natalie's hair aside, wanting to pinch the strange fruit, to rip off a little piece, keep it as skin treasure, and hide it among all her shells.

Natalie, running back toward her now, hurdled a piece of driftwood and pulled up in front of Dede, sand streaking her tan legs, sun squinting up her eyes.

"Did you see that? Bloody brilliant, right?"

Bloody great show-off, more like. Dede felt the shell's serrated edge with her thumb pad. Sharp enough to slice off Natalie's birthmark before she knew what was happening.

"God, Deeds, you're bleeding." Natalie reached for her hand. "And you've stained your shirt."

"It's nothing." Dede tossed the worthless shell toward the ocean, sucked blood from her knuckle, spat out onto the sand. Worth nothing. Same as her friendship with Natalie. Then she jangled the real treasure in her pocket. Amber sea glass. She would not share it. Well, maybe with Ethel. Besides, Dede had secrets of her own.

"Do you want to get some lunch? I'm starving. We could head to the Grill?"

Dede checked her watch. 11:25 a.m. Perfectly accurate because she'd called the time from Natalie's house this morning while everyone else was asleep. The man with the low tide voice had said, *Tanqueray gin is the in gin. Imported by Butler & Sons. Time 7:01.* Mum had worked last night which meant she'd still be asleep; Ethel would be painting because it was Saturday. If she wanted to go home now, her ride would be Johnnie Angel, and she was sort of sick of him.

"Lunch would be lovely."

Natalie talked the whole way to the Coral Cove. Nonstop prattle about her lacrosse skills. "I am definitely going to play right wing attack. My oldest cousin, Phillipa plays first home. Scored in every single game last year. I guess I could play second home, but with my speed, I really want right wing." On and on about her twists and cradles and checks. Then another round of how bad the food would be at boarding school: porridge for breakfast, tinned meat for lunch, boiled beef and boiled potatoes for dinner. "Just awful for vegetarians." The fake misery on her face barely covered her smile. She already loved the drama of British boarding school life, having something to pretend-moan about, when mostly what she loved was leaving.

Dede understood wanting to leave Sunland Academy, but why would anyone want to leave the Fryers' house? Since the Wahoos' group project, back in March, Dede had spent loads of weekends there. Natalie had two younger brothers, and her parents didn't seem to mind having an extra person in the house. Mr. Fryer was tall, red-haired, and funny in that understated English way. Natalie's mother, Cilla Fryer liked talking to the girls as if she were their age. One weekend, she even took them to see Jimmy Connors play Ilie Nastase, whom she called Old Nasty, at the Xanadu. She tried flirting with a security guard so she could get Old Nasty's autograph, but it didn't work. Now that Natalie was leaving, Dede probably wouldn't have the chance to step foot inside the Fryer home again.

The beach at Coral Cove Hotel—raked clear of seaweed and jellies—spread flat from the dunes to the water. There were a few deck chairs laid out, a couple of sun umbrellas, but no one was on the sand; no one playing in the turning tide. No one watched the gray sky reflecting the roiling ocean; or was it the other way around, water reflecting the troubled sky?

Dede followed Natalie along the boardwalk. Her scraped knuckle stung as much as the jelly-fish welt on her foot. She'd have to ask Clarence, the cook at the grill, for a plaster. Did real Bahamians say Band-Aid like the Americans or plaster like the Brits? So much about this island was a mish-mosh: American words, British spellings, and, of course, Bahamian pronunciation. Rubbish bin or trash can? Petrol or gas? Crisps or chips? The British built the roads, the Americans imported the cars, and all the island drivers steered Chevys and Olds from the curbside. Strange and disorienting, that's what Mum said.

Many times, lately, Dede felt as if her body didn't connect with her brain. Who was she after three years—a quarter of her life—on Grand Bahama? And who would she become if she had to stay and attend Freeport High? A Conchy Joe like Jethro? A perpetual expat? The expats closed themselves off in posh circles—Dede only got access through the Fryer family. Conchy Joes and Black Bahamians circled each other like the potcakes in the settlements where Ethel was from. And nobody, nobody liked too-friendly, money-talking Yankees who only came to gamble. Dede knew enough about the island to realize that she and her mother belonged with the temporary workers group: croupiers and oil rig grunts, but Silvio had upgraded them to respectable. Silvio, everyone knew, was in a class by himself.

Dede took her usual stool at the counter, by the hibiscus, and close to the soda snake. Natalie sat to her immediate right, started munching on peanuts set out in a bowl.

"And how are my two lovelies?" Clarence had on mirror shades, as usual, one of his zig-zaggy shirts, and white trousers. He slapped two huge beef patties onto the flame without being asked. Dede and

Natalie were his only customers, and they had his full attention. The massive pool deck and the beach strip in front of the resort were theirs, too, on a day like this: off-season and bad weather brewing. Clarence filled two tall glasses with ice chips, then hosed in Coca-Cola. Dede took a sip of the sweet, frothy brown. The syrup from Clarence's sprayer always had a slightly antiseptic taste that she'd come to expect and enjoy.

"Any good beach finds today, then? A Perigean high tide last night if I'm not mistaken."

"You're not mistaken," Dede said, as she emptied her pockets, and organized her finds, piece by piece, on the counter. Even the amber sea-glass.

Clarence patted through the shells without removing his glasses. He claimed he was partially blind, but Natalie said he was completely pissed most of the time, that if you watched him closely, he drank shots all day long. His fingers paused on the first amber shard as if he saw its color and value right away. "What will you do with this then?"

"I just collect it." Dede said. "But my friend, Ethel Edgecombe—sometimes she makes mobiles from sea glass."

"Ethel Edgecombe?" Clarence said, his face suddenly serious.

"Do you know her?"

"Indeed."

"Can I have some more peanuts?" Natalie asked.

Clarence reached for a jar under the counter and filled up the bowl.

"How do you know Ethel?" Dede sensed a secret.

"I knew her very well, back in Hanna Hill, when she was Ethel Tootes."

"Did you ever see her sea glass collection?"

"Can't say that I did." He tapped his sunglasses. "Don't see much of anything these days. Haven't seen Ethel in what, fifteen maybe twenty years, before she left the island on some fancy scholarship. Water and bridges, water under bridges, if you understand my elocution."

Natalie drained her glass then banged it down on the counter. "Hello? It's *my* last weekend on the island. My last meal here. Can we please talk about something—someone—else besides Ethel bloody Edgecombe?"

Clarence cocked his head. "You leavin' me, girl?"

Natalie nodded. "Boarding school." She fake-frowned and took a long swig of Coke.

"Time to get yourself a proper ejjification, eh?" Clarence fake-frowned right back at her. "We couldn't have seen that coming, now, could we? No way we could have predicted this unlikely and unfortunate turn of events." He shrugged and re-filled Natalie's Coke. "Another one heading back to dear old Blighty."

"Father's making me go." Natalie said.

Liar. Dede thought and chomped her ice. *Big fat bloody beef-loving liar.* Natalie couldn't wait to get away. Who would pay for Dede's lunches at Clarence's after Natalie left? Mr. Fryer had an account at Coral Cove and whenever the girls ate there Dede didn't worry about paying. Clarence just put it on the Fryers' tab. Losing Natalie meant losing lunches with Clarence, too. And all Natalie could do was sit at the counter, insult Ethel, ignore Dede's tide treasures, and lie, lie, lie about her true desires.

"You can't wait for London and lacrosse," Dede said. "It's all you talk about lately, so why not admit that you want to go?" Dede's head felt as if it might explode.

Natalie shrugged.

"Well, what about you, Dede?" Clarence asked. "You don't want to get ejjified in England?"

"I'm staying put." Saying it out loud didn't make her less furious. She could kill Natalie for leaving. She could kill Prudence for taking her scholarship. And most of all, murder Mum for keeping her here against her will.

"But we'll always be friends, right Deeds? When I'm at Roedean, you can be my Commonwealth pen pal."

Stay friends? Not on your life.

Clarence turned back to the grill, flipped and pressed. Eight minutes start to finish was how he prepped the meat. Buns—twenty seconds of toasting right at the end. He served the burgers on white china plates, gold *Coral Cove* written on the rim. A slice of tomato and a ring of onion resting on a lettuce leaf; two ridged pickle coins and a scattering of potato crisps. Or rather, potato *chips*.

"Bone appetite," he said.

He also brought out miniature sealed jars of tomato ketchup and mustard. Clear glass. Twenty or fifty years from now, maybe someone would find a sea-frosted shard of this very Heinz bottle washed up on the beach.

Dede ate the burger first, then dipped the crisps in meat drippings, and saved the pickles for last. The salt from the crisps stung her knuckle-cut.

When Clarence refilled her Coke, Dede asked, "How did you meet Ethel anyway?"

"I could ask you the same thing."

"Well, if you did, I would tell you that she is my next-door neighbor and she's my friend and she taught me to paint earlier this year and now she does lots of ceramics. She's a clay maniac, in fact."

"And if I told you, I'd be telling tales out of school."

"Does that mean you went to school together?" Dede insisted. "Were you classmates in Hanna Hill? You can tell me, Ethel wouldn't mind. We're very close, actually."

"Then ask her yourself" he said. "Go ahead and inquire about her old friend, Clarence Lawler. Be curious to hear what she has to say about me." He removed his glasses and wiped them on his white apron. His right eye looked normal, but his left wandered away, milky white, willful. Hurt. "Like I said, water and bridges."

Maybe they had been boyfriend and girlfriend. Maybe Ethel had broken his heart. Maybe he'd blinded himself in the left eye when she left him. No. Ethel seemed too practical or just too something, too no-nonsense or focused, perhaps, for any boyfriend. And Clarence seemed, well, not old—no gray in his hair—but more broken down somehow, with his potbelly and his milky eye.

"How old are you, anyway, Clarence?"

"Old as my tongue and a little bit older than my teeth."

"I think you're forty. Maybe a little less?"

He took away the plates and condiments, wiped down the counter. "Do you girls want dessert today? Before the storm rolls in?"

Dede turned to face the ocean. Bruises spread across the horizon towards the west, brown and black and purple.

"We should get going," she said.

"I'd like dessert," Natalie said. "Remember... it's my last week-end. I leave in four days' time."

As if she would let Dede forget.

Natalie ordered two Knickerbocker Glories, and Clarence assembled them quickly on the back counter: sponge cake, strawberries, pineapple chunks, chocolate and vanilla ice-cream, chocolate syrup, coconut flakes and whipped cream. Two blood red cherries on top. Dede ate a mouthful and felt sick; she pushed the parfait glass aside. Natalie didn't do much better eating hers, but she wouldn't rush. On some stupid principle, she sat upright in her stool, stirring her ice cream into a soupy mess, pretending she was still eating, pretending to love the taste, pretending she wanted to stay, as clouds coagulated into danger.

"Phillipa says that they don't really have cakes at Roedean," she said at last, pulling the long metal spoon out of her sludge and licking it front and back. "Only puddings for sweets. I am going to turn thirteen in September without a proper birthday cake. Will you please write to me Dede? Will you at least send me a birthday card?"

"Of course." There was no way on earth. Not a gift, not a card or a note. Not a shell from the beach or even an easy-to-find sea-glass shard. Let Natalie's cousins and her lax team take care of her now.

Natalie pushed the ice cream away. "Shall we have a good-bye toast? How about it, Clarence? Pour us all a stiff drink. Then we are off for a sail. My last one probably before I leave."

"You're not sailing in this weather." He took down three shot glasses, set them on the counter and reached for a bottle, filled each glass with caramel colored rum. "To two fine English ladies," he said and drained his shot with a quick, flicking motion. He poured himself another.

"*For the finest drinks under the sun, mix them with friendly Appleton rum,*" Dede said, and took a sip that stung her throat like a jellyfish, and then sunburned her chest from the inside out.

Clarence laughed loudly, smacked his lips, and said, "You call the time clock, too?"

Dede nodded. If she tried to talk through the heat of the rum, she would choke. Yes. She called, especially late at night or early in the morning when she was the only one in the flat. It brought her some comfort to hear that familiar, unflappable voice.

Clarence said, "I try to ring right at 1:23 or 2:34 or 3:45 in the morning. If I hit it *exactly,* then good things will happen."

Dede liked the *exactly* game. She swallowed. "My favorite is when the man says, *Time: 1 a.m.,* because I think, "here I am at 1 a.m.""

Natalie finished her rum and pushed the empty shot glass back across the bar towards Clarence. "Well, murky buckets for the drinks, but I suppose it's time to say Cheerio, Toodle-loo, Pip-Pip and all that. This time next week I'll be somewhere over the Atlantic."

Clarence took the glasses, put them in the sink, then turned back to Natalie and reached across the bar to shake her hand. "Good luck, young lady. Forward, upward, onward."

Words from the Bahamian motto. Either accidentally or on purpose, Clarence had omitted the final and most important qualifier, *together.*

"Put it all on Dad's account," Natalie said, as she stood to leave, "And give yourself a ruddy great tip."

They walked back down to the beach. An older man, slightly grizzled around the temples, was lowering the sun umbrellas and carrying them to the storage shed.

"Storm any minute," he said as he hurried from one spot to the next. "You young ladies better hurry now and find some shelter."

"We want to take out a sailboat," Natalie said.

He laughed. "It's hurricane season, ladies, and a strong storm is coming. Look at that sky. Run home quickly if you don't want to drown."

Dede stared into a thick black brow curving in the sky over the West End. "Maybe we should go into the hotel, call your Mum or Dad for a lift?"

"It's my last Saturday on the island," Natalie said, "so we're sailing."

"Look at the waves." The ocean had starting churning, green, froth topped. Spiteful.

"Such a spoilsport, Deeds," She said and punched Dede's arm. "Be a daredevil for once."

What did it matter? Why not go along with Natalie for the rest of the day? Didn't she always? Why stop now?

"Say you'll sail, and I'll tell you a secret." Natalie said. "Can I trust you?"

"All right. I s'pose."

"So, you're game?"

Dede's gut churned. She checked her watch—1:30 p.m.

"Come on," Natalie turned east and took off—running away from the hotel, away from the approaching storm clouds, running even farther from her home. Dede followed, walking first, then jogging as fast as she could with her swishing stomach. Her bikini top felt too small and tight across her back, and her breasts were painful, bouncing up and down, so she slowed down. The beef burger and the Coke and the ice cream and the rum turned somersaults inside her. Beyond the resort's swept beach, the line of seaweed picked up again, but she didn't dare slow down to look for tide treasures now. The wind from behind threw sand against her back; hair whipped against her cheeks. She burped rum and ice cream. Her pockets clinked with shells and sea glass.

Down the beach another half mile or so, Natalie turned into the dunes where two aluminum masts rose stark and silver out of the sea oats.

"Come on, slow poke," she said as Dede caught up to her, stood panting on a sandy flat between two dunes.

"What are you doing?"

"Getting us a boat," Natalie said. "Jethro won't mind."

Dede took in the vista beyond the dunes—a palatial home with a pool the size of a football field—Jethro Ingraham's place, probably the largest home on the Lucayan beach. These were his family's boats; two brightly painted Hobie Cats. Dede prayed they were locked up, but Natalie was already unknotting the first boat. No padlocks, no chains, just a line of rope looped around the mast, then tied to a giant piece of driftwood. Bahamian security, Johnnie Angel would have said.

"We take them out all the time." Natalie said, as she untied the rope. "I know where they keep the sails." She walked down the path towards the house. Dede tried to keep up.

"What if someone sees us?"

"It's okay. I swear. So..." she smiled and laughed into her hand. "Here's my secret. Jethro and I have been sort of going steady. I was keeping quiet about it, but I don't really care who finds out anymore. Since I'm leaving next week."

"You and Jethro—together?" Dede saw his cocky grin and swagger. "For how long?"

"A few months. We got together after we worked on that school project. Don't act so shocked. He's pretty great when you get to know him."

Natalie had kept this secret and not said a word during all the sleepovers. Not once had she mentioned him. What kind of friend was she?

Now, she led them along a sand trail, through the tall oats, past a few cocoplum bushes that rustled in the wind. A hundred yards down, a little hut stood off to the left. Natalie thumbed down the latch on the door and shoved it open. Inside, on a wide wooden shelf, two sails sat folded into neat triangles. Natalie picked up the top sail, blue and gold and black like the Bahamian flag, and walked out without a word. Dede followed her back out to the beach.

Even if he were Natalie's boyfriend (the idea made Dede want to vomit)—would Jethro not care about them taking the sailboat? What about his father—if he found out? Or worse—if the girls damaged the boat? Natalie might be leaving the island, but Dede still had to live here and live with the consequences. Stealing a boat was a very big deal in the Bahamas. Even the most callow expat knew that.

"Are you in love with him?"

"Jethro? God no. Just a dalliance," Natalie set the sail on the trampoline of the first boat. "That's how Mum said I should think of it. A little fun before my real life begins."

"Your Mum knows too?"

"Of course. I tell her everything. She's okay, my Mum. Though she did insist on giving me the birds and the bees lecture." She rolled her eyes.

"You haven't, you know, done it, have you?"

"Oh, don't be a prude, Deeds! It's just a little fun."

Dede wanted to punch Natalie right in her gob. She began to thread the main sail into the mast. Wind snapped at the cloth, making every inch a struggle. Jethro. Natalie. Christ. Dede's stomach churned and she tasted bile in her throat.

"Shouldn't we have life jackets? Just in case?"

"You're not chickening out, are you Deeds? Not on my last weekend? Because I'm a bloody great sailor. The sail's ready. Now get back here with me, and push. This wind's going to be amazing."

Dede unzipped her shorts, folded them in half and dropped them in the sand. She stood shivering in her yellow bikini and t-shirt top. Sea oats whipped against her shins, but she positioned herself at the back of the boat. They pushed the Hobie through the plants, over the fine sugary sand, over the seaweed line and close to the water's edge. Natalie made some adjustments to the main sail and the rudder as the wind slapped hair around her face and neck.

"Ready?"

No. *NO.* Dede's last chance to say it, but she felt Natalie testing her. And she was dizzy and nauseous, and about to fail another test, a social one—Natalie deciding whether she was worthy, had ever been worthy of receiving her attention, her friendship. Was Dede a superbly fun boarding school kind of girl or was she the kind who deserved to get left behind? An adventure lover or a timid book-worm? A true Brit or an island hanger-on?

The waves chopped around her thighs, between her legs, tickling her private parts, rising over her waist, the water was warm, warmer than the cool air blowing against her back. The boat lurched for-ward. Okay then. Screw Natalie. Screw Jethro. Screw them both for screwing each other. Dede was ready. She could do this by herself. She gave a push, hoisted herself up on the pontoon, then flopped across the trampoline.

"Wait." Natalie yelled instructions, "Grab the line. Tighten..." but her voice got lost in the crash of the waves. Dede found a rope, held on; the boat skipped through the water, fast and offshore. Natalie screamed and dived into the surf, trying to catch up, but when she emerged from under the white caps, she was already twenty yards back. Left behind. She'd be furious Ha. How do you like that feeling? The waves crashed and splashed and drowned out Dede's voice, and the distance between them grew fast and faster. The boat lurched again as the boom swung towards Dede; she ducked and lay flat on her belly. She crawled forward and managed to tie the rope around a metal thingy. The wind snapped at the sail and the boat raced fast and faster offshore. Dede had no idea how to stop or steer. She gripped the frame. Sea spray blasted her arms, legs, and back, while wind ripped through her hair. Sea and wind fighting over her like nobody had before.

CHAPTER 10

Ethel's heart drummed her awake, but the dream still clutched at her brain. She pushed up to sitting and grasped the couch arm, anchoring herself to the now: her living room, her flat in Freeport. Was it still storming? The room was dark. The clock on the bookshelf read 9:15 p.m. Night, then. But still Saturday. God, she was thirsty. She'd driven out to High Rock mid-morning, walked past the coppice into the thick pine forest, and dug for a couple of hours, filling four plastic containers with black soil and humus, picking out palmetto fronds and the limestone chunks which, she'd learned the hard way, were disastrous for her clay. Later, she drove closer to the water, parked, and took a swim. She'd floated above the reef, occasionally holding her breath and diving down for a closer look at a particular specimen. When the afternoon weather moved in from the Northwest—a strong offshore wind—she'd swum back to shore, dried off as best she could and started home in a pelting rain, only to give up and stop midway for an awful late lunch at Hank's American Bar: An undercooked burger, a platter of onion rings, the food made worse by the pina colada she ordered in an out-of-body moment. A tourist drink, for God's sake—maraschino cherries bleeding in the froth. No wonder she'd passed out when she got home.

She stood up, went to the kitchen tap, let the water run to cool. The dream flashed through her mind: Scabby yards, tin-roofed shacks, mottled clotheslines. She was in a car, no, an old black truck, racing through Jonestown, Hanna Hill, Pinedale—the luckless towns blurring together, in dream as in life, while knock-kneed boys and mangy potcakes raced beside her. Asphalt streamed in front of her, a straight road to her adult life, and she pushed the accelerator until the vehicle was shaking and spewing, seventy, seventy-five, eighty; almost free, when something suicide-streaked across her vision. She swerved, too late, and hit it. A hen? A dog? A child?

Christ, she was fully awake now, but her head throbbed. She walked back into the living room and tried to steady herself, but the boom, boom, boom intensified. Not in her head this time but coming from outside. A silhouette behind the living room curtains; someone pounding on her glass doors. Ethel checked the buttons on her work-shirt; sweat beaded between her breasts and she hurried to pull aside the drapes. Pool lights cast an eerie blue glow behind, not Dede, but her mother. Anita. Anita Dawes, dressed in her Casino uniform, blonde hair spilling out of a ponytail, and worry, annoyance, or perhaps a mixture of both, tugging at her pretty mouth.

Ethel gestured, just a second, slid the glass door open. "Everything all right? That was quite a storm." The pool deck was a mess. Chairs tipped over, leaves and branches everywhere.

"Sorry to bother you." Anita tucked a vagabond strand behind her ear. "It's Dede. I wondered if you'd seen her tonight."

Ethel moved the screen out of the way and tried to push aside her own grogginess, the day, the drink, the dream. The strangeness of this visit. She and Anita had lived in the same building for close to a year now, but rarely spoken, just the occasional wave or hello in the parking lot. Even though Dede had spent countless hours with Ethel—gardening in the courtyard, cooking in her kitchen, painting at a variety of beaches, walking at low tide—the mother had remained out of the picture and Ethel hadn't sought her company. She was a familiar type: petite and sexy and vulnerable all at once, man-oriented, not caring about what other women might think of her. She looked ready to cry. Strange, when most of the time she didn't seem to know, or care that much, where Dede was.

"I haven't seen her since—let's see—a couple of days ago." Yes. Thursday. Dede had stopped by in the evening, so they'd played around with clay for an hour or two in Ethel's studio. Poking at it with chop sticks and toothpicks for coral effects. After seven, they'd skipped a real meal and made an awful key lime pie. Three-quarters of it was still sitting on the top shelf of Ethel's fridge now, drying out under tin foil. "What's going on? Would you like to come inside?"

Anita stepped into the living room, jiggled keys in her hand. Eyes moving, a shaking or twitching in her cheek. "She spent last night at her friend's house. She was supposed to be home for dinner, to check in with me before my shift. I thought maybe she came to visit you again and had forgotten about the time. Sorry for troubling you. It's just with the storm that came through... I got a bit worried."

Ethel shook her head. "She hasn't been by. Was she with her friend Natalie?" Ethel knew Natalie's father, Chris Fryer—to nod and say hello. He was high up in Barclays; he had a hunched-over, slightly self-effacing manner that made him well-liked among underlings. "Did you ring up the family?"

"Yeah. 'Course I did." Anita bit her top lip. Ethel offered her the couch, but she didn't sit—stood uneasily on the shag. "I spoke with the maid first and then Natalie. Dede and her were on the beach all morning. Had lunch at Coral Cove, like they do. When the winds picked up, Natalie ran home along the beach. She thought Dede must have done the same. Why wouldn't she?" Anita's voice wobbled and thickened, the Brummie accent that she probably tried to hide most of the time coming out. "What's the stupid girl playing at?"

Ethel tried to think of the most logical explanation. Dede spent a lot of time alone. Maybe she'd got caught up in her beachcombing after the storm. Or perhaps she'd headed to the library and got lost in a book. Still. Seven or eight hours was a long time to be gone. "Maybe she ducked into the hotel, decided to wait out the weather?"

Anita shook her head. "She'd have telephoned by now."

"The library?"

"I tried already, didn't I? Closes at noon on Saturdays."

Ethel sensed that if she said anything reassuring, the slight woman would dissolve. But she could tell Anita wanted something from her. Someone to take charge. She seemed liked the kind of woman who needed someone to guide her through life. Probably why she'd latched on to Silvio Bruti.

"We should check with all the other tenants here. The guys upstairs—I've seen Dede play cards with Sebastian a couple of times, by the pool. Also Mr. McGuinn; doesn't he drive her home from school now and then?"

"She chatters on and on about you. You're her favorite's why I come here first."

Ethel tried not to show her ridiculous pride in this, but her cheeks flushed. She wanted to prove herself worthy by knowing what to do, where to look.

"Let's start with McGuinn," she said. "Maybe Dede called him to ask for a ride home." Ethel didn't like the way he allowed the girl to call him Johnnie Angel. Ridiculous. *Unseemly*, Nora would have said in her English way. When she'd visited in March, *so American*, was the phrase she used for anything excessive or gaudy; surely, she would have found McGuinn's doting on the girl to be that. The way he'd bring her cold drinks by the pool. If Dede'd called him for a ride, he would have picked her up from the beach. She would be safe. Maybe she was watching one of her TV shows there right now—maybe she'd simply forgotten about the time.

And, if not? Ethel's mind flashed on the three guys they'd run into down at the West End after Christmas—the ringleader with his thinly veiled threats, the gap-toothed muscleman with the machete. The third man who'd warned Ethel: *the island is not what it used to be, Miss Tootes.* What if Dede had bumped into the likes of them? Ethel wanted to push Anita back outside, close the door, and head into her studio, so that none of this was real. She didn't need another family's problems invading her peace and quiet. She'd worked so hard to escape her own. But Dede. Damn it.

"I've got his number somewhere."

Anita offered a worried thanks. Skinny as a wraith, dark circles under her eyes. Too many late nights at the Casino? Drugs? Silvio was apparently into moving drugs and competed with the crew from Eight Mile Rock. That was the reason those thugs on the beach had backed off when she'd used his name. But did he use? Did Anita? Maybe cocaine came along with the flat and croupier job he'd given her. Anita

131

had high cheekbones, a pointy chin and a fine nose. That's what pulled men like Silvio to her. The feline structure, the fragility on display. And she would be drawn to his power and money, if not his looks. She clearly was not a woman used to figuring things out on her own.

Ethel walked into the kitchen, took a deep breath. Poured a glass of water and chugged it down. Think. Dede had some TV show she liked to watch with him during the week. But McGuinn was often away on weekends. A lackey for Silvio's sketchy business dealings? She opened the drawer under the phone and pulled out a list of all the names and numbers of the residents in the flats. Probably outdated—tenants came and went quickly through the units—but written on the top corner of the first page, in red ink in her own handwriting, J. McGuinn: 373-4234.

Ethel dialed. Waited. Seven rings, eight, nine. She rarely called him because even when he answered the phone, he was evasive. Better to pound on his door when his lights were on, or corner him in the parking lot, or when he was cleaning out the pool with the girl—the one job he didn't shirk. She hung up after twenty rings. Ethel refilled her glass with water, poured another one for Anita, and carried both out to the living room.

"No answer."

"No surprise there," Anita said. "I usually send Domini over when I need him." Anita took the glass but didn't drink; her leg jittered, her eyes welled. Ethel took it back, set it on the table.

"I'll walk over, knock on the door. That's how I usually get his attention, too."

"I'll come with you."

Ethel slipped on her sandals, opened the glass doors again, and followed Anita outside. Night thick as a wet towel wrapped around

132

them. Summer storms never cleared the air, just pumped more water into it. Everything—trees, bushes, leaves—drip-dripped, or threatened to. Twigs and blossoms littered the concrete walkway; an over-turned chaise pushed against the stucco apartment wall, and a broken pot spilled soil into the pool. They stepped around the recliner without righting it.

"When I lived in England, I missed the drama of a good tropical storm. All the rain, but never any of this—the winds, the noise, the damage."

"English drizzle." Anita said, "My whole life there, I felt I was drowning in the gray. How long did you spend over there?"

"Fifteen years. Went for a final year of secondary school in Nassau—took my A levels—then University in London. Got a job in the Bristol area with Barclay's. International investments."

"A long time to be away from your home."

Ethel nodded.

"So, you must be what? Thirty-two, thirty-three."

"Close—just turned thirty-four."

"We're almost the same age. I turned thirty-two in March. I don't think we'll ever be going back to England." Anita said. "I love the weather here, truth be told, and it feels more like home to me than England ever did."

Home. Ethel tried to remember the last place she'd thought of that way. Certainly not her flat now. Nor Bristol, where she'd always felt like an outsider—had been called "an over-sized darky" on more than one occasion. Not the purple painted cottage where she lived with the Edgecombes for a year in Nassau as she prepared for University, nor even Auntie Gert's shack; she'd always felt like a cuckoo in that nest.

Ethel led the way with Anita trailing; they cut through the corridor to the car park—several palm fronds had come down near the street. A large branch had hit someone's car. They turned down the sidewalk to McGuinn's front door. Ethel banged hard. They waited without speaking, then she banged again, louder, harder. Anita shifted beside her, from foot to foot. No lights on inside. No sounds except the usual clicks and chirps: cicadas, tree frogs, and that churring nightjar.

"He goes away on weekends sometimes," Anita said. "Lord knows where. Helps Silvio with imports or what have you."

"Let's try the guys upstairs."

No answer at Sebastian's.

"Probably at work, already," Anita said. "Both of them do nights."

They walked back to Ethel's unit without talking. If Dede had been caught on the beach or the roads in the storm today, they should be worried. The fear hit hard. Once inside, Ethel made herself say the word.

"Police?"

Anita looked down and shook her head. "Silvio."

Half an hour later, he appeared at Ethel's front door, escorted by two police officers. Silvio had that way about him. Always in charge. Squat, tan, muscular through his neck and chest, with silver hair rolling off his forehead. Well-dressed, of course, in black trousers and a blue silk shirt.

"Miss Edgecombe. Very kind of you to help us out."

Ethel nodded, shook his hand. She'd met him before, a couple of times; he stopped by somewhat regularly to see Anita. His demeanor most of the time was too busy, too powerful, too important to stop and chat. Ethel wondered how much cash he'd handed over to have the police show up with him tonight. Was it an event-by-event kind of payment arrangement, or was the whole force essentially working on retainer? To his credit—or discredit, perhaps—Silvio didn't make any effort to hide his relationship with Anita. He bent down to kiss the top of her disheveled head.

"Don't worry, baby girl," he said, "We'll find her."

He gestured to his companions. "Detective Horatio Hayes and Officer Trevor Nelson. Two of the very best on the force."

Ethel bit her tongue. No secret that most of the high-ups in the police department were on the take; the rest were thugs and louts—they'd always been hated in the settlements, that was for sure.

Both men nodded at Anita and ignored Ethel. The taller, darker one was dressed in full police regalia: black pants with red side stripe, a white jacket. The other, light-skinned, freckled, with reddish hair, wore dress slacks and a teal shirt; a shark's tooth hung from a gold chain in the v of his shirt. He looked as if he'd been planning a night on the town. Ethel wanted them out of her place but offered to make them tea.

On the counter by the stove, she kept clear containers, one held loose tea leaves, the other white sugar; the third was half-full of blue sea-glass. Cobalt blue on the bottom, then aquamarine, an almost cerulean layer on top. Most had come from Deep Water Cove, where she'd taken Dede just a couple of weeks back. And the girl, usually full of questions and ideas, had spent hours working silently, walking seaweed threads, picking and rinsing hundreds of shards.

Where are you girl? Where did you go?

Ethel found a tray, took out her mismatched cups and teapot. She spooned in five round scoops of orange pekoe—a dark brew for what might be a long night. Found milk in the fridge, fresh at least, and filled a small clay sugar bowl. She set four teaspoons on the tray too, and carried it out to the living room table, as if she were acting in some kind of poorly scripted comedy of manners starring the stalwart police officers, the debonair silver-haired gentleman, the damsel in distress; and Ethel, big-boned island woman, pouring tea for her strange company. She passed out cups. No saucers. The sugar bowl made its rounds and Ethel wished she had biscuits to offer. Stupid. Still trying to impress a social club that had no room for the likes of her.

"What if she calls home?" Anita said. "I should be by my phone."

Silvio whispered something to the uniformed officer, handed him a key, and he left.

Detective Hayes took a sip of tea, then put his cup down, opened a notepad, licked his pencil, as he must have seen it done on some British police procedural, and asked for a description. Silvio began as if he'd done this before. Female. Twelve years. Anita added the DOB: 10/23/63. Height about five foot. Weight? Approximate? Anita didn't seem to know, she'd filled out a lot lately, so Ethel ventured a guess. Dede couldn't be more than seven and a half or eight stone. Hair color? Brown with blond streaks, Anita said. Blonder, really, Ethel said. Long or short? Medium, choppy or rather streaky, hard to describe. But they tried. Long enough for pigtails. Just barely. Sometimes she cuts it herself. Distinguishing marks? No. Did a lisp count? Moles, scars? None. Last wearing? Unsure. Probably a yellow bikini under a t-shirt and shorts. If she was wearing any shoes at all, probably sandals. Would she have worn sandals on the beach? Any pictures? Anita said she might be able to find some at home. She stood to go, but Ethel remembered she had a Polaroid the girl had given her and offered to get it.

She walked into her studio, turned on the overhead light. From the bulletin board, Dede smiled. Tilted smile, smattering of freckles on her nose. Dressed in her favorite brown shorts, white shirt and a straw hat in her hand. It was from a while back—last September or October, perhaps. She looked much younger than now, certainly, but also much younger than her age. Ethel untacked the photo. Be okay. Please, be okay. She felt reluctant to give the shot to the Officer. What if she never got it back? What if they never found the girl? She'd want the photo for a makeshift memorial. A photo and also memorabilia: Sea glass. Shells. Dede's best paintings. Stop it. Life was crazy enough without inventing drama.

Ethel walked back into the living room and handed over the image.

The detective asked Anita for a list of Dede's friends. Anita came up with two names: Natalie Fryer, and a girl named Rowena who'd left for boarding school in England a year ago. Ethel added a couple—Prudence, and the Ingraham boy. Jethro. They'd all worked together on a school project and spent a lot of time together in the Spring.

"Is he a boyfriend? Barry Ingraham's son?" The detective asked.

"Nothing like that," said Ethel. "He pesters her. You know boys that age."

"You sure? Barry's boy has got a reputation. His father's pulled strings on more than one occasion to get him out of trouble."

"I'm sure," Ethel said.

Anita nodded confirmation, then added, "Dede's young for her age."

"Has she been in any trouble at school? Or any recent fights with you, Mrs. Dawes? Any chance she's taken off—avoiding punishment?" He laughed, too lightly for the situation.

"You mean run away?" Anita shook her head, hands trembling in her lap. "No," she said. No argy-bargy. Dede was an easy child, entertained herself, never got into trouble.

"Does she keep a diary by any chance?"

Anita nodded, blushed. "I've peeked in it before. Not much in there. What time she woke up. What was on the telly. That sort of nonsense. No secrets that I uncovered. Like I said, she's young for her age."

"And the father? We had a custody kidnapping just a few weeks back. Some little boy picked up walking home from school. An American father grabbed him, had him on a plane before we could close the airport. Any problems like that with your husband, your ex, Mrs. Dawes? Is he the kind likely to swoop in and grab her?"

"We separated more than three years ago. He's got a new girl-friend." Anita said. "Domini doesn't know that yet, but her father hasn't shown much interest in her for a long time. Hasn't called in months. Last time, he reversed the charges. Always was a cheap bas-tard." She shook her head. "I suppose I'll have to call him."

"You can give it 24 hours, I'd say. Most of the time these missing persons calls turn out to be miscommunications... not that we won't take this seriously, of course."

Ten minutes later, the detective said his thanks, made promises, and walked out to meet his fellow officer and do whatever it was they did in these cases. Silvio put his arm around Anita and escorted her back to her apartment.

Ethel undressed and took a shower, tried to wash off the day's sweat and accumulating anxiety. She let the water pummel her scalp. She soaped her legs, her cracked yellow heels. What could she do? She stood naked and dripping on the bathmat. Jesus. The poor kid. Wherever she was, she must be terrified. It was after eleven. McGuinn. Maybe he'd picked Dede up and taken her to dinner or perhaps a movie at the drive-in? Would he be that stupid—to cart her around at night and not check with the mother first? She found a clean towel and dried off, racking her brain to think of a more likely scenario. Maybe Dede was at another friend's house. Maybe she had a secret boyfriend, after all. But Dede was not boy crazy—not even boy-focused. If anything, she belonged to Ethel's tribe. None of this made any sense. None of it. She wanted to call Nora, talk it through; Nora was always good in crises, both analytical and compassionate, part of her job requirement, working with teenagers. But she couldn't just ring her up middle of the night. Besides, she'd promised that next time she called, they'd make solid plans for Ethel's visit in September, before Nora went back to school.

Think. What would the girl do in a storm? Alone, independent, too sure of her own resilience. Ethel knew what moved and interested her: The beach. The offerings of the sea. Ethel should be able to find her, to pull her home safely. God, let me find you. Let me bring you home.

Ever since their time together at Deadman's Reef, Ethel had felt a deep connection, more than she wanted, with this girl. The run-in with the three men had left Ethel with a sense of responsibility, too. For several months Ethel had fought against the feeling, but she knew it was no good to flail and deny it. She found a flashlight in her kitchen cabinet, grabbed her keys, and headed out.

Ethel started her car, rolled down her window; the sky like a sponge ready to drip. She'd left all her buckets in the truck bed, and they were overflowing with water and dirt. What a mess. And despite her recent shower, Ethel was already sweating again. But she needed to hear the island, what it had to offer, and remind herself it wasn't a dangerous place. Dede would be all right. The kid was smart, knew the roads and streets, its beaches and bays, and she could find her way home in the dark if she had to. She'd probably just gotten too absorbed with a project; the kid always loaded herself up with facts and information as if miscellanea could fill up the holes in her life.

She parked at the end of Sea Gate Lane—the same place she'd brought Nora back in March—and walked through cocoplums and palmetto scrub. When she got to the sand, she took off her sandals, left them as a marker by the path, and walked toward the water. Low tide now—like it had been that first night here with Nora. Moon full or close to it. Maybe Dede had got caught up with finds, picking up shells, searching for glass—always so plentiful after a storm. No footprints on the sand. Even if she had walked here earlier, the storm and the tides had washed out the evidence. Ethel walked east. Overhead, the clouds had finally cleared to reveal a black sky colandered with stars. Sand shimmered silver ahead of her; at the water's edge, it phosphoresced under each foot strike. Swaths of seaweed paralleled her path; she stepped over driftwood, a Coke can, jellyfish and horseshoe crabs. If she'd had the time to spend, sifting each strand of Sargasso, what would she find?

Just a few lights shining from behind the dunes, expat homes, the thumping bass sounds from the Sandpiper disco, then close to a mile of uninterrupted beach towards Coral Cove. It was there that the girls, Dede and Natalie, had eaten lunch. Ethel would walk there first, then, talk to the staff, check out the story. Surely someone at the hotel would remember seeing them.

When she got to the resort, the beach pagoda had shut up tight. She walked up the steps and onto the deck, with three inter-connecting pools, lights on, and the pool water clear, clean, flat. A couple sat in the hot tub at the far end of the deck area but didn't notice as Ethel made her way around the deck. She entered the hotel through the glass doors on the south side of the building. Almost as deserted inside as outside. She asked the lone desk attendant—a pimply, young man with a high-yellow complexion and frazzed orange hair—who had worked the grill during lunch.

The young man stared at her, not impressed by Ethel's rumpled clothing, her humidified Afro. "You mean Clarence?"

"Do you know where I could find him?" She asked, "Is he still around?"

"The bar's always a good bet with him and his fellas." He pretended to chug from a bottle, rolled his eyes back in his head.

She thanked him. Cheeky bastard.

No one was sitting on the stools at the bar, but four men occupied a table in the back of the room; they had a bottle of rum and shot glasses and were playing cards. Cigar smoke funked up the air. She was walking into a private party. One of them spoke as she approached.

"Can I help you, sister?"

"Is there a Clarence here? I'd like a word if I might."

"And you are?"

"My name's Ethel. Ethel Edgecombe."

The man seated with his back to her set his hands on the table and pushed up out of the fog. "Well, well, well. Look what the storm conjured up. Miss Edgecombe is it now? More highbrow than Tootes?" He turned to face her.

Clarence Lawler; Jestina's son and Ethel's best friend from the All-Age School. She felt her heart thumping. They had been so close, top pupils, both sent off on a scholarship year in Nassau to prepare for a British university. But he'd cut her off when she'd won a scholarship and left him behind. In his last correspondence, he said that he hated what she'd become.

"Clarence. It's good to see you." Did her voice sound as quaky to him as it did to her? "Could we talk somewhere?"

"I'm about to win big, Miss Edgecombe. Surely, you don't want to take that away from me?" He was drunk.

His card mates chortled, and Ethel felt a wave of disgust. Is this what he'd done with his life? He'd been so clever.

"Please, a quick word?"

He bowed theatrically to his colleagues. "Well, I can't keep the lady waiting," he said. "She's an ejjified English woman, you see. Did you hear her accent? So perfectly proper, eh?"

His friends laughed themselves into a collective coughing jag. Bloody fools. Ethel followed Clarence out of the lounge into the hotel lobby. She sat on one of the many empty beige chairs scattered in the large area. Clarence took the one next to her.

"How are you, Ethel?" He sounded suddenly much more sober.

"I can't complain much, though sometimes I do."

"Heard you'd landed at Barclay's, some years back. In London, wasn't it?"

"Bristol. But I'm back here in Freeport now. Transferred to offshore banking."

He scratched his head. "England not all it's cracked up to be? Not so special after all that?"

So, he still wasn't over it. Still full of anger and self-pity. "I don't want to talk the past, Clarence. Maybe sometime we can hash it out. But please. I need your help."

142

"Somebody sick? One of the Tootes? I used to like the Tootes family, back in Hanna Hill."

She put a hand on his arm. Maybe a touch would settle his angry soul. "It's about Dede. The English girl. She came by your place today."

"You asking or telling?"

"I'm only asking. She lives near me—same flats—she didn't come home this evening and her mother's worried out of her mind. Got the police on the start-up, looking and such, but I just wanted to come by, see what I could find out. Her friend—Natalie Fryer—she says the two of them ate lunch here today."

"That's right. The Fryer daddy got an account. They are regulars—always running down here, swimming in the pool, eating burgers and such. Running up a tab, without a care in the world."

"You seen them today?"

"I fed the two lovely ladies lunch. Burgers and fries. Ice creams. Likely my only customers since it's off-season. Dede—she showed me her treasures. And told me she was friends with one Ethel Edgecombe. Can't be, I thought to myself, but she said you been back on the island for a while, said you took her out to Eight Mile Rock a few weeks back. Can't be true, I thought, because you would have surely come and said hello. If not to me, then to Jestina. My mother still talks about how she misses you. So, it's quite the coincidence, isn't it? Dede meeting you. You and me meeting like this again? After all the years."

"Dede didn't come home tonight."

Clarence shook his head. "And what? You coming all the way over here to question me? Like I know something?"

"I had no idea you worked here. I just heard she'd been here today."

Was he smirking at her? Did he think it ridiculous that Ethel was out searching for a lost white child when there were so many kids running barefoot and hungry around Eight Mile Rock? Did he know something he wasn't saying?

Ethel said. "Do you know where she could have gone?"

"All I know is all I told. They had lunch. The Fryer girl said she'd be leaving soon, and Dede was acting kind of put out about it, but, you know, they had Knickerbocker Glories, then rum shots. A goodbye toast. And yes, a storm coming, so they ran off down the beach."

"You poured them drinks?"

He nodded, daring her to criticize.

"You remember which way they went on the beach?"

He shook his head. "Can't see that far, even if I had my old eyesight."

"The police may be sniffing around here tonight, or tomorrow. They got the casino boss behind them so they going to try to at least look like they are working hard to find her."

"Oh, she'll show up soon enough. Probably just after giving them a scare." Clarence stood and walked back to his game. "All girls that age be drama-mamas. You remember that. You were full of the theatrics, too."

When she got back to the apartment building, Ethel decided to try McGuinn's apartment again. She approached the back door this time, slapping her hand against the glass. The curtains were closed, but she could see through a chink that the TV was on. She continued rapping until she saw a shape—yes—someone rising off the couch. He pulled back the curtain, looked out at her, running a hand over his hair. Dressed only in tennis shorts, his soft white belly sagging over the waistband. She gestured for him to open.

"What the hell?"

"I came by earlier. Me and Anita Dawes. You didn't answer. It's an emergency."

He smelled of cheap aftershave and booze. He swayed slightly as he stood with one hand on the sliding door. "You know how late it is? You woke me up."

"It's Dede; she's missing. I could see your television was on... I thought...."

He looked at his watch, "After midnight." His big body blocked her view into the apartment.

Ethel nodded impatiently. "She didn't come home tonight. Her mother's going crazy with worry. Did you see her today?"

"I have no idea where she might be."

"The police were over here talking to her mother; now they're out looking." She wanted to rattle him. "They'll probably be stopping by to talk to you."

He scratched his chest, swallowed a yawn. "Like I said, haven't seen her. But I'll keep my eyes and ears open."

Inside her own apartment again, Ethel lay on her bed, drifting in and out, half-dreams, half-worries, and full-on regret. Auntie Gert with a laundry line in her hand. A chicken with its neck wrung. McGuinn's fat white belly. Had he been trying to block her view? Did he have someone in there with him? A woman? One of the foreign girls who hung around the casino? She wouldn't put it past him; there was something about the man she didn't like, didn't trust. She felt uneasy. She had to get up and do something. Talk to someone.

The phone rang as if she'd willed it. She raced to the kitchen and picked it up on the third blare. Please, let it be Nora.

"Hello?" Ethel said.

"Hello yourself, Miss Tootes."

"Clarence?" How had he found her number? "What time is it?"

"Here I am at 1 a.m." He laughed. "Our mutual friend, Domini Dawes, she likes to call the time, too."

"Are you drunk?"

"Yes, ma'am. But listen to me anyway. Gus, one of my poker boys, he was on the beach tying things down before the storm. He say the Fryer girl and Domini come over after lunch asking him for a boat. They wanting to go out on the water. Gus say no, but the Fryer girl, she a pushy one, you know. She run the show all right. Said she hell bent on sailing and the two of them run off to the east. No idea where they'd get a boat in that storm but just in case they fool enough... I thought you should know."

"Thank you," she said. "I owe you."

"Put it on the tab," Clarence said and hung up.

PART II

CALLOW CAY

AUGUST 1976

CHAPTER 11

Dede comes to lying flat on her stomach, sand rimming her eyes, her nostrils, and coating her lips. When she pushes up onto her hands and knees, the skin across her back and shoulders stretches so tight that she thinks it will rip. Snarled with seaweed, her hair hangs in front of her face; she tosses it aside, tries to spit, but her tongue is swollen and dry. Her head hurts. All the muscles in her neck and shoulders too, every inch of her scraped, sunburned and sore.

Is this real?

The words form in her brain and she grabs a handful of sand. Yes, the grit digging into her palms; and yes, the burn of ocean in the back of her throat. And the thirst. God, the thirst. She needs water. She tries to move, to crawl, one hand, then the other. Her seaweed hair swinging left right left. Water. The word echoes in her skull, like ocean sounds in a shell, but when she tries to push herself up to standing, her knees buckle and the beach kaleidoscopes towards her. Her stomach heaves. She retches, emptying ocean, black kelp, speckled grit. And she is flat on the sand again, spent and stupid and ashamed of what she has done.

What on earth were you thinking, getting on that boat? Mum's voice.

The words bounce around in her skull and change.

What on earth were you thinking getting in his car? Whose voice is this?

Where is she?

Damp sand beneath her; the soft shush of the ocean. She rolls onto her back and she cannot find the sun. The sky is gray, not black enough for deepest night. No moon, no stars. She closes her eyes and senses him above her, his eyes wet and his voice pleading. Our little secret. She hears the words and wants to silence the voices in her brain and lie down until her bones bleach into limestone, her body another accretion on the coral landmass. She tries to cut out all sound except the waves, tries to cut out the pain. But the thirst is stronger, starts her body moving, pulling her forward, away from the ocean, without her consent. She crawls over packed sand, across a thick rope of seaweed, and toward the fine white stuff higher up. There's somebody else lying on the edge of the beach. Not moving. Asleep? Who is it? The shape sighs and trembles.

"Please," she says, the sound hissing across her chapped lips. She must find help, get water. She moves until she can almost reach her hand out and touch the hunched body. "Please, wake up." The shape rustles and shifts into a bush. She grasps at the leathery leaves, pulls back a branch, and grabs a cluster of familiar fruit: Cocoplums. Unripe. Hard. Her teeth pierce the skin, and her mouth works the recalcitrant flesh—like sucking on a rock. She tries again to spit—to expel the bitter taste—but there's nothing, no saliva, no bile. She closes her eyes and freefalls.

When Dede wakes again and rolls over, opens her salt-crusted eyes, the clouds braid gray and mauve over the land. Morning then? But where? She stands up, staggers along a sketch of a path leading away from the beach. Maybe she's landed on one of the afterthought cays that drop off the end of Grand Bahama. She passes an old fishing boat, half hidden in sea oats, its wooden planks parched and splitting; years since it's been on the ocean, but it means someone has lived out this way. Her head splitting. She needs water.

The path broadens but she sees no buildings, no vehicles, no people, no animals. She makes herself stop, listen, try to figure it out—where she has landed, what she should do. Ahead of her, the thick bush filtering sun. East. She continues until the path dead-ends into a rutted dirt road. Which way to go? Ocean behind her, jungle ahead. Never Eat Shredded Wheat. She turns left—north—and staggers on. As she walks, the bush begins to rustle beside her, high and low and in between, birds and lizards and cicadas, other noises, too—a strange bark and then a quick scramble in the trees. Maybe dogs, or wild pigs? Livestock abandoned? Or the chickarnees—half-bird, half-lizard creatures that torment travelers. She doesn't believe in fairy tales, she reminds herself, and she's always been good with dogs. Just keep walking. Water. The terrible thirst. She counts steps to keep moving.

To the right, sunlight needles through the thick bush. Overhead, the sky remains gray—the color of amnesia? The color of compromise, Ethel once said, of giving up on yourself. Dede is lost, has no idea what to do. How long until people give up on her? Forget about her? Her so-called friends at school? Natalie? Prudence? Miss Evans? What about her family? Mum? Ethel? Dad? If she died here, would anyone find her body? What day it is? How long since she got on the boat? She checks her wrist and sees her watch. 6:46. Same backwards and forwards. Stopped time.

She rounds a bend. Rubs her eyes. Something flutters into her vision, off to the right—a white sail? She moves closer. No, laundry hanging on a line. Whose sheets, left out to dry in the middle of nowhere? She steps off the road, crosses a narrow gulley, and enters a scabby plot, littered with dried corn kernels. No car, no driveway, no house. No one here. But maybe water? She staggers toward the laundry line. A rooster squawks as she comes closer. She pauses, watches him until he loses interest, turns and chases after a cluck of hens that are pecking at the ground. She continues.

The rooster turns back to check on her, charges at her, its crest blazing red and bumpy as fire coral, its beak open in full screech. She jumps back into the gully, and the rooster holds its ground, challenging her to try again. Then, set back, beyond the laundry, she sees the blurry outline of a shack. Faint, so faint. She strains her eyes to find the edges, to fill in the details—wooden planks. She can just make out a tin-roof. Is that a rain barrel beside it? Is she dreaming? But the rooster is real... and that's laundry on the line, and yes, she smells something cooking. Please, help me. But what if it's a crazy person living out here all by himself? Or a ghost she's conjured up? She pinches her arm, feels the sunburn pain, she kicks a rock. She does not know where here is, but she is alive in this moment and the smell of food is stronger now, sweet and starchy. Rice? Bread? Would a crazy man or a ghost be baking? The smell draws her forward through her doubts.

The rooster pecks at her legs, screeching bloody murder. Dede tries to shoo him, stumbles, and falls. Get away, get off me. The words stick on her blistered lips. The rooster puffs his feathers and eyes Dede sideways, daring her to move. He squawks again and she thinks she will die here, die of thirst, right here in the gulley.

Someone, please.

The front door swings open. "Go on, Mistah Biggety. Leave them hens alone."

A woman stands in the jamb. She shades her eyes and takes another step into the yard.

Dede tries to scream but only air comes out, a tire deflating. She waves her hand, tries again to stand.

"Sweet Jesus of the Seven Seas," the woman says.

Dede pulls herself from the ground, stumbles towards her, past the outraged rooster, across the bare and gritty yard, moving towards a voice that she might be conjuring from desperation, a voice that sounds like healing, like home, and she is falling. *Catch me*, she can't quite say, *catch me*, her mouth moving, and the woman's arms are open and strong and cool against Dede's burning red skin.

"Lord! How you come Bight side, child?" She holds Dede up, looks her over. "Easy now. Don't talk, don't even try to say a word."

She half-carries her into the shack, toward a table in the middle of the dark room. "Sit you down right here. You sun-fried for sure. I'm gonna fix you some quench."

Dede sinks into a chair, puts her head down on the table and closes her eyes.

A hand lifts her head, holds a cup in front of her. "Your lips all chap-chap. No need to chug. That's right, just be sipping. Little sips."

Coconut and tart lime burning her lips but opening her throat. Dede empties the cup and wipes her mouth with the back of her hand. She needs more. She blinks and blinks again, looks around as the room comes into focus. At one end, a counter stacked with

153

pots and plates, an open window, curtains rippling turquoise like a shallow sea. At the other end, a mat on the floor. A set of shelves and beside it, a rocking chair. The woman takes and refills Dede's cup, then pulls up another chair, sits down beside her. She watches Dede drink again, waits until she puts the cup on the table, empty.

"You walk down here from Hard Bargain? That's a long and lonely stretch of road."

Dede shakes her head. "Freeport." Her tongue is like a dead animal in her mouth. She swallows, tries again. "A storm. The sailboat capsized. I held on—a long time, through the dark—and then, then I swam. I think that I must have swum into shore. Is this the East End?"

"East End of what, child?" The woman stares at her, shaking her head, "You on Callow Cay. This here's the Bight settlement. Least what's left of it."

Dede closes her eyes and shakes her head. Callow Cay? She can't place it on her mental map. She tries to run through the archipelago north to south but can't hold onto the names.

The woman walks over to the window beside the door, pushes aside the curtain and looks out over the yard.

"Where the others?"

Dede shakes her head.

"They behind you?"

"It's just me."

"All by yourself? And the boat you come on? Where's that?"

"I don't know."

"You saying you sailed it alone. And ship-wrecked, too? Washed up at my beach, walked to my doorstep?"

Dede nods, her body remembering the hours on the boat, lurching and holding on, the churning of the sea, the boat upside down, gripping the pontoon in the dark and the night and the waves still coming. At some point, she must have let go. Did she let go?

She nods again, imagining or perhaps remembering how she breast-stroked towards the beach.

But this woman doesn't believe a word she is saying. "Maybe you from the Abacos. Lots of smooth-headed children there. White people lived there since slave time." The woman pats Dede's shoulder. "You from Marsh Harbor? You one of Captain Albury's grandbabies. Maybe ride the mailboat over here with your granddaddy?"

"I live in Freeport. My name is Domini Dawes, but everyone calls me Dede."

"You run off then? Got yourself in some kind of pucketery?"

She pushes her chair back. "I told you. I didn't run away. She tries to stand and her legs buckle. "I am not lying. You can call my mother if you don't believe me."

"Easy, now. I'm not much used to visitors, especially no white girls down this way." The woman's voice is deep; she returns to the table and sits. "How 'bout we start this conversing over again. My own name Miss Harmony Knowles and I am glad to make your acquaintance. You free to call me Harmony."

Harmony's face matches her voice, full and smooth and not so much friendly as calm. Her short hair is orange brown, her cotton smock a similar shade.

"Do you live here by yourself?"

"That's right. Last Knowles left in the Bight. Used to be four houses out back—had to walk through that bush to get to the family houses. One for my big sister Aggie, my three brothers and me. Uncle Harcourt, he had his own place but watched over us when all the menfolk left on the Contract. Uncle Harcourt lame so he can't work

155

like most of the others. Hurricane Betsy flattened all the houses and took Aggie and no one wanted to build again after that. All of the other Knowles done moved on, but I stayed and the government built me this no-good shack, right out here on the range."

"Do you have a husband?"

The woman laughs. "You a terreck one, all right, spilling out questions." She shakes her head. "No husband. Most of the menfolk gone off picking crops in the Carolinas or head to the big islands. Gone and never come back. Even my own boy, Fulcrum, left. Had to follow his uncles to Nassau. These days, it's me and my biggety rooster, some laying hens and what's left of Aggie's fruit trees. But I'm talking too much when we got to get you taken care of. We got to tell your daddy and momma you all right; let them know you ain't drowned out there in the Tongue of the Ocean."

Harmony grips Dede's forearm. "Think you can walk with me up to Clementina's? She two miles up from here, living in the old plantation house with her idiot son. They got a radio to signal Hard Bargain and Hard Bargain can roust Captain Albury, and get you home."

Dede shakes her head. She cannot walk another step. She doesn't know what to say, or how to explain what she is doing here. She can't say what she is running from or even whether she is running. She cannot say how she landed here. She can barely remember walking up to this shack. She wants to cry, but she's still so dried out, there's nothing to give but body shakes and chest heaves. She rests her head on the table, feels the ocean tossing her again, feels the dark coming down.

"Okay now," Harmony strokes her hair, snags a strand of sea-weed, and untangles it. "Don't worry none. You flat exhausted. Don't need to decide nothing now. What we gone do is feed you first, and then get you clean and let you rest some. Step-by-step is how we do in the Bight. Step-by-step. We can get word to your family soon enough."

From a tin pot, Harmony spoons up a plate of food, talking softly the whole time. "Only last night's pigeon peas and rice, right now, and I got no relish to pile on because I ain't fished all week. Got no corn left because I shucked and chucked the last to the hens before you stumbled up here. But there's cassava bread just come out of the rock oven. Oh, you gonna feel better after a feeding."

Soon she sets the food down on the table. "Eat now, then maybe you be ready to tell me your story."

Dede lifts her head, props it up on one hand and eats a few mouthfuls, but her eyes are closing as she chews. The story? Where would it start? When she arrived in Freeport? In Johnnie Angel's apartment, Happy Days on the telly. *Feels so right, it can't be wrong*...feels so wrong it can't be right. The lyrics jumble in her brain and the world is upside down. The time still 6:46. Where is she? She startles; she must have fallen asleep with food in her mouth because Harmony is wiping at her with a cloth and clearing the plate, picking up rice from the floor.

"Can't let you sleep sitting up, all salt-soaked and crispy, like some smelly old fish washed up on the beach." She half-leads, half-carries Dede from the table to a big wooden rocker. She goes outside for a few minutes and returns with a bucket full of water.

"A cowboy wash, like I used to do with my own boy." Harmony bends down and wipes Dede's salt-speckled legs, then pulls her forward in the chair, gently removes her crusty t-shirt and rubs her neck and back, her cheeks and forehead. "Yessir, I did Fulcrum this way once a week, from baby to heart-breaker, but he still run off on me."

When she finishes, Harmony dries Dede with a thin towel, then goes off into a side room and finds another shirt—Fulcrum's favorite, she says—soft and bleached from too much wearing; Goombay Punch written on the front, the letters half-gone, but that cartoon face Dede knows so well still smiling big. Dede takes it, pulls it on over her bikini top, and Harmony leads her to a mat in the back corner of the shack, where she lays down a sheet and a pillow for her.

"Go to sleep now, girl; I'll be right here, watching out for you."

Harmony sits in the big chair and Dede lies on the floor-bed. Their eyes meet and Dede wonders if she will be able to sleep with someone staring at her, staring into her. Will this woman read her thoughts, know what she's done? She keeps her eyes open as long as she can, holds Harmony's gaze, and she feels thoughts and feelings swirling between them. Harmony's thoughts and feelings coming into her brain—*hush now and peace, peace and easy seas, easy seas and calm*—Harmony's colors and shapes soothing her, letting her sleep. Dede watches herself fall asleep, feels her mind letting go.

CHAPTER 12

Near night now and the island is putting itself to sleep, the sun hovering over the bay, a breeze kissing the trees, and the leaves starting to curl in on themselves. Harmony sits in her rocker keeping watch over the girl. She thinks of Aggie, how her big sister used to do the same when Harmony was a child and feared the dark. The girl's been sleeping for hours and she's still on a rolling sea, twisting, turning, and crying out. Harmony pulls herself up from the chair and walks over to the bed on the floor, kneels as best she can with her knobby joints, and touches the girl's forehead. Hot as a bush fire. Harmony shuffles to the pitcher on the counter, fills a cup and brings it back, holds the quench to the girl's scabby lips and wakes her just enough so she can sip-sip and fall back down. Then, she's back in her chair, rocking and watching, watching and wondering. Where did this girl come from? Aggie, what you know about this?

It seems like years since she had a visitor inside this place and the girl has her rattled, tapping at the mother in her, making her worry like she's on duty again, even though her own son is long gone. How did this child find her? Soon enough, the screams start again, dreams crashing around inside the girl's skull. Harmony sees her story needs outing, or it will poison her. A poultice for the brain. Cascarilla or a Billy Webb decoction? Leaves of sour sop—good for a fever? She wants to ask Aggie—her knowing all the medicine plants—but Aggie's dead and only visits when she's got a mind to. All the family gone, and Harmony is alone, a Knowles without the know-how.

"Please," the girl moans. Her eyelids flutter and her arms cross over her face like she's staving off blows. Her body wants rest, but the dreams keep hammering. Harmony frets and rocks and tries to figure this out. Why she come stumbling into my yard? Why did I pull her inside? She's got half a mind to leave right now, walk up the road to Clementina's and have her radio help, have someone come take the girl away. But what kind of help gonna come this way after night fall? And what kind of authority ever helped Harmony anyhow?

"Please," her voice raspy from the sea.

A wet rag, leastways, to cool the brain. Harmony can do that. Back at the sink, she fumbles around in the dark till she finds a flannel, douses it in the clean water and wrings it out. She folds it in three and lays it on the girl's head. "Easy now. You safe here."

The girl sighs as if she wants to believe. Her arms relax and her eyes open for a second and meet Harmony's; her fingers rest on the cloth like a thank you.

"A touch of sun fever is all." Harmony straightens out the sheet, so it covers her up, tries to tuck it under the mattress, but the girl twists away. Harmony takes her wrist to feel how fast her heart is pumping; but again, the girl jerks away, kicks off the top cover and lies on her back with her mouth open, gulping at the air like a porgy fish out of water. Her skinny arm drops down the side of the mat and her hand's a-twitching on the floorboards. Under Fulcrum's t-shirt, she got a hard-bubble belly from too much quench, most like, and all the rice and peas she shoveled in. Yes, Lord, she ate too much, too fast. Harmony should have slowed the girl down.

The girl's quieter. The cool cloth on her brow settling her thoughts. The sleep gonna help whatever she's been through. Her face burned and blistered, her arms sun-mottled too, and her hair twisted as love vine. Dede—what kind of name is that? The girl is short and patchy enough to fit it. She more hard scrabble than pretty, more Tom-Tom than girl. Harmony heads back to the rocker. Whatever you done, girl, you gonna be all right.

These in-between-years tough on most all children. Fulcrum, he always been a real pretty boy. Even at this girl's age, when other boys were all pocked and gangly, Fulcrum got the smooth high yellow skin, the soft orange curls like most of the Knowles, his eyes brown and round and shiny as new pennies. Yes, he was so pretty and so clever that the Hard Bargain girls wanted to brand him for themselves. She remembers watching from the street, all the children at ring play in the schoolyard, and the girls be trying to pull him in, pull him in, even when he not wanting to stop and dance, and they singing and teasing: *Hey Fulcrum put de hand in de pocket, Fulcrum lick. Hey Fulcrum put de hand in de pocket, Fulcrum lick.* All the pretty girls singing and shaking their bodies at him. Oh, he pretended he agitated but he couldn't help himself when they pulled him in, neither; he stepping this way and that, and soon he be mashing the roach like the best male specimen. All the girls wanted to take him home, but none of them, not even the prettiest town girl could keep him here on this island. Sixteen and he run off to find his no-good uncles, Thaddeus, Crusader, and Bertram, all the men that had already up and left to make their livings anywhere else. Some money came back for a month or two, then nothing. More than ten years and he can't even write her a letter? Her own son. Harmony's brain complains again, Why? Why? What she ever done except love him? Then, she catches her thoughts, scrabbling like hens in the yard. She has to smile at herself.

Aggie's smiling too. *Same old song, Harmony Knowles? You sitting there and still complaining about that boy of yours? How many years now?*

Aggie the wisewoman of the Knowles clan. The oldest child who learned her ways somehow without a mother or a teacher except for Uncle Harcourt who drank too much and slept too long to be much use. Aggie always knew how to calm a brain, how to pull out a fever, how to settle a stormy stomach. Aggie gone out of the world, all right, taking her bush medicine ways with her, but she still pays visits, offering her wisdoms to Harmony, even when they are not wanted.

The girl sits up suddenly, stares at Harmony like she seen a ghost.

"It's just me setting here. You safe in my home."

Her chest is heaving, she's gripping the sheets. Maybe she's in one of those underwater night-scares that swallowed up Harmony when she was a child.

"It's okay, child. Put your head down. Hush now and peace..."

The girl falls back on the mat, eyes closed again, breathing easier.

Why this white child come stumbling up to my stoop, Aggie? What am I supposed to do with her now?

Calm yourself and sense what you should know.

Well, Aggie, how I am supposed to know what's gonna help this here situation?

Harmony pushes herself up off the floor, rubs her aching knee, and walks to the front door. She opens it and looks out on the night. Hens gone into the seed shed, tired of waiting for Harmony to shut

162

them in. Sun's hit the water. Harmony missed the hiss, and the sky's turned dark purple. Off in the bush, a potcake barks–short and sharp, just twice. Maybe that pregnant dog she caught last month stealing a loaf from the oven.

Harmony's got no idea what she's supposed to do with this child, what this child want with her. She's got no notion what Aggie's trying to show her. *Sense what you should know?* Sometimes she wishes Aggie would stay out of her business, keep her opinions to herself, but Aggie is as much a part of the island as the birds and the insects and the potcakes in the bush. And she will be heard, Lord, she will be heard. She is going to correct Harmony every chance she get.

Back inside, she cleans up the place in the dim candlelight, rinsing plates and cups in the basin, setting them on the rack to dry. Then she wipes down the table where she fed the girl. Sure enough, there's rice where she spilled from each and every forkful, rice on the chair and under the table too. Harmony finds the broom and sweeps it up, her brain worrying with every stroke. Maybe she'll make up a pallet on the floor next to the girl, maybe she can pull out that old mattress that her boy used. She knows where it is, pushed in the back room, tied up tight, like the memory of him, ready to spring open any moment. But no. She doesn't want to smell that boy scent of sweat and soil mixed in with the sisal. So, she takes a thinned-out sheet from the shelves, returns to her rocker, sits down and covers her lap. She kicks off her slops and pushes them to the side of the chair. Then she closes her eyes and listens for the ocean.

For a long time, her mind won't settle. It keeps reaching out to the girl in her fevered sleep, trying to understand where she come from, what has she done. If you know, Aggie, tell me. Don't make me wait. I need to know. I need to understand so I can help her. But

Aggie is silent while dark swallows the sky. The nocturnals and the spirits taking over, thronging in the bush and spiraling in the night.

CHAPTER 13

Harmony wakes before sun-up, still in the big chair, with a crick in her neck. She turns her head slowly, shifts it side to side. Then she remembers. The mat on the floor—sheets all scrambled, and the girl is gone. *Was she a dream child then? Conjured up to break my lonelies?* Harmony stands up as fast as her knees allow, walks over to the privy, splashes water on her face, tries to clear her head. The girl had to be real; there is sand all over the floor in here and yes–the shame-shame bikini, smaller than a kerchief, right there on a nail by the basin. A living girl. Evidence everywhere. But where did she go? *Maybe she just came here to be thieving from me? What did she steal?*

Hush, Aggie says. *What she gonna take from you save some food and some mother love? She got a story to tell if you calm your crazies and set beside her long enough to listen.*

Harmony picks the girl's bikini top off the nail. It is salt-baked and hard as husk. She hears yapping outside, pushes her face up against the small window and there's the girl, setting on the laundry rock, with three potcake puppies jumping up at her, trying to crawl on her lap. Light seeps through the thicket behind her, and the girl's sleep-wild hair glows orange gold, same color as Fulcrum's, Lord, same color as her own, and Harmony can't stop smiling. She raps on the glass and the girl lifts her hand, searches for a minute, and then waves back. I see you. You see me. Our stories got crisscrossed here on Callow Cay.

You been lonely, Aggie says.

Ah, hush, Aggie. I like my quiet.

You been lonely these years and you pulled this girl to you.

Harmony rinses the girl's bikini in the water bucket, slips her slops back on, pushes open the front door and looks out at the yard. A light gray sky stretches across a gentle sea. Miles and miles of ocean from here to Grand Bahama Island and the girl wants her to believe she sailed it all alone? Naw. Harmony never been clever like Aggie, but she won't be the boukee in this girl's story. She twists out the bikini and takes it round to the line. The girl's still on the rock, wheedling at the potcakes that's climbed up there with her. One pup is scratching her legs and she's laughing and shaking her hair-spikes, another pup chewing on them with needle teeth.

"Good morning," the girl says.

She sounds better today. Her voice less raspy.

"Don't let the dog do that," Harmony says. Her first words this morning crosser than she intends them to be. "You gonna make him a biter."

"Sorry." The girl pushes the puppy down.

Harmony hangs the bikini to dry on the clothesline above the laundry rock. Takes down the sheets from two days back and throws them over her arm.

"Come on inside, now. We got to see about getting you home to your folks."

The girl looks like her face got slapped. And, don't you know it,

166

Aggie chiming in: *She been through something, Harmony. Why not let her set there a while and play?*

Harmony sighs. Aggie's right, like always. The girl and the puppies just being young in the morning rise.

"You feel like yourself this morning?" Harmony asks.

"I feel much better thank you. Just sort of achy all over."

"You crazy-talking in your sleep."

"Did I say something bad?"

"You yelled out some, asking for help, thrashing at the sheets, but you done slept near twenty hours. Let's get us some breakfast and then we talk some more."

Harmony walks to the seed shed and finds two baskets. Sure enough, the girl and three puppies soon standing behind her, sniffing out something interesting.

"What are you doing?"

"I'm going to the patch, pick the ripes. You coming? You and your potcakes?"

"Yes, please," she says, so polite.

Harmony hands her a basket. "Never seen those puppies before. I expect they been too scared of the rooster to come into the yard. Mistah Biggety don't like no dogs."

"I coaxed them out with some food," she said. "I took some bread from the kitchen. I hope you don't mind."

"Well, I suppose one time won't hurt, but don't go spoiling them. Potcakes got to fend for themselves out there."

What's the girl thinking? She will be gone by the end of the day, leaving Harmony with three puppies that want home cooking. Smooth-headed children don't know nothing about settlement living. She's seen enough of them in her days, coming over from the big island on boats their white daddies built, looking at Aggie and Harmony and the boys in their patchy clothes at Market Day, and smirking, or worse, pitying them.

Harmony leads the way to the bush path, trying to get ahead of her irritation. The girl and the puppies chase after her. She's none the worse for her boat accident if there was an accident. Strong enough to play with the puppies. If the girl's momma saw them at this very minute, she'd likely lose her mind. She'd likely say, why you keeping my daughter from me? She'd likely be a small white woman, all delicate and righteous in her accusings. You trying to steal my girl? Harmony shakes her head. The girl found me, came stumbling up to my door and pulled me into her story. But she knows that's no kind of answer. The girl's daddy likely gonna show up with a gun, ask no questions and take what's his.

Step by step. Just pick you some breakfast and let the story out.

Harmony leads them through the scrub, down a narrow path to the clearing. "This here the orchard. My big sister Aggie planted most of these trees. Spent most of her days here taking care of them too. Pruning, feeding, watering, picking, making her tonics and decoctions from the fruit and the bark and from plants in the bush. I try to keep the fruit trees going but they never been the same since she gone. This here pear don't give much no more. All the citrus dead from the cankers last year. The mangoes okay, though. And see down the path there? Still plenty of strong dillies. Aggie loved her dillies. They're flowering right now. You ever eat a dilly, Dede?"

The girl laughs and shakes her wild ocean hair.

"Never ate them on your island, then?" Harmony just curious. "Well, they not ready just now. But once you sample your first sapodilla you won't want them other fruits."

"What do they taste like?"

"Hard to say what they like exactly. Maybe Coca Cola and pear all mixed up. Couple of months from now, we'll have all the dillies you could ever want. We'll make dilly jam, dilly puff, fresh dillies."

But the girl would be long gone by then. Back in Freeport where she say she's from. Or somewhere in the Abacos if it turn out she a liar. In a couple of months, she be back home with her momma and daddy, and she won't remember Harmony Knowles. Or Harmony be like a dream she can't quite figure out. And Harmony would be still here, blaming herself for getting left behind and forgotten all over again.

Stop it. You walking down this path right this minute.

Aggie right, of course. No need to fix the brain on some past that could have been or some future that may never happen. Be here and stop worrying how the story goes, who writes it, or where it will end.

Dede pulls on a green tentacle. "What's this tree?"

"Genep. Bite the skin and suck the sweet stuff, then spit out the seed. And right next to it, this here's a sour sop tree. Grows real big fruit like apple-pineapple. Good for the fever and sugar sickness. My Uncle Harcourt, he died of the sugar sickness. Took his leg first then his life. Aggie tried and tried, but sometime even the bush medicine not strong enough."

Beyond the last of the orchard, the garden patch. Harcourt worked it year after year, and the soil was deep and black, not like the hard scrabble sand by the ocean. And he planted enough to feed the children, not one of them his own, but all of them his family, fed them from here with the peas, the corn, cassava, tomatoes, okra, yams. A light rain falls on the land now, no more than a mist coming down. The bush has reclaimed some of Harcourt's garden, but

Harmony still tends it and gets more than she can eat. Plenty to share each week with Clementina up the road a couple of miles. Some to take up to market if she so inclined to walk all the way into Hard Bargain. And lots right now for her visitor.

"Feel that spry? Just a kiss of rain, perfect for planting corn. You can plant it every month if it's wet. I gonna pick us some tomatoes for our breakfast. I got mush melon over there. See that hole? You can fetch it. Pass by those poles. Them the pigeon peas. Yep. Just past there. See? There's two maybe three nice mush melons left. Just pull one clear off the vine."

They fill up Harmony's baskets with tomatoes and okra and peppers. The girl carries a melon in the upturned bowl of Fulcrum's t-shirt. Puppies fix on her like she their momma, circling her legs, whining for pick-up, chasing after her when she walking. And she loving it all, the garden in the morning, the drizzle, the pups. Harmony can't bring up what she should be saying. How she should be planning for her to go back to where she come from.

"Do you grow all your food?" Dede asks as they back-track the path to the house.

"Flour, rice, sugar and black tea come off the boat in Hard Bargain. But we Knowles grown up eating from the garden."

"My friend, Ethel plants flowers in the garden, all kinds of flowers, but no fruits or vegetables. I wish you could meet her. I think you'd like each other."

"Where she at?" Harmony asks all clever-like, "back in England where you come from first, or in the Abacos where you live now?"

The girl's walking ahead on the path, so Harmony can't see her eyes.

"She's my neighbor in Freeport. Grand Bahama." She stops and turns and shakes her tousled hair. "I know you think I'm fibbing but

I'm not. She lives in the flat next to me and my Mum. But her passion is painting. I bet she'd love to paint your house."

"My house don't need painting."

"Not the outside; I mean paint a picture of it—the whole scene, with the hens and the rock oven and your laundry line and things. She did all these people in Eight Mile Rock; the way they live, fishing and farming. Now she's making lots of things out of clay—corals and fans and things."

"Why?"

Dede shrugs. "It's what she loves to do, I guess. Maybe like you love to garden?"

Did Harmony garden out of love or because she had to? There must be love in the day in day out tending. Uncle Harcourt, he had loved it, hadn't he? Even if he didn't like being left with all the children, even if he sometimes yelled and cussed at them for messing up his life. Harmony supposed there was a love that pulled you to certain things even when you were tired or sick or wanted a break. Love in keeping things going even when all your family has gone and died or left you alone on the island, left you not much more than a ghost watching over the past. Was there love or just self-sorries in fretting over a no-good son who never in ten years writes to his Momma?

"Dede, we got to get word to your family. Your Momma and Daddy must be worried sick about you. After breakfast, we gonna walk you up to Clementina's and try to raise somebody on the radio."

The girl kicks at the dirt with her big toe and shakes her head slowly.

"You in some kind of trouble?"

This time she shake-shakes hard.

"You ran away?"

171

"No. Please believe me. The boat was an accident. I got on and there was too much wind and I just held on. I couldn't turn back."

"Any fool can turn a boat, child."

"The waves were terrible. You have to believe me. I didn't run away, but I can't go back."

"That don't make any sense." Couldn't? Can't? The girl's legs look like they crumbling underneath her. She struggles to hold up the melon and sinks to the ground. Harmony drops her baskets and sits beside her, peers into her face. Getting the truth from this child is going to take time, take patience. Harmony has plenty of the first, and yes, Aggie, she's working on the second.

"All right now, don't fret. Come on now, we got a meal to make. Let's get you back up and go on inside."

"Potcakes stay out," Harmony says when they're back at the house. Got to have some rules, even if the girl only staying a day or two. Harmony sets the melon and the baskets on the table, then sends the girl out to find eggs, tells her the best places to look, behind the seed shed, over by the outcrop and on the bush-edge. And soon she comes back in with five in her shirt basket, smiling again. All children like egg-hunting, finding the secret spots, making off with the perfect treasure. The girl gently places each egg on the counter. She also likes the fixing and the cooking; she cracks all five eggs for the scramble, slices the tomatoes, and warms up the beans and rice on the stove top. Then she set two places real pretty at the table: Orange napkins, fork and spoon and knife each. Real glasses to drink the fresh quench Harmony teaches her how to make, this batch with tamarind pods.

When they sit for the fixings, Harmony takes both the girl's hands in her own: "Gifts of land, gifts of sea, for Your people living free. Amen"

172

"Amen," the girl echoes.

"Don't have to always be grateful in this life," Harmony says, "But when you are, only right to say so. I'm grateful you landed safe."

"Amen again," she says, and laughs. "Amen squared." Then she eats fast and furious like the day before, shovel-in, shovel-in, until her plate lickety-clean. Harmony passes the cut melon and the girl stuffs in more, until her belly presses up against the Goombay smile shirt.

"Easy now, don't make yourself sick. Uncle Harcourt's mule ate too much Jumbie plant and got colic and died."

She tells the girl a second time to slow down but she keeps on eating, making up for whatever she's been through, days without, hours on the water. Harmony doesn't know what to believe. When she finally stops shoveling in, the girl pushes back her chair and burps loud and long, like Fulcrum used to do. She apologizes, which he never done, but then she lets out another deep burp and soon they're laughing to tears. Then Harmony clears the table while the girl heads back outside to play with the pups. Harmony watches them through the window–a game like hide and seek, and the girl is always the hider, of course, behind the laundry rock, behind the sour sop tree, behind the seed shed, the girl always the hider, because puppies can't hide good from children, just like children can't hide too good from adults.

Who else is looking for her now? Her Daddy? Her Momma? Her somebody, for sure. She's wanted and not forgotten, that's clear to see; she's singing out a little song to help the puppies find her, here pup-pup-pup-pup-puppy, and they find her and climb on her and they all start over again. Harmony keeps watching while she dries the fry pan, thinking this seem like a dream now, but this is what real life is. Lost and found and found and lost, over and over and over again. In the end, most everyone wants to be found.

Later in the day, when the sun's full up, Harmony carries one of the small chairs outside.

Dede is flat on her back on the laundry rock, pups sleep between her legs, her yellow bikini top dangles overhead like bait on a fishing line. She and the pups so tired out from hide and seeking? Tired from the walk through the bush? No, they all so tired out from their lives before this moment; they all of them skinny and scrawny, too thin in the limbs, too fat in the belly. Stick legs, swell bellies. Not a pretty group, it's true. Harmony sighs. She could get used to their company, though.

What's wrong with a little company?

Aggie's gone quiet.

Harmony watches the girl. She a strange one, this child, but kind with the animals. Yes, she a strange and familiar child. Her belly going up and down, going up and down, going up and down with each breath. A tight melon under her skin, way too big for the rest of her. And then, Harmony sees.

Oh, she's so young, so very small. She can't be. Can she? Aggie— talk to me. She going to be okay?

Aggie doesn't say a word. Or maybe she already said all she needs to: the girl's got a story to tell and needs someone who'll listen. Only choice now is how Harmony going to play her part. She sits in her chair and waits. Harmony watches the girl. Harmony breathes in and out until her own breathing matches the girl's: in and out, in and out. In like the waves that brought her to the Bight. Out like the waves that will carry her away soon enough. Who counts them? All the waves. All the girls with babies in their belly. All the children that leave and never return. All the mothers waiting.

When Dede's done her napping and the puppies start squirming, Harmony scoots her chair closer to the laundry rock. She sits with the girl while the sun arcs from bush to beach. They talk about nothing and everything—the garden patch, catching sweet water from the sky, hurricanes, rock ovens, and fruit trees. They talk about taking a walk to the Bight, pulling some conch from the sea for their supper. And when the sun is hovering over the water, they trek down the ocean road, over the coral ridge, out in the shallows. Harmony sees no sign of a boat, nothing on the reef, no wreck, no sail, not even a scrap of wood, but she doesn't ask Dede about it. Not today, no way. The girl's got her reasons for running. The questions can wait another day.

Near Crooked Rock, where all the waters meet, they haul in conch for supper. They toss a dozen shells in a gunny sack and when they get home, out in the yard, Harmony clonks each one with the machete, cuts the muscle, and pulls out the white bodies, drops them into a bowl. Dede says she got the know-how to make fritters and Harmony lets her lead, pounding the conch on the cooking rock, cutting it into pieces, chopping onions and peppers from the garden, tossing them in with the mixings.

"I don't know about the spices."

"You go on and find me another two eggs out back—look under that neem tree past the laundry rock."

Harmony finds her spicy mix in the kitchen, pours out a half handful, finds the flour tin, and takes it all outside. When the girl returns, she cracks two eggs in the mix, stirs it up.

"We gonna have us a feast. Now pick up them shells there and take them out back to the pile."

"I never found a pearl," Dede says as she gathers the conch shells scattered around the rock. "Did you ever?"

Harmony smiles, "Wait here," she says. Back inside, she goes to the chest beside her bed and pulls out the old tobacco tin. She carries it out in the yard, opens it up to show the girl.

"Oh wow! How many are there? Where did you find them?"

"Where all the waters meet."

"But how did you get so many?"

Harmony shrugs "Twenty-three conch pearls. I'm more than fifty years old so… one every couple of years, I guess."

"My Mum got a conch pearl necklace for Christmas last year and it had twenty-two pearls. It cost a fortune." Dede pokes around in the tin and picks out the darkest pearl—the same color as her sun-fried lip. "You could sell these, you know. Thousands of dollars, I bet you could buy yourself a bigger house. You could move to another island."

Harmony laughs. "Too old for moving. I'm gonna stay right here and hold on to what I got."

Later, while the girl shares more of her crazy ideas about rescuing potcakes, painting pictures, writing story books, Harmony fries up all the fritters. They eat more than a dozen for dinner, sitting out front in the yard, watching the giant melon sun suck up the sea.

CHAPTER 14

The sun says it's morning again. Time stretches out on Callow Cay, each moment extends, like in boredom or in the deepest dreams. Is anyone looking for Dede now, or have they given up hope, imagining her disappeared, drowned, dead?

She lies in the sun on the laundry rock, letting the puppies scramble all over her.

I'm okay Mum, she tries to telepath across the sea. *But I can't come home just now.*

The girl puppy, the one she's named Tuppence, nudges at Dede's pocket, nudges her back to this place.

Dede tears off a pinch of conch fritter in her pocket and gives it to her. Patches and Luc, the two boys, roll in the dirt. Dede claps her hands, and they stop wrestling for a moment, look at her with a mixture of fear and curiosity.

"It's okay," she says, but they don't come closer. Bush shy, that's what Harmony calls them. Both boys have yellow fur, but Patches has red splotches across his back and legs; Dede wants to get a closer look. She claps again and whistles, then holds out the whole fritter in the palm of her hand. This time, the smell gets their attention, and they come to her. She rewards them each with a taste.

"Good dogs."

Patches stares up at her, all bone and angles, his skin, bumpy and red. Dede neck-scruffs him, then runs a hand across his flank. Fleas? Ticks? His back leg jitters, trying to scratch the sores. "Easy boy," she tries, but he won't settle. The pups sleep in the bush at night. Harmony says she hasn't seen the mother lately, says that sometimes a bitch tires out, leaves her litter because she's got nothing left to give. Pups are on their own now. Dede wishes she could stop Patches' itching with cream or lotion or something. Once when she had psoriasis on her knees and elbows, Mum took her to see Dr. Antonio at his clinic and he said stress caused the skin condition. That made Mum laugh. Stress? She said, go on, pull the other leg.

Dede lies flat on the rock, arms out to the sides, drawing down the rays of warmth. Ten a.m.? Maybe not that late. She checks her watch out of habit. No use; still 6:46. She has to judge by the angle of the streaming light, and the sun's not above the tree line. Tuppence jumps on her belly, licks Dede's hand and settles down next to her thigh. Dede closes her eyes and breathes in the morning: sea and salt from the Bight, a thread of scent—something citrusy and sweet. Maybe those limes that grow in clusters—Genep? Harmony knows so much about the plants, the fruits, the island. She knows so much about so many things here on Callow Cay, but not much about the rest of the world. She has no radio. No television, of course, because there's no electricity in the Bight.

What was missing except maybe company? Harmony says she likes it this way; but Dede can tell she misses her son. Still has all his things in his tiny room, his t-shirts washed and folded on a shelf, as if he never left. The room is like a conch shell without the snail inside it. Dede reaches out a hand and rests it on Tuppence's side. The puppy's ribs vibrate like guitar strings. Three breaths in for each one of Dede's. Hadn't she read somewhere that animal skeletons, even human bones, are made of the same stuff as seashells? Calcium something. Dede's own ribs not much different from a conch shell. What would it be like to carry your home with you everywhere? Or the inverted question, to float freely like a coral polyp until you found a place to anchor yourself?

Tuppence twitches; does she dream of chasing land crabs or maybe juicy agouti? Dede keeps her eyes closed with a hand on Tuppence's warm belly. The boy pups whine at Dede's feet, too timid to jump up. Tuppence whimpers. Then she barks and jumps off the rock.

"What is it, girl?" Dede says, but she hears it too, a noise that pulls her out of her half-dream. An engine chuck-chucking down the road. A horn honks once, twice, then a man yelling, "Good Morning, Harmony." Mistah Biggety squawks in the front yard. All the puppies scurry into the bush. Dede turns and follows them; she falls flat on her belly in a cluster of saw palmetto, her pulse thumping through her ear. From the hideout in the bush, Dede cannot see the road, but she can feel the ground rumble. Another honk, long and loud. Dede holds her breath. Waits. The engine rumbles and fades, lost in the rush and rustle of the jungle.

"Dede?" Harmony calls. She stands in the middle of the back yard, scanning the bush. "Where you hiding? It's all right."

Dede crawls out of the undergrowth and stands up. "I heard a car."

"Captain Albury in his truck. That man always make the biggest ruckus when he come down this way, yelling and honking like the whole world got to know he out doing his business. I don't know where he's going, but you and me, we got to talk. We got to make a plan we can live with before it gets made for us. It's market day in town and we need to get you sorted."

Dede stares at Patches. "I wonder if I might get some more food for the puppies. Give them a real meal."

"Not now, child. You gonna spoil them," she says. "And no one here going to feed them when you gone."

"Please, Harmony. Just this once. Let me give them a proper breakfast."

Harmony sighs. "All right. There's some rice and peas leftover." She waves her hand. "Go on and fetch it. But then we talk for real."

Dede shakes her head, then runs inside, digs up a slab of the thickened potcake, breaks it into three portions and brings them outside. The pups rush over and swallow the lumps down in seconds, and then look at Dede expectantly.

Harmony lounges in her outside chair again, near the rock. "You ever have a puppy back at your home?"

"No. Mum said the flat's too small."

"You good with them."

Dede nods because every living animal just wants to be gotten. Dogs seem to get her, and she gets them. She rubs Patches' head. "This one needs some medicine for his itch. Maybe we could get some from the vet in town."

"No vet in Hard Bargain. Bring him here to me."

Dede picks him up, carries him over. Harmony reaches out to run a hand through his coat, pulls out a tuff of fur, sniffs at it. Patches yelps.

"Only the mange." Harmony says.

"See how skinny he is compared to the others," Dede says. "They're all thin, but he's a skeleton."

"You tender-hearted, Dede, but sometimes nature knows what it doing. Lot of dogs out there in the bush got mites and mange and fleas, got to live with a little patchiness. Not the worst thing in the world."

"Do you have any Calamine lotion?"

Harmony shakes her head. "Back in the day, when we Knowles get the poison oak or the jelly stings, Aggie made us Kamalamee wraps. Pick some leaves from the tree, boil them up, make a poultice."

"Can we try it?"

"On a potcake? Oh girl. You got to understand—on this island, potcakes is a nuisance. The boys in Hard Bargain, they beat dogs that come there begging. Some of the businesses, they leave out poison for them dogs to eat. Got to let nature do what nature do."

"Putting out poison is not nature though. It's murder."

Harmony sighs. "What we gonna do, Lord?"

"He's just a little puppy."

"I suppose. Let's go get us some bark. But listen, when we come back, we still gonna have us a little talk. Woman to woman. It's high time we figure things out. Like why you landed here; like how we getting you home."

The girls is already up and eager, not listening to a word she doesn't want to hear.

Harmony fetches a basket and her garden scissors from the shed. The puppies follow them down the path past Aggie's orchard trees, across the vegetable plot and over to the edge of the untamed bush. Five or six Kamalamees—tall, V-shaped trees—line up as a make-shift fence.

"Tourist trees," Dede says. "That's what the kids at my school call them."

Harmony begins to tear off the papery red bark.

Dede works on the tree beside her. It's a satisfying feeling, to tug at the strips. When she first moved to Grand Bahama with Mum, she burned and blistered after every long day at the beach; a few days later, she'd pull skin off her shoulders and nose with that mix of pain and pleasure. Sometimes, Mum would ask if she could peel off a piece of Dede's skin. Sometimes Dede let her and sometimes not, depending on her mood. Sometimes it felt as if Mum were scratching an itch, other times as if she were stealing something precious. Dede's skin is red brown these days, not much lighter than Harmony's. She could pass as a light-skinned Bahamian. Maybe even Harmony's granddaughter. Then she'd never have to go home. Would that be so wrong, to stay here forever and always?

While the puppies play at the edge of the Bush, Harmony and Dede lay bark strips into the basket.

"Maybe a dozen more long strips," Harmony says. "Don't take no more you need. Aggie's first bush medicine rule."

Dede stops collecting and stares out at the thick jungle. A bird chuck-chucks. A hum of insects so loud it seems to come from inside Dede's brain. A few trees she can recognize, but so many are new to her, tubular and snakelike, yellow and hairy, prickly like pines. "Do you know all these plants? What to use them for?"

"Not near all. Aggie knew them all. She the expert everyone come to see back in the day. That there's Inkwood," she says. "And that yellow rope all wrapped round it there, Love vine. Poisonous. Aggie's second rule is don't use nothing you don't know nothing about. But come on now, we got plenty."

Back in the house, Harmony fills up a pot of water and tosses in the bark. She says it will take a couple of hours to boil the decoction on the kerosene stove. They go back out to sit, Harmony on her chair, Dede on the edge of the laundry rock. All the puppies are lying nearby in a small spot of shade. It must be close to noon now, the sun firing overhead. Dede worries about that Captain Albury man coming back up the road, showing up unannounced. What will he do if he sees her here? But Harmony wants to talk. She leans back in her chair and asks sideways questions.

"How old is your Momma, Dede?"

"Thirty-one, no, thirty-two."

"And you say your daddy live in England still? You miss him?"

Dede asks her own questions, too.

"How come you never got married?"

"Never fell in love, never saw no need. And Fulcrum had good-enough uncles to help raise him up. Too bad they had to steal him from me."

"Don't you ever get lonely living out here all alone, with all of them gone?"

When Harmony answers, her voice is softer and breathy. "The onliest place I lived these fifty years is here in the Bight. I miss Fulcrum, sure enough. Nothing as empty as a loved one leaving, except a loved one staying gone. But I ain't too lonely, truth be told. I got Clementina up the road, a couple folks I still know in Hard Bargain. And Aggie with me here most days, still talking at me, still bossing me about."

"What do you mean?"

"The hurricane took her body, but her spirit pays visits. A tingling in my brain and her words inside me and it almost like she right here. Not exactly like how you visiting with me here now but not too different neither."

Dede wants to say that she could live here always, stay with Harmony. She wants to say that she could do that—be someone more real for Harmony to talk to, not some sort of ghost or memory. She would take care of the puppies, too. Help with Aggie's orchard. She'd learn how to use all the plants for medicine. Become an herbalist like Aggie, help all the people and the animals on the island. She'd train the puppies and they'd be as smart as Miss Evans' Border Collies and learn how to hunt food and keep away enemies. Like Harmony, she wouldn't ever need to marry.

"What about your poor Momma?" Harmony says, as if she's listening in on all of Dede's thoughts. "Leaving her not knowing if you alive or dead?"

Dede gets a funny feeling in her belly. She wraps her arms around her knees and closes her eyes. She pictures Mum getting ready for work: ironing her white blouse, blow-drying her hair, putting on her baby-blue eye shadow and her poinsettia lipstick, then coming in to say good-night. Leaving a lip-print on Dede's cheek.

She rubs the spot where the kiss would be, tries not to cry. "I can't go back."

Harmony pulls her chair closer. "Why?"

"I just can't."

"You still young, Dede; you don't know how a mother's heart aches."

Dede's hands crisscross her chest. "Mum's got her own interests; she won't miss me *that* much. And I don't miss her." She says the words, but her body doesn't listen properly. Harmony sees the tears spill out; quiet tears first, then heaving sobs. Dede feels her stupid traitor body showing her up. All right, she misses Mum, she wants to see her, but it is impossible to go home. Why doesn't Harmony understand. "Mum has Silvio to take care of her, to buy her things, to treat her special."

Dede can't bear to be anybody's Princess again.

"Okay, now," Harmony says and strokes Dede's back.

"Please let me stay here," Dede says. "I'll write Mum a long letter. I'll tell her it's best for me and probably best for Mum, too. She won't ever have to worry about me. I will help you so much, Harmony, I promise. I'll help with everything."

Harmony sighs and shakes her head. "What about your boyfriend? Don't you leastways want to see him?"

"I don't have a boyfriend."

"Is there someone in your school you sweet on?"

"The boys in my class are idiots. And mean. They chase lizards and rip off their tails. They cut open frogs. I hate them all."

Harmony leans forward and takes Dede's chin in her palm and turns her face so she can peer straight into her eyes. "I know you been with someone. Your body say it's so. You caught yourself a baby."

Dede pushes off Harmony's hand and stands up. "I'm thirsty. I need a drink."

Harmony stands, too, and follows her to the water barrel, close as a shadow. Dede senses her there, and keeps moving, round to the other side of the house. Harmony closes in and grasps Dede's arm. "Tell me the reason you come up on my island, tell me the reason you bust into my life. Don't you run from me, child. I'm the onliest one can hear what you got to say, so you might as well say it to me."

Then they both hear it again, a vehicle coming close, closer. Two loud honks of the horn again. Dede freezes. Mistah Biggety squawks intruder, intruder.

"Jesus Lord," Harmony says. "Get inside, get on the bed. Under them covers, quick."

As the truck turns into the yard, Dede slips in the front door, scrambles across to the back of the room, crawls under the sheets and shuts her eyes tight. Mistah Biggety is going crazy. The engine gets louder, then chokes and dies. A car door slams. Talking and laughing. A man's voice, deep and island speckled. More loud laughter. More talking. Harmony's voice this time, smooth and easy. Dede begins to shake. What if he sees her yellow bikini hanging on the line? What if he saw her running into the shack? What if he demands to look inside?

The front door swings open. "Quiet child. Don't you move." Harmony pours something into a glass. Then the door slams again and she is gone.

Dede tries to still her thoughts, but her brain won't stop. What if Harmony tells him she has a white girl hiding inside? What if the man drags her out of the shack? Tries to load her in his truck and carry her away? She will not get in. She will not get into his car again. She squeezes her eyes shut. No. Never. No.

More laughter outside, more talk, several more minutes pass by, before the engine splutters and starts again, chugs out of the driveway, honks once, twice, then heads off down or up the road.

"Oh, Lordy girl," Harmony says when she comes back inside. "That was the Captain." She puts a glass by the sink, sits down at the table. "You can come on out, come on over here now. Look at you—all shakin' again. Child, listen now. Some bone-fishing idiots found parts of a boat snagged in the Marls, south of the Bight—got to be yours. They radioed the Harbor earlier this morning and Captain Albury drove down to check it out, now he's waiting till high tide to pull it back to land. He's got the boat's numbers and gonna make some calls and find out where it come from. He stopped by here to drink my quench and to brag about his doings and wanting to know had I seen anybody, any folks don't belong on the island. He weren't asking about you, about an English girl, but soon as he radio Freeport, they likely gonna connect it to you, Dede, and they gonna be back down this way, Captain Albury and all his sons and their friends. You know them Conchy Joes from the Abacos, them wreckers and scavengers, they love any kind of hunt, so now we need a real plan."

Dede cannot meet Harmony's eyes, afraid of what she might see in them.

"All I am asking is all of the truth from you," Harmony says. She reaches her hand toward Dede, again cups her chin and tilts it upward until their eyes connect. "Which boy you been with?"

Dede can't speak, but she shakes her head once, twice, ever so slightly. Her mind flashes on Johnnie Angel. She tries to close off the thought, but Harmony has seized it, and is taking in more.

"Not a boy? A man?"

Dede does not move. Her throat is sealed. No words, no words.

"A grown man." Harmony whistles softly and retracts her palm, as if it's been singed. "And you caught his baby, Lord."

Dede shakes her head. No. Never. No.

Harmony says it again. "A baby inside you. It's clear as the shallow seas. That's why you left Freeport and that's why you found me here."

Dede puts a hand on her stomach, her traitor body. How she cried that first time, and then later, the next few times it happened, how she stopped crying and counted instead, counted on and on as far as she could remember, 3.14159, slices of pi, forward and then backward, until he was done, and then how the shame came rolling in, wave after wave of shame, flooding her body. And the shame is in her now and she feels so sick, suddenly, awfully sick and oh God, a noise, a wail coming from inside.

Harmony walks around to Dede, wraps her in her arms. "You didn't know you was having his baby, but still you ran away? You didn't know. But you knew."

She squeezes her eyes tight and sees his face. His forehead above her. His hands wanting more. His body so heavy. Heaving. She didn't think—those times in his car, how could she imagine—a baby inside her? Not possible. But suddenly, completely, true.

"We've got to get you someplace safe before they all come back out this way."

She pushes Harmony away. "You could get in trouble for hiding me. Why not let them find me and take me back to Freeport?"

"I can't, Dede. Not with that man there."

"He said he loves me. He said no one will ever love me as much as he does."

"Maybe he said it, maybe he even fool enough to believe it, but he's no good. That ain't no kind of love. And somehow your Momma opened the door to him, open the door to all your troubles."

The words buzz like mosquitos. The room swirls. Dede needs to lie down. She staggers across the living area, and falls on the mat, her head pounding. Harmony brings her a drink, lays a hand on her shoulder, whispers to her as she falls into sleep, "You gonna survive this, Dede. Sometimes it so hard to see how you gonna make it through, but I'm with you even if you think you alone, I'll be watching out for you, just like Aggie always do for me."

188

CHAPTER 15

Seems like days later when Harmony shakes her awake again, speaks softly in her ear.

"You been down for a while—two hours, maybe—but now we got to get to Hard Bargain so I can go on into the harbor before nightfall and find us a boat. Then we ship out first thing tomorrow, get over to Nassau and find some of my folks to help you out."

She tells Dede to bring a chair over to the kitchen sink. "First thing, we need to tame and hide that hair."

Harmony stands beside her with a pair of ancient kitchen shears and cuts the knots and the last of seaweed from Dede's hair and slathers her head with a thick paste—nuts, tea, and vinegar, she says—and spreads it from roots to tips, slicking it back, singing while she works:

Right then they was talkin' about a storm in the island. Run come see Jerusalem... My God it was thirty-three souls on the water, swimmin' and prayin' to the Daniel God. Run come see Jerusalem...

Dede wants to ask if it's true, all those souls drowned in the sea– but Harmony's voice is too beautiful to interrupt and the story seems too sad to be made-up. Sound vibrates in Harmony's chest, like waves in a cave. When she sings the last line, *'Cause I've seen Jerusalem,* she wipes dye-drips off Dede's neck, tosses the black splotched cloth into the bucket and assesses her handiwork.

"Well, you'll fool any folks we might run into, I suppose, once we put a cap on you. Anyone ask, I'll say you're Fulcrum's boy, finally come here for a visit, and we need to rent us a boat." Harmony hands Dede her bikini and another faded t-shirt, and a dingy baseball cap. Dede takes them from her and walks into the toilet, sheds her stained Goombay Punch tee and pulls on the new gear over her clean bikini. She hides the shoulder straps as best she can, puts the cap on her head. A passing glance in the mirror flashes back a jut-armed, pot-bellied, mottle-skinned boy.

"What we gonna do about shoes?" Harmony says when Dede comes out of the bathroom. "Can't walk through the bush barefoot."

Dede's managed that way since landing at the Bight. Three years of island living have toughened her soles. She shows Harmony her heels as hard and creviced as reef-rock.

"I'll be all right. My soles are tough."

"Jungle walking is different. Fire ants, poison-pins, burr-boys bury between your toes and never come out, no how." She rummages again, this time through shelves in the back by her bed. "Fulcrum took his tennis shoes with him when he left me. I'd give you my own extras, but my feet are twice too big... "

She peers under her bed. After a while, she finds what she's looking for, a pair of flip-flops, with cheap plastic flowers on the straps. She carries them back to the table and waves them triumphantly. "I'm going to fix you some bush-trekkers."

She snips the flowers and straps off and has Dede step on the foam soles. She scores a line around the outside of each foot with the blade of her shears. "While I fix these up, you go get you some lunch. Gonna be a long way to town the way we have to go."

Dede slices a piece off the cassava bread, nibbles on that. Her stomach twists every which way with wants and worries: She likes being here with Harmony and the pups, but now she can't stay because people are searching for her. Captain Albury and his crew.

Harmony says she has a plan to get Dede away.

"What you think?" Harmony holds up a shoe sole, cut out. "Right size?" Now she's plaiting strips of cloth to make straps.

Ridiculous. Dede won't wear those. Why would Dede even listen to anything Harmony says? Her escape plan will never work. Even if she manages to get Dede, disguised as a boy, all the way to Hard Bargain, even if they find a boat to rent, even if they make a sea journey to Nassau, then what? How's she going to live in Nassau? Who will she stay with?

"Looks like you ate something poisonous," Harmony says. "Why you turned all twisty-mouthed?"

"I'm okay. Can I take some bread outside, say goodbye to the puppies?"

Harmony nods.

As Dede pushes the door open, two small planes approach from the west. She watches the sky, listening for their hum as they move in over the sand flats. Before they hit the Bight, the planes turn north side-by-side and fly parallel to the coast, white bodies gleaming against the bluest sky.

"Close that door," Harmony says. "They searching for you, Dede. I'd bet my life on it. They connected that sailboat with you. Now they be flying up and back the island all day. Like before when that drug plane went down. Everyone be out looking; everyone be talking in town."

Dede comes back into the room, but she can't sit. Are they really looking for her? Silvio owns a Cessna Skymaster with a push-pull engine, 712 Whiskey Quebec, and once, when he was trying to get Mum to like him, he took Dede along island-hopping; they stopped for a picnic in Eleuthera. While Mum and Silvio sat on a blanket and drank champagne, Dede ran along a beach of pink sands, collecting shells. Would Silvio have his plane out now, searching the coast? Would Johnnie Angel be looking, driving his car along the highway, walking the beaches, looking for any trace, a dropped necklace, a note she scrawled in the sand? Johnnie Angel had told Dede more than once that he'd die without her. That if he couldn't be near her, his heart would just shrivel up and turn to dust. He loves her that much that he just can't help it.

Harmony ignores the buzz of the planes; she finishes the shoes and holds them out for Dede to try. The final version looks much better than expected, and when she jimmies them on, ties them up tight, they are pretty comfortable, like fitted socks with a hard sole. She gives Harmony a quick hug.

"Child." Harmony touches her cheek. "Go on, now. You've got a few minutes to say goodbye before the planes circle back this way."

In the backyard, she calls, "Here Tuppence. Here boys."

No barking, no rushing, yapping. She walks over to the laundry rock. "Puppy, puppies." Still nothing. Over near the bush, where they like to nestle in the day's heat, a shadow slinks into the undergrowth.

"Tuppence?"

A growl. Dede can't tell if it is her. "Easy girl; I brought you a treat." She holds out a hand with a small bread offering. Waits. Takes a step forward. Do they hate the smell of her dyed hair? Not recognize her in the new clothes and cap? Or maybe they sense Dede is deserting them already; maybe they've hardened their hearts. Another growl, louder this time, then a large brown dog rushes through the saw palmetto, teeth bared, and disappears in the bush.

Dede throws the bread after it. "Stupid bloody mutts. Don't even know who your friends are."

In the front yard, Harmony tosses corn to the hens, then wipes off her hand. "You fixed and ready to leave?"

Dede kicks a rock. Puppies didn't care a damn about her leaving. Stupid tears again, and she swipes at them. "They wouldn't come out for their food. A big dog growled at me."

"They survivors, Dede. Potcakes born that way. Don't take it personal." She hands Dede a flask to carry, while she hitches a sack over her shoulder. "Come on now. No self-sorries. We got miles to mark before the dark downs us."

As they pass by the shed, Harmony grabs a machete, and then leads them along the orchard path. At the last tree before the vegetable patch, she slashes off a branch of geneps and tosses them in her sack. Then she edges around the garden, pushes out onto a half-hidden trail. An old mule route, she says. Uncle Harcourt pulled his team to the sisal plantation this way, back in the day. Two miles to the crops, then two miles back. They'd be going farther—more than six miles to town this way. Harmony says that when she was young, younger than Dede's age, she'd race through here, following Uncle Harcourt and the mules, hopping onto the cart when she got tired. But no one used it anymore. Not since the Contract pulled most of the men from the Bight.

Wheels have rutted the rocky base of the path; a few plants spike the midline. Red ant colonies throng and thin every few yards. Dede is glad for the makeshift shoes. Overhead, branches meet and tangle together; love vines braid the canopy, making the route seem more like a tunnel than a road, too narrow for side-by-side travel. Dede follows close behind Harmony. About a half-hour into the walk, another plane buzzes overhead; it swoops so close Dede feels that she could raise up a hand and touch it. Through the trees and vines, she sees flashes of its silver underbelly. Harmony keeps walking at her steady, long-stride pace.

"They gonna be searching for you all day most like, and they won't stop till sunset. So, we gotta be clever and hide best we can."

"Is that why we're walking inland instead of taking the easy road?"

Harmony doesn't bother answering, just picks up the pace.

The bush thickens and Harmony begins to swing the machete blade out in front of her, then uses her body to clear branches and vines. Her arms and legs bleed, but she keeps going at a good clip, hacking and pulling and sweating and swearing. Her smell trails behind her, like fermented fruit. Dede's underarms smell too, like puppy pee. Or maybe it is the dripping hair dye. She is getting thirsty, still not hungry, but what she mostly wants is a bath. A warm bath and her favorite nightie and one of those boarding schoolbooks. *Tilly's Great Adventure* or *Pippa Gets Lost in the Jungle*.

They've been walking for what must be over an hour when the bush thins out; before them, an open field, plants push up in rows, blades dark green and sharp enough to slice a finger.

"Teh Kinset," Harmony says. "The old plantation." She pulls a thin cotton blanket out of her pack and spreads it on a bare patch at the edge of the field. "Quench?" They sit side by side and swig from the water jug. Harmony finds the loaf and breaks off a chunk, picks a genep from the bunch she packed, puts it in her mouth and works off the peel, spits out the green, and sucks on the yellow flesh. Her eyes rove up and down the half-hidden rows. She spits seeds into the bush behind them.

"Back in the day, all the men burned this here bush and turned the soil, buried them little shoots, them little spark-tops, buried them down in the black and they growed good here, in the sun and the rain and the island heat. Nine months, maybe more, then the men and the oldest boys, they cut off the barbs, and stripped the leaves, washed the leaves in the bay. When they dried out, we helped load bundles on the dray. The mule hauled the dray to town."

Dede starts to ask questions, What's a dray? What happened to the mule? But Harmony's eyes stare off across the abandoned field.

"Harmony?" Her squinty look scares Dede. "You see someone out there? What is it?"

"Hard work, sisal. Then no one wanted to buy it no more. Most men folk gone off on the Contract. My Momma dead from birthing me, so that left Aggie in charge, left her in charge of me and all the brothers when she only twelve herself. Uncle Harcourt helped us of course. The boys grew up and left, can't blame them, I suppose." Harmony shakes her head and packs up the picnic, tosses peels and seeds deep into the bush.

"Why doesn't your son come back to visit?"

Harmony looks as if Dede has smacked her cheek.

"No one comes back to Callow Cay. No sense hoping things different then they are. Now get the water and come on."

She leads them long-ways through the plantation; they skirt the agave fields to stay away from the sharp plants and stay close to the bush cover. They walk maybe another mile, maybe two, quick-paced, no talking, the fields changing to pine-studded bush, the bush to scrub-dotted limestone. Harmony stops at the edge of a rocky plain.

To the west, above the pine line, the sky weaves strands of orange and red and gold. Dede strains her ears but can hear only jungle thrumming: birds shrieking, insects buzzing, tree frogs glugging. Harmony says all the planes have probably gone for the night—have to land before sundown.

"Over that way," she says, pointing ahead and to the left, "through the bush there is the road to town. Tomorrow morning early, we'll head into the harbor, get going before the fishermen. Right now, we got to set you up at the resting spot. You can set there awhile, while I head into Hard Bargain and find us a boat."

She starts to walk across the wide-open rock to their right, looks back over her shoulder. Dede feels timid, exposed after two hours under the jungle canopy. Harmony walks a few yards ahead and up a slight incline. "Come on, now. Planes gone and we are almost there. You can rest in another while. Got us a fine spot for some recuperations."

The homemade sandals have lasted well, but Dede has blisters blooming on both heels beneath the straps. She is more than ready to sit. Shells stud the limestone flat. An old reef? Didn't she read once that all these islands were reefs risen out of the sea?

Harmony stops and as Dede catches up, she reaches her arm. "Steady now." Two steps ahead the edge of a drop. Beneath them, maybe twenty feet down, a perfect aqua circle, as if some giant has speared through the rock bed, deep and deeper, puncturing through layer after layer of limestone, until dark water bubbled up and filled the hole.

"You ever see a blue hole before?"

Dede shakes her head.

"That hole drops deeper than anyone knows." Harmony says. "And the walls all around it, holding the blue, they made of bones and skeletons. Crazy mystery how the ocean creatures make up this land we standing on. This island nothing except layer upon layer of past lives, and you and me here standing and breathing on our ancestors' bodies and memories."

Dede feels cool coming up off the water, cool rising up the craggy walls, cool blowing in and out of the crags and crevices that lace the rocky walls. Heat rises, she learned in school, cold air falls. But here in this topsy-turvy island, cool blows up at her, as if blasted from a fan. Cool air and cooler water beckon her like a beautiful blue death.

"Don't that feel nice, now?"

"What is this place?"

"Anne Bonny's Hideout." Harmony says. "Ever hear of that lady pirate? Got herself caught with Calico Jack Rackham and sentenced to hang beside him, but she caught a baby in her, so the Governor took mercy. She fled Nassau and landed here, and her children's children and their trickle-down families still live on the island, fiery and red-haired like their mama." Harmony laughs. "I suppose I got some pirate in me too."

She points to the other side of the water. "See those caves over there—in that wall? When Betsy came, it was Market Day in the town and devil winds roared over the island, tore roofs off, pulled solid trees right out the ground. Most everyone from Hard Bargain ran inland, many of the people from town come right here. Maybe fifty souls huddled in those walls for three days. Most all survived."

She doesn't need to say, everyone except Aggie. Dede can read the memory running across Harmony's face.

They walk around the edge of the cliff wall, then scramble down a rocky route, over small rocks, and large boulders, to the mouth of the caves. They are six feet below the rocky plain they crossed, ten feet or more above the water. They step into the dark chamber, Dede's eyes trying to adjust. Harmony runs her hand on the craggy walls. "Inside here we was safe but the roaring got louder than any noise can be." She reaches out for Dede's hand, guides her farther into the cave, pointing out the side wall where lines, dots... words maybe... are scratched in the limestone; it looks like inverted Braille and Dede runs her fingers over each indentation and furrow, as if she can pull meaning from what is missing. The place feels like a church, not the kind of place to move things around or ask too many questions. Deeper inside the cave where dim gives into darkness, three large rock slabs form a makeshift table. Harmony drops her sack and unpacks all the provisions: A towel, a change of clothes, food, even some fritters wrapped in a napkin. More water.

"I got to leave you here go on into town. Two hours top until I come back round." She finds her small tobacco tin and rattles the conch pearls. "These should get us a real fine boat, get us over to Nassau in no time. So, you set here and eat, then try to rest in the cool until I get back. You safe here, Dede."

"Can't I go with you?" Dede imagines Anne Bonny wandering around the blue hole, venturing into the cave, lost and angry, wanting revenge. No telling who she might want to hurt.

Harmony shakes her head. "End of Market Day and the folk gonna stay in town, eat and drink and talk. They see you, even with your cap, and your boy clothes, you show up strange in their eyes. They gonna ask questions. They gonna speculate. You safe here waiting till I get back, then tomorrow we gonna walk to the harbor early, get on our boat and get us away before folks start their day."

"What if someone comes here while you're gone?"

"No one comes this way no more. And you safe here in the cave.

You scared in here? Take one of these for your own." She opens the tin and places a bumpy shape in Dede's hand. "This pearl is gonna keep you protected. You be just fine here."

Even with ghosts? Pirate ghosts? Dede swallows hard, tries to find a brave face as Harmony packs a water bottle for herself, stuffs it back in the sack. Dede follows her back outside as she gives final instructions. "Stay by the cave, down low and out of sight, and don't go near that water."

Dede nods. She sits at the cave's entrance and watches Harmony scramble back up the boulders and disappear. It's okay, she reminds herself, you are used to being alone. All those nights in the flat. You can do this. But she won't go back in that cave. It's too dark and full of ghosts. She scrambles back up to the upper edge of the blue hole. When she looks at the water, its inky center is like no color she's seen in the ocean before. She wants to touch it, such a broken-hearted blue. She sits on a flat rock, takes off her cap and sandals, and dangles her feet above the water. She shakes her wrist, the watch still stuck at 6:46. How long has she been gone from home? It's evening time, after sunset, so Mum must be getting ready for work, putting on her uniform, brushing her beautiful blonde hair, slipping on her comfortable heels. Dede tries to finger-comb her own hair, but it's disgusting from the paste. Everything she is, everything she does, patchwork and makeshift, a disappointment to her beautiful mother. And now her shame.

She picks up a clump of limestone and hurls it into the water, imagines it sinking below the surface, down past bone-coral and coral-bone, through a narrow black tunnel to another world. Another world. A way to start over in a different place. That's what Anne Bonny did. Was that what Harmony was trying to buy for her? A boat ride to a whole new life. How could that ever work? The sky above fades from the day's translucent blue to the color of forgetting. If she could lose herself in that gray—forget the images in her brain. She grips the pearl in her palm. Closes her eyes. She hears a rumble. The sky is too dark now for small planes. She squeezes her eyes tighter, hums to herself. *Run come see Jerusalem. Run come see Jerusalem.* But the rumbling gets louder. Maybe it's a truck on the road to town, its sound carried through the porous limestone. Or maybe it's coming for her. She pushes herself up to standing, tired from the day, the days, the heat, the worry, and she stands on the edge of the blue hole. She cannot stay here. She cannot go home. This is the loneliest alone she can remember. She makes herself move—shaking out her arms and legs, twisting her neck both ways till it cracks. Then she begins to walk the rocky perimeter. Clumps of limestone and rock press into her bare feet and she's grateful for pinpricks of pain. How many times could she walk this perimeter before Harmony returns? What is the circumference of the blue hole? Circumference equals pi times diameter. Geometry seems a thousand years ago. She walks around the edge of the circle, singing out slices of pi: Three point one four one five nine, this is Pi, followed by, two six five three five eight nine... Her heart is racing. What if Harmony never comes back? Maybe Dede should leave now. Where would she go? Harmony said to stay in the cave. She said she'd be back. Directly, she said, but she is long gone now. An hour? It could be more. Why would she trust her to return? Mum said stay inside at night. She'd be home in the morning. Johnnie Angel said this is what you like. I would never hurt you; I would never, ever hurt you.

She sees a shape standing on the rocky plateau. A ghost. A man. A white man. "Dede," he yells. "Don't move, I'm coming."

No. No. Get away. She scurries lower down the rock wall, stops on a ledge, peers into the water below. Her toes grip the edge.

The white man is stumbling, running, stumbling towards her. "Wait," he yells, "Domini, wait. It's okay, I won't hurt you."

Never, ever.

She closes her eyes, counts to three, and dives. The water swallows her, wrapping her in a delicious cool and she propels herself with butterfly kicks forward and up to the surface. She swims, still gripping the pearl in her right hand, swimming toward the middle, swimming and counting, counting and swimming, seventy-five full strokes to what must be the center. When she stops and treads water, shivers rise up her feet and calves and into her thighs. Water between her legs, finding her shame. Wherever Dede goes for the rest of her life, wherever she lives, the shame will burn inside her.

She stops treading water, lets her legs go vertical, points her toes, streamlines her arms above her head, lets her body sink arrow straight. When the saltwater holds her up—too buoyant—she flips over and makes herself swim headfirst, arms pulling her down, her lungs squeezing tight, her ears popping, the walls narrowing, closing in around her. She pulls another stroke. And another. If she dies here, she will become a skeleton turned to coral. Her shame fossilized inside her. She takes another stroke, deeper still, the pressure in her ears, the water in her mouth, burning her throat, filling her lungs. She closes her eyes and drops the pearl so she can take one more urgent stroke into blackness.

But then hands grab at her, from below or above, or maybe from the walls, hands on her ankles and now her arms, thick arms circling around her chest, squeezing her body, pulling her out of one story and back into another.

CHAPTER 16

The jungle spits Harmony out on the coastal road a mile shy of town. Empty both ways. Market day traffic long gone now. Behind her, sky dusks the bush; trees and scrub and tangled vines hiding under a soft grey blanket, but out over the bay, the sun hovers blood-orange, all proud, all look at me.

One minute can't hurt. One minute to catch her breath, rest her torn and tattered feet, one minute before the next dread part—wheeling-dealing in town for a boat. If anyone still at the docks. The girl would be safe in the cave with food and drink. She'd be okay for a while. Sun says near eight o'clock now. Been a long time since Harmony was in Hard Bargain past stall closing. Been a longer time since she did any kind of bartering. What she has to offer today is more than nothing, but would any right-headed fisherman turn over his boat to a chewed-up island woman hauling a Georgie bundle of pearls?

Doubts pull at her ankles, slowing her worse than the yellow vines that tripped her all day in the bush. Shins slashed bloody, not as bad as the girl's, though. Dede would need some tending later. Sisal juice good for that, but Harmony hadn't cut spears where they grew tall, back at the old plantation. Maybe some shooting up wild around the caves; she'd find them later and treat the girl.

Harmony crosses the concrete road, scramble-falls down the bank and onto the beach; there, she squats like she's bean-picking until her aching knees force her boongy flat on sand, Lord, eyes dried out, legs spread wide. So tired. More so since worry mixing with the usual aches and pains. Thirsty, too. She reaches in her sack, pulls out and uncorks the bottle, swills an inch of water—warm as soup, but still, she's glad for it. Six hours in the bush will do that—make you fool glad for simple things, like puh-toohey water.

Had she left the girl enough to drink? That half bottle of quench won't last long. Harmony'd forgotten how an afternoon jungle works the body; how tired and thirsty can dredge up doubt even in a sound mind. And what about food? Would half a loaf, plus four or five of them geneps be enough to feed her and the one growing inside? The girl knows how to find cocoplums if she gets desperate...but maybe she'd be too frightened to leave the cave. And she'd never find fresh quench out there. Hard Bargain got its name because sweet water so scarce people be trading their everything for it. Oh Lord. Harmony worries, of course, about leaving a girl alone, but she couldn't see another way round it. How could she walk a skinny white child into town? Even disguised. People talk and talk, the children asking who's that with Miss Harmony? Grown folks knowing she got no kin left on the island. And if people talking... Captain Albury'd be there in a flash. That white man and his boys always listening to island talk, always working themselves into some situation. Calling the police out on Clementina's idiot boy just cause he playing on the radio. Reporting Avery Nottage for taking that old car and trying to fix it. Weren't enough they run the mailboats, run the harbor, they got to get in the peoples' lives, Lord.

Best stick with the plan—or at least, the half of a plan she got: get into town and see about a boat. Steer clear of folk all the way in.

And what if no one gonna rent you a boat?

Oh Aggie, always showing holes in my big ideas. Truth is, I don't even know what I'm going to do. Even if I get a boat from some fool-needs-the-money, even if I get him to take me and the girl to Nassau, I got no idea what come next. Just walk up and down Bay Street till I find the brothers? I sense my Fulcrum's long gone from those parts.

Sure got yourself in a pucketery this time.

Seems like trouble just found me, Aggie. Just walked out of the shallow seas, crossed the sand, stumbled up the path and tapped me on the shoulder.

Shoot, Harmony. You opened up the door, caught trouble in your arms. Gave that little girl a cowboy bath and a bed to sleep in. Can't pretend like she ain't your worry now.

The sun sinks another inch. Harmony stares at the edge of the world—a purple-grey thread trims the black sea. She doesn't blink, doesn't want to miss it. How many nights had she and Aggie, chores-done, bellies full of rice and pigeon peas, stood side-by-side where all the waters meet, waiting for this moment? She strains her ears now, listening for the *pssht*.

So even if you get to Nassau… what you gonna do then? Drop her off with some family you ain't seen in years and you be done? Like you was done with Fulcrum when he left Callow Cay? Why you let go of everyone you love?

Aggie's words like needles in her heart. Harmony sighs so loud she surprises herself. Fulcrum gone. All her brothers before him.

Her father before them. And her own mother dead before Harmony full on born. In the hungry weeks after Hurricane Betsy hit the Cay, after wind and water took Aggie and all the family homes, Crusader begged Harmony to leave the Bight. Move to Nassau with the rest of the family. Not worth taking government money to rebuild a shack that the next hurricane going to blow down anyways. She shook her head, then and now, at the old voices, at so many boys always telling her what to do. Telling her what she wanted to do. She wanted to stay.

"It's my mind." She says to the ocean, to the setting sun. She wants Aggie to hear her now, too. "My own choice, Aggie, to stay here with you, to keep us woven together."

Harmony is tired, yes, tired from her walk, and tired from worrying about the girl and how to do right by her, but she's not tired of this island. She will never tire of the thrumming bush in the early morning; waters spreading blue and green and slip-silver in the midday sun; and how many sunsets like this does any person have in life? Harmony isn't miserable, not close to it. Not poor. Not starving. Gets what she needs from the land and the sea and the market. What she doesn't have, she doesn't need. What does she want, save for now and then, a little more company? She misses the brothers some, all right, and misses Fulcrum hard—especially when he first gone. But she's always had this place. She still has Aggie.

Feels good to have the girl though, don't it? Someone real to talk to, someone live like you.

You still real to me, Aggie. Don't pretend you ain't.

Why not go with her? You're woven with her too now.

Harmony closes her eyes. Mosquitoes jazz her face and arms, smelling sweat and opportunity. She swats her arm blind. She would

205

never leave this land. She isn't like her father, her uncles and aunties, her brothers or even her son. She would never leave Aggie here alone. When she opens her eyes again, the sun has already dipped itself into the sea.

"I missed it again, Aggie. Tried to see it, tried to hear the pssht. I really did. Don't that trying get me something?"

Get you disappointed and bug-bit is all. Now get yourself up and figure this thing out.

No matter how old Harmony gets, Aggie still gonna be her know-it-all bossy big sister, never could bide doubts and excuses.

Harmony pushes herself to her feet, scrambles back up the bank and onto the road, continues walking north toward town. All right. She'd get the boat. Get the child over to Nassau. Get her to Bay Street, where Crusader, last she heard, is a storeowner, *a civic leader* he called himself in the postcards he sent. If he true-talking, then maybe he could get something sorted for the girl. Find her a place to stay, a white doctor, too, when she needed it. Maybe he and some of his boys would even take care of the man that done this to Dede.

She moves quicker now, easier going on the coast road, without the bush grabbing at her shins and shoulders, with her doubts stamped down for a while. Swings her arms, a trick that Thaddeus taught back when they were kids. Even when the legs get tired, the feet get dragging, you fool them into moving if you swing the arms. Right, left, right, left. Just swing. That's the way. North a half mile and round another two curves, to Mule Point. At this pace, she'll be in town before hard night. Still her feet hurt, all pounded out from the path; her ankles too, pounded, picked and pocked from plants and insects. Truth is, she can't hoof it like a pack mule anymore.

Truth is, you turned soft.

Harmony laughs in spite of herself.

Ten years I been gone, and you turned into an old lady. Moaning and groaning like you almost dead. Where that solid little mama who birthed herself a baby boy out on laundry rock? What happened to that tough woman knocked Joe Bethel's lights out when he rumored things about her son?

Harmony shuts her brain off, blocks out Aggie's tomfooling, hoofs five more minutes up the road. She passes the hitching post. No one ties mules here these days. The cross-rail grey and splintered. Market Day traffic is now all trucks, scooters, a few bicycles with baskets. In the sand near the picnic table, a Coca Cola can, a chicken carcass, potato chip bags. Someone lunched here on the way back from market. Bones still fresh with meat, not dried out yet. Potcakes will clean them up soon enough—probably eat bones and the can, too, if they get half a chance. More goats than dogs, truly. Harmony feels near as hungry. She longs for her chair, a bowl of hot rice and fresh relish. All right, maybe she has grown soft and old. Body and feet sensitive because most market days now she rides into town with Clementina in that ugly piece of equipment. What else is she going to do, though, at fifty-plus some? Walk by herself, every week, both ways? And Clemmy always chit-chat-chitting about that idiot son of hers, as if she can't remember Harmony's lost her own boy; as if she can't understand Harmony bored out of her mind hearing about Bertram's doings. How he got three radios in his momma's house; how he listening always to fishermen and pilots and police and fig-uring out who doing what where. Makes Harmony want to say, if that boy of yours is so clever, why he still living with you, Bight-side? Why he eavesdropping on working peoples' conversations? Why the police come calling twice last year? Least Fulcrum been curious enough to leave.

Beyond Mule Point Bay, less than quarter mile from town, a half-dozen potcakes slide out of the sea grape bushes and trail Harmony, like her disappointments. As she nears the first row of houses on the edge of Hard Bargain, she turns to yell, "Go on, get." But the only language town-mutts understand is rocks coming hard and fast and she doesn't have that in her. Harmony always been too easy on animals. And children. So, she keeps walking, ignoring the dogs as they get bolder, move in closer. She makes it to the half-broke fence around Avery Nottage's place. Or rather, his boy's place. Avery been dead since soon after Betsy, too, and the boy—what's his name? Bain?... He not like his father with the upkeep. Tin cans flash in the dirt. An old truck rusting up on blocks. Two snot-nosed kids—Bain's boys or his sister's—sit under the laden clothesline, drawing with sticks. When they see the potcakes trailing Harmony, they race to the fence, screaming. "Yah, yah, yah." One boy banging a stick on a can. The other tossing chunks of coral. "Get outta here you uglies mugglies."

Dogs turn and run.

The older boy stops, wipes his grubby face with the back of his wrist. "Evening, Miss Knowles."

Harmony keeps walking. "Evening, young man. Say hello to your grandmother for me." Pleasant Nottage losing her mind, folks saying around town, ever since Avery gone. Every rainstorm since Betsy like to put her in a fit. Hurricane season hell for the poor woman.

"Yes, ma'am. I'll tell her." He whispers something else under his breath and both boys laugh. She feels their eyes on her as she passes two more yards, turns the corner and heads toward the square.

No cars or mopeds gunning around this evening, just a couple of old fellas on bikes, a tall man leaning against Sam's store, smoking a cigar, looks like Chauncey Tynes from back in the day, when he still tall and handsome, before he met the white girl from Hope Town and turned into a sick, old fool from all the longing.

On closer look, it isn't him.

All the stalls are folded up, all the fresh gone from the square, save for a few mango pips scattered in the dirt. She's timed it right, after all, waiting for night fall. Fewer folks that see her in town the better. No one likely to blab to Captain Albury. The tall man not Chauncey didn't even acknowledge her when she passed by, which is good, even if it means people not as friendly as they used to be in Hard Bargain; used to be everyone said hello even when they can't remember your name or don't know your face.

She walks toward the harbor, hoping she isn't too late to catch some fella still working on a fishing boat. Someone who might help her out. At the start of the short pier, Obie Meadows sits on a wooden crate beside his chowder pot, fire beneath it close to dud. He sucks on a bottle, stares out at the blackened sea.

"Harmony," He crooks his neck and scratches an unshaved cheek. Always been something hound-dog in his face, eyelids slung low, cheeks big and jowly like he chewing leaves. He smells of fish and pepper and stale brew. There's five or six empties by his crate. But Mr. Meadows handles himself better boiled than many men do sober. Hadn't he straightened out Uncle Harcourt once or twice after Market Day bartering led to drinking and drinking led to fighting?

"Your legs all torn up, there." He points with the bottle and waits for an explanation.

The lines she's rehearsed stick in her throat.

"How's business, Mr. Meadows?"

"No use in complaining." He takes the top off his pot. "Chowder near gone. Suppose I got one more serving if you wanting it."

Harmony can smell the green peppers and onions, tomatoes and some of the day's best relish in there, no question. He always pulled the finest fish off the docks first thing in the morning, prepped and cooked it right there. Grouper, most like. Always plenty of conch, too, of course. A pile of shells next to the pot. Lord, she is hungry, but she can't take time to eat now. Not with the girl waiting alone. Night comes black in the middle of the bush.

"I'm well fed, thank you. Here and wondering though, where would I find me a boat for tomorrow."

"What you want with a boat?"

Harmony shifts from foot to foot. This man's known her since before she knew herself. Even though he is drunk, that's his steady state; he'll feel her lying right away. Still, no point telling the whole truth neither.

"I got me a situation, Mr. Meadows. Need to get over to Nassau fast-like. See my own family. Need me a boat and a clear-headed, close-mouthed skipper for about a day or two. Can't talk much about it, you understand."

"Can't you wait for the mail boat on Friday?"

"No sir. This closer to an emergency."

"You all right, Harmony?"

"I am. I truly am. Just... needing to fix some things with my brothers directly. You know families." She shakes her head again, hoping he'll commiserate.

He probably won't because he always been bottle-lonely. Still, he nods. "Clear-headed, close-mouthed, you say? That rules out Albury and all his big-talk white boys. They'd be an easy hire,

210

course, and the boys with their fishing fleet always hungry for money, but they been gone all day off on some search. Maybe you seen them racing up and down the island in trucks and cars and boats like they found Blackbeard's treasure. Sea rescue planes out, too. S'pose you heard them?"

Harmony shows him nothing. Doesn't trust herself to act interested, ask questions. Doesn't know what he'll think if she stays silent. "I heard them, sure 'nough. But what they looking for?"

"Adventure, I suppose." Meadows shrugs, takes a long pull to empty his bottle, and wipes the back of his hand across his mouth. He sets his empty down. "Them Whitsun boys chugged into harbor just a half-hour ago. Long day out on the water. They still cleaning up their boats—they good fellas. Hard workers and eager to make a dollar. Dock off the long pier if you want to give them a try."

"You're too kind." She turns again on her torn, tired feet, and listens for his usual goodbye.

"Take care of yourself, Harmony Hibiscus. I knew your Daddy."

She doesn't want to walk past Red Beard's, but no other way to get to the long pier. The air rum-sticky before she gets close enough to see the crowd. The drinking and the drunk fill the rickety balcony; their talk and laughter spilling out on the street. She puts her head down, shields her face, as she hurries past. Doesn't want to get seen by anyone and doesn't want to get caught in the old stuff neither. Memories like the top of the sea—glints of green, specks of blue glimmering at you—but who knew what waited down deep? Between Callow Cay and Nassau, an underwater canyon ran deeper than deep. The Tongue of the Ocean and thousands of souls drowned and buried in those waters, ghost hands and ghost memories always reaching for the living.

At the end of the long pier, a young man stands beside the petrol pump, filling the tank on his boat. Tall, reddish-brown curls press tight across his scalp, he smiles big as Harmony approaches.

"You Virgil Whitsun's boy?"

"One of them." He extends his free hand. "Virgil, Junior."

"You don't remember me, do you? I'm Harmony Knowles. I knowed your Daddy, back in the day. We good friends at one point in time." A small lie might help her cause.

"Yes ma'am, Miss Knowles," he pretends to recall. They do the exchanges. His parents now living out near Adelaide. Retired or close to it. Virgil, Junior, and his twin, Homer, still fishing up a living, deep water off the Abacos with American tourists; lately, got a flat boat for some bone fishing too, around Callow Cay—a growing business. Rich white men loved it. Bone fish in the shallow seas as common and as hard to hold as dreams.

"I'm looking for a boat tomorrow morning," Harmony says. "Early. Gotta get my grandson over to Nassau. Visiting all week now, but got to get back home to his Daddy, fore he like to drive me crazy." She laughs as true as she can. "Can't be waiting on Friday's mail boat. Any chance you can help me out, Virgil, Junior. I'll pay good enough, of course I will."

He eyes her curiously, one eyebrow tilting like he not believing much of what she said no how. Why would he?

"How much you need make it worth your while?"

"Need to pay for my petrol. And make up for my time not fishing, not earning. Thirty dollars let's say for one day there and back. Time gonna be near six hours in one day if the weather hold. If you need me overnight and for a second day, then sixty all told."

He must know he's asking a fortune. Maybe this his way of saying

212

no, can't be doing favors, for some Bight-side nobody his Daddy once knew but he sure can't remember.

"Well, here's the thing, Virgil Junior," Harmony reaches in her Georgie bundle. "I got a $5 bill I can give you right now," she says. "Not much, I know. But then, there's this here, too." She opens the tin.

Virgil closes in for a look. "Oh, Lord. They conch pearls?"

"Good, solid color. See? Deep pink, fiery, like the ladies want them. Twenty-two here. And if you willing to keep this arrangement just between you and me, then we can sell them once we get to Nassau. My brother Crusader knows all of them new Bay Street jewelers. We get them to value up these pearls, and I give you half of whatever they worth."

"May I?" Virgil picks up a pearl, rolls it between his thumb and finger. "How long you been collecting?"

"A good long time now."

"Ten years of daily fishing, a lifetime on these waters, and I never found one. Where you find them at Miss Harmony?"

She smiles. She has him. "Can't say I remember, exactly. Not now, at least. But meet me here just before sunrise ready to go. Bring some fresh quench, and maybe a little food. And if you can keep all this close to you then half of all these are yours. Half these pearls are yours, Virgil Junior, and well earned."

"And your spot? Tell me your conch spot and we got ourselves a deal."

"You get me to Nassau and back first. Then we talk about the source."

"All right then." He extends his hand again.

Harmony takes it. "You drive a tough bargain, like your old Daddy did. I'll see you tomorrow."

She puts the tin back in the bundle, turns to walk back to the girl. She'll stop for water, maybe at the Nottages. If she swings her arms again, if she sings herself a marching song, she'll make it fast, make it back to Dede long before sleeping time. Another mile, maybe a mile and a bit; she can handle. And tomorrow, tomorrow, she and Dede finish what they started today. Walk one step after the next, keep on going, climb on the boat and work the troubles out.

You think so, Aggie?

But she gone quiet. What you not saying, Aggie?

Harmony's on the outskirts of town, not quite at Mule's Bay, when she hears an engine revving, tires screeching and headlamps in the distance, coming toward her from the south. One of them market-day drunks? She raises her hand, shields her eyes, and steps off to the side. The truck comes fast round the turn. Maybe he doesn't see her? She takes another step back onto the verge. If the driver notices her, he doesn't slow. But she sees him, yes, she sees Captain Albury. Just a flash, but it's him all right, wide white face glistening through the windscreen, fishing cap on his head, usual cigarette stuck on his bottom lip. And next to him on the seat, Lord, a boy, no, no, Dede. She is bouncing around from the speed and the bumps, one hand pressed against the glass, her eyes meet Harmony's for a desperate second before the truck rounds the corner.

PART III

FREEPORT, GRAND BAHAMA ISLAND
AND
FORT LAUDERDALE, FLORIDA

1976 - 1977

CHAPTER 17

There was no way Ethel could leave Freeport while Dede was still missing. She'd told Nora during their phone call on Sunday that the girl was lost. It was all they talked about, and Nora was concerned and caring, asking all the right questions, saying all the right things. But would she understand if Ethel delayed her flight—scheduled for Saturday, in three days' time—or would she see this as another evasion, a familiar and annoying indecision? Ethel bailing out again. They'd planned to spend a fortnight together before Nora's autumn term started at Red Maids. Time in London at the outset, including a day at the Tate Britain (the Turner Collection, Ethel's demand), then a drive to Nora's family's holiday home in Aberdyfy for a week. At the end, they'd return to Bristol, settle into the cottage, leaving several days to talk without interruption and, yes, to come up with a decision. They both agreed that they needed to decide. Move forward together or let one another go.

That evening in her studio, Ethel had success shaping corals out of a revised clay recipe. Firm, but malleable, holding shape even as she rolled out the lengthy antlers of a stag coral. She gathered her tools to rinse off with the hose outside and checked the kitchen clock as she passed: 8:15 p.m. Too early in Nora's world for a call. She'd leave it until tomorrow. Nora might be frustrated with a postponement of their holiday, but she'd understand. She'd met Dede, after all, she knew Ethel cared for the girl.

After a light, late supper—toast and jam, and a cup of weak tea, her spinster special—she decided to start a load of washing. Around 11 p.m. as she was in the laundry room, switching from washer to dryer, Anita showed up out of nowhere.

"Dede—she's been found, she's alive. She's all right!"

Ethel dropped a lump of wet clothes on the tile. "Jesus. You startled me…"

"Sorry. Sorry. But I had to find you, to tell you. I knocked on your door, then I saw the light on in here. Dede's been found. She's safe."

Ethel took a step back, leaned against the washing machine. Her heart raced from the scare, from this news. "Where is she? Who found her? Tell me."

"A man—a Captain Albury—he heard the radio alerts over the weekend and then someone found the boat on a sandbar and the Captain, somehow, he tracked her down just a couple of hours ago. She's in Marsh Harbor now—at his home, resting." Anita grabbed her hands. "She's okay, Ethel."

"Oh, Sweet Lord Jesus. Did you talk to her?"

Anita shook her head. "She was asleep when Silvio got the call from the police. But he's going to fly me over first thing in the morning."

What to say? What to feel? Relief? Joy? Nothing. Ethel felt numb. She tried to take inventory of her emotions, but Anita was everywhere, talking, crying, spilling emotion.

"After all we've been through. The waiting, walking, wandering the beach. Four days. It's a bloody miracle. I thought we'd lost her, Ethel. Honestly, I was readying myself for the worst. That's why I had to let you know tonight. You've been such a support to me. Sorry, again, for startling you."

Ethel pulled her hands from Anita's grip. "Where was she found? What island?"

"I don't even know the name. So many cays, aren't there? I'm not sure which one. I think west of Great Abaco—near where they found the Hobie Cat."

Ethel bent down and picked up the clothes she'd dropped, tossed them in the dryer. The Abacos? Dede would have had to survive what forty, sixty or more miles on the open sea. In a storm. Could she have done that? And then made it another three or four days on her own? She must have found fresh water, somewhere. Shelter, too, from the sun, the elements. Jesus. Ethel shook her head, tried to calm her own breathing, turned, and closed the dryer door, then faced Anita again.

"I am so relieved." Sometimes saying things made them true, and if she couldn't feel relief yet, well, maybe it was because she had been preparing for the worst. Maybe she needed to lay eyes on the girl. Watch her again in the pool. See her sitting on the deck with her nose in a book. Hear her annoying prattle. "And you're sure she's all right?"

"Domini's a tough little nut. She'll be fine once we get her home. Her father was supposed to come this weekend if we'd had no more news." She put a conspiratorial hand on Ethel's forearm. "I don't know what I'd have done if he'd actually showed up. Don't know how I would have handled it. With Silvio and all. We haven't had a proper talk in... well, years. But Domini's found, she's safe, and things can go back to normal."

Ethel didn't know what to say. Normal? Was she joking? And now words threatened to spill out angry and uncharitable. You careless slip of a woman. If you had done your job in the first place none of this would have happened, anger coming fast and furious, like a freak wave. She swallowed it back.

"I'm glad you told me. We'll all sleep better tonight."

Back in her flat, Ethel laid her clean tools out on a towel in her studio, began to prepare her clay for tomorrow, carrying a pail of slurry outside and pouring it through the strainer. Could Dede really be sleeping safely in some stranger's house? How could her mother be so vague about where she'd been found? Ethel remembered the map that she had buried somewhere in her desk. She wanted, needed, to picture Dede's route, figure out how she'd survived, and see where she was right now.

She rummaged through the drawers: A jumble of notes and pencils, half-finished sketches, a box full of different corals that she'd used recently as models, and there, under a cookbook put together by students at Sunland (she'd paid Dede $2 for it), she found the map. Unfolded, spread out on her desktop, it showed all the islands, the tiny no-name cays, as well as the surrounding waters, the shallow seas, and the underwater canyons. She traced the bow-shaped Abaco archipelago, from Crown Haven in the north down to Hole in the Wall on the southern tip. Only two or three named landforms were dropped west of the chain: Moore's Island and Gorda Cay, along with a handful of smaller, presumably uninhabited cays and sandbars. If Dede's boat had hit one of those dots, well, that was some kind of miracle. Had she drifted past them, past Sandy Point at the southern tip of Abaco Island, she could have ended in the Tongue of the Ocean, the deepest trench every Bahamian child had been taught to fear. Blind Blake singing about the '29 hurricane: *thirty-three souls on the water, Swimmin' and prayin' to the Daniel God.*

She shuddered at the thought of Dede alone out there on a flimsy boat. Ethel wanted to call Nora and talk it through. Now that the girl was found—well, maybe Ethel could make the trip to England, after all. She wouldn't have to disappoint Nora yet again. Still, she'd need to call her at a more reasonable hour—tomorrow morning, or better yet, after she'd seen Dede.

Clarence. She should let him know. They hadn't spoken since the night Dede went missing but she knew from Anita that the police had talked to everyone at Coral Cove, patrolled the beach for hours. The next morning, an officer had found Dede's brown shorts, pockets full of sea glass and shells, in the dunes in front of the Ingrahams' house and Barry Ingraham soon confirmed that one of his Hobie Cats was gone. Jethro swore he never would have lent her his boat—especially not during a storm and Natalie insisted she was a trained sailor who knew better. Dede must have taken it herself. But why? Dede was not a thief, not a risk-taker.

She found the number for Coral Cove on her notepad in the kitchen, dialed and reached the front desk at the hotel and asked for Clarence. The receptionist connected her to his residence on the hotel grounds and he picked up on the first ring.

"Dede's safe," Ethel told him. "I thought you'd want to know. Some sea captain found her in the Abacos."

Clarence whistled lightly. "Well, the Lord watches after sailors, drunks, and children."

"She's supposed to arrive home tomorrow." Ethel said.

221

"With a story to tell, no doubt." Clarence said. "But she won't be so happy to see us, now, will she?"

"Meaning what?"

"Well, it's no secret she wanted to get away from Freeport. Must have told me that a hundred different ways over the past few months."

So, did he believe the police hypothesis that Dede had stolen the boat, in a stupidly dangerous attempt to run away?

"You told me that Natalie was the one hell bent on sailing that day. Dede wouldn't... I don't see her taking that risk alone."

"Natalie didn't go out on the water though, did she? Natalie was leaving Freeport and bragging about it nonstop, driving Dede crazy. Maybe Dede wanted to get off this damn island so bad that she might well have..."

"In a storm? No. I don't believe she'd be that stupid."

"Jealousy make clever people stupid."

Was this an admission? What was he saying? What wasn't he saying?

"Meaning?"

Clarence cleared his throat. "Only that some people will do anything to get away from this island. Want it so badly they're willing to hurt others, even hurt themselves, to leave."

He had to get in one more dig. But she didn't rise to the bait. Not now. She wasn't going to apologize again for all those years ago. She waited for him to find his better self, holding her tongue through a long and awkward silence.

"Well," he said at last. "Coming tomorrow, eh?"

"That's right; her mother's flying over to collect her. On her boyfriend's—Mr. Bruti's—plane."

"Kind of a coincidence, don't you think? You showing up at

Coral Cove the other day, looking for Dede and finding me instead. My mother always said coincidences be God's way of keeping anonymous."

Ethel flashed again on Jestina Lawler, sitting on a rocker, chickens pecking up the yard, all her kids and some extras sitting cross-legged in a circle in the yard, playing biddy hold fast or ring. Jestina saw Clarence and all her younger boys through school, even after her husband died. Made sure they finished high school and found real work.

"I miss your Mama. Jestina... she was always..."

"Take care of yourself, Miss Tootes."

"Clarence, wait...." But he'd already gone.

A wave of energy kept Ethel moving. She swept and mopped her kitchen, hall, and bathroom, where she'd spilled dirt and sloppy clay. Maybe when Dede got home, got settled, she'd help Ethel figure out the best spots on the island to find the right kind of soil. They'd go digging together. She emptied her pail, then mopped a second time to clean off a streaky residue on the floor. Then she showered to get the day's grunge off her, slipped on a clean tee shirt and shorts, before collecting and folding her laundry, putting it away in her bedroom dresser.

Around 12:30 a.m., she lay on her bed but still couldn't sleep. Her mind all over the place. Thinking about Dede alone in the Abacos, Clarence drinking himself into an early grave. Nora sleeping under flannel sheets in their old double-bed, windows wide open, the way she liked. Or perhaps she'd already woken. She was an early riser... was she getting excited about their upcoming holiday together? Planning the details: where they'd eat in London, the route they'd take to Wales? Nora was such a good planner—not the sort to act spontaneously. Which made her surprise visit to Freeport back in

March such a shock... a move bold enough to restart their dying, no, their moribund relationship. Five months since they'd spent that unexpected week talking, making love, planning a maybe future. And soon they'd be together again.

If Ethel were honest, if she pushed past her pride, she didn't want to be stuck in Freeport anymore. What was her life here? But she didn't have a certain answer for Nora either—what she wanted, whether she'd move back to England, how it would work if she did. So...this familiar existence, Ethel Edgecombe tapping at the edges of everything and committing to nothing.

No use fighting the thoughts knocking at her brain. She got out of bed and walked through the living room, outside, and onto the pool deck. She exhaled, blowing out her worries, then lay down on a chaise, closed her eyes. The night air thrummed—birds whispered about her past decisions and poor judgment, her never fitting in anywhere, never making friendships or building relationships that lasted. Her parents. Auntie Gert. Jestina, Clarence, the Edgecombes who'd let her take their name. She tried to shut them out, but they grew louder. What now? What now? Stay or go? Loneliness or love? Past or future? Island or England?

She heard a scuffle of feet across the courtyard. Anita again? She didn't want to talk; she still felt furious with the woman, but she opened her eyes and strained to see in the dark. Someone was dragging a large box or a sack. Doing late night laundry? No—headed in the wrong direction. Far too tall, too burly for Anita. It had to be McGuinn. She lay low, tried to blend into the lounger. He pulled alongside the tool shed. She heard metal clattering. McGuinn cursed. And Ethel knew she was seeing, hearing something she wasn't supposed to. The prickling danger she'd felt that day at the West End beach with the girl when they ran upon the drug deal. Whatever McGuinn was up to, skimming from Silvio, stealing from a unit, smuggling, he wouldn't want her nosing around. She remained immobile and quiet, watching him come and go with a few more boxes and bags from his flat to the shed, the rubbish bins, and back inside. What was he doing?

Five, ten minutes. Ethel waited, uncertain why she continued to do so. But he re-emerged again, this time with a suitcase in hand, a duffel over his shoulder, and walked around the building toward the car park.

So, was he moving out? In the middle of the night?

Ethel pushed herself up and, before she realized what she was doing, trailed him on the pavement. She heard her own voice, disembodied in the night air.

"Wait." She didn't know why she'd spoken. She saw him stop, turn around.

"Who's there?"

"Ethel," she said. "Ethel Edgecombe." She stepped off the curb. His Olds was next to her El Camino. Her heart was thumping so loudly she thought he must hear it. "Are you leaving?"

"Looks that way."

"For good?" She laughed awkwardly. "I mean, permanently?"

"Is there something you need Mrs. Edgecombe?"

"No. No. It's just that, I don't know if you heard. Dede will be home tomorrow," Ethel blurted out.

He pulled keys from his pocket. "That so?"

"They found her. She's going to be fine."

He opened the back door of his car, tossed his bags on the seat. "Well, terrific."

"Wait," she said again, without knowing why.

He climbed into the driver's seat.

She grabbed the door handle and threw out words. "Aren't you at least going to wait and see her home safe—to say a proper good-bye?"

He inserted the key, turned it, and the engine shook to life. "Doesn't look that way."

"It's just, she liked you so much." She leaned in, so her face was inches from his. In the glow of the dash lights, she watched his expression shift—from annoyance to confusion to something else. He shook off the moment and jerked the door out of her grip. She stepped back so he didn't run over her feet as he accelerated out of the lot.

Crossing back over the courtyard, she took a short-cut through the weeping fig bushes, and, stupidly, stepped down hard on something sharp—a shell or a piece of broken glass. She hopped up onto the pool deck and balanced on one foot to inspect her toe. Bleeding, definitely bleeding, but it was too dark out to tell how badly. She'd need to wash it out. She cautiously put her weight on her forefoot. Blood surged and spilled on the tile. Jesus. That's what you get for meddling in other people's affairs. What did she care if the caretaker ran off in the night? She'd always known he was a slippery sort. Her toe hurt... she had to take a look at it... hoped she didn't need stitches. Where would she even go at this time? Bloody great fool.

In her apartment, she hobbled to the bathroom and ran the water over her foot; the cut was jagged and deep and painful. She wrapped it in a clean flannel, found an elastic band in her desk drawer to hold it in place. Tomorrow morning if needed, she would call in sick and drive to the clinic for stitches. Finally, in bed, tired beyond belief. Her mind racing and her throbbing toe trying to keep up with it.

She would doze off, then jerk awake again, in and out of worries, imagining and revising scenarios, always unsure what to do. With her work. With her art. With Nora. With her life. What was she doing with her life?

She must have passed out at some Godforsaken hour, for she woke up just after 9 a.m., much later than usual. She called her office and took a sick day. Tea and toast again for breakfast. She sat at the kitchen counter, thinking, trying to clear her foggy head, her toe still wrapped in the blood-soaked flannel. She'd drive to Chappie's in a bit, buy some antiseptic and gauze, dress the wound properly. That was the kind of caregiving that Nora excelled at—*Come here, love, let's have a look. Stop pushing me away, just let me take care of you for once.*

Bright light flooded the room. A beautiful and clear late summer morning. Daytime always helped with her ruminative moods. And later today, Dede would be flying over the shallow seas, the reefs and the cays and the canyons that lay between missing and home. Ethel—with a properly dressed wound—would wait on the pool deck, hope to see her when she arrived; she wanted to hug the girl, look into her eyes, and find out that she was okay. Maybe then she would understand what had happened. Would Dede feel like a captive, a failure, a delinquent, returning to Freeport, as Clarence had suggested? Or would she feel relief to be back? And what did it mean that McGuinn had made a cryptic getaway in the middle of the night? Seemed everyone was moving in different directions while Ethel waited alone in her shabby apartment, unsure of where her home could ever be.

Oh, Christ, woman. You have a lover waiting for you in England with open arms. Stop the drama. Finish your tea, take a bath, a proper English bath, then call Nora. Stop fighting against yourself so hard. She loves you. Talk to her and work things out.

227

Ethel stepped down hard on her injured foot and pain shot through her body. Jesus God, the pain. And with it, understanding—like another stabbing wound. Oh God. McGuinn.

Ethel sat down on the floor in her kitchen. That haunted look on his face, his eyes last night when she said that Dede cared about him. He'd done something... Ethel felt it. Done something to scare her off. She knew it. She'd seen it, for Christ's sake, last night. What had she seen? She half-limped, half-ran outside, across the courtyard. His sliding door was unlocked. She lost her bloody flannel midway across his living room, not caring about dripping blood on the carpet. Oh, if he'd hurt the girl...

In his kitchen, open drawers, a sink full of dishes, cups, silverware. Down the hall and into the only bedroom. A mattress on the floor. Had he touched her? She would kill him with her bare hands. She slid aside the flimsy slat doors of the closet. Only an old windbreaker on a hanger, and on the floor, a scented candle, a book of matches. Nothing. She would call the police, tell them that he'd run off in the middle of the night. She'd explain the guilty look on his face when she tried to stop him. She would call Anita and Silvio and get it all out in the open. She hurried back out to his kitchen, picked up the phone that hung on the wall next to his fridge—the mirror image of her kitchen layout. What would she say exactly to the police? That she saw the caretaker leave late last night? That a strange look came over his face? Think. She needed more. She hung up the receiver. Slow down. What had he done? What had she seen?

She hobbled to the back of the building, the shed, the rubbish bins. She felt edgy, endangered, but she was not doing anything wrong. She lifted the top of the first bin; inside plastic bags spilled open, papers, magazines, receipts, all smelling as if he'd doused them in aftershave or alcohol. Standing awkwardly on one foot, she rummaged through the piles of papers. In one bag, there was a broken tape recorder; its door snapped off, and a cassette half inside. She pulled out the player, removed the tape, but it spooled out and she tossed them both back in the bin. She dug through two more bins, but the contents were similar—damp, half-destroyed papers, a few clothes, useless knick-knacks, an expense ledger, girly magazines. *Penthouse, Hustler.* Empty beer bottles. Then, near the bottom of the last bin, she found a soggy paper bag and inside a few sticky Polaroids, held together with a pink pigtail holder. She pulled them out carefully, slid off the band. On the top, a woman with long blond hair. No, not a woman, a girl, looking at the camera, her lips in a pout, one hand on a jutted hip. The photo was blurry, too much light and water-damage, but surely it was Dede. Yes, those were her favorite dungarees. And she was wearing a wig—a blonde wig—her mother's? Trying to be funny? Beneath this image, stuck to it, were more pictures, half-developed or damaged, the colors blurring together, Dede in her school uniform standing next to McGuinn's car, in shorts and a t-shirt, sitting on a couch eating a bowl of cereal or ice cream.

Ethel limped back to her apartment with the photos. If she called the police, what else could she say? That McGuinn had a few Polaroids of the girl? That he'd tossed them out before he left? Proving what exactly? Would this information only make things worse for Dede? Or was it irrelevant? After all, Ethel had kept a picture of Dede in her studio, pinned to the bulletin board. She'd even offered it to the police to help their search. She sat on the edge of her bathtub and rinsed her foot under warm water.

Nora. She would call Nora. Nora had met the girl. Nora was good at working things out. Nora would listen and would help her make sense of it all. She had good instincts. And perhaps after they'd talked it all through, Nora would say something—just a few days until I'll meet you at the gate. And then she'd have to tell Nora what she now realized was true... that although she was ready to return to Bristol, although she would soon, there was a complication with the girl. Ethel didn't know what had happened exactly, but she felt a certain way. She couldn't fly to England before she laid eyes on Dede, before she'd taken enough time to find out what had gone on and whether the girl would be all right.

CHAPTER 18

D ressed again, Dede sat erect and silent on the couch, next to her mother, waiting for Dr. Antonio in his office. Mum's right leg jittered; she chewed her thumbnail and kept glancing at the door.

"Why would he keep us waiting in here?"

Dede shrugged. *No idea.* But she knew.

When Mum looked at her watch for about the tenth time, Dede could hear the secondhand ticking or maybe it was her pulse, thrumming in her neck. No. It was the fan. Placed on the top shelf of Dr. Antonio's bookcase—whoosh, click, whoosh, click—it punctuated the silence. They'd been waiting about forty minutes, but time slowed as Mum became more fidgety, Dede remained immobile. Mum picked up a magazine. Put it back down. Rifled through the stack on the coffee table, trying to find something else, anything to take her mind off the waiting. She had nowhere to be, but this morning's appointment sliced into her usual sleep routine. Puffy-eyed and ponytailed, her sundress sagging, she fished out another magazine, turned the pages fast, not even pretending to read. Dede tried not to twitch; she didn't want her body to give anything away. She only allowed her eyes to scan the room. Right, center, left.

Unlike the sterile box where Dr. Antonio had examined Dede a little earlier, his office had personality. To her right, the bookcase spilled medical texts, journals and novels, as well as miniature puzzles—wood cubes and metal rings—things to take apart and try to put back together. Across the room in front of the only window, Dr. Antonio's desk lay solid and thick as a fallen tree trunk. Maybe it was made from that island wood, *Lignum Vitae*, supposedly the heaviest in the world. Too heavy to float. The desk surface rustled with letters, envelopes, and pamphlets, caught in the fan's periodic breeze. Even the paperweights pinning down the documents seemed, if not alive, then close to it: A chunk of brain coral, a bleached sand biscuit, and an orange starfish. They looked like Ethel's ceramics, but these were the real thing. Dr. Antonio must be a beachcomber, too. Perhaps he walked quietly in the mornings, enjoying his solitude before clinic hours. Or maybe he strolled at sunset with his wife. And kids. Did he have children? Two framed pictures looked away from Dede on his desk, so Dr. Antonio would see the images when he was seated. A daughter, Dede guessed, close to her own age. Off at boarding school most likely.

In the examination room, Dr. Antonio had pushed up Dede's flimsy gown and pressed down on her belly, his hands moving in a circle. He could feel her shame growing inside. "Do you have a boyfriend?" he'd asked. Dede turned to face the plain white wall. "How long have you been sexually active?" Dede didn't speak, not to be difficult, but because she didn't know how to answer either question. Johnnie Angel had said that he loved her bigger than the whole world, that no one would ever love her as much as he did. But he'd left the island without saying goodbye. Before she'd even returned from Callow Cay. And, sexually active? Most times, she'd done nothing, letting him do what he had to do. Only sometimes, she shook, out of control and ugly as a dying fish; only sometimes she couldn't stop her stupid body from moving when he did things. Dr. Antonio said he needed to run a few tests. He directed Dede to the bathroom first, gave her a funnel and a flask. Then the nurse came and drew some blood. Dr. Antonio told Dede to get dressed again and have a seat in his office; he'd like to bring in her mother from the waiting room so they could chat. All together.

Any minute now.

Dede's throat felt thick with sand, but she didn't want to move, speak, go for water.

"Are you hungry?" Mum asked.

Dede shook her head. Mum turned another page. Then another. A door slammed down the hall. Footsteps approached, walked past, then faded. A distant phone trilled, trilled, trilled. And the persistent click whoosh click of the fan. Mum finished thumbing through *Time,* dropped it back on the table.

"Well, I could eat a horse," she said.

On the cover of the discarded magazine, Nadia Comaneci, all pointy-toed concentration on the balance beam at the Montreal Olympics. *She's Perfect,* the caption said. Only fourteen, and the whole world eating out of her hand. Dede had spent the last week of July at Natalie's house; the two of them parked on the sofa, eating Pringles from the can and watching Nadia compete: Snaky and aggressive on the balance beam; bold and belly-banging on the uneven-bars. Number 73 on the back of her white leotard.

Seventy-three: The year she and Mum had moved to Freeport, supposedly for a three-month stay, but three years later, they were still here and all the while Nadia had been practicing in Romania, flipping and twisting, falling and getting up, training for the moment after she'd landed, when she stood by her coach shrugging her shoulders, shaking out her arms and knowing, just knowing her own brilliance, expecting what the scoreboard didn't yet know how to record: A perfect ten. She had seven of them by the end of the games. And three gold medals, too. 73. *Her* lucky number.

Mum looked at her watch again. "I'm going to be a wreck tonight if we don't get out of here soon. Are you sure you're not hungry? Maybe for Beefy King? A thicky and cheesy?"

"I'm fine."

"Or we could drive over to Coral Cove. You love that place, don't you? Quite a tab you and Natalie worked up there, according to the police." Mum was trying to act all chummy ever since Dede returned two days ago. "Why don't you let me buy you a burger for once, rather than making poor old Mr. Fryer pay?"

"No." Dede's voice bounced off Dr. Antonio's serene blue walls, much louder than she'd intended. She held her stomach. The thought of seeing Clarence made her nauseous all over again. Apparently, the police had questioned him for hours after she'd disappeared because they believed that he was the last person to see her. Ethel said they'd kept him at the police station until someone found Dede's shorts at the Ingraham's place, and then they started talking to Jethro. Stupid bloody Jethro. Dede hated him. She hated Natalie even more, though. Natalie had not even reported Dede missing, and when she was questioned, she said that sailing was all Dede's idea; she never would have been so stupid to go out in a storm. Now she was off in England, avoiding all responsibility. Which left Dede here. "I don't want a bloody burger."

Mum stared at Dede. "Mind your manners, Miss. I know you've been through a lot, but you can't talk to me that way."

"Sorry," Dede said, but she couldn't make her lips smile apologetically like they were supposed to. Nothing, nothing was going the way it was supposed to. Natalie had left for England while Dede was gone. Johnnie Angel had left without saying a word to anyone. Even Ethel was acting strangely—she'd been waiting outside on the pool deck and hugged Dede tightly when she saw her, whispered in her ear that she was available anytime, if Dede wanted to talk. Next week, she told Dede, she was flying over to England to see Nora. But she'd be around, day or night, if Dede needed her between now and then. And she'd told Dede she'd write from England.

"Where's my old Domini?" Mum said. "My sweet little girl?"

Dede shrugged, tried to move her lips again. Nadia smiled at the end of each routine, but Dede could tell how exhausted she was. What her body had been through. Dede wanted to be straight and thin and pale like Nadia. And beautiful like Mum, when she dressed up, her hair hanging long and glossy down her back. Dede's hair was a choppy mess from the sun and the sea and the bush, and her body lumpy beneath her too-big t-shirt—stomach protruding as if she'd eaten unripe cocoplums. Couldn't Mum see that? Her skin was disgusting: arms and legs red-brown and patchy. Like those tourist trees shedding bark. Sometimes Dede looked at her limbs and thought *Whose arms? Whose legs?* Nadia's body was a disciplined warrior under her command; Mum's body was a gift she could wrap up beautifully. But Dede's had turned on her again and again. Traitor body.

"Well, I should go see what's taking the doctor so long," Mum said, but she didn't move from the couch. She liked to pretend she could talk a tough line, but she never backed it up with action. She needed Silvio for that. "I hate sitting around here for nothing."

Not for nothing, Dede thought. She'd peed in a beaker. She'd given two vials of blood. She didn't know how the pregnancy test worked, how long the results took; she didn't want to think ahead to the moment when Dr. Antonio came through the door. And she didn't want to see Mum's face when she looked over at her and started to understand what Harmony knew so fast. What Ethel might have already guessed. Mum had brought her here to the clinic for a quick check-up, she said, because it looked as if she might have contracted some kind of skin disease—maybe from the hours in the ocean, or maybe an allergic reaction to something she'd eaten out in the wild. She'd told Dede perhaps ten times the story of how she ate mussels in Mallorca on her honeymoon; flared up red all over her face and neck. *Perfect start to a marriage, right? Should have known, then.*

Footsteps again, coming towards the office, getting louder. Dr. Antonio knocked as he opened the door, walked in, and sat down behind his desk. He had a file and he set it on his other papers. He clasped his hands, made a church and a steeple, under his chin.

"Sorry to keep you waiting. We had to run the specimens over to Rand Hospital. We use their laboratory."

The way he said laboratory—what was the accent? Trinidadian?

"Skin tests?" Mum said.

On the wall behind him to the right of the open window, Dede noticed for the first time a large, framed photo of a lady with shoulder length brown hair and a funny lopsided smile. Dr. Antonio's wife was white. Or at least very light-skinned. Dede wanted to turn around the frames on Dr. Antonio's desk and expose the children—the daughter, reveal her, see her skin, her plaited hair. Dede wanted to replace her.

"So, you're no longer dehydrated. Potassium and sodium are just a little lower than I'd like, but drink lots of fluid, some Lucozade over the next few days and you'll be fine in that regard. And your skin condition is nothing to worry about. *Tinea versicolor.*" His eyes met Dede's. "That's what it is called when we doctors want to sound educated. Sun fungus, among friends. It's quite common. The result of too much sun exposure. I'm going to give you a topical ointment, Domini, apply it twice a day and it will be gone in a couple of weeks."

Mum tapped her fingernails on the edge of the couch. Her ponytail stretched her skin tightly over her cheekbones. Nadia wore a ponytail, too, but she had a black fringe covering her forehead. Mum's hair swept back off her face making her thinner, older, more worried looking than usual. "All right, then," She bit her bottom lip. "Is it contagious, this *tinea* what have you?"

He shook his head. "A yeast infection, basically—we all have it in our systems. Sometimes it grows out of control. Especially in teenagers. Especially in hot climates. So, Dede's at high-risk for this kind of infection. Even more so after the recent incident, and the stresses in her life."

Mum nodded as if she understood. Dede picked a scaly patch on her arm. Mum reached over and grabbed her hand. "You'll make it worse."

Dr. Antonio plucked a pen from a blue glass jar on his desk, began to write out a prescription. "Use this liberally all over your rash. And stay out of the direct sun, too. It aggravates the condition. You could try wearing long sleeves," Dr. Antonio said, "As long as the fabric is lightweight, and doesn't make you sweat too much."

Mum stood and reached for the prescription. "Skin fungus? So that's it? Everything else checks out okay?" She looked at Dr. Antonio, then at Dede, then back at him. Her head, side-to-side and back, like the fan. She sat down again—her back rigid, her bony hands clasping the armrests. Did she know now? She must know. If she squeezed any tighter, the truth would come out of the furniture, out of the humid air in the room. Dede wanted to punch her hard, so hard in the mouth. She must have seen or heard something. The truth had been in her reach for days and weeks and months and why could she not see smell sense touch taste it? The change in the way Dede walked, talked, the clothes she'd been wearing to cover her shame. And most of all, how could Mum not have asked what happened to Johnnie McGuinn? Where did he go? Why did he leave right before Dede got back?

Dr. Antonio's smile had gone. Worry lined his forehead. Dede knew he wanted her to voice what Mum hadn't figured out yet—what she either couldn't or wouldn't believe. His eyes stayed on Dede as Mum grew more and more irritated.

"Are we finished, then?" Mum asked.

"I wanted you both to join me in my office because there is something else that we need to talk about. More serious than sun fungus, I'm afraid."

"What's going on?" Mum said.

"Do you want to tell her, Dede? Or would you like me to?"

Dede didn't move, didn't flinch, didn't blink.

"Tell me what?"

He waited. His right hand found the starfish on his desk and gripped it, but he kept his eyes on Dede—focused, as if he could wait for a decision all day. And he would have to because Dede wasn't going to say a word. Not to Mum. If she couldn't figure it out. Not ever. No. Never. No.

"Somebody tell me something right now or I swear..."

He turned slightly in his chair, looked to her at last. "What Domini does not want to tell you, what I therefore must, because she is a minor, is this," He coughed again, glanced at Dede. "Your daughter is pregnant."

"Pregnant? What are you talking about? She won't be thirteen until next month. She just started her period at Christmas. This is ridiculous. Dede, tell him it's ridiculous."

Dr. Antonio's eyes grew larger, rounder behind his glasses. Dede stood up. Her heartbeat like Junkanoo drums. The moment stretched the office. The blue walls moved like waves.

"I'm afraid that the test results confirm it."

"Tests? What tests?"

"We ran a urine test that detects pregnancy hormones and had the lab look at her blood, too. For confirmation."

Dr. Antonio's words sailed from him to Dede and across to Mum. Dede saw her catch them, a spasm in her face, felt her mind trying to give meaning to the sounds. Dede turned to watch the small white fan oscillate. Small. White. Fan. Os-cill-late. Such an amazing word. Almost an onomatopoeia, pushing the breeze. Right-Center-Left. How many smaller words could she get out of Os-Cill-Late? *Sit. Sea Silt.* Papers fluttered on Dr. Antonio's desk. She could do better than that. How about *social*? She would never have a social life again. Where would she go? Not back to school at Sunland, that was certain, and no English boarding school would take her now.

Mum stood up beside Dede, her hands covering her mouth, like a stricken woman in a bad TV show. "Oh, Domini, darling," she said. "What have you done?"

Lie. Steal. Sail.

Dede could sense Mum's brain racing, trying to put the puzzle pieces together, trying to make sense from the bits inside her head.

"Who's the boy? Were you trying to run away because of this?"

239

No one really wanted to know the story. No one wanted to hear Dede's buried secrets. She walked toward the bookshelf and picked up one of the puzzles. She twisted it in her hands, tried to pull it apart.

"What are we going to do? What the hell are we going to do?"

The clock behind Dr. Antonio's desk said ten forty-five. *Happy Days* came on at 11 a.m. Reruns. Dede had seen most of last season's shows with Johnnie Angel, sitting beside him on the couch eating ice cream. Mint Chocolate Chip. She'd never eat it again. He'd gone. Poof. She'd never see him again. He'd told Dede once that it made him crazy how much he loved her. That was a lie. He'd run off before she came home. Silvio said he always had been a shifty bastard, that he'd stolen the car, probably sold it by now and taken off with the cash. But Silvio knew nothing. Mum knew nothing squared. Ethel knew something, Dede saw it in her eyes. But no one, no one, no one really wanted to know the whole story. No one ever would. Except, well, maybe Harmony, and she didn't matter to the rest of the world. She didn't even exist to the rest of the world. She might as well be a dream. Was she a dream? Harmony?

I'm here with you child.

Dr. Antonio took off his glasses, squeezed the piece of skin between his eyes.

"Domini, come sit back down, dear. Your mother is surprised, naturally. But we both want to help you. We're here for you. Really."

Dr. Antonio's eyes were almond in shape and color, his curly hair slicked back off his round face. Where was he born? *Isle. Locale.*

"You are quite young," he said. "Did the boy—did he push himself on you?"

Dede stood as tall as she could in front of him, let her head move right, center, left. No. No. No. She didn't need Dr. Antonio for a father.

She didn't need parents at all. She should have stayed with Harmony. She would have taken care of the potcakes, all the dogs on Callow Cay.

"Was it someone from Sunland, or an older student from the high school? Some of these Bahamian chaps, they don't understand about the age of consent."

"It wasn't a black boy, was it?" Mum moved towards Dr. Antonio's desk, extended her hand. "Sorry, I don't mean to sound prejudiced—I'm not—it's just . . . I should call Silvio," she whispered. "He'll know what to do."

"No." Dede screamed at her. "I don't want Silvio here."

"Calm down," Dr. Antonio said. "Let's keep our heads. Domini, we are here to help you. Other girls have weathered such situations, and you will too. We need you to say, though, how did this happen?"

"I want my Dad. I'll tell him."

"Are you that thick?" Mum said, "Your father never came to see you once, did he? Not once in three years. Not even when you were missing."

"When he comes, I'll tell him."

"He's not coming, Domini. He's... he has a new girlfriend, all right? He didn't come when you were missing. He's still a selfish sod." She shook her head. "And you're making the same bloody mistake I did. Falling for a bloke who's only after one thing."

Dede shook her head. She would not cry. *Stoic.*

"Why didn't you come to me?" Mum started to cry. "I could have helped. I could have told you some things before this happened. I'm not old-fashioned, we could have talked about birth control."

Dede would never ever tell them anything; her story would harden to coral. Dr. Antonio slumped in his chair. Not as great a man as Dede first thought. Probably not even a decent father. His

241

own daughter probably hated him. Dede looked straight ahead, over his head, stared out the window. A parking lot. Beyond that, another building. Mary, Star of the Sea Church. The white spire pierced the sky. A loud click. The fan hit extreme right, clicked back to center. The breeze in Dede's face, and she was back on the sailboat. Back on the water. Leaving all this behind.

She held on tight to the boat's frame, but she was in control, she knew what to do this time, how to steer, how to direct her path. The water ahead calm, flat, miles and miles of clear blue, and below it, thriving reefs: Sea fans and brain coral and starfish and conch and angel fish. She'd skim over these worlds, sailing miles and miles south to the Tongue of the Ocean, where she'd dive into the deepest waters and a new language would fill her, until ocean-tongued, she could tell her story the way that it should go.

"Can you tell us his name, Domini?" Dr. Antonio's said quietly, "Please."

Mum grabbed her arm. "Who was it? Tell me right now."

"Jethro," she said.

Her face burned. *Lies*. She was embarrassed to claim him. Natalie's discard. Sloppy seconds, as they said at school. But she knew as soon as she saw Mum's reaction, what he offered: plausibility. All the girls in school liked him. A handsome, white Bahamian boy with a reputation. A known troublemaker.

"Jethro Ingraham." She repeated it clear and loud and certain this time. And once his father heard, Jethro would be packed off to military school. Serve him bloody right.

A shudder passed between Mum and Dr. Antonio, confirming the power of her choice. "He said he loved me before we did it. Then he stopped speaking to me after. I didn't know what to do."

242

She could see that they believed her. How wonderful that his name had spelled itself onto her brain at exactly the right time. Jethro's father was a powerful man. Ingraham roots spread deep and wide as the saw palmetto that covered the island. The family would not tolerate a scandal. And the only way to make this story disappear would be to send its teller far away.

CHAPTER 19

D ede lay thick-tongued and nauseous with a white sheet pulled up to her chin and the hospital bed angled so she could watch the television and block out what had happened. Mum sat beside her on a plastic chair, giving her sips of lukewarm water through a straw. Every now and then, Mum fed herself a spoonful of green jelly from the ten-thirty lunch tray.

"Did you know Americans call it Jell-O?"

Dede nodded but kept her eyes on the set. Unlike her telly in the flat back in Freeport, this one in Fort Lauderdale got wonderful reception on all the stations. Plus, she had her very own remote control attached to the bars of the bed with a thick white cord. Dad would have been so jealous. Back in England, he used to pay Dede to get up from the sofa and adjust the sound, just so he didn't have to budge. *Oh, Tuppence,* he'd say, *Come and help your poor old Dad.* He'd called her last week and said *Good luck, Tuppence,* as if she were about to take an exam, not have a baby. Then he'd gone quiet. She'd had to finish up the conversation. *All right, then, Dad. Bye now.*

"Sure you don't want to try a bite of something?" Mum said. "You need to get some energy back after all that work you did."

Dede shook her head. Everything looked disgusting—grey chicken, gummy mashed potatoes, Play Doh carrots. Even if the hospital food were half-way decent, Dede had no appetite. The anesthetic had made her stomach sick. Either the drugs or the pushing and pulling to get the baby out. She shook her head again.

Bob Barker announced another name: *Andrea Walker, come on down. You're the next contestant on the Price is Right.* Lights flashed, the camera zig-zagged, people in the audience clapped and cheered and a huge white woman in a pink Adidas tracksuit jumped out of her seat in the very last row. She squeezed out into the aisle and made her way to the front, blowing kisses into the air. On stage, she swept Bob Barker into a hug and swung him around like a ragdoll. When he escaped her embrace, he straightened his tie and grimaced.

"Why do contestants always play the fool?" Mum asked, as she unwrapped a margarine pat and started to spread it on a bread roll. She'd always disliked the telly because she claimed that it sucked Dad's brain out when they first got married, but she capital L - Loathed American TV. All the sit-coms and gameshows made her want to scream. So, the fact that she was sitting here beside Dede in the hospital room, after being up all last night for the delivery and all through the labor pains yesterday, meant she was trying—really, *really* trying—to provide support. Exactly what Dr. Antonio and Monica, from the South Florida Adoption Center had encouraged Mum to do.

At the meeting last week to sign the initial papers, Dede was returning from the toilet when she overheard Monica tell Mum that birth mothers are very fragile in the first few days after delivery, that they needed lots of support before the "final surrender." Even more so with teens. Dede coughed loudly before she walked back into the conference room with them. Monica and Mum looked up and smiled too big—they knew they'd been caught talking about her. *We're proud of you*, Monica said, *you're handling all this like a champ.* Dede didn't reply, *What's the alternative?* She knew Monica meant well. She sat back down on the uncomfortable chair and waited while Mum completed the last forms. Dede didn't want to cause any trouble, but the word "surrender" had fish-hooked her brain.

Now Mum took a bite out of the bread roll and then spit it out in the napkin. "Why is it so hard to make decent food in a hospital setting? How does anyone manage to mess up a roll, for Christ's sake?"

A knock on the door and another nun-nurse—this one grey-haired, dressed in blue like the others, but with a different hat. She walked fast but a little hunched over, didn't smile or say hello as she approached Dede's bed. Had she heard Mum swear?

She pointed to the armchair by the window and said to Mum. "Over there, please, out of the way."

Mum arched her eyebrow at Dede when she stood and moved; she had a new silent language since they were in the hospital, as if she thought they were a team now, mother and daughter against the world.

The nurse stuck a thermometer in Dede's mouth, took her arm and placed two bony fingers on her wrist. She gripped tightly for what seemed like forever. Maybe her senses were bad because she was so old, or maybe Dede's pulse was faint—too faint for her to detect, or maybe she could hear secrets echoing through Dede's blood stream. Did she know Dede was a liar? That she'd made up stories about Jethro Ingraham? Could the nun part of her sense what Dede had done? What had happened in Johnnie Angel's car?

"Hold still."

246

The thermometer still hung precariously in her mouth. "*Mmmmhh*," Dede said, through tight lips.

The little nurse shot her an evil eye and straightened the bed covers. Finally, she removed the thermometer and flicked it down.

"No fever." She glanced at the lunch tray. "Did you eat anything yet?"

She harrumphed at Dede's answer. Then she put on her granny glasses and recorded her findings in the chart.

"Urination? Bowel movement?"

Dede shook her head.

"Neither?"

She shook again.

"You better start eating and drinking, then," the nurse said as she turned to the door. "Doctor's not going to let you out of here until you're regular again and you won't get regular until you take in some solid food and hydrate yourself."

After she'd gone, Mum returned to the bed and sat down on the end. She placed her hand on Dede's foot and began to massage it through the sheet and blanket.

"It's high time someone retired." She rubbed her eyes and scanned Dede's lunch tray again—as if she might have missed something edible on the first few looks.

"She doesn't like me," Dede said.

"She doesn't like her life."

Dede rested her head against the pillow and lowered the bed. Her stomach felt sore as she shifted but eased once she repositioned. On the game show, Andrea Walker made it through the bidding round and won the chance to play a real game. She fanned her face with her hand, as if she might pass out from the shock. Bob Barker explained

247

the rules—all Andrea had to do was match three grocery items to three over-sized price tags. He revealed the products: A tin of ravioli. A large bottle of shampoo. A jar of peanut butter. Andrea was so excited about being back on camera that she couldn't focus. She put the $2.53 tag on the Chef Boyardee and the 79 cents tag on the Herbal Essence, even though the audience kept yelling *switch, switch*. She got the Skippy right, but one match wouldn't be enough to move on to the next round. Everyone knows that you have to listen to the audience. When she lost, Andrea turned her face skyward as if to say, *how could I have known?*

Bloody idiot. Dede switched channels.

"Do you want to talk?" Mum said. "I remember after you were born feeling so exhilarated and terrified at the same time. I'm sure you must be reeling."

Dede shook her head, flipped channels. She didn't feel exhilarated or terrified; she wanted to be left alone.

When the *Days of Our Lives* hourglass filled the screen, Mum popped out of her chair. She blinked a couple of times and said she'd rather poke out her own eyes than watch another American soap opera. Then she caught her unsupportive tone and coughed into her hand. "Sorry, but I'm completely bushed." She poured herself a cup of water in a Styrofoam cup, drank it fast. "I'm a bit sick of the hospital. Would you mind terribly if I went out for some fresh air?"

Dede shook her head, again. Of course, Mum needed a break from the hospital. She'd left her croupier job and left Silvio to come over to the States with Dede. They'd been together every minute, every hour for the past few weeks.

Easier to watch the telly than listen to her anyway. "You can go, Mum. I'm fine, really."

St. Bernard Hospital was only a few blocks from the ocean and just a short walk from the place Silvio had rented for them. Mum could go to the beach to clear her head or walk back to the apartment for a nap. Yesterday, when Dede's contractions had started, really started and Mum knew they were the real thing, they'd walked together along the dirt brown sand, which was nothing like the white sand beaches of the Bahamas. The January Atlantic churned muddy and froth topped. Dede and Mum were alone on the shore—a good thing since she didn't particularly want people staring when she was grimacing and squatting every few yards. When pain hit and doubled her over, Mum held her and whispered into the back of Dede's neck, "That's it, you're doing well." She walked beside her for three hours and told her when it was time to get ready for the hospital.

Now Mum slipped on her trainers, brushed her hair into a fresh ponytail.

"I won't be away too long. Can I bring you back some real food? A beef burger?" She bent over Dede and tucked in the top sheet. She rolled the side table with the lunch tray away from the bed.

"Maybe a Ginger Ale," She sipped her water. Sipped again. "Please."

"Of course. Try to sleep." Mum kissed her cheek before she walked out and it almost made Dede cry, this tenderness coming now, coming too late.

Dede was alone and she was tired. She'd spent so much time over the past few years fighting aloneness, but what was so bad about it, really? She would watch telly a little longer, or turn it off and stare at the ceiling, think things through; if the thoughts came too strong, she would sleep. The medicine was wearing off. A deep ache anchored in her tummy and dug in lower down between her legs, where the doctor had cut her to get the baby's head out. She clicked off the

TV, lowered the bed to 180 degrees and lay flat. Square, white tiles, textured and thick, covered the ceiling. Silvio must have paid extra for a single room, though this one was certainly not glamorous. No color. No art anywhere, just a wooden Jesus on a cross. Mum said Dr. Antonio had trained at this hospital years ago, so now he sent all his high-risk patients from the island here for delivery. Dede knew there had been lots of arrangements made. She'd overheard some of the phone calls. Part of the deal worked out between Mum, Silvio and the Ingrahams was that after Dede left the island for "confinement and delivery," she would never come back again. The adoption would be finalized in the States—just another two days until the final surrender—and after Dede recovered in Florida, she would return to England and live with Dad and his new girlfriend, Polly, for a few weeks. As soon as she was ready, she could start at Red Maids. Ethel and Nora had helped with that part, arranged for Dede to enroll at a proper English boarding school and all expenses would be paid by the Ingrahams. It sounded almost too good to be true; it was what Dede had always wanted. Why didn't it feel that way anymore?

Dede counted ceiling tiles. Length and width, then multiplied. One hundred and fifty in all. Sponge-like, porous—when she half-closed her eyes, they seemed to move, as if they could breathe, sense, see. Did they absorb sound? What had they heard and observed in this room? The air conditioner hummed lightly. A few voices from the hall filtered through the background noise. Was that a baby crying next door? How many women were on this floor now? How many girls had lain in this very bed staring at this exact ceiling, counting tiles? How many had surrendered their infants?

Surrender was a bloody idiotic word for what had happened. Dede kicked off the bed sheet and the pain seared through her abdomen. She ran a hand from her hip over her half-deflated tummy. The middle felt tender and swollen, but the skin above had loosened and sagged. She grabbed a handful and pinched it hard, another sharp knife. The anesthesia had worn off. She needed to pee now but felt scared of how it would burn. She wished she hadn't drunk all that water. Shouldn't have listened to that stupid ancient nun-nurse. Could she hold it a little longer? She looked at the clock on the wall. The baby was still less than a day old. A girl, they'd told her, 5 lbs, 5 oz, and 18 inches long. Dede had heard her cry. Where was she now? What was she doing? Dede was not supposed to wonder; she'd agreed to surrender. Not to struggle or resist. To admit defeat. To hand over all control.

She stood up and held the bed railing, then shuffled across the green linoleum toward the tiny bathroom. A shower, really a thick hosepipe, hung over pine green floor tile in one corner. A small toilet tucked into the other corner beside a tiny sink. Dede held onto the edge of the sink with one hand, while she pulled down the granny knickers they must have put on her after stitching her up. When she sat, a giant sanitary pad fell out of the knickers and onto the floor, dark and bloody. She kicked it into the corner and started to cry. She cried and cried and couldn't pee. She wanted Mum to come back and help her return to bed and give her some more medicine to stop the burning and a different kind of medicine to stop all the sad thoughts in her brain.

Medicine, yes, or an herbalist's potion that could reverse time, take things back to how they had been on Callow Cay. A thin nylon cord by the sink attached to an alarm; the sign above said pull for assistance. Should she pull? If only it would work that kind of magic and bring back that place. Bring back Harmony. But the last thing she needed was that mean nun-nurse hobbling back into the room to berate her for being a tramp. Isn't that what they thought? So, she just sat there for a long, long time, letting the pee dribble out, letting more tears come, then stop, then come again until she felt dried out. After she was done, she found a clean pad behind the toilet, put it in the knickers and hobbled back to bed.

She closed her eyes, wanting sleep, but her body hurt all over. She'd seen herself in the bathroom mirror—puffy, red-eyed, her breasts grown ginormous in the last few weeks. She looked nothing like the girl who once lived in England. Would Dad even know her when she returned next month? Inside, she felt nothing like that girl either. Mum would go back to Freeport and Silvio. Dede could start at Red Maids *as soon as she felt up to it*. Strange that the new Dede didn't feel happier. Give it time, Ethel had said on the phone last week. "I still think you'll find it's the best option for you. And Nora and I will be close by, we want to be your home away from home. We've got a small bedroom ready for you whenever you'd like to come and stay."

She had no home so how could she have a home away from home?

She pushed up to sitting on the bed. She couldn't think of anything she'd like to eat, except maybe something citrusy, like geneps from Harmony's patch. They'd tasted like lime and grapes mixed together. She wished she had a bunch now. Not just geneps. She wanted Harmony with her. If she could appear now, the way she did when Dede needed her on the island, Harmony would understand. Yes, she'd understand how frightened Dede had felt when that Captain dragged her into his truck and took her to his home. She'd know how good it felt when Mum came to collect her; and again, when Dede arrived back at the flats and saw Ethel waiting and then running to her with her arms outstretched and tears spilling onto her painting shirt. But would Harmony realize how forlorn and crazy Dede felt when she learned that Johnnie Angel had gone away; that he had not loved her enough to stay and see if she were alive? Would she understand the lies Dede had told and kept telling? Protecting Johnnie Angel, blaming Jethro. Would she now look at Dede with nothing but disappointment? Would she say, *Oh, girl, what have you done? Secrets and more secrets? Lies and more lies.*

From the time Mum found out about Dede's shame in Dr. Antonio's office, and later, during all the meetings and consultations and appointments, no one said Dede was ready to be a mother. And Dede didn't waver when she went to the adoption agency. Of course, the social workers and the lawyer asked lots of questions: Did she understand what she was doing, did she know it would be a permanent decision, was she sure, did she consent, did she acknowledge, could she speak a little louder, was this her choice, was that a yes, was anyone pressuring Dede, coercing her, could she speak a little louder please, would she sign on the line, could she step outside while the lawyer talked to her mother about the fee arrangement (Did she need to use the restroom? Was she thirsty? Would she like a Snickers bar from the vending machine), would she mind coming back inside to initial two more pages, was there anything else she wanted to add, did she understand? Did she know she'd have 72 hours after delivery to re-consider?

Dede signed. Mum signed. Silvio handled all the negotiations with the Ingrahams in Freeport. Mum said that Dede now had the chance for a new start, the chance to go to a proper school, get a good education, all paid in full; a clever girl like Dede could put all this behind her in no time, and not let a past mistake define her. When the baby was born, he or she would be well loved and wanted by a new family. Dede wouldn't have to worry anymore.

Except now Dede was lying here worrying. She had pushed out her shame and after that last agony, she'd heard the spluttering noises. The nun-nurses murmuring and cooing and the baby crying and the doctor asking if Dede wanted to see the baby girl. She shook her head and closed her eyes. Are you sure? The doctor said. "This will be the only..." Dede closed her eyes, shook her head again. The doctor had cut the cord and the nurses carried the baby away. The American couple would take her away tomorrow and after the final signatures, the baby would have a mother and a father. A home of her own. Dede didn't want to picture the new parents or think about what the baby's life would be. Putting a face on any of them, imagining their home, the nursery, the art on the walls, the books on the shelves, would be too much to carry. She had to stop thinking. She had to let the baby go, uncontaminated by her shame. The baby should be a blank canvas to be filled, when the time came, with her own thoughts and feelings. But if Dede could have some influence over the life she had chosen to surrender, then she hoped the baby might dream of shallow seas, waters with color and shape always evolving, and the sound the waves made would be *hush now and peace...* Dede listens for the waves and Harmony is sitting beside her on the edge of the hospital bed, tucking in her covers, holding her hand, whispering words to settle her thoughts... *peace and easy seas, easy seas and calm.*

PART IV

FLORIDA

2001

Chapter 20

Up to his elbows in warm sudsy water when the phone rang again, McGuinn glanced at the clock. 3:45 p.m. Same time as yesterday's call. Shit. He shut off the faucet, wiped his hands on his shorts and grabbed the receiver.

"Hello?" He cleared his throat. He sounded like an old man. He was an old man, for Christ's sake. Not that anyone gave a good Goddamn about that. He coughed—a long, phlegmy rattle—leaning on the countertop where Peg kept her address books, Post-it notes, a macramé basket full of pens, pencils, and an assortment of reading glasses. She was a packrat, but he was in no position to complain about her housekeeping. Or anything else she did for that matter. He tried to calm his breathing. Not for nothing had Peg told him to see a doctor. Asthma, she guessed, McGuinn suspected worse, but he had no patience for all that prodding and poking, the questions, and the assumptions. Never liked doctors. Arrogant hucksters, most of them. The phone smelled of Peg's hairspray and some other old lady smell, roses maybe, and he thought he was going to hack again, but he pushed against the Formica, straightened himself up and got control of his voice.

"Who is this?"

Silence rolled back down the line.

Had the crazy bitch tracked him down again? Or was his mind getting the better of him? Whoever had called yesterday around this time had hung up fast, without saying a word. McGuinn had let himself assume it was a wrong number and gone about the evening. He'd fried up a steak, baked potatoes in the oven, and opened a bottle of wine; he'd had a glass with Peg out on her patio, even though he didn't like wine or patios, for that matter. Small concessions for the haven. He hoped he could stay with her a while. She was lonely, he was desperate. But now...two calls in two days; both at the same time of day? He knew the pattern. McGuinn's heart raced, his lungs burned. He knew the signs; this is how trouble always started.

"Who is this?... Hello?" He wiped a hand across his sweating forehead.

Nothing.

"Well, it's your dime, buddy."

He hung up, exhaled, and tried to calm himself. He'd lived with this for years. Sometimes, months would go by with no calls, no interference; he'd begin to settle in to wherever he had made his next home. But she'd track him down again. Phone calls, letters, once even a note on his car: He wanted to put a name or a face on her, but she hadn't given either away yet. She seemed to want to keep him guessing. He assumed she was a playground find from years ago, a girl who'd been cute as a button, eager and accommodating, but somewhere along the way grown up, grown old, and turned batshit crazy, completely obsessed with tracking him down. Making his old age miserable. Each time she found him, he had to leave again, find another home, another town. He'd get a few months, maybe a year without hearing anything, then it would start again. He had no idea how she did this... *No rest for the weary, John.* Sister Mary Pat would have said.

If she'd found him again, where the hell would he go? He had no family to take him in. Burned all those bridges years ago when he left without any kind of warning. There had been a skinny young thing, a girl with a penchant for cowboy boots and flouncy skirts. She'd loved his attention, let him teach her all kinds of things. But for some reason, she'd told a teacher that he'd been messing with her. Two Orlando cops had showed up at his apartment, escorted him to the station, taken a statement, a picture, fingerprints, and even held him overnight. In the morning, when an old-timer judge let him go on his own recognizance, McGuinn didn't wait around for second thoughts. He'd taxied home, packed a suitcase, took off, without a word, not even to his ex-wife and kids. He was spooked all right. He even spent a couple of years out of the country—working shit jobs in the Bahamas—and when he returned to Florida, in what, 1977 or '78, he kept a low profile, closed all his bank accounts, never listed his phone number, or bought property in his name.

Still, she'd tracked him down. He couldn't remember now exactly how it had started, maybe a phone call? Or was it a letter full of accusations? Time and time again, he'd moved, and time and time again, with dogged persistence, she'd found him. Left voice mail messages, letters full of threats, she even made anonymous calls to the Department of Children's Services that resulted in nosy caseworkers stopping by on several occasions. And now, presumably with help from the goddamn internet or perhaps a private eye, she must have located him at Peg's. How long would he have before he'd need to leave again?

Peg's condo had been a haven since she'd let him move in almost a year ago, a few months after her husband, Randall, had died. Randall—owner of the Rainbo Lounge, and McGuinn's onetime boss long ago in Miami. So, he washed her dishes, fixed things around her place, filled her car with gas. He kept her company when she asked, playing bridge when she needed a fourth, taking her to dinner at her dingy tennis club, or sometimes joining her for a sappy matinee at the Citrus Cineplex. They could have passed for any old Floridian couple—sun splotched and slow-moving on the hot sidewalks. And he left her alone when she felt moody. They'd come up with an arrangement as comfortable as McGuinn could hope for. He'd almost let himself believe that the stalker had finally given up on him. He wanted to believe it because he couldn't take another beginning. Not at his age; not in his condition. This goddamn cough, the pain in his ribs with each hack.

His hands felt clammy and his chest tight. He leaned against the counter, made himself breathe, in and out, that's the way. Probably just a wrong number after all. He turned back to the sink and began washing up the Greats Plates that Peg used for all her meals: Stan Musial, Ozzie Smith, Dizzy Dean, Lou Brock caught in action, their uniforms fading to pink from too much use. McGuinn wiped each one with a soapy sponge, then rinsed it, barely glancing at the stats rimming each picture. He'd always hated baseball, but he kept his mouth shut around Peg, who'd shared her passion with Randall. They'd moved north an hour to this neighborhood several years ago to be near the Cardinals' spring training site.

Through the window, out on the usually empty streets of the condo community, a flash of red. A kid on a bike zipped past. Crimson cap on backwards—the way boys, even grown men, wore them these days. An idiotic look. Probably down here for spring break. Peg said that several permanent residents in the condo park would rent out their units to snowbirds, or have their grandkids come visit during March and April. McGuinn had never been friends with the boys who slept with their mitts on and showed off their sliders at the playground. Little pricks, all of them, in his memory. McGuinn had always been different, had his own interests, his own passions from early on and pursued them as he got older. When other men pored over Major League stats, he kept photo albums of his girls so he could pull them out in dry spells.

A dark van crawled along the street, stopped two doors down.

The phone again. Jesus God. He dried his hands on a dishrag and picked it up. He had to. If she left a message on Peg's voicemail, it could screw up everything again.

"Yes?" He held his breath. He couldn't show anger. Or fear. He wouldn't give the caller that satisfaction.

He heard music in the background but couldn't make out the song. He should hang up, pack his bags, and leave before Peg got home. He could take some of her jewelry, the little bit of cash she had stashed in a Folgers can. His heart kicked against his chest. He needed to sit down. He needed to get a drink. He needed to think. *Just think, goddamn it.* McGuinn was panicking, but it might not even be her. Just take it easy. Play along. Let the caller speak if she wanted.

"Hell-o-o? Anybody there?" So friendly, so re-laxed, atta boy, nice and easy, as he opened the freezer door and grabbed one of three bottles he'd buried in ice thirty minutes ago—his reward for doing the lunch dishes. He tried to help Peg out whenever he could, so what if he hadn't quite finished the job; she'd appreciate the effort.

"So, you gonna talk to me this time or what?"

261

He popped the bottle cap off with an opener that attached magnetically to the refrigerator door. A Mark McGwire opener. Peg's place was full of this MLB paraphernalia: playing cards, beer mugs, key chains; she hung onto it all as if it were gold. He slipped his beer into a squishy Cardinals koozie walked out to the living room. He sank into the leather armchair in front of the TV. Randall's brown leather LaZBoy. Set the bottle on a pressed cardboard coaster. A goddamn Willie McGee coaster. McGwire, McGee, McGuinn. Maybe in another life, another time, if he'd been given a real chance, maybe he, too, could have been a baseball star. The hero of the playground; the guy everyone worshipped.

McGuinn ran his hand over the smooth leather armrest. A comfortable enough chair, but Christ, another man's leftovers?

Did the caller sigh too? Was she still there?

"If you've got something to say, do us both a favor and say it."

He shouldn't let the agitation show in his voice, but he could feel the caller waiting. Taunting him?

"Or don't say a word. No skin off my back. I've got time. Plenty of time. I can wait all day if you want to play games. Is that what you want?"

McGuinn didn't want this. Truth was, he needed a nap. He was tired of living this way, scared of creditors and ex-business partners and people who thought he'd screwed them over. Tired of running. Tired of the past. His own kids had grown children of their own, making him a grandfather, possibly a great-grandfather, and all of them thinking he'd done them wrong; all of them hating him. Last time he'd tried to call his daughter, Barbara, she'd hung up on him before he even completed his explanations. He'd never hurt them, he'd never hit his wife, rarely slapped his kids; he'd left their home when he had to. And the girls—his princesses--all of them, he'd only ever wanted to spoil them with attention and gifts, to show them their own beauty. He'd only wanted to teach them about their power.

He held the phone close to his ear in the crook of his neck. He'd lost many names but could conjure up faces. There was the dark-haired one back in Jersey, two long braids that hit her elbows. Then the girl with a limp—Linda, was it? It was so easy back then, coaching tennis or softball, helping a novice learn the serve, showing her where to place her toes, how to toss the ball just so. In the Bahamas, there had been the English girl, with her satchel and sagging socks, and after her, an American teenager living in Nassau—she'd had big breasts, too old for his needs but he hadn't had many options at that point. He'd returned to Florida and once again coached tennis for a variety of clubs and summer camps. So many Chris Evert wannabes. He'd helped them with their double backhands. So many memories he could lose himself for hours. He could lose himself again all over, just remembering.

The phone was dead. He strained to hear... nothing. Or maybe... a sound like a small wave shushing up on the shore. Then, was he imagining it? Words... soft and slow at first, but he swore he could hear that song from years ago, one of his princesses, with a voice so sweet. *Suck 'em slow, chew 'em fast, fun on the tongue, flavors that last.* Oh dear God. Which one had sung like that for him? When he lived in Miami? He'd made a tape, hadn't he? Listened to it on his most lonely nights. And this voice on the phone now, she would be so young, so sweet, so pure. How young? He liked them ten, eleven tops.

"Aw, honey," he said. "You've got a beautiful voice." His heart skipping at his creation. A girl still shy and undeveloped. He had always liked them a little clumsy. Not the graceful ballerinas. Too

263

much attitude from them; no, he needed them embarrassed by their bodies, girls on the cusp. *Now giant lifesavers on a stick, Lifesaver lollipops fun to lick. Hey Lifesavers.* The voice just perfect, the way it snagged on the esses. He'd always been a sucker for a lisp. A knee scrape. Ponytails and dimples. Tomboys, tennis players, skinny and shy and intense. He still walked along the beach some days. He could make it a mile out and back if he went slow. Past the rental condos, past the Sheraton resort. Not the college girls, but the younger ones, trying so hard to act older. They ran in and out of the waves, they stopped for shells and sand dollars, danced in the sand. These days, the mothers kept the girls so close, even on the beach, made his work harder than it should be. Maybe Peg's granddaughter would come down to visit at Easter, again. Would the parents send her alone? What the hell was her name? Jessica or Jennifer? There was a picture stuck on the microwave, probably pinned under Mark McGwire's mug. Ha. Blonde curls around her dimpled cheeks. Blue eyes. Peg probably looked like her a century ago. A hundred pounds ago. Still, he was grateful that Peg had asked him to stay, needed him to stay, asked him to help. He couldn't screw up. He had no other options.

"Are you coming to see me again soon?" The stirring in his stomach. Desire. It had been a while. Years now since he'd had a regular visitor. The feeling in his gut sank lower, into his groin, moved inside him like a school of fish. McGuinn might be almost bald, his skin fragile as dried paper, but inside, where it mattered, he was still a kid, for Christ's sake. And the cute little girl he imagined on the other end of the line, oh yes, she would be sitting on a stool at some kitchen counter, her legs apart, just to tease him. Wearing what? A plaid skirt—Catholic school, knee-highs that started the day white, but now had a little grass stain on them. Maybe she had a scraped knee he could kiss better. Put a Band Aid on it. Maybe she'd just come home from school. A latchkey kid with nothing to do, making herself a snack. Her mother still at work. She'd found him just like so many before her. A kind of magic really, how it happened. Always had been easy for him. There should be a fucking Greats plate in his honor. All the princesses dancing around the circumference. He felt Buddy Boy harden, thick as the handle of his tennis racket. And when McGuinn unzipped, Buddy still fit perfectly in his grip. After all these years. McGuinn let his head drop back against the smooth supple leather of the LazyBoy neck rest.

The flesh on a child is different, stretched tight and smooth. The love of a child is different, too, and not for the faint of heart, not for the weak, not for the cautious. But the rewards, dear God. Each girl had her own tastes of course. Some let him take pictures; some let him record songs, ditties, silly girly things. He'd thrown out most of that stuff along the way, precautions he had to take with all his moves, but he had one book of memories, a couple of cassettes buried somewhere in a box, and he kept other images in his brain so that during dry spells he could visit them, call up their supple skin, their high voices, how they would squirm on his lap. He could conjure them when he needed to recall how it felt, how he missed it even now—the love of a child.

Who was he fooling? The phone was dead. He felt bereft. Robbed. Then the doorbell buzzed loudly. Christ. She'd got him all hot and ready to go, then let him go. Buddy was confused, but the fucking doorbell again. The mailman? Two loud long rings. He tried to calm his breathing. He coughed. Buddy fizzled out. Three more rings. He sank lower in the chair, didn't move. Curtains drawn, no one could see him inside. He counted to fifty and strained his ears. Did he hear footsteps on the walkway up to the front door? Footsteps receding? A car driving off or was that the roar of trucks from the AIA in the distance? His pulse throbbed in his ears. He waited for another minute or two, then pushed himself up. Legs tingling. Neuropathy, Peg said, he should get it checked out; she knew a neurologist. Fucking doctors. He walked into the foyer straightening out his toes, flexing his foot in between steps, to try and get the feeling back.

Then the phone again. Jesus. He walked back to the recliner, found the handpiece.

"Yes," he said, trying to catch his breath. Jesus. When did walking a few steps become such an effort? "Is that you, Princess?"

"Ha!" Peg said. "That's a good one. Listen. I'll pick us up some dinner on the way home. Home in fifteen, twenty minutes. Mix me a drink?"

"All right," he squeezed out.

He needed a drink, too. More than a beer. He grasped the back of the couch, supported himself across the living room, towards Randall's liquor cabinet. He took a shot glass from the 1982 World Series collection that lined the top shelf, filled Whitey Herzog, Manager, with Jameson's and took a gulp, enough to revive him before he walked back to the front door and peered out through the white lace curtains. No one there on the front stoop or the walkway, but something on the bottom step. He opened the door, grasped the siderail, walked down two steps to the sidewalk, and bent to pick up the envelope.

"Let me get that for you, Sir." A tall, uniformed man appeared out of nowhere, picked up the envelope.

"John James McGuinn?"

"Yes."

"You've been served."

The officer hit McGuinn with the package and left as quickly as he'd appeared. McGuinn looked up and the down the street. Nothing. No car. He'd lived long enough to know good news did not arrive like this. He closed the door behind him, carried the envelope back to the living room. He could just throw it away. He was tempted. He'd been happy living here with Peg, things were quiet. No problems. Should he open it? Open himself up to God knows what?

He didn't want to know. He could smell himself. Beer and sweat from the day, the dry catch of scotch in his throat. The lightest layer over it all: The smell of sex and frustration—the smell of his life. He'd have to shower before Peg got home. He sank back down into the recliner, set the shot glass on the side table, let the envelope fall on his lap. His head hurt. His chest burned. He took a breath. Christ. He fumbled with the seal and pulled out a sheaf of papers held together by a giant clip. He pulled off the clip, lifted the top page: *In the Circuit Court of Broward County...*

The back door opened. Footsteps in the laundry room. He could hear the garage door closing.

"Peg?" he called out. He tried to stand, but his legs gave out and he collapsed back in the chair. The papers fell from his lap onto the carpet. Footsteps from the back hall, coming closer now, closing in.

"Is that you?"

He had to pick up the documents... didn't want Peg to see what was in the Complaint. All the old stories and lies, he had to hide them, but his hands felt big and clumsy. Every movement required so much effort. Hands gripping the leather arms, his feet flat on the floor, knees bent and ready, and, Christ, he was not six inches off the cushion when again, a pain, so sharp in his chest. He couldn't breathe. He grabbed at his throat, tried to call out, but he couldn't speak. His brain flickered. His eyes couldn't focus; the room was spinning, he was on the floor, the ceiling fan whirring. Peg was there and not there, hovering over him, her lips moving, she was speaking into the phone, her tongue thrust between her teeth, her perfect fake white teeth. He couldn't hear her words. He was reaching for her as she turned away, *please help me,* he said, but she kept talking into the phone. Didn't she see them? So many girls holding hands, girls in a circle, so many faces from before, so many names he'd forgotten, girls dancing and swirling around him. *I would never hurt you* he told each of them, all of them, all twenty, twenty-one, maybe more of them, *I would never, ever...* but they closed in on him, pointing, whispering, waiting, watching as he gasped one last time, *please...*

PART V

TONGUE OF THE OCEAN

2013

CHAPTER 21

2013

Ethel had asked me months ago to come back to the island for her opening. It would mean so much, she'd said, with Nora being gone. Her work would be featured in an exhibit, *Art from the Archipelago*, at a new gallery in Freeport, on Friday, July 12th, a celebration of the 40th anniversary of Bahamian Independence. Almost two years since Nora's death and Ethel said she'd acclimated to life alone, dividing time between Bristol and Grand Bahama, but that she wanted—no, needed—family beside her for the first night. She hated openings, the stress before, the spotlight during—so many eyes on her, the glad-handing patrons, and the inevitable let-down after. Would I please come and stand with her? Only if I were ready to return, of course, and she'd understand if not, but, if I arrived a few days early, we could spend some quality time together, walk the beach in front of her home in High Rock, search for sea treasure as we did years ago, swim again, off the shores of our separate childhoods.

I said yes last December—from the distance of 1,200 miles and the cool remove of seven months—sure that I'd find an unassailable reason to back out before the summer. Work pressures, I'd tell her, maybe an intractable deadline from my editor. Ethel knew I was making revisions to a collection of my short stories that would require time. Or family demands. Wouldn't you just know it? Yondi's got another trial and I'm needed on the home front. So sorry, I'd say, I hope you understand.

As the plane descends, I press my forehead to the window, and try not to think of all the damn good and half legitimate excuses I could have given her. My better self wants to show up for Ethel, as she has for me, so many times over so many years. I check my watch—which I've already jumped ahead an hour from Chicago time. It's 6:38 p.m. here, a beautiful Wednesday evening over the Atlantic. The decision's made; no turning back. White clouds scallop the sky for as far as I can see, and below, the ocean shows off the piercing palette that I learned so long ago—the navy of the deepest troughs, the bright blues of the open sea, and the cyan over shallow reefs. And now, the white, rocky West End community rising to greet us, as Grand Bahama grows from a dot to an island. The undercarriage groans as the plane lowers and floats for a couple of minutes over the Eight Mile Rock settlements before a jarring landing at Freeport International Airport. Spontaneous applause from the sparsely populated cabin. Midweek, midsummer, means few if any tourists among the fifty-or-so passengers.

While we taxi to the terminal, a chummy Bahamasair flight attendant welcomes us all back to paradise. "A clear and balmy eighty-five degrees outside. Whether you're visiting for the first time or coming home from your travels, welcome to Freeport/Lucaya. And remember, folks: It's always better in the Bahamas."

When I emerge—travel-worn and jangly—from customs, Ethel is waiting. Her arms, still lean and muscular, open for me. A gentle smile. At seventy-one, she's shrunk a couple of inches, her shoulders round forward more than I remember from when she visited us in Chicago at Christmas, but she still towers over me. Her close-cut hair, whiter than gray, gleams under the fluorescent lighting, while her face remains remarkably unwrinkled by the years—certainly less than mine. True to form, she's in khaki shorts and a paint-stained t-shirt, no doubt coming straight from studio to airport.

"My Dede!" Her hug feels like homecoming. "You made it."

"Of course. I wouldn't miss it for the world. I can feel your ribs. Are you eating enough?"

"I'm fine, fine. Not cooking as much as I used to. How was the flight? Yondi, Laila? How are they? I so wish they could have come."

"They wanted to. Yondi wanted to see you and the show, of course, and Laila begged and begged. But this way, we get more time together, time to catch up and really talk. Just the two of us with no interruptions. Laila's not one for sitting quietly by while the grown-ups talk."

"Oh, I know. Couldn't get a word in edgewise last time we Skyped. She's a bit like someone else I used to know."

It's seven-thirty by the time we leave the airport, turn onto what Ethel reminds me is Grand Bahama Highway, the island's west to east through line. I've traveled most of the day, from Chicago, my home since grad school at UChicago, to Palm Beach International Airport, for a two-hour layover and a change of airlines, then a quick flight into Freeport. My body feels as if I've downed a carafe of coffee before going to bed—over-tired and jittery at the same time—my hands shake as I buckle the frayed lap belt. Ethel's home is another thirty minutes east of downtown in a quiet and remote part of the island. High Rock. She and Nora bought the place in the late '90s—a flood sale, literally, after Hurricane Floyd. At first, Ethel would spend time alone on the island during the autumn months when Nora was busy with school. She could work long hours on her art and then, when the term ended, Nora would fly over to join her. It worked well for them; even after Nora's retirement in 2003, they kept it up—Ethel coming over in October or November, and Nora arriving before Christmas, when the dreary weather swallowed Bristol. Many years, they came to Chicago to celebrate the holidays with my family, though it would have made more sense meteorologically speaking, for us to fly to them. For obvious reasons, I've never wanted to go back to the island and Ethel had never pushed the point until now.

She's tied back the canvas roof of her ancient Land Rover, so the evening hits us, breezy and warm, as she drives more slowly than necessary, even taking a couple of quick detours, to point out several sites that I vaguely or vividly remember: El Casino—where Mum used to work—shuttered and ramshackle, not as tacky in its decrepitude as it was in its heyday. The faux Asian pagoda still marking the entrance to the International Bazaar, and Mary Star of the Sea Church, with the white steeple which used to be a guidepost on my walks to the library still piercing the blue. The roads are potholed, and the buildings seem dirty, dated, and smaller than they should be, so the power of this place, the island's grip on me, should have deliquesced with time, but my gut fills with familiar dread the farther we drive; my ears buzz with something like fear.

"Do you want to swing by Sunland School? The Baptists took it over a few years ago—same spot, Gambier Road, but they got rid of those rusty old trailers and built a nice new building. Or we could snoop around the old apartment building. I'm not sure who owns it since Silvio's death."

I shake my head. Picture the flat where Mum and I lived. The kidney bean pool and the hours I logged in it, beside it, alone and longing for attention. Ethel's voice is A.M. radio breaking up—distant, choppy. I inhale—four counts in, exhale—four counts out, repeat until her words become clearer through the muffled distance.

A mile or two down the highway, she points out spots I can't recall: A dive called Beefy King, where she insists that I used to order the "Thick and Cheesy." Remember? I shake my head. The tower of onion rings? Nothing. Next, a side road that leads to the ex-pats' tennis and squash club. Your Mum was quite good at squash, wasn't she? Nothing. The Freeport Players Guild where Ethel says she and Nora took me to see *The Sound of Music*. Not even a flash of recollection. I don't doubt her memory but where have I stored those places and events?

East of town, the highway is increasingly cracked, jarring even in a four-wheel drive, and the verge flashes with broken glass and litter.

"Hurricane Irene took a real toll as you can... feel."

I laugh half-heartedly, pull myself into the here and now. But I have not forgotten that two worlds coexist here: paradise and poverty, beauty and desolation. And the roads were always rough outside of downtown.

"Is it strange for you, spending so much time here? Does it feel like home again?"

"Home. That's a tricky one for people like you and me, isn't it? After Nora died, well, I suppose I didn't want to stay most of the year in Bristol, being reminded of her at every turn, in the kitchen, our garden—her roses, walking to the shops, riding the bus into town, seeing all the Red Maids students. Being here most of the year has helped because she was... and I don't mean this disparagingly... not

275

a major part of my life here. It's less painful, not being tripped by memories."

"I get that."

"I'm thinking about selling the cottage. Getting the money of it. Prices are crazy high in England. Lord knows I never thought I'd wind up my years in the Bahamas but here I am. And to answer your question, I can't say I am fully at home. But maybe as much as anywhere. It helps that I am closer to you and Yondi and Laila. At least in North America and a similar time zone. Plus, unlike in the old days, I can get materials shipped easily from suppliers in the States. Blick's in Miami has everything I need."

"Remember when you used to make your own clay? That was a labor of love."

"Fool's errand, more like. You probably don't recall but there was a spot I found inland near Bevan's Town, just a couple of miles from here actually. It had the richest soil on the island, though that's not saying a lot. I'd dig through an inch or two of mulch to find a thimbleful of that reddish pineapple soil before hitting limestone. When I first returned to England, must have been in '77 or '78, Nora took me to a farm in East Sussex where you could wade into a stream and dig up bucketsful of clay—the good stuff; you could roll it, shape it right out of the water, so easy it felt like cheating. But I don't mess with that anymore. My clay arrives in perfect cubes. Fifty pounds for twenty dollars. You'll see my studio—I've simplified things a lot, reduced the amount of manual labor I do. I even pay an assistant to come once a week and give me a hand with the heavy work, materials prep, and clean-up."

We are maybe fifteen miles out of town, driving a straight gray line, with pine-splayed brush on either side. The investors' promises of the sixties and seventies never amounted to much, Ethel says, and if you turn left or right onto any one of the side streets, tarmac quickly changes to gravel, then dead ends.

My mind snags on a hot day. Me sitting on his lap in the front seat, my hands on the wheel at 10 and 2, like he taught me. These were "driving lessons," turning the car onto a gritty and jarring road, my legs too short to reach the accelerator and brake. We came to a stop before a deep, empty canal. The Olds Cutlass Supreme. The afternoon heat. His thick hands on my thighs. I steered myself to this place. The wracking guilt that comes on like nausea. I need to get away, to get out of here.

"You okay?" Ethel asks and repeats before pulling over on the verge. She reaches for my hand and squeezes my fingers. "Dede?"

I nod and try to stay present. Find five things you can see, four things you can hear, three things you can touch... a palmetto bush, cloudless sky, the seat beneath my jeans, my tennis shoes resting on the thick rubber floormat. My hand in Ethel's.

"Domini?"

Birds chirping in the bush, a small plane overhead, Ethel's voice.

She knows my story, or at least the broad strokes of it. She knows more than anyone. McGuinn, the sexual abuse, the baby I surrendered, and the lies I told to cover it all up. She knows these things, but we have barely mentioned them in the years since. No one wants the details—the flashes and shards that come out of nowhere to knock me to my knees—here and then gone. Only not gone, not really, never gone, just buried again.

"I'm good. Twinge of a headache from the travel but I'll be okay once I get some water."

A mile off the main highway, her home is one of several on a single-lane street parallel to the beachfront. Yellow clapboard, with white shutters and trim. One story. Her studio's another mile down the road, she says, in the middle of the town, which, she adds, is nothing like a town. After Frances flooded the island a decade ago, she bought the old High Rock supply store from the government for $100, converted it slowly, cheaply, over time into her perfect workspace. I've seen it in photos she's sent—she's proud of it—and tomorrow she'll walk me through it.

I grab my suitcase and backpack from the rear of the jeep. Inside, the house is clean, cool, artsy. Lots of windows, ceiling fans. An open floorplan for the kitchen and living areas. White marble floors, white walls, minimal modern furniture. A slab of tempered glass on a massive knot of driftwood for a coffee table. On one of the walls, she's built a set of shelves to show off sea treasure: Large jars and vases full of weathered glass, whelks, shark eye shells, and sunrise tellins.

My bedroom is on the west side of the house. It's small, barely large enough to hold the double bed and a dresser, but the large windows on the three external walls are open and air flows through, giving it a spacious feel. The sky has darkened to periwinkle and I can make out dunes in the foreground, sea oats gripping the sand; the ocean spreading to the horizon. She's filled a vase with yellow flowers, set it on the dresser. Wild Unction, she tells me. Above the headboard, a painting that is not hers... an island boy lost in contemplation as he cuts into a Queen Conch... a pile of discarded shells beside him. The image is timeless and private— capturing an intimate moment in this everyday act—and I can see right away why Ethel chose to hang it. By a friend of hers, Sheldon. He's also in the show. You'll like him, she says. She points out two towels and a bar of soap in the small half-bath which is closet-sized, tucked into the corner of the bedroom.

"This is perfect."

"Feel free to freshen up. Maybe a quick cowboy splash while I finish supper? I've made all your old favorites. If you want a real shower, though, you'll need to use my bathroom."

The meal fills an array of colorful ceramic plates laid out on the kitchen counter—fresh conch salad, of course, Ethel's famous conch fritters, cassava bread, and an array of island fruit. Six bottles of Kalik, a Bahamian lager that she says goes perfectly with every conch-coction, sweat in the humid air. We heap food on our plates and grab beers, head onto the screened-in porch that she added after Nora retired, doubling the footprint of the house. She's filled it with a sisal rug, a circular dining table, four dining chairs. Off to the side of the porch, two rockers, for looking out over the ocean. We sit side-by-side in the rockers, plates in our laps, beers in hand. Night rolls towards us, along with the sounds of the upwards sea. We clink our bottles, dig into the meal.

"This is all right."

"I'd agree. Thank you for coming. It means the world to me."

After seconds of everything, including beers, I ask Ethel how she's doing, really doing, in adapting to life without Nora. She shares parts of the cancer journey that I've not heard before, things she didn't mention last Christmas in Chicago. How Nora quit chemo without consulting her. How Ethel had begged her to try new drugs, experimental ther-apies, homeopathy, anything out there... all of which Nora rejected. Ethel stops herself. No point in rehashing this now, I don't want to sound bitter, she says, and tells me a happier story, about a walk they took in Gloucester on a drizzly day, Wellington boots on, Nora march-ing down a bridlepath—ten yards ahead of Ethel, as always—hopping merrily over a stile and landing in a field of cow slurry. Nora up to her knees in it. And soon we are laughing together, recalling Nora's quirks—the abundance of headscarves, her adoration of Sir Edward Elgar and the Proms, the Cambridge boys' choir she insisted we listen to every Christmas morning while drinking mugs of Horlicks.

We clink bottles again and offer up a toast. To Nora. Keep calm and carry on.

"I should let you sleep," Ethel says, eyes down, picking clay from her fingernails.

"I'm okay. I can sleep late tomorrow." I reach for her hand, kiss the back of it, the knuckles now knobby with arthritis. "I know you must miss her like crazy."

She nods. "I'm grateful that you're here. I do okay on my own but would have felt bereft without family here for the opening."

"Do you want to tell me about it? The installation—coral reefs, I presume."

"Indeed. Still stuck in the same gear. This exhibit's called *Geometry of the Sea*. Like the earlier walls, but I've changed point of view and it's got a few Bahamian specific references. But I don't want to say more—you'll see."

In the late nineties, she received her first grant for a public installation, a massive exhibit of an endangered reef that debuted in the lobby of the High Commissioner's office in Australia. That led to several other commissions, including one from the U.S. Department of State through their Art in Embassies office that made her semi-famous.

"Can I help with anything at the gallery? Set-up, lighting, anything?"

"No need, love, they've got paid workers for that. Young people with strong backs. Besides, I want you to experience it opening night with the full effects."

"You sure? I've got nothing else to do."

"You know how you won't let me read early drafts of your short stories? I want it to be like that, for you, immersive, not piecemeal. Anyway, the concepts I'm exploring are not new. Damaging effects of human influence, pollution, overfishing. Me going on about the same old things. Only now climate change is at the forefront of public debate. Suddenly I'm in my seventies and quite popular."

"You were prescient, Ms. Edgecombe."

"Ha." She pushes herself up off the chair. "More like stubborn as a mule. Kept doing the same thing until people finally paid attention. But listen, we'll have all weekend after the opening to talk about my work. After you see it, we can do a full debrief. Tonight, I want to hear more about the family, if you're not too exhausted."

"I've actually got a second wind. What to say? Yondi's good. She's working on a huge death penalty case. While there's no capital punishment in Illinois, this is a federal trial—with like, ten co-defendants—gang-related. Drugs and guns and conspiracy charges that make them all eligible for the death penalty under federal law. She's coordinating the defense, strategizing with all the other attorneys on how to best present their arguments. Not for acquittal but for mitigation. It's very consuming, as you can imagine, finding character witnesses, interviewing family members. I thought for a while that it would mean I couldn't come—that's why I was so cagey last month—but we worked things out."

"You mean care for Laila?"

"Yep. Our girl." I picture her and my heart fills. She's a touch over five feet, long-legged, athletic, talkative, inquisitive, probing. Almost eleven... about the same age that I was when I first came to the Bahamas. "She's enrolled in a Park District art camp for all of July. I'm evil to deprive her of time with you and seeing your show.

Evil. But it's better that she stayed at home. She bikes herself to and from camp with another kid. And we hired a college student to watch her in the afternoons, drive her around to the pool or soccer practice, so Yondi can work a full day. They'll do lots of messy, late-night baking. Especially without me around to curb the fun. That's their nickname for me, you know. Professor Funbuster."

"With a PhD in ruining their good times?"

"You've got it."

They've been a team since I cut the cord and laid Laila on Yondi's chest. It works this way—the two of them together, my stepping back; it's a dynamic that I have fostered because my adult self wants, craves time alone for my writing—while Yondi loves to be fully present in whatever she does. At home, she's Laila's buddy and confidante and go-to. Sometimes it hurts a bit, but if I am completely honest, I have been scared to carry the full weight, the care of a child since day one. *You take her,* I would say to Yondi in the early months, when I couldn't tolerate the worry of keeping her safe, *please, just hold her,* when I was losing my mind wondering if she was still breathing. And Yondi is a perfect balance for me. Even-keeled in court and in life, she sees it as her mission to help me relax, to point out the good in people, the joy in parenting, enjoy small pleasures and the occasional extravagant ones, too. My wife, both the breadwinner and our household steady, a Chicago lawyer who enjoys her work, a mother who enjoys spending time with our child, even when Laila's an utter pill, which is more and more often these pre-teen years. She laughs off Laila's moods in a way I can't, even when I'm well rested, even in my calmest moments. She takes Laila to her parents' house in the South Shore community most weekends for "proper church," hair-braiding by Grandma, and dinner with the extended family, giving me time alone to read students' papers or to plod away at my creative work.

"Yondi's a lot more patient as a parent than I am, honestly. Laila pulls the Old School British out of me when she acts spoilt or sometimes simply childlike. I want to send her to her room, or tell her to shape up, to be grateful for all she has. I hear myself saying things Mum would have, *you don't know how good you have it, young lady*. Or *no one likes a precocious child*."

"Ha! I can hear your mother in that. She had a… a certain tone. Not exactly gentle."

Mum died in a plane crash, along with Silvio and two of their friends in 1991. Clear day, good weather, no sudden storms, but the Cessna dropped 100 yards shy of the landing strip on Eleuthera, smacking into a rocky plateau, and killing everyone instantly, the investigator said. They were flying to Pink Sands for a friend's wedding. I was twenty-eight years old, dating my first serious girlfriend and half-way through my PhD program. Mum and I were coming back around, after years of estrangement. Maybe it's a strange kind of loyalty, then, that has me recycling Mum's words for my daughter when I swore that when the time came, if the time ever came, I'd never parent the way she did. Or didn't. In the seventies, "parent" was a noun and decidedly not a verb.

"Sorry if I upset you, saying that about your mum—her tone."

"No. No worries. I was the one who conjured her up—*precocious*—God, she loved that word. Overused it on me. Besides, it's not as if I could come back here and not think of her. I knew it would happen. I'm prepared for the memory rush. Somewhat."

"Dede, there is one more thing… I should have told you before, but I was afraid you wouldn't come if you knew. The gallery—where the exhibition is—well, it was built with money from the Ingraham family. It bears their name. Jethro and his wife, they've pumped millions into the island over the past couple of decades; some say it's drug money. I don't know. They've built resorts, restaurants. She's a creative sort and must have encouraged him to invest in the arts, too."

I take a long pull on what will be my last beer of the night and feel my head spinning. I'm not a big drinker and I'll have a raging headache tomorrow. Jethro. God. I try to block a picture of him... smirking, standing over a frog with a scalpel in his hand...

"He may not be there, of course. It may be his wife, or neither of them. But... I wanted to tell you... yes, I should have told you before you came, but I needed you here."

I put down my beer bottle. "Thanks. I want to be here. And it will be all right. I can handle Jethro," I say the words, but dread fills me. I am not sure I can handle any of this.

In bed, clean sheets encase me, and the smell and sound of ocean fill the room. It's too late to call home so I send Yondi a quick text. *All's good. Will call in the morning.* When I am less tired, less drunk. My head spinning from too much beer, my body exhausted from the travel, the stress of being here, the news about Jethro. What would I say if I were to run into him at the art opening? That I am terribly sorry? Is that even true? Didn't some part of me relish wounding him? My pulse pounds in my ear. I need to breathe, try to relax. I exhale and begin backwards counting, 99, 98, 97—my fail-safe soporific—96, 95—but my brain is buzzing, sleep taunts me. Through the south-facing window, the moon is a thin sliver above the Providence Channel, dark water filled with forgotten memories, silenced stories.

Ethel said that she wants her exhibit to create the effect of immersion rather than narration. *Geometry of the Sea*. Geometry: Questions of shape and size and relative position in a particular world. I am a daughter, a wife, a mother, and a writer, finally returning to this crooked island, with the chance to look at what happened. Was it my fault? Did I cause it? Did I crave attention? A cock tease, he said many times, and I believed. Now I know that a child cannot consent, that a child cannot be complicit, that a child does not seduce. I have an eleven-year-old daughter. I know Laila, I know she has no such power. Yet I still believe that *I* should have known better. I was clever... a precocious child... aware of my effect on him. I saw how he looked at me, how he gave me things, bought me treats, said he couldn't help himself when his body took over. I must have known that what he did was wrong because I didn't tell anyone. I remember that I kept a diary back then and would write in it each night about the details of the day. Dry facts that told nothing. I am sure that I didn't ever mention what was happening on those drives with the man I called chauffeur. Was I afraid that someone would see or was I worried that by writing it down I'd make it true, in a way that it could not be true, if I locked it up in a priest hole of memory?

I was a liar. Lying by omission. Lying by commission. I hated Jethro for good and childish reasons, so I lied and put McGuinn's blame on him. Now I wonder whom I wanted to protect. McGuinn? Mum? Myself? All three, perhaps. The twelve-year-old self, the princess of ellipses, didn't know that the lies I told and the things I left out would haunt me. How the unsaid rustles through our minds when the world goes quiet and we are alone.

I pad to the bathroom, drink lukewarm water straight from the tap. I'm okay. I am almost fifty, and I am all right. I left the island and went away to boarding school in Bristol; and Ethel and Nora were there for me when I needed a family. I got through college and graduate school and made myself a good life—teaching and writing. Each week I have lived is a week beyond McGuinn and the Bahamas. And there have been days, maybe even weeks when I didn't think of him. For years I thought I would never be in a relationship, enjoy sex, have a permanent home or, God forbid, a child. But I met Yolanda Imani Jackson in Chicago more than fifteen years ago and now there is Yondi and there is Laila and there is our life together. It has shape and meaning. Our own geometry.

McGuinn is dead. I know that. Spring of 2001. West Palm Beach, Florida. Heart attack. He can do no more harm, Yondi said, when she showed me a copy of his death certificate and a pile of other papers that she'd hired an investigator from the Public Defender's office to find. It's time to let him go. But when the scene of the crime is your own body, how do you forget?

I check the clock radio on the side table. 12:59 a.m. All those long nights in the flat when I had to call the time. *For the finest drinks under the sun, mix them with friendly Appleton rum.* Here I am again, still holding the secrets, still ashamed of the omissions and the lies that I told. Is admitting that I had no control, no ability to stop McGuinn, worse than taking the blame for it? With blame, at least I keep some of the power.

The next morning, after a quick breakfast of fruit and toast and tea, Ethel and I head straight to the ocean in swimsuits, sandals, and shorts. The white sand spreads flat and empty; the teal sea licks at the shore. We walk for maybe a half mile east and the beach ripples under our feet, tiny ridges of sand formed by last night's tide. As we near a rocky promontory, we stop and look out across the sea. We are farther east by twenty miles, but on the same beach as the one I was on so many years ago, wandering along the shoreline, one Saturday in August picking up shells and sea glass shards, and trying to hold on to Natalie's friendship. Grateful for her time and attention and jealous of her life. Lunch at Coral Cove. A storm coagulating in the sky. I didn't know I had a baby in my belly yet. Or maybe I knew and did not want to believe. Maybe that is why I did whatever Natalie told me to do—shook my fists at the storm, stole a Hobie Cat from the Ingrahams, and pushed out alone onto the raging sea. Maybe I was running away, even then, before I knew the truth that I would have to face.

How many miles did I sail on that storm-tossed sailboat? How did I survive the hours on the ocean? I think that I remember waking with sand in my mouth and eyes. Salt patterns crisp on my body. My thirst pulling me along a pocked road to a lonely shack. Callow Cay feels like someone else's life, a story I read and co-opted for myself, or a vivid dream that went on and on for days. Did any of it happen? Could Harmony still be alive? Memories of her voice, her calm, have come to me over the years. Who is she to me? Maybe it's a story that I still need to write.

"What are you thinking?" Ethel asks.

"Nothing."

Ethel bends to pick up something… a perfect white sand-dollar half-buried. She washes it off and shows me, before tossing it back into the sea. "Forgive me if I find that hard to believe, Dede. Nothing going on in that head of yours?"

How nothing covers the memories that burst in my brain, how nothing swallows the words I still hear. McGuinn's face, the hot vinyl seat, his hands. *I will tell. I will tell someone. I will tell my dad.* I told no one. All the nothings that he did—those that I remember, and those that I have forgotten. All the nothings I never spoke of. Where do they go? Do they attach to the limestone seabed or swirl deep and unspoken in the Tongue of the Ocean?

Late morning, after we've had a swim, showered, and dressed, we drive into Freeport, and I drop Ethel at the Gallery for her pre-show meeting with the curator. It's a beautiful modern building near Port Lucaya, but she doesn't want me to come inside with her, tells me to take the Land Rover, maybe get a bite to eat and write for a while, there's a lovely spot on the water. She gives me directions and says to take my time before collecting her. She's got plenty left to do before the exhibit opens tomorrow evening.

My nerves feel jangly, super-sensitized to the heat, the colors, and the sounds. As I drive away from the gallery, I veer onto the left side of the road. An oncoming car honks. I downshift and the Land Rover lurches. My ears are ringing, a familiar flash of pain behind my left eye. I brought along a bookbag with a pen and a notebook, but I didn't think to throw in Sumatriptan, the wonder migraine medicine, for today's trip. A mistake, but I don't want to drive all the way back to High Rock. Maybe a cup of strong coffee will help me through.

At Sunrise Highway, I make a left turn, then at the first round-about, spin off on Gambier Road. When I walked to or from school several times a week, this road seemed to go on forever, but today it's not much more than a glorified driveway. Less than a half mile, and on my left, *Sunland Baptist Academy*. I pull over, stop the engine, and sit for a couple of minutes. The gates are closed, the parking spots in front of the administration building empty, the trailers out back gone. I have no stomach for walking around the grounds, visiting the scrubland where we played tetherball, dodgeball, jump rope. Where the boys trapped and tortured lizards. I try to recount the names of my classmates: Natalie Fryer. Prudence, who took my scholarship. What was her surname? Enid. And that Timmy kid, with the glass-bottom boats and the encyclopedic knowledge of blue holes, his fixation on pirates and buried treasure.

The teachers: Miss Popplewell, Mrs. Morley. Miss Evans—Janet Evans—was the last teacher I had. Welsh. So young and so well-intentioned that first day she arrived and faced us all. How Jethro terrorized her... terrorized me, too. How I found my revenge. I am hit with a fresh wave of guilt. Jethro sent away to boarding school but returned now to take his place in the family line. In the end he's okay, it seems, married, financially successful. But what I did... it must have cost him something. Maybe a lot. I am ready to learn what happened. If I see him, I am ready to tell him I am sorry for what I said, for the lies I told.

I do a U-turn and drive back to the traffic circle, continue west past the International Bazaar where a few straw-plaiters are hawking their fare: hats and fans and baskets. I used to walk past here after school, on my way to the library, where I'd sit at a table in the A.C. for hours. I'd read anything. History books, scientific studies about bush medicine, back issues of *National Geographic* that I'd ask the librarian to special-order from Nassau. Encyclopedias, too. Sometimes, I'd pull out maps and memorize island names or listen to oral histories on tape; old Bahamians talking on about their childhood on the out islands where their families fished and sponged or raked salt. If I were to close my eyes and concentrate, I could probably still hear the island-tinged voices, remember the lyrics to traditional songs.

The library is still housed in a two-story structure, but it's had a recent face lift, painted fresh white. I park in the small lot, next to a beat-up Volkswagen bug. Inside, modular furniture, banquette seating, study carrels, and computer stations. A blue-haired, white woman in a proper English frock like my gran would have worn staffs the thoroughly modern front desk. She asks if I need help and I explain that I am a tourist, here for *The Art from the Archipelago* opening. She knows about the show. "Wonderful building, the new gallery. Took years to finish," she says, "Construction started and stalled, started and stalled through all the hurricanes."

I tell her I am searching for information about a resident of a tiny cay in the Abacos. "Is there any way to access public records for the Out Islands? Births, deaths, marriages, that kind of thing?"

"We call them the Family Islands now," she says, "Less pejorative, I suppose. Anyway, we don't store that kind of information here, but I can help you access a government database, if you have a legitimate purpose for the research?"

"It's for the exhibit," I lie. "My friend, Ethel Edgecombe, is one of the artists and she asked me to see if I could find a current address and date of birth of a woman she wants to credit. Someone she worked with long ago."

"Oh, I so love Ethel's work. What a trailblazer she is. I hope to get to the opening tomorrow."

She sets me up on a computer in the main room and spends a few minutes connecting to the right site and shows me how the data tracks by island groups. She clicks on a link for the Abacos.

"What's the name you're looking for?"

"Knowles. First name Harmony. Or her sister, Agatha or Aggie Knowles, would be good, too."

"Quite a common name, Knowles, especially in the Abacos," she says, "and there's lots of inter-island movement as you might expect. You can limit your search by a time period or a category—birth, marriage, death records—but you might inadvertently exclude some information. There are already many omissions because record-keeping was so haphazard, especially before the 1990s, when the handwritten records were transferred online. And, of course, many life events were never reported."

I take a seat in a sturdy wooden chair. The air is cool, the librarian goes back to her station. I am the only customer and I have plenty of time before I need to pick up Ethel.

First, search of birth records: Knowles + Callow Cay + date after 1900. Nothing. I try again, listing the Abacos instead of the cay. This time I get multiple hits, but none of the Christian names match. Then, I look at marriage and death records. Again, plenty of Knowles, but not the ones I need. Surely, Aggie's death in 1965, a hurricane death, would have been recorded. Or maybe there was a newspaper article?

I find the librarian and ask if she can help me with press archives— anything on Hurricane Betsy. She pulls out some old microfiche and together we look at a dozen newspaper articles from August 27 through September 8, 1965. A story in the Nassau <u>Guardian</u> mentions one person killed in the hurricane: A man who was out on his boat when the storm hit. Several pieces report flattened houses, dislocation, crops ruined, dead animals, but no other human loss. No one reported missing or dead in the Abacos. And no mention anywhere of a Callow Cay.

Back on the computer, I click on an interactive map from the National Hurricane Center that lets me trace Betsy's path. The storm started in the Atlantic and moved west and north over the Bahamas, pushing towards Florida, then stalled and looped back, striking the

Abacos a second time, before heading on to Louisiana. I pull up a map of the islands on Google and zoom in. There is a small group of islands to the west of Great Abaco where the hurricane made a direct hit, but none with the name Callow Cay.

I walk to the front desk again. "Do you have time for one more question?"

The librarian laughs. "You can see there's not a lot going on here these days." She follows me back to the computer.

I put my finger on a line of dots west. "Do you know anything about this chain of islands?"

"That's Moore's Island, at the top, there, if I'm not mistaken. Let me see. Yes, yes. I went there once, many years ago, with my husband. Great bone fishing in those waters. But that island's terribly poor. Originally settled by Loyalist plantation owners from the States, I think, came over after the American Revolution, but when they realized the land was barren, they took off, leaving many of the slaves behind. They survived—figured out a way to survive, but Moore's Island is the poor cousin of the Abacos."

"Have you ever heard of Callow Cay?"

She shakes her head. "Sometimes the locals have their own names. Different names for all kinds of things. Places, plants, fruits. Maybe you're thinking of Gorda Cay—that's the second one, just below Moore's, it's now called Castaway Cay—Disney bought it for their cruises. Other C names, well there's Cat Island and Crooked Island—but those two are not in the Abacos, much farther south."

So much I can't be sure of, but I remember waking on a beach, stumbling up to Harmony's door. *East End of what, child? You on Callow Cay.* I thank the librarian and say I will come back later if I have time.

"Tell Ethel that I'm sorry I couldn't help her find her friend."

It's a short drive back to the museum, and I'll be early if I go straight there, so first I swing by the old apartment building. Run down, and so much smaller than I remember. I pull into the parking lot, but don't get out. Don't dare to venture into the courtyard and look for the lounge chairs where I'd sit for hours, reading from my latest stack of library books or scribbling nothings in my diary. Ethel's flat nearby. Across the courtyard, McGuinn's unit. My head hurts. Behind my eye, a painful throbbing. I restart the Land Rover and drive back towards the gallery.

No other cars on this stretch of road—there are no street names either—maybe those came down in the latest storm. But I'd come along this route to Natalie's house, walking on the rocky verge sometimes, and sometimes he'd drive me here, Royal Palm Way. Sometimes, I'd be the one steering. The pain behind my eye is so intense that I turn down a side street and pull over. I can't drive when I am like this, each thought a pickaxe in my head. Why no Callow Cay? No record of Aggie's death in the hurricane? No birth or property records or death records for Harmony Knowles? I squeeze my head in my hands and God, this cracked side road and his car pulled over. The snow cone melting. Him teasing me because my lips and tongue are turning blue. My head against the passenger door. He covers my mouth with a padded hand and his body bearing down. My head splitting open. I breathe, try to breathe, the pain is blinding. I am screaming. Let me out.

I open the door, stumble out of the Land Rover. Eyes half-closed, I stagger toward the bush, lean against a skinny tree with red and flaky bark. The memories like blood vessels rupturing in the brain. Jagged pain. I hold onto the tree, try to ground myself. Touch its bark, like peeling skin. Kamalamee, Harmony called it.

Good for rashes and poison ivy. We can make a decoction for the potcake. Harmony shows me how. Harmony, strong-boned and clear-headed; she's always standing in the doorway, and I am still running to her, stumbling into her arms. She's holding me up, even now. *You are not alone.* You will survive this. Five things I can see, four things I can hear, three things I can touch… I start the exercise to bring me back to the current moment—the Bahamas, where my past overwhelms my present and I cannot get away. I shade my eyes and walk gingerly back to the car, dig my phone from my bag and call Ethel.

"Dede?"

"My head…"

"Where are you?"

"I'm not sure. Close. Off Royal Palm somewhere, I turned on a side street. Sea Grape maybe? I don't know, everything from back then. I can't do this…please."

"Oh, child, I shouldn't have left you alone. I'll come."

I nod and the tears come. "Please."

"Okay, love, I'm walking to you now. If you can't talk, just listen to my voice. You hear me?"

"Yes."

"Hold tight. I'm on my way. You are not alone."

And soon she wraps me in her arms, and I am sobbing on her shoulder. Years before on this island, she listened to my jabbering, she taught me how to paint. She came to worry about me, to care for me, despite her better judgment, and in England, she and Nora let me stay with them every weekend and on school holidays and they became my chosen family. When I married and had a child, they became Laila's grandparents. By the time Ethel helps me back into the passenger seat, my headache is easing.

She climbs in her side but doesn't drive yet. She sits with me until my breathing calms. "Getting better?"

"I'm okay now."

"Are you sure? Can you tell me what happened?"

I shake my head.

"Did something bring it on? Tell me, Dede. I can handle anything you need to say."

"The time I was lost, the time I took off on the sailboat..."

"You scared me half to death. I walked up and down that beach most of the night looking for you."

"What else do you remember?"

"Well, someone found your shorts, I think, on the beach by the Ingraham's place. Yes, that's right, we knew they were yours because the pockets were full of shells and sea glass. We realized that you'd taken the Ingrahams' sailboat. There had been a bad storm, and everyone feared the worst. Me... I walked the beach, over and over."

"Harmony Knowles?"

Ethel shakes her head. "Who is she?"

"She lived on the cay where I washed up—in the Abacos, I think—I must have told you about her place, how she took care of me?"

"A captain found you. The guy who ran the mail-boat to all those small islands if I remember right. You were half-crazy from the sun and dehydration. He took you back to his home. Was it Green Turtle Cay? Or Marsh Harbor? One of those old white Abaco families. Boat builders, I think. Silvio and your mum flew over to get you."

The pain in my head starts again. I close my eyes and I am back in McGuinn's car on the side of the road. I asked him once, before he ever did it, to put his dick inside me. I didn't know what I was

295

asking, didn't imagine... I could be pregnant... I didn't understand until Harmony.

"Dede? Are you with me?"

"I went to the library because I wanted to track down Harmony Knowles. But Callow Cay is not on any of the maps and her name isn't in any records. But I remember her home, Ethel, I remember it as if I could touch the earth, taste the fruit. Genep and dillies in her orchard. Kamalamee trees by the vegetable patch. She had a rock oven. A rooster and hens scrapping in the yard. I can remember her voice, her words calming me. Could a memory be so wrong?"

"Not wrong, love, maybe just incomplete. Trust yourself. Start with the pieces; that's all any of us can do. Look at the parts and try to put them together. Remember way back when we swam over the reef down in Eight Mile Rock? How we got the panoramic view from above, then dived in close? And when we painted from memory later, do you remember how all the details came back to us—the stag coral, its arms orange and branching? The purple sea fans waving. A prickly black sea urchin. Things we didn't even know we'd absorbed found their way into our paintings. I still work that way, start with one detail, place it next to another, and after a while I figure out where I'm going, begin to understand the bigger picture. But let's go home, get you a drink, get something for your head. You can take a rest this afternoon and later, maybe not tonight but after the show, before you leave the island, well, we should talk. It's high time we got the poison out of you."

"There are things I can never say. Even to Yondi."

"I have never wanted to pry, but I see how it still pains you. Here, well, it's obvious, but even when you're at home in Chicago, I see what you carry. So, we can sit on my porch in the rockers or lie on the High Rock beach with our eyes closed or float on our backs in the ocean staring at the sky. It doesn't matter, but this week, before you leave, you need to show me the pieces."

CHAPTER 22

Friday evening, we arrive at the gallery, an hour before the exhibit opens. Ethel wears a black shirt and black jeans; only a colorful scarf, made by a family-owned batik factory in Andros, reveals that tonight is a special event for her. I feel overdressed in a gray and flowy Eileen Fisher outfit that I bought for tonight, but once the guests start to arrive, that worry dissipates. It's an elegant and well-dressed crowd, old and young, ex-pats and Bahamians, Black and Brown and White all mingling in ways that wouldn't have happened in the seventies. Not in the Freeport that I knew. I can't help but scan the room for someone who looks like Jethro, four decades since our years together at Sunland.

The reception room is set up with a podium and microphone up front and several rows of folding chairs for the audience. By 6:30 pm., the three well-stocked bars, spaced evenly across the back, are serving G & Ts, Pimm's Cups, and a colorful line-up of British and Bahamian beers. Ethel and the other two artists leave to check in with the curator in a back room. I ask one of the bartenders for a glass of tonic with lime and stand self-conscious and alone in the growing crowd. A few vaguely familiar faces look my way and occasionally make eye contact, but I can't muster the will for chitchat. I wish that Yondi were here to keep me company, to help me with the glad-handing I should be able to manage alone. A column in the back corner holds me up.

Ten minutes after seven, the curator introduces herself: Beatrice Kermode. She is a tall woman, completely bald and effortlessly elegant, with slim gold earrings and ruby-painted lips. She begins a somewhat lengthy introduction about Bahamian independence, art on Grand Bahama Island, the opening of this new gallery. She thanks the Ingraham family—who had hoped to make it here tonight, she says, but evidently didn't. She recognizes a few other patrons, some of whom get a turn at the microphone, talk too long, and recognize their own special people: Couldn't have done it alone, wouldn't have been possible without…. When the curator reclaims the mic, starts to talk about the three artists, I find a seat in the back row.

Third in order, Ethel stands when introduced and bows slightly to the crowd, then retakes her seat to hear her work described—a process which I know she must hate. But as Beatrice talks—and she goes on for a good while—Ethel seems calm, serene, so beautifully herself that she's hypnotizing. I read the paragraph summarizing her work in the Exhibit Guide.

> *Ethel Edgecombe's obsessive, large-scale sculptures portray an underwater world in which corals own the narrative space. Hardy, voluptuous forms impart to her subject matter a robust and eroticized presence. Using complex layers and subtly mathematical line-work in each coral piece, her nuanced reefs teem with echo and response. The effect leads the viewer into a trance of meditation, a secret sea-place of beauty and force. For this anniversary show, the artist—a Bahamian citizen by birth, a longtime resident of the UK,*

and now living and working back in High Rock on Grand Bahama Island—invites us to immerse ourselves in her world, to walk—or perhaps, more accurately, to float—though her understanding of the Baja mar—the wide, shallow sea.

As the introductions wrap up, uniformed attendants open the side doors to the gallery. I stay in my chair for a moment, waiting for the crowd to clear so that I can find Ethel and walk through the show with her.

The blue-haired lady from the library approaches. "Hello again. I hoped I'd see you tonight. After you left yesterday, I did a little more digging around. I plugged the names you were looking for into our library catalogue. Did several searches with Knowles and the Abacos and wandered through the stacks. Well, have a look at what I found."

She hands me a book. On the front cover: *Island Memories: Bahamian History Told by Those Who Lived It.*

"Thanks." I see Ethel talking to three or four people by the dais. I want to go to her. "That was very kind of you."

"Open it, open it." She's reaching for the book again, taking it from my hands in her excitement. "Almost 300 pages, with some photos and letters, population tables, too."

"Yes. Very interesting. Thank you so much."

"Here's what you really need to see." She rifles through the pages, smiles at me triumphantly before she starts to read. "Chapter 4: Interviews with Bush Medicine Practitioners. Right here, page 122, there's a woman who grew every kind of plant imaginable, a well-known herbalist in the Abacos... Her name is Aggie Knowles."

"Aggie Knowles?" I say the name and my head is spinning. Her voice is fading. The crowd is dispersing. I should get to Ethel. "I'm so sorry, I can't... I have to go."

"Well, look, I know this is a busy night. But please, keep the book and show it to Ethel later. Maybe this is the family she's looking for. Ask her to drop it off when she's done."

I tuck it under my arm. "Thank you. That's very kind." I make my way over to Ethel.

She's talking with a well-dressed couple in front of the dais. She looks my way and holds up a hand. Just a minute, she indicates, or is it, come on over? I make my way towards her but this time she holds her palm up like a stop sign.

Too late. A tall white man turns. Muscular through his tight-fitting dress shirt, well-tanned. His hair is sun-streaked, long, and stylishly unruly. His eyes meet mine before a wave of dread hits me.

"Well, well," he says. "I wondered if you'd ever show your face on the island again." Same old smirk. "Remember me?"

"Jethro... This is a surprise."

"You look exactly the same," he says. "Except for the gray hair."

I nod, but my mouth won't work.

Ethel tries to extricate me. "I've promised Dede that we'd walk through the show together. It was good to talk with you both."

"Hold on, hold on. Before you pull another disappearing act, Dede," The smirk again, as he places his hand on the back of the woman beside him who looks me up and down, "I'd like you to meet my wife. Olujinmi, this is Domini Dawes. We knew each other years ago."

I extend my hand. "Nice to meet you."

She says hello, shakes my hand, though her face shows nothing but boredom. Her eyes are looking past me to where the gallery doors have opened, letting the guests into the exhibit space.

"Dede and I were classmates at Sunland for what, three or four years? Not so much friends as... what would you say... competitors? At least until Dede made a rather dramatic departure."

I try to read his face, see what he is after. I don't want a scene. Not here. Not now. Not on Ethel's night. I look from him to his wife, not knowing what more I should or shouldn't acknowledge.

"Jethro, I owe you an apology. Long overdue. I am so very sorry for all the chaos I must have caused you... Maybe we could talk, another time perhaps?"

"She's the one?" His wife asks, and now her eyes are boring holes through me.

"Yep. She's the one. Coming to say sorry forty years too late."

I try to stand tall, take responsibility, take the anger that I deserve. "I made a lot of mistakes back then and I truly regret pulling you into my mess."

"Mess?" Jethro says. "That's one way to describe it. Four years in military school, for starters. My father wouldn't believe me, practically disowned me after your lies. I wasn't sure I'd ever be welcome here. It took me years to get back into his good graces."

"I am so sorry."

"Well, that doesn't help me much, does it? But you know what? I'm doing just fine. Better than fine," He reaches for his wife's hand. "We're in my parents' old place on Sea Gate Lane. We've got two amazing kids." He meets my eye with a fierce dislike. "My life is great, despite what you tried to do." His voice goes quiet. "I built this gallery, Dede. That is how well I am doing."

"Again, I didn't mean to hurt you." Even I can hear the lie in my words. How could it not have been about Jethro? He was the one I selected to take the hit. "I am happy for your successes."

"Come on, J, she's not worth the trouble." His wife walks towards

302

the exhibit, but he stays behind, takes my upper arm a little too tightly in his grip, pulls me away from the flow of people to an empty spot by the wall. "I know about what happened to your mother. She didn't deserve to go down like that. Terrible thing. Silvio's fault of course, for taking her on that run."

"They were on their way to a wedding with another couple. The plane just... just dropped. No one's fault, the investigators said."

A cruel smile I remembered from years ago. "Is that what they told you? And you believed them?"

"What do you know about it?"

"I know that it's stupid to mess with my family or my business. Now if you'll excuse me, I will join my wife. I trust you won't be staying beyond this weekend."

I watch Jethro catch up, take her elbow and disappear through the swinging doors into the first exhibit.

My face is burning—as if I am a teenager again—my hands are trembling. Ethel joins me. "I'm so sorry. I thought they hadn't shown up at first. I didn't notice them at the reception. But they found me after the talk. I haven't run into any of them in years. Turns out that his wife is good friends with another artist in the show, Jane Antonio. Are you all right, love, you're shaking?"

"I'm okay. That was long overdue. I survived it. And, apparently, Jethro's still a complete bastard. So, come on. Let's go see your beautiful work."

"No hurry. Let's give them time to get through the exhibit. I don't want him souring tonight for us."

I am grateful for the moment Ethel gives me to calm my breathing, to steady myself. I go to the bar and ask for a water, no ice. While Ethel waits beside me, I sip it slowly, focus on the present, why I am here. It's not about back then. Even if I made mistakes, Jethro cannot take this. It's Ethel's night.

We walk arm-in-arm into the first room. Incredible watercolors, by her friend, Sheldon, a self-taught painter who grew up here. Like the painting hanging in Ethel's guest room, the series installed for the exhibit shows Bahamians involved in intimate, private moments. The subjects seem to have stopped time for themselves. They are island people, not wealthy, but they seem to luxuriate in the world they inhabit. They are at home.

The art in the second room is starkly different. *Island Bound,* by a performative artist named Jane Antonio—who Ethel tells me is the daughter of my onetime GP, Dr. Antonio—is a giant fishing net woven from her own and her family's belongings. It hangs about eight feet above the floor, and as we cross the room, awkwardly angling our heads, each section of rope provides intimate, even disturbing details: hanks of someone's long black hair, strips of clothing, lacy under-wear, leather belts, fishing line, a man's tie, colorful scarfs, all plaited together to form a giant web. Only as we get most of the way across the 20-foot room can we see that the artist is herself cocooned—or is it trapped? —in the family web.

Finally, Ethel's gorgeous world. We walk through another set of doors to the base of a staircase, climb up to a balcony that stretches the length of the room. The doors leading onto the balcony close behind us and the room darkens slowly, quiet, except for the breathing of the twenty or so individuals on the balcony with us, peering over the railing into the darkness. Gradually, lights and a jazz flute solo fill the room below us, and one by one, pieces of coral are illuminated: red antlers, orange lobes, purple fans, greens and golds glowing in the dark; sounds of an ocean, alive, thriving. The big shallow sea. Then slowly the color leeches out from the edges first, whitening each piece of coral, each stag branch, each brain bulge, until the intricacies of each life form disappear into the white, dying, dead. As the music fades and ends, only one thing remains illuminated in the middle of the white graveyard—a single queen conch, unmoving in a bed of seagrass.

By 10 pm, when all the guests have left the gallery, when Ethel has been hugged and praised and talked to for so long that she can barely stand, I drive us home to High Rock. I drop the book that the librarian brought for me on my bed while I change into comfortable clothes. A blurb on the back cover says, "A social history told by those who lived it, *Island Voices* is at times more like poetry than history, weaving vivid, poignant memories of Bahamians from the first half of the twentieth century." It feels painfully familiar, and I open it up. On the inside of the jacket there's one of those old index cards that libraries used to use to check out books. This one has only been signed out a few times, so it's easy to see, up near the top of the list, a curly girly script that I recognize oh so well. *Domini Dawes*. The smudged date next to it, April 8, 1975. I must have found this book on the library shelves and signed it out, carried it home in my satchel. I check that date of publication—1962—and I skim the index and turn to Chapter 4—a series of interviews with practitioners of bush medicine and photographs of them in a few cases. Fred Ramsey, born on September 2, 1909, Smith Bay, Cat Island, photographed standing next to a mule. One Olive Simms, born in 1934 on Exuma. And Aggie Knowles, born in 1910 and pictured out front of her home in the Bight Settlement, Moore's Island. Nothing about Aggie or her homestead looks familiar. I read her interview quickly—several paragraphs, describing her decoctions and how she developed them, how she treats her neighbors in the community for all kinds of ailments, from sugar sickness to high blood pressure to infertility. Her obvious pride in being the island's only bush medicine practitioner. No mention of any family—parents, aunts, uncles, siblings, children.

Ethel's in the kitchen, back in khaki shorts and a t-shirt. We eat leftovers straight from the fridge. Then we carry a bottle of wine and a blanket to the beach. The sky tonight is cloudless and black, pinpricked with stars. We spend an hour talking about the exhibit, who came, the surprise of Jethro—how he was what we might have expected, only more so. Still cocky, still arrogant, with more than an edge of danger, these days. A bad boy grown into a bad man. I tell Ethel what he said about my mother's death, about the plane crash. His cryptic comments about drug trafficking. She tells me that there have always been rumors about that—with Silvio, the Casino—from way back in the seventies. Stories about local drug kings and fights between different factions. She always felt Barry Ingraham was clean—a straight politician—but she wouldn't be surprised to learn that Jethro was in on the drug trade. Where else would all that money come after the tourism industry collapsed. Maybe he clashed with Silvio? "But the plane crash," she says, "there's no basis for what Jethro was telling you. He's just being an asshole, trying to intimidate you, don't you think?"

I don't know what to think. I tell Ethel I suppose I deserve the treatment Jethro gave me, the tongue lashing at least, but not the veiled threats, I don't know what I am supposed to do with those. I am glad to be heading home tomorrow. "I'm so glad I came to see the opening, though. Your work was always incredible but what you've done… its scope and wisdom… it's staggering."

"Thank you. I guess I never could have imagined, back in the seventies when I gave up painting and began dabbling in clay that I'd get here—shaping these reefs, making money from my art, living the life I wanted."

Ethel talks about the brilliance of the curator's decisions in selecting the artists, how the sum of the three bodies of works resonated with the larger story of the islands: individuals, families, lands, and waters shaped by the best and the worst of humankind.

Then we sit for a long time looking out over the water. I think maybe Ethel is too exhausted to say another word. It must be close to midnight.

"Are you ready for some sleep?" I ask, "It's been quite a day. You are a superstar, you know."

She picks up my hand from the sand. "There's one thing I'd really like," she says.

"What's that?"

"I know it's hard, but it's time for you to talk."

"Not on the first night of your show. It doesn't feel right. You must be shattered. We can talk tomorrow, before I leave, I promise."

"The time is never going to feel right. But you're ready. You came back to the island. You met Jethro tonight and you handled it. You're never going to want to revisit that time, but you're safe, it's just the two of us."

She doesn't say more for a while and I close my eyes, try to think what to say.

"I don't like to go there because some of it, well, it knocks me down... like yesterday morning when I was driving to pick you up. A memory of being in his car. A memory of his face above me, his slicked back hair, his pleading eyes, his hands on me, and I want to scream. I still have nightmares of him, too, even though I know he's long dead. That's like one part of it all. Danger. Beware. Then, there are the thoughts and memories that are okay, even good—tastes, smells, faces that I remember. Harmony. I picture her a lot, hear her voice. See flashes of her shack, her garden, even hear her loud-mouthed rooster squawking at me. But now I think it's possible that I made her up. Created a person, a life, her world? That book the librarian gave me tonight... it's full of all kinds of names and facts and details that I must have read and held onto and maybe used to build what... an alternate reality?"

"Memory is tricky. Maybe you could think of the flashes like sea glass we used to pick up on our beach walks. There's no way you could rebuild the original bottle from the bits you find. But when you collect hundreds of different shards—reds, ambers, greens, blues—and arrange them in a new way, maybe layered in a vase, or strung to make a mobile——well, you create something beautiful, more beautiful than it was for suffering the sea change."

Ethel says that after Nora died, she came across some of my things in a box, stored up in the attic back in Bristol—items that she's held onto for years but will need to clear out when she sells the cottage. A yearbook and report cards from Sunland School. My old swimsuit and some clothes. A necklace I made for her out of shells. Cards and letters that I sent to her over the years. Some photos of potcake puppies. A few Polaroids that she held onto. Even an old diary of mine. She can ship them all to me if it might help me fill in blanks.

"Mum gave me that diary one Christmas. It had those girls on the front cover—wearing pinafores and clogs. The picture of white girl naivete—how my mum imagined me? I remember scribbling entries at night when I was bored, all the quotidian details of my life. I doubt I said one word about McGuinn."

"You were protecting yourself when no one else was looking out for you. The grown-ups failed you, Dede. Me included. I should have trusted my gut sooner. I knew that man was bad news. But so much was, well, if not unimaginable then unspoken in those days. If you read through that diary now, with your perspective as a mother, with your writerly sensibility, maybe you'd find the seeds of the story that the twelve-year-old did not yet know how to tell."

Maybe Ethel is right. The moments that I wrote about are not as important as the way I connect them. The way I fill in the unspoken between the written words. Memories are not static like library books on the shelves. Any retrieving changes the memories. Writing the story must change the teller. Should I begin with a mother and daughter arriving in the Bahamas? A dozen kids in a tin can classroom. A lonely girl night-swimming in a bean-shaped apartment pool. Or maybe... yes, a girl on a boat on a thrashing sea. And she's walking a scorched, scabby path up from the Bight. A squawking rooster named Mistah Biggety. An island woman with flaming orange hair and a broken heart. There's bush medicine for a potcake's mange. More and more images—each one as real as the sand granules beneath my hands. Twenty-three conch pearls stored in a rusty tin. And a blue hole honeycombed with caves. They come to me now, memories that are not lies, not make believe, but pieces that I pulled from books and maps and tape recordings, collected from teachers and painters and writers, picked up from beaches and the bush, and all of them shaped by sights and tastes and smells and sounds, calm waters and raging seas, all of them I gathered and stored then later collaged to carry me through. My story to poultice the raw and jagged truth.

Acknowledgments

Olga Culmer Jenkins' work, *Bahamian Memories: Island Voices of the Twentieth Century*, at times more like poetry than social history, provided me with stories, textures, and sounds of the islands. I am deeply indebted to her.

To everyone who helped me find the words to write this book and get it out into the world, I want to say thank you.

I begin with Robin Condro who helped me acknowledge and honor Blue. I will always appreciate your wisdom, unorthodox approach, and your undeniable gifts.

Todd Cooper, for endless hours of laughter, giddiness, tears. For your amazing art. For my book jackets. For your even more amazing heart. For listening to the memories and thoughts that I thought I could never say aloud. For helping me find the colors and shapes to answer the questions. For lifelong friendship that has helped me grow, evolve, and find gratitude.

To my writer friends, especially the women of Writers' Bridge—Jan English Leary, Arlene Bremer, Lynn Sloan, and Mary Beth Shaffer—who read many versions, provided invaluable feedback, cut excesses, offered unflagging support through my doubts and stumbles.

To the Ragdale Foundation for time and space and letting me roam free during COVID.

To Alex Kotlowitz, for friendship all along, and for guidance through the joys of writing and the perils of publishing.

To Abby Geni, for your kindness and openness when you didn't know me and certainly didn't owe me.

To Fred Shafer, for one-of-kind teaching, endless patience, painstaking care, and making me a better writer.

To Donna Bister and Marc Estrin at Fomite Press for considering, editing, improving, and then publishing my work.

To Virginia Justicz, for eagle-eyed copy-editing, for laughter, love, and friendship.

To all the friends who have shared meals, laughter, tears, and encouraging words along the way, especially Larry Wood, Gwenan Wilbur, Alex Kotlowitz, Maria Woltjen, Kathy O'Donnell, Ellen Somberg, Nancy Blum, Mary Roberts, Allison White, Peter Nolan, Karen Steward-Nolan, Melissa and Don Manning, Steve Wood and John Kennedy, Bonnie Allen, and Caroline Lawler.

To my brothers, Alex, Nick, Max, and Dan. I love you all so much.

To my father and mother, who imbued our family with love and kindness and a special kind of Justicz craziness.

And to my family: Mary, Thomas, and Lilly. You are my everything.

Fomite

Writing a review on social media sites for readers will help the progress of independent publishing. To submit a review, go to the book page on any of the sites and follow the links for reviews. Books from independent presses rely on reader-to-reader communications.

For more information or to order any of our books, visit:
http://www.fomitepress.com/our-books.html

More novels and novellas from Fomite...

Joshua Amses — *During This, Our Nadir*
Joshua Amses — *Ghats*
Joshua Amses — *Raven or Crow*
Joshua Amses — *The Moment Before an Injury*
Charles Bell — *The Married Land*
Charles Bell — *The Half Gods*
Jaysinh Birjepatel — *Nothing Beside Remains*
Jaysinh Birjepatel — *The Good Muslim of Jackson Heights*
David Brizer — *The Secret Doctrine of V. H. Rand*
David Brizer — *Victor Rand*
L. M Brown — *Hinterland*
Paula Closson Buck — *Summer on the Cold War Planet*
L.enny Cavallaro — *Paganini Agitato*
Dan Chodorkoff — *Loisaida*
Dan Chodorkoff — *Sugaring Down*
David Adams Cleveland — *Time's Betrayal*
Paul Cody— *Sphyxia*
Jaimee Wriston Colbert — *Vanishing Acts*
Roger Coleman — *Skywreck Afternoons*
Stephen Downes — *The Hands of Pianists*
Marc Estrin — *Hyde*
Marc Estrin — *Kafka's Roach*
Marc Estrin — *Proceedings of the Hebrew Free Burial Society*
Marc Estrin — *Speckled Vanities*
Marc Estrin — *The Annotated Nose*
Marc Estrin — *The Penseés of Alan Krieger*
Zdravka Evtimova — *Asylum for Men and Dogs*
Zdravka Evtimova — *In the Town of Joy and Peace*
Zdravka Evtimova — *Sinfonia Bulgarica*
Zdravka Evtimova — *You Can Smile on Wednesdays*
Daniel Forbes — *Derail This Train Wreck*
Peter Fortunato — *Carnevale*
Greg Guma — *Dons of Time*
Ramsey Hanhan – *Fugitive Dreams*

Fomite

Richard Hawley — *The Three Lives of Jonathan Force*
Lamar Herrin — *Father Figure*
Michael Horner — *Damage Control*
Ron Jacobs — *All the Sinners Saints*
Ron Jacobs — *Short Order Frame Up*
Ron Jacobs — *The Co-conspirator's Tale*
Scott Archer Jones — *A Rising Tide of People Swept Away*
Scott Archer Jones — *And Throw Away the Skins*
Julie Justicz — *Conch Pearl*
Julie Justicz — *Degrees of Difficulty*
Maggie Kast — *A Free Unsullied Land*
Darrell Kastin — *Shadowboxing with Bukowski*
Coleen Kearon — *#triggerwarning*
Coleen Kearon — *Feminist on Fire*
Jan English Leary — *Thicker Than Blood*
Jan English Leary — *Town and Gown*
Diane Lefer — *Confessions of a Carnivore*
Diane Lefer — *Out of Place*
Rob Lenihan — *Born Speaking Lies*
Cynthia Newberry Martin — *The Art of Her Life*
Colin McGinnis — *Roadman*
Douglas W. Milliken — *Our Shadows' Voice*
Ilan Mochari — *Zinsky the Obscure*
Peter Nash — *In the Place Where We Thought We Stood*
Peter Nash — *Parsimony*
Peter Nash — *The Least of It*
Peter Nash — *The Perfection of Things*
George Ovitt — *Stillpoint*
George Ovitt — *Tribunal*
Gregory Papadoyiannis — *The Baby Jazz*
Pelham — *The Walking Poor*
Christopher Peterson — *Madman*
Andy Potok — *My Father's Keeper*
Frederick Ramey — *Comes A Time*
Howard Rappaport — *Arnold and Igor*
Joseph Rathgeber — *Mixedbloods*
Kathryn Roberts — *Companion Plants*
Robert Rosenberg — *Isles of the Blind*
Fred Russell — *Rafi's World*
Ron Savage — *Voyeur in Tangier*
David Schein — *The Adoption*
Charles Simpson — *Uncertain Harvest*
Lynn Sloan — *Midstream*
Lynn Sloan — *Principles of Navigation*
L.E. Smith — *The Consequence of Gesture*

Fomite

Printed in the USA
CPSIA information can be obtained
at www.ICGtesting.com
LVHW041246290923
757987LV00033B/227